Beauty of the Beast

Fairy Tale Retellings, Book One

Rachel L. Demeter

Beauty of the Beast
Fairy Tale Retellings, Book One
Copyright © 2017 Rachel L. Demeter

Cover Art: Sarah Hansen
Beta-Reading: Shelley at *2 Lovers of Books*
Editing: Stephanie Parent, Jenny Quinlan
Proofreading: Jenny Sims

All rights reserved. No part of this book may be used or reproduced in any way by any means—except in the case of brief quotations embodied in critical articles and reviews—without written consent of the author.

The characters and events portrayed in this book are fictitious. Any similarity to real persons, living or dead, or places or establishments is purely coincidental and not intended.

RachelLDemeter.com
Twitter: @RachelLDemeter
Facebook.com/RLDemeter

ISBN-13: 978-1542972567
ISBN-10: 1542972566

For my grandma "Bella,"
the most beautiful person I know.

Prologue

LAVONCOURT, THE KINGDOM OF DEMROV, 1808

PRINCE ADAM DELACROIX, the fourth of his name, jolted awake as a thunderous roar splintered through his bedchamber. Overhead, beyond the lush canopy and intricately carved bedposts, the crystal chandelier tinkled and swayed. Its illumination flickered across the parquet flooring and caused the shadows to crawl like living creatures.

Another roar resounded—and this time Adam *felt* it. The entire bed trembled beneath him and rode the penetrating drone.

His heart pounding, he clasped the silk coverlet until his knuckles whitened with strain and his breathing turned shallow. He stared at his family's royal sigil, which was carved into the floorboards countless times, and recited his house's words: *Nutrisco et extinguo. I nourish the good and extinguish the evil.* He chanted them with the audacity of a prayer—drawing strength and comfort from the age-old mantra.

Another crash resonated, much fiercer than the last. The entire castle vibrated from the force of the impact. Dust particles and chunks of plaster rained from the lacquered ceiling. He watched in despair as the debris blanketed the sigils like fresh-fallen snow.

Or perhaps ashes.

He prayed for courage. He was eleven years, almost a grown man—not a frightened babe.

Yet blinding terror filled him, overwhelming his thoughts and paralyzing his limbs. Alas, it felt like a stone had been laid upon his chest and was shackling him in place. He tried to scream—to cry out for help—but only a strangled gasp surfaced.

Maman, Papa... *Rosemary.*

Somehow he forced his legs to move and stumbled from his four-poster bed. The billowing canopy fluttered like the wings of a bird as the room shook beneath him. Quaking with fear, each step was a struggle and his feet felt like lead. He uttered a prayer, then rushed to the conservatory window and swept the crimson drapes aside.

Air whooshed from his lungs at the sight.

Balls of fire filled the courtyard. They bobbed within the dark expanse and appeared to float in midair. One soared through the sky like a shooting star, streaking the night with a ribbon of flames...

I must be dreaming. Adam rubbed the sleep from his eyes and exhaled a fortifying breath. He counted backward from five—but the ritual did nothing to sedate his nerves or chase away the nightmare.

Torches—hundreds of them, maybe thousands—swamped the courtyard. Yells and hollers rose from the chaos in a unified chant: *Vive la Révolution! Vive la Demrov!* Tricolored banners waved amid the sea of men and torches, painting the night with red, white, and blue. Rain descended from the bruised skyline, and a crack of lightning split the horizon. Thunder mated with the sounds of cannon fire and shouting, uniting the clamor as one.

In the back of the mob, clusters of men yelled among themselves and wheeled the cannons forward—past the castle's destroyed gate and straight into the heart of the courtyard.

Straight into my home.

It was a siege.

Shrouded in terror, Adam stumbled from the window and raced into the hallway. Sconce lanterns flickered within the abyss, summoning irregular shadows across the burgundy walls and hanging tapestries. Rough shouts and the rumble of footfalls—dozens of men, if his ears didn't deceive him—reverberated from below. And they were storming up the stairwells... coming for his family. He heard them fast approaching... heard their eager, overlapping voices draw closer... *closer*...

At the end of the corridor, light bounced off the walls and ceiling. His family's royal sigil—two interlinked salamanders twisted around a blazing shield—returned his stare from its home on a polished coat of arms. Likewise, the portraits hanging in the corridors seemed to observe his every movement like silent sentries. Adam felt as their eyes tracked his steps, felt as the ghosts of past ages strengthened his spirit and set fire to his resolve.

Watch over me, Adam silently called out to a portrait of his great-grandfather. *Keep watch over us all.*

Three men emerged from the stairwell holding flaming torches. They were tan and gruff-looking—clearly members of the working class. Raindrops rolled off their tattered cloaks while streaks of mud stained the parquet floor. Red, white, and blue badges, which boasted the infamous revolutionary symbol, decorated their jackets and tricorne caps. Pistols and crude daggers hung from their belts and swayed with each step.

Adam shrank against the wall, which was painted an unsettling blood-red, and shrouded himself behind a tapestry.

"Little prince... come out, come out, wherever you are..." That sardonic voice sank below Adam's skin and crept like a living thing. Manipulated by his ragged breaths, the tapestry wavered forward slightly.

"You hiding somewhere? Now, now, don't be shy."

His heart was beating so fast; he was sure the sound would give him away. The footfalls loudened as the men drew nearer... nearer. Soon they stood scant meters from his hiding spot.

He slapped his palm against his mouth and nose to stifle the sound of his own breathing... to keep the tapestry from waving. Mercifully the fabric grew still—and he could just make out its silhouetted design: a salamander wearing a bejeweled crown, its elongated body jutting out from a field of fire. Adam mutely counted backward, craving the distraction—needing some way to relieve the coiled pressure.

Five.

The inside of the tapestry glowed as the men stopped directly in front of him. *Mon Dieu.* They lurked less than a meter away. Another few steps and they'd discover his hiding place. Or if they simply brushed the material aside and checked behind it...

Four.

Heat from the torch penetrated the tapestry and beat against his face, causing sweat to rain from his brow. The salty rivulets leaked into his eyes and blurred the world around him. What if the men saw his silhouette? What if the tapestry wasn't heavy enough and gave him away? The hanging had been in his family for generations, existing as a symbol of their eternal valor and might. *And what if it betrays us now, on this eve?*

"Suppose he escaped?"

"With the castle so guarded? Not likely."

Three.

A great crash reverberated; the sound blasted down Adam's spine and caused the tapestry to quiver. *Thunder? Or more cannon fire?*

He inwardly called out to the salamander, imploring its protection—seeking its wisdom and guidance.

Two.

"Thought I heard something," one of them grunted.

Adam held his breath until he grew faint. The very thought angered him and caused bitter resentment to rise in his gut. Silently he muttered a prayer—and hoped someone, anyone, would listen.

One.

"Let's go. Let the little wretch burn with the castle."

His prayer was answered. The torchlight shifted away from the tapestry, leaving him in blessed darkness once more. Finally able to draw breaths, Adam inhaled a gulp of air and listened as the footfalls receded. Sparing the tapestry a final glance, he sprang out from his hiding spot and hurried down the twisting corridor. Sconce lanterns flittered, casting wavering shadows along the blood-red walls and low ceiling. Adam's heart raced. He'd never reach the end of the hall. The corridor appeared to physically expand and lengthen... The doors floated farther and farther away... He felt the walls and ceiling closing in, coming together and lowering...

An eternity seemed to flash by before he reached the end of the corridor. He shoved open a door, which led to one of many formal sitting rooms, and jackknifed toward the lofty bureau. His hands violently shook as he ripped open the drawers and rummaged through them. Nothing. Yet he knew Papa had hidden it somewhere in this room. Adam craned his neck back and focused on the very top of the bureau.

Yes, that's where Papa keeps it. At the top, where I couldn't ever hope to reach it. And where I still can't reach it...

He'd watched his father hide the pistol once after he'd polished the barrel to a shine. Papa had always been impressively tall—a God among men in Adam's eyes. Since his eleventh birthday, he'd showed promise of reaching Papa's impressive stature—but he still had almost half a meter to go.

Adam grabbed hold of a luxurious wingback chair and dragged it over to the bureau. The thing felt monstrously heavy and emitted a loud screeching noise as it clawed at the parquet floors. What if someone heard? What if he was discovered? Adam knew well what had become of France's king and queen nine years ago; Papa had made certain of it.

Non, no time to think of such things. Lightheaded and trembling, Adam leapt onto the upholstery, stretched his arms, and strained for the pistol. His bare feet covered the embroidered salamanders, though a part of him felt the emblem's searing flames.

He could *barely* reach. The chair swayed below him. His fingertips grazed the pistol's well-oiled barrel. Beyond the high arched window, a flash of lightning illuminated the horizon. A heartbeat later, a resounding crash shook the castle and nearly threw Adam off the chair. Fighting back his tears, he regained his balance, then gave a desperate hop. *Yes.* He managed to latch on to the barrel and retrieve it from the bureau.

As the castle shuddered and shifted below his naked feet, he dashed down the corridors while booming voices and footsteps bellowed in all directions.

Only one thought occupied his mind: *Rosemary.*

His breaths grew labored as he threw open the nursery's door.

Flames rose from his baby sister's bassinet. Crying filled the room and caused vomit to sear his insides. Adam read the engraved letters several times—*Rosemary, Rosemary, Rosemary*—as the bassinet's wooden frame withered and blackened. His knees gave way and buckled, sending him to the floorboards.

Non. She's still alive. Suffering, but alive. He struggled back to his feet, thinking of nothing but the feel of her tiny, pale hand gripping his finger.

In his mind's eye, he saw himself standing before her birthing bed, saw Maman and Papa's joyful expressions as they gazed down at Demrov's crown princess...

Smoke flooded his lungs as he shot across the nursery. His eyes watered and burned from the agonizing temperature.

Muttering his house's words repeatedly and clinging to their meaning, Adam reached past those roaring flames... felt as the fire blistered his skin and drifted into his face. Perspiration and tears mingled, tracking down his inflamed cheeks, thrashing the breaths from his lungs.

Time became suspended—and a mere second held the weight of an eternity. Sweltering heat engraved his flesh, each tendon, every muscle. He paused, breathless and immobile from the mind-bending pain, feeling as his skin smoldered down to the bone like wax melting from a wick.

Rosemary's brittle cries warped until they were no longer that of an infant baby; they were the screams of a dying person. They sounded inhuman—like the panicked shrieks of a horse suffering an agonizingly slow death. Adam had witnessed this once, years ago—and those horrific cries still haunted his nightmares. One of the groomsmen had put a bullet through his beloved Arabian, granting the creature a quick and merciful death.

But there was nothing quick or merciful about Rosemary's fate.

His father's voice whispered in his mind and fueled his resolve: *Be brave, my dear boy. Endure and be strong.* Madly coughing, tears of pain running down his cheeks, he reached toward his sister's screams, fought the instinct to run far away... and pulled her motionless body from the bassinet and into his scorched arms.

Rosemary's cries fell quiet a heartbeat later. It was the loudest silence he'd ever heard.

Adam jerked away from the bassinet and into the corridor, her tiny, swaddled body clasped against his heaving chest. The pain hit him at full force as he rolled across the ground, dousing the fire and praying in vain.

But it was already over. Barely breathing from the smoke and anguish, Adam unwrapped Rosemary's blanket while the inferno raged on.

Half-immobilized by the sight of his sister's crumpled, burned body, Adam scuttled backward until he crashed into the wall. And at that moment, he and Rosemary became connected, one and the same. As he felt her spirit fade away, he too felt a part of himself disappear. His body grew cold and numb, resembling an empty shell.

His chest heaved in violent spasms. The smoke made him grow weary and faint. Vomit dribbled from his mouth and splattered onto the parquet flooring. He couldn't think. Couldn't draw breaths. The entire castle spun in nauseating circles... The heat of the flames singed his skin, its infernal light blinding him.

The nursery had transformed into the depths of Hell, and all nine of Dante's rings were branded in his flesh. The sight of Rosemary's countless strewn pull toys and blocks, now consumed by flames, summoned another wave of bile. Vomit gushed from his mouth, tracking down his neck and the front of his nightshirt. Despair, unlike anything he'd ever experienced, coursed through his veins. As the fire's heat grew and flashed across his face, he closed his eyes and recalled the first time he'd held Rosemary.

Always remember, my son: A kingdom is only as strong as her leader...

Now those flames were rushing toward him—straight into the corridor—devouring everything in their path. He struggled back onto his feet, using the wall to steady his body. His limbs felt like jelly, and the burns on his arms bubbled, flooding him with excruciating pain.

"Forgive me, Rosemary... I'm so sorry..."

His mind drew blank with shock. Somehow he managed to collect himself and continue his quest; quitting now meant losing everything.

Securing the pistol in his blistered hands, he charged through the hall, overwhelmed with hopelessness, dry-mouthed and lightheaded. The hard rhythm of his pulse thundered in his chest, his neck, his temples, even behind each eye. A black void expanded in his soul, and he felt himself perishing from the inside out.

I must be brave, just like Papa...

Despair took root deep inside Adam's heart.

The entire weight of the world fell upon his shoulders while his father's words echoed in his mind.

We, the Delacroix house, shall stand for a thousand more years, because we are the true pillars of Demrov.

And now those pillars were collapsing.

Chapter One

THE VISION MIGHT have been stolen straight from a fairy tale. Gusts of smoke ascended from a wickerwork chimney and clashed against the baby blue skyline. Beneath the cottage's tattered walls and shingled roof, Isabelle Rose lounged before a hearth. Warm flames enveloped her like a blanket and tugged at her imagination. She flipped through her book's well-loved pages, allowing the sentimental words to wrap her soul and lift her into another time and place.

Hairline cracks spidered overhead, adding insult to injury to the low ceiling. From the corner window, sunlight trickled inside the cramped drawing room and illuminated each imperfection.

Yet Isabelle felt at peace.

Like most other days, Papa relaxed beside her in his Windsor-style rocking chair. She paused her reading and glanced at his ashen features. The cataracts had grown so severe that he was almost blind. Her heart gave a painful ache at the unsightly slump of his shoulders, the wan complexion of his parchment-thin skin, and the deep wrinkles that burdened his brow.

I'd be utterly lost without him.

Shoving away the gloomy thought, she lowered her book and exhaled a rigid breath. "Papa?" He responded with a wheezy snore.

She basked in the tranquil moment—something of a rare occurrence—and savored the simple comfort of Papa's companionship. A unique blend of scents sweetened the air and helped pacify her spirit: a cauldron of stew cooking over the hearth, the bitter aroma of dark coffee, and the chill of winter as a breeze penetrated the cottage's beams.

Once upon a time, when Demrov was still a kingdom, and Isabelle existed as nothing more than a whisper on her parents' lips, Papa had been a renowned merchant. She'd often rejoiced in hearing the tales of his journeys, of the colorful noble ladies and men, farmers, and tradesmen he'd met during his travels. But as the tariffs and taxes rose, and the gap between the working class and nobility grew, Papa had lost his touch. Even after the great revolution, he never regained his momentum. And whatever modest savings he'd stashed away had depleted after he'd married Theresa and inherited the woman's two insufferable daughters...

Speak of the devil. The front door thrust open with a loud crack. Harsh voices imbued the drawing room. The wind howled, filling the cottage with its mournful song. Ice-cold air blasted against Isabelle's face, and the hearth wavered, threatening to snuff out.

Clarice and Elizabeth, Isabelle's stepsisters, volleyed inside, their voices overlapping with frantic chatter that made her head spin. The complete lack of blood ties showed well; Clarice and Elizabeth were as similar to Isabelle as day is to night—and they'd inherited their late mother's animosity for her.

As usual, they both wore long shawls and even longer scowls. They flung the garments over Isabelle's head as if she were a designated coatrack. She expelled a long-suffering sigh and flipped the page of her book. It was all very ritualistic and exhaustingly expected.

"And no wrinkles! I daresay those shawls are worth more than your wardrobe," Clarice said before resuming her chatter. Isabelle peeled the shawls away without batting an eyelash or stopping her reading. Then she tossed the garments into the hearth with a rebellious smile. Justice prevailed, and the shawls shriveled into ashes.

The commotion quickly crescendoed. Lowering her book, Isabelle stopped her reading to observe the scene. Papa tensed in the rocking chair while Clarice and Elizabeth flanked either side of his body. Manipulated by Clarice's arm, the chair dipped into a deep and unsettling sway. A familiar rage flushed through Isabelle as Papa clutched his chair for dear life.

"*Mon beau père!* I hardly recognized you when I walked in." Clarice pinched one of his sunken cheeks. "Why, you're looking better by the moment. Don't you think so, Elizabeth?"

"I shall say so. Finer than any prince!"

Dust rose into Isabelle's face as she slammed her book shut. She watched from her spot by the hearth, inwardly seething while Elizabeth idly meddled with Papa's shirtsleeves. "Oh, Papa, you shall never guess what happened! I took a walk with the baker's boy today. You should have seen him, looking dreamy as ever!"

Mutely Papa nodded as Clarice and Elizabeth shared a sly glance; it was a look Isabelle knew all too well. She clasped her fingers together, overcome with the urge to slap those grins off their wretched faces. Inhaling a calming breath, her eyes descended to the silver cross hanging from her neck—a precious keepsake that had once belonged to her mother.

Give me patience and strength...

"He asked me to the Lachances' ball! Can you believe it?"

"How come you always have all the luck? Well, you and Isabelle," Clarice added with a scoff. "How she managed to land *Vicomte Dumont*, I shall never comprehend..."

Whatever semblance of peace Isabelle felt moments before faded away. The mere mention of Vicomte Raphael Dumont eclipsed her mood and sent shivers racing down her spine. She hung her head and massaged the tender skin of her temples, nursing what promised to be a splitting migraine.

"Bah! What's wrong with you?" Clarice spat, poking Isabelle's shoulder with her index finger.

Elizabeth huffed and flicked her long, plaited hair over her birdlike shoulder. "Oh, enough about her for once! It's unfortunately tragic that I won't be able to go. To the ball, I mean," she pouted, slinking closer to Papa. "See, all my dresses are tattered and terribly stained. Why they wouldn't even let me through the door!"

Anger welled inside Isabelle as she examined Elizabeth's crisp, *clean* dress. She was taking advantage of Papa's deteriorated vision; that much was painfully obvious.

"Can't I buy a new dress, Papa? Just one!"

"Oh, I really don't know. I—"

"*Please,* Papa! Courting the baker's boy shall make me happier than anything in the world! You want me to be happy, don't you? Maman would have ensured I went, looking my very greatest..."

A protective instinct flowed through Isabelle. Nearly shaking from her anger and frustration, she clutched the book against her chest and shot onto her feet. "That's quite enough! There's hardly money for food, let alone dresses. And Elizabeth—the one you're wearing could pass as new."

Elizabeth slinked toward Isabelle, wearing a sneer on her thin, pale lips. Snatching the book away with a shrill giggle, she said, "And when did you get *this*? Let me guess. When you were out buying 'groceries'? You're just a little hypocrite, nothing more."

"Papa gave it to me years ago. On my birthday, you might recall, had you been around."

"Why should we care about your stupid birthdays? Everything revolves around you. It's not fair. Papa's always favored *you*, always ensured *your* happiness." Tears sprang to Elizabeth's silver eyes; they looked foreign and cold to Isabelle. They were Theresa's eyes. "You both are so cruel to us."

Isabelle didn't doubt the sincerity of Elizabeth's words, no matter how twisted and delusional they sounded. Guilt stabbed her as she was reminded of Elizabeth's young age. Even though they'd only seen fourteen and seventeen years respectively, Elizabeth and Clarice made themselves impossible to love. "Oh, if only Maman were here to witness this cruelty." Elizabeth spun toward Papa and gave his chair a hard kick. "You—you are glad she's dead, aren't you? Go on, admit it: You let her die, right in this room, and now Clarice and I have no one. No one!

I shall never forgive you, you old, useless fool."

"Please, Elizabeth... do try to settle down," Papa cut in, his thin chest spasming from the force of his coughs. "You know very well I did all I could. The pneumonia was quite past any help. Now I—" Another chain of coughs shattered his words. They sounded thick, dangerously guttural.

S'il vous plaît, Dieu. Not another infection.

"Shh... it's fine. Don't unsettle yourself. Hush now, Papa, hush..." Isabelle stood behind him and gently massaged his shoulders until the coughs subsided. Then she moved in front of his body—blocking Clarice and Elizabeth's paths—creating a flesh-and-blood barricade in front of her beloved father. "What's the matter with you two? Can't you see how sick he is?" As usual, her plea fell on deaf ears and stone hearts.

"About as sick as Maman was before the wretch let her die," Elizabeth said with an unsettling smirk.

Those words cut far deeper than she dared admit; they struck with the audacity of an ice-cold wave.

"The book—may I see it for a moment, my dear, sweet, lovely sister?" Clarice asked Elizabeth with mocked politeness.

"Most gladly," Elizabeth replied, dipping into a well-practiced curtsy and passing the book along.

"Hand it back." Isabelle thrust forward and attempted to grab her book. "You are upsetting Papa again."

Elizabeth shrugged, then tossed the book to Clarice. They made a game of their cruelty, throwing it over Isabelle's head and baiting her with it each time. Clarice drew backward and flipped through the pages with feigned interest.

She made an elaborate show of clearing her throat, then read from the pages: "'He therefore turned to mankind with regret. His cathedral was enough for him. It was peopled with marble figures of kings, saints, and bishops who at least did not laugh in his face and looked at him with only tranquility and benevolence. The other statues, those of monsters and demons, had no hatred for him—he resembled them too closely for that.'" Clarice surrendered to a harsh laugh and shook her head. "What kind of senseless melodrama is this?" Continuing her dramatic narration, she strutted over to the hearth and threw the book in the roaring fire.

Horrified, Isabelle rushed past her stepsisters and collapsed to her knees. The flaming hearth immediately drew sweat from her brow. Hardly thinking and overcome with anger and despair, she reached into the fire and attempted to rescue her treasured book.

Elizabeth clutched her stomach while her reed-thin body rolled with laughter. "*T'es un imbécile!* You never were the smart one. If only Maman could see you now!"

Silent and still, Isabelle watched the pages curl and disintegrate into ashes. Then she felt Clarice's hand on her shoulder and heard her voice in her ear. "My sweet sister... now, you have nowhere to hide."

RUILLÉ'S MARKETPLACE WAS an engine of chaos the following morning. Lost within the sanctuary of her private thoughts—grateful to be free of her stepsisters—Isabelle wandered the unpaved walkways in silent contemplation. This part of Demrov lacked the manicured appearance of Lavoncourt and the other surrounding provinces, which mimicked Paris's cobbled streets. Indeed, ever since France had adopted Demrov and taken the former kingdom beneath its expanding wing, the island had lost a little of its rustic nature in exchange for Paris's rising culture.

Yet Isabelle felt perfectly at home. She knew these paths like the back of her hand and could blindly maneuver them without a single misstep. Weaving in and out of the booths and rolling carts, she dodged her fellow citizens and returned their jubilant greetings.

Off to the side, a handsome couple embraced under the bough of an old elm. Isabelle paused in midstride and watched them with an ache in her heart. The gnarled trunk hovered above their hugging bodies, its mass grotesquely deformed and fraught with age. In contrast, the young man looked dashing, clearly in the prime of life. He leaned in close and gripped his darling's waist, never intending to let go. Beneath an earnest sigh, he whispered sweet nothings and peppered kisses upon her brow. The wind carried her heartfelt laughter as she reciprocated his affection. Ever so gently, he cupped her cheeks and lured her into another timeless kiss. It was a kiss she'd remember for years to come, a kiss that whispered a thousand unspoken secrets. Standing below that monstrous elm, the two of them were shamelessly head over heels in love...

With a reverent sigh, Isabelle tore her eyes away and continued down the path. Years ago, Maman and Papa had read her a certain fairy tale. She'd been only six years old, yet the story of the maiden awoken by true love's kiss had spoken to something deep inside her. She'd never forgotten those beautiful words, which seemed to have been spun from an unworldly magic. The stories had planted themselves in her heart—and throughout the years, they'd blossomed into a throbbing desire. One, she'd come to realize, that would never be fulfilled.

Although she was a grown woman, Isabelle knew she remained a child in numberless ways. Fanciful. Seduced by pretty stories and romantic dreams. Far too curious and impulsive for her own good. Half the time, she floated on a cloud, which drifted on a horizon that only she perceived—

"Fresh caught oysters, straight from the coast of Demrov!" Isabelle nearly collided into the passing oyster cart.

Snapping out of her inward thoughts, she mumbled an apology, then inhaled and welcomed the crisp air into her lungs. The clamor intensified and reached a crescendo while society awoke for the day. Men and women opened shop, greeting their awaiting clientele. The clatter of hooves and creaking wheels filled the air as phaetons, mail coaches, and even a lacquered carriage whizzed by.

"*Bonjour*, Mademoiselle Isabelle! So good to see you again," a merchant called out as he pushed a cart full of hand-blown glass wares down the dirt road.

Isabelle returned his enthusiastic wave. "Ah, *bonjour*,

Monsieur Reyer! Aren't you looking well this morning?"

"The madame has no cause for complaints, I suppose." He turned to her as he passed, wagging a playful finger in midair. "Your father and I never did complete our trade. Let ol' Bernard know I'm still holding him to it!"

Isabelle pushed back the uneasy sensation. She nodded, then journeyed on again. The town baker rolled his cart, whistling a cheerful tune with his bread rolls still warm and steaming. Without warning, his cart gave a violent lurch and dipped into a gaping hole. Isabelle rushed over as he attempted to pull it free. Despite the overcast weather, sweat beaded down his face in a matter of moments.

"Monsieur Lafitte! Wait—let me give you a hand!"

His wrinkled features brightened at the sound of her voice. He loosened his grasp on the cart and reeled back. Blotting the perspiration from his brow, he said in a breathless voice, "Ah, Mademoiselle Isabelle! Stop that now, *ma chérie*. I won't stand for it. You mustn't exert yourself so!"

His portly belly swung as he attempted to aid her. She playfully slapped his beefy hand away. Then she grunted and flashed a strained smile while she released the cart. Brushing her dirt-covered hands against her dress, she said, "There we are! I assure you, monsieur—I'm quite stronger than I look."

"Well, yes, one can't argue that." He adjusted his spectacles, pushing them up a hooked nose. "Say... a congratulation is in order if I'm not mistaken!"

Isabelle gave a small laugh and adjusted her grip on her basket. "For my newfound strength?"

"Why, no, no—because of your engagement, of course! To our very own Vicomte Dumont."

The words felt like a punch to the gut. She fought to retain her smile, though a quaver rocked her voice. Bowing her face to hide her disdain, she replied, "Oh, yes, how silly of me. *Merci*, monsieur."

Monsieur Lafitte edged closer, eyeing the errant buzz of Ruillé. Several Demrovians yelled greetings to Isabelle; she shifted her feet and returned them with an uncomfortable smile.

Monsieur Lafitte gently nudged her in the side, as if he were about to share a well-guarded secret. "To be completely honest, I never cared for the Dumonts much. I've heard, well, unsavory things, to say the least. Didn't want to believe the whispers."

Isabelle empathized with his apprehension. Unlike France, the nobility still held the upper hand in Demrov, though the hold had loosened ever since the rebellion twenty-five years before. And the Dumonts were the worst kind of nobles. Extortion, brutal slave labor, and fraudulent business deals were only the tip of the iceberg. It was common knowledge they'd climbed France's political ladder through bribery and even bloodshed; in turn, they'd sold privileged information to Demrov's representatives before turning their backs on their homeland. Striving to see the best in Raphael, Isabelle found his charming demeanor had acted as a blindfold.

Raphael is a decent man, she'd reassured herself each night. *A good man. The tales of the Dumonts wrecking lives and building their name off the misfortune of others are rumors built from ignorance and jealousy. Nothing more.* The truth had quickly come to light, of course—as did Raphael Dumont's genuine colors.

Monsieur Lafitte patted her shoulder with a tender touch and smile. The warm gesture extracted Isabelle from her meandering thoughts. "To know you're to marry the vicomte... Well, the rumors must be nothing more than wagging tongues. I'm sure of it now. And that knowledge gives me hope."

Isabelle nodded and forced a smile that failed to reach her eyes. Absently she clasped her silver cross and gave the necklace a tender squeeze. "Hope is a beautiful and magical thing. Grasp it tight, monsieur, and never let go."

"Pretty words from Demrov's prettiest girl." He flaunted a charming, toothless grin that caused Isabelle's heart to melt. Then he gestured her forward again with a sly wink, wheeled around his cart, and lifted the linen sheet with a flick of his wrist. Isabelle had nearly expected him to cry out, "Ta-da!" as he did so. Beneath the checkered sheet, a bounty of fresh-baked rolls glistened in the morning light. Winking again, he placed four inside her basket, his handlebar mustache twitching from the magnitude of his smile. Glancing from side to side, he cupped his mouth and said in a playful, conspiratorial whisper, "A humble gift from me to your family."

Isabelle couldn't suppress her laughter. "*Merci*, monsieur. That is most kind of you!"

"But of course, *chérie*. Say... how is your father's health as of late? It pains me that I haven't seen him for months now. Always rather enjoyed his company and quick wit. I rarely see you anymore, come to think of it. Shame on you, depriving us of your bright face! Now, why is that, mademoiselle?"

The world shifted. Darkened. Isabelle swallowed against the knot in her throat. She inhaled a calming breath, then met Monsieur Lafitte's eager expression with an enthusiasm she didn't feel. "Ah, forgive me, monsieur. It's quite simple. I don't like to leave Papa alone for long stretches of time, see..." She ignored the first part of his inquiry, not able to confront her worst fear in such a tangible form—refusing to put the reality of Papa's declining health into words.

If I don't say it, if I try not to think it, perhaps it won't be true.

Once again, Isabelle allowed herself to slip inside the fabric of her dream world—a beautiful realm of make-believe.

GATHERING THE SULLIED hem of her dress, Isabelle sprinted up the dirt road that led to her modest cottage. In the wake of her steps, dust rose from the ground and flooded her lungs. She fanned the debris and covered her mouth and nose with a faded handkerchief.

Then she stopped dead in her tracks at the sight of a grandiose parked coach. The ornate detail and gilded coat of arms summoned a queasy sensation in her gut. DUMONT was emblazoned across the black-lacquered door in sprawling

script—and each letter deepened her nausea.
Not this morning. Not now.
The blood drained from her face and her heart jackknifed. How she wished the ground would open and swallow her whole.

Monsieur Belmont, a kindly coachman with slick white hair and a set of bushy, tight-knit eyebrows, grinned at her from his perch in the box seat. Then he dropped his chin and lifted his bowler hat with that ever-growing smile. "Ah, *bonjour*, Mademoiselle Rose! Fine thing to see you again."

Hesitantly Isabelle returned his smile as her eyes darted across those emblazoned letters. "I must say this is quite a surprise," she said, pocketing the handkerchief. "I... I didn't expect Monsieur Dumont this morning." The stunning team of horses gave amicable nickers, their tapered ears rotating toward her voice.

"Yes, well. You know how the vicomte is—impulsive and erratic."

You aren't joking, she sardonically thought; though the coachman seemed to find humor in his words. He tossed his head back with a hearty laugh, then blew into his gloved palms and rubbed both hands together.

"Now don't tell me he left you out here in the cold?"

He chuckled again and shrugged his hefty shoulders. "Ah, well... it's not so terrible. I've got my girls for company. See," he said, motioning toward the six striking horses.

"And what lovely *beautés* they are." Isabelle glanced into her basket and withdrew two rolls. "Here. They're still warm. For you and Geoffrey."

"Oh, no, no. I couldn't possibly—"

"Don't be silly, monsieur. I insist!"

Monsieur Belmont nodded and accepted the rolls. A smile curled his lips and brought an irresistible light to his eyes. The transformation visibly stripped the years from his face.

"Tell me—how is little Geoffrey coming along?"

"Quite well! Pox aren't much more than an itch now."

Isabelle smiled at that, enjoying the small talk. Anything to keep the inevitable at bay. "And your father? I suspect he's faring well?"

Monsieur Belmont frowned at the word "father," the empathy in his blue eyes unmistakable. "I can't say. Each day is so different. So unpredictable."

Such is life, she thought. "Well. As always, the two of you shall remain in my prayers."

She gave a last smile, gathered her nerves, and headed for the cottage's front door. Inhaling a rigid breath, she removed her engagement ring from her apron, where she kept it stashed for such occasions, and then slipped it on her finger.

How despairingly heavy it felt.

THE DOOR EMITTED a treacherous moan as Isabelle slid inside and struggled to remain discreet. Her heart quickened at the sight of Vicomte Raphael Dumont; she inwardly cursed herself, not believing he could still affect her so. Sinfully handsome, he sat in the rocking chair next to her papa's, looking every bit the perfect gentleman with his polished, golden hair and cognac eyes.

But Isabelle knew better.

His proposal had come as an utter surprise several months back; he'd appeared sincere and truly besotted with her. The memory of his tentative glances and touches still set her heart aflutter. Paired with Papa's ailing health and the rising costs of medicine, his interest couldn't have come at a better time. Isabelle had been happy, hopeful—even, dare she admit it, in love.

Then everything had changed.

She quickly discovered that, above all things, Vicomte Raphael Dumont was an excellent pretender.

Foolish dreams and false hopes. How naive and blind I'd been.

The floorboards creaked.

Raphael swung toward her, shooting Isabelle a knowing grin that displayed his stark-white teeth. He paced across the drawing room, eliminating the precious space that stood between them. She stiffened with each of his steps and instinctively drew backward until she bumped against the doorjamb. For the first time ever, she longed for her stepsisters' company. They were quite enamored with Raphael's charm and golden looks and would have created a buffer between him and Isabelle—albeit, a noisy one. His amber eyes flashed, turning a golden hue; they took in her five-carat engagement ring before sliding down the rest of her body in a leisurely perusal.

"Ah! That you, Isabelle, *ma petite*?" Papa's voice gave Isabelle a start. She attempted to wheel around Raphael's large body without luck.

"Yes... I'm back, Papa."

"Good, good. Look... look who's come to see you. Isn't that a lovely surprise?"

"Very nice, indeed. Now kindly move aside, monsieur."

Raphael swept to the side with a regal bow. Isabelle pushed past him, then pressed a kiss to Papa's forehead. *Mon Dieu,* he felt warm again. She set the basket of rolls and fresh fruit on his lap and gently combed the sparse tufts of his hair with her fingertips. "Some fresh bread rolls. Don't they smell wonderful?"

"Very much so. Few things bring more pleasure than the feel of fresh-baked rolls on one's lap." Papa withdrew one of said rolls, then continued through a mouthful of bread, "Raphael has kept me company for the past hour."

Collecting the basket, Isabelle crossed the room again and struggled to find her voice. Her throat was raw. She felt overwhelmed, alone, trapped. Raphael's mere presence unnerved her, shocking her back into cold reality. Keeping the antipathy from her tone took a monumental effort. "I see. This is quite unexpected. What are you doing here, Raphael?"

He gave no response. He merely returned Isabelle's stare and leaned against the round, chipped table. She turned away and set down the basket, willing her hands to quit shaking. Then she unclasped her cloak—and froze as his unwelcome body heat closed in on her. He towered behind her, intimately near. Her insides coiled into tight knots, and the beat of her pulse blasted in her eardrums.

Next to hunting, it was one of his favorite sports—toying with her, knowing well that Papa couldn't see his wandering hands.

And that Isabelle could hardly voice her resistance. If Papa learned the truth of his nature, he'd throw Raphael out on his head and never allow their marriage to take place.

"Why don't you two come sit by the fire?" Papa obliviously asked. Indeed. He gazed directly into the wavering flames, seeing *nothing*.

"Yes, Papa. In a moment."

"I missed you terribly, you know." Raphael leaned forward, whispering the words. Hot breaths singed her nape and caused her gut to quiver.

"I know what you missed."

Rotating her body, Raphael made an amused sound and perked a thick, blond brow. "What's this? I'm not permitted to miss my fiancée. Hmm?"

Fiancée. Suddenly the five-karat ring felt like a manacle. Her skin crawled as Raphael pressed his torso flush against her back. He swept away her curls and twisted them in his long fingers, kissing the side of her neck with cold lips, his hands everywhere at once...

"Why... why are you doing this?"

Raphael spun her body around with a chuckle. He grabbed her left hand in a gesture that could only be described as rough and lewd, and forced her palm against the front of his trousers. His size swelled in her hand, causing vomit to climb inside her throat. She swallowed it back and fought to detach herself from the here and now. But his voice was a husky whisper that added to her disgust and kept her anchored in place. "Don't play daft. I think you know precisely why."

Isabelle recoiled her hand, scandalized and shuddering with anger. "You repulse me."

"And you intrigue me." Raphael's arms crept around her body again. His hands broke through her cloak, provocatively parting the material with a jarring whoosh of air. "Yes, indeed... there's something about you... something I can't quite place my finger on... something so alive, so very tempting. You're different, Isabelle, refreshing—unlike all those blue-blooded chits Father demands I shackle myself to. Just look at you, *ma chérie*. You're a diamond among a sea of mere pebbles. And I'd be a damn fool to ever let you slip away," he said, tightening his grasp. "You are *mine*."

Those words told Isabelle all she needed to know: She'd been thrust in the middle of a father-son battle—one she wanted no part of. He intended to make her his property, an insult to the comte.

"Spare your false sentiments," she scoffed, elbowing him in the chest. He gave a small chuckle and loosened his hold a fracture.

"You wound me, mademoiselle. My affection for you runs deep."

Months ago, Isabelle would have fallen for such a line. But this was now.

His fingertips resumed their perusal, skimming over her hips, her breasts. All the while Papa stared at them while he ate. Detachedly she watched as he broke off a chunk of bread and finished the roll. Raphael's thumb and forefinger pinched her nipple straight through the garb, twisting the skin, summoning a flash of pain and anger. "Please. Stop. You've had your fun. Stop it now, Raphael."

"Stop? Stop what?" Raphael asked in a mocking, amused voice. He cupped one of her breasts, and continued through a breathy whisper, "Stop this?" Cupping her other breast with a harsh squeeze, his voice sunk impossibly lower, "Or rather *this*?"

"What kind of sadistic monster are you, tormenting me in this way?" She battled to maintain a low whisper, but her frustration emerged like water spilling from a broken dam. "Knowing well I can't cry out, can't even—"

"Come now, Isabelle. Indulge a bit. Free that fire that stirs within you," Raphael said as he ran his palm down her arm. Up and down. "The fool is blinder than a mole. He would never know—"

Isabelle turned in his grasp and stared daggers into those cool, placid eyes. "Don't you dare say a word against my father. You hear me?"

"Or what? Hmm?" Only silence. "That's what I suspected. Your threats are as empty and pathetic as your tears are."

Isabelle silently cursed herself as the tears returned to her eyes. She fought them back and raised her chin, meeting his gaze as an equal—refusing to back down. "You *are* a monster, Raphael. Make no mistake about that. And one day you shall pay for your cruelty."

Pure silence again. Alas, it was unbearable. The loudest silence she'd ever heard. For a moment, Isabelle felt certain Raphael would strike her. But he merely stepped back, smoothed down his navy frock coat, and said, "You need me as much as I need you. You and your useless, ill-fated father. Never forget that."

"Isabelle... now, where'd you run off to, *ma petite*?"

"I—I'm sorry." Isabelle fought to disguise the tremble in her voice. Despite her valiant efforts, it shattered her words into breathy fragments. She clasped her chest and filled her lungs with fortifying breaths. "I'm right here."

As deep as Raphael's words had cut, they bore an unshakable truth: They depended on his funds.

Raphael traced her jawline with his gloved fingertip—a gesture of both genuine and mock affection. She tensed even further, if that was at all possible, and battled the urge to cry out her rage and frustration. Instead, her eyes fixed on the gilded buttons of his double-breasted frock coat and starch-white cravat. Concealed under that finely tailored clothing, he carried a wretchedness that paralyzed her very soul.

"Go on, then. Go see your dear papa... while you still can."

Exhaling a shaky breath, Isabelle pushed past him and joined Papa by the fire. She crouched in front of him, kissed his warm cheek, and then smoothed her fingertips over his scalp. "You exercised quite an appetite, I see. Feeling any better this morning?" Miraculously her voice sounded normal and unaffected.

Papa's wrinkled lips broke into a toothless, childish grin. "Like a man reborn. I must say... Raphael here lifted my spirits."

Isabelle gazed into the hearth while silent tears streamed down her face. Hastily wiping them away, she glanced down at the imposing engagement ring, finding no beauty in the glittering diamond or sleek gold band.

A rough, guttural cough shook Papa's body. Isabelle reached out and gently clutched his arm. "That's enough excitement for now. Why don't you come lie down and rest for a bit?"

Papa paid no regard to her words. "You are a good man, Monsieur le Vicomte. When I've passed on, you'll take care of my Isabelle for me, won't you?"

"Of course." Raphael paused. "How could I do otherwise?"

Papa exhaled a long breath, as if a burden had physically lifted from his shoulders. "Then I may go in peace."

"No. Don't talk like that. You will get through this. Raphael's already made arrangements with some of Demrov's finest physicians." Isabelle swallowed the lump in her throat and met Raphael's hard, unwavering gaze. "Haven't you?"

His eyes flickered down the front of her bodice—and Isabelle felt his intrusive stare as if it were a tangible thing... as if his fingers were prying into somewhere sacred, forever leaving their taint.

"I'm sure we could work something out."

Reality slammed against her thoughts with a startling force. She realized that to save her loved ones, she'd need to sacrifice much more than her flesh and happiness. Alas, by the time this nightmare ended, she'd be forced to sacrifice her very soul.

Papa opened his mouth to speak, but his words were cut short as he exploded into another fit of coughs. He raised a trembling hand, which Raphael clasped in midair. "Isabelle is right. You should take care not to exhaust yourself so much."

Papa shook his head and gave a full-bodied laugh; in spite of the circumstances, the unexpected and joyful sound lightened Isabelle's heart. "I've always been a stubborn brute. Age hasn't changed that. Death shan't change it, either." Silence hung between the three of them. A poignant chill cut through Isabelle's veins as she locked on to Raphael's icy stare. The challenge was unmistakable in his cognac eyes—and it chipped away at her soul.

ISABELLE LOVED NIGHTS such as these the most. Her tiresome stepsisters had departed for the evening, leaving her and Papa in the soothing warmth of each other's company. Contentment flooded her spirit while they relaxed before the crackling hearth. She watched as the fire tempered into glowing embers. Their bellies still felt warm and soft from the stew, and a pot of tea sat between their two rocking chairs. Tea was a pricey luxury—one they could scarcely afford—and together they found a rare joy in the indulgence.

The night had drifted by like some dream, and her vile encounter with Raphael felt like a distant nightmare. She and Papa had spent countless hours laughing and reminiscing about when Isabelle had been a girl and the entire world had laid at their feet. Now, a comfortable stillness filled the cottage, broken only by the sounds of the whispering wind and snapping logs. Isabelle stared into the wavering flames and gently caressed the book in her lap, stroking her fingers over its fragile spine; an unexpected sadness, a strange sense of loneliness and solitude, eclipsed her mood.

Within the confinement of her thoughts, Raphael's words came storming back and seized her spirit in an iron clasp. *Go on, then. Go see your dear papa... while you still can.*

How dare he? Revulsion and red-hot rage flowed through her veins. She gripped the edge of her book until her knuckles grew white and numb.

"Do you care for him, Isabelle?"

Papa's quiet inquiry woke Isabelle from her train of thoughts. She silently turned to him, then collected her chipped cup from the end table and downed a sip of tea. The warm liquid raced down her throat in a waterfall of spice and mint. "What a silly question. Of course I do." The lie left a bitter taste in her mouth. She took another sip and battled to still the quaver in her voice. "Why do you ask, Papa?"

"Because you are my little girl." He shifted in his chair and released a pained groan. "You shall always be my little girl. You deserve warmth, kindness... a gentle touch. It hurts my heart and fills me with sorrow, knowing you might have found true love with another."

Isabelle held her tongue, refusing to expose the truth of Raphael's character. What was done was done. "Vicomte Dumont is a gentleman and an important person here in Demrov. He—"

Papa waved off her words like swatting a fly. "Blast it. Never mind all that. That's not what I'm asking. I—" Hard coughs shook his body. Isabelle set down her cup and gently clutched his arm.

"Papa. It's late. Quit being a stubborn mule. You really should—"

"Now, now. I'm quite fine, *ma petite*." He heaved a sigh. A mutiny of emotions surfaced in his glassy stare. "I know why you have accepted Monsieur Dumont's proposal. I may be blind, but I'm not *that* blind." He cracked a small grin, and Isabelle couldn't help but return the gesture. Then his sightless eyes danced and filled with raw emotion, as if he was watching something beautiful unfold within his mind. The smile on his lips grew with each passing second—and for a heartbeat, he appeared fifteen years younger. "I fell hard for your mother the first time I laid eyes on her. Was she a beauty like I had never seen. Indeed, her beauty stole half my wretched heart. Her spirit stole whatever remained. There was nothing I wouldn't do for her... Nothing we wouldn't have done for each other."

The mention of Maman filled Isabelle with a painful longing. She hadn't known her mother for very long—she'd died when Isabelle was only seven—though, through Papa's tender stories, she felt like an old friend. Papa's sentimental words rang inside her heart, loud and clear, deafening the world around her. In the back of her mind, the echoes of a fairy tale joined the song and tugged at her core.

Finding true love. It was a dream Isabelle was willing to sacrifice if it meant buying a couple of more precious years with Papa. More years and more nights like these. Such was a price she'd contentedly pay.

Visibly overcome with grief, Papa brought two wrinkled fingers against his temple and massaged the frail skin. "You were gifted with your mother's strength and gentleness, Isabelle. Both her strength and beauty. Never abandon those things, *ma petite*. But greatest of all, you have her heart. Guard it well."

Tears stung the corners of her eyes. She tried to speak, but tumultuous emotions all but constricted her voice. She exhaled a long breath, then managed to whisper two words. "I shall."

Papa turned to her as another small, sad smile graced his lips. The hearth's wavering light softened his expression and smoothed out the wrinkles that embedded his skin. Indeed, at that moment, he almost looked vibrant and youthful again. Tender memories tugged at Isabelle's mind and heart, urging her into another time and place.

"I should have never married her," Papa whispered as he shook his downcast head. Isabelle knew he spoke of Theresa, her stepsisters' late mother. The topic was never breached, yet it often echoed within long silences. "It's a great regret I have."

Isabelle reached out and patted Papa's trembling hand. "Don't have any regrets. No regrets—only peace. Peace and hope and love."

He smiled as the tears rushed to his sightless eyes again. "You deserve true love. A man's undying, unconditional love."

Now it was Isabelle's turn to swat the air. "The only man's love I need is *yours*," Isabelle replied as she battled the lonely feeling in the pit of her stomach. "Truthfully."

He grinned, surrendering to a rigid sigh. "That you shall have until long after my last breath. Forever and always, *ma petite*."

The mood shifted. Beyond the walls, the wind howled a grim melody and rattled the nude trees. Branches clawed against the wooden panels and sent tremors racing down Isabelle's spine.

Studying Papa's pale complexion, she seized his hand. She smoothed her thumb pads across the delicate web of bones and raised veins. He felt impossibly fragile... like he might slip from her reach at any moment. She increased the pressure of her hold, as if the movement might prevent him from ever leaving her.

"I love you, Papa. More than anything else in this world. You know that? And there's nothing I wouldn't do for you. Nothing I wouldn't do for us."

Chapter Two

"There is many a monster who wears the form of a man; it is better of the two to have the heart of a man and the form of a monster."

—Jean-Marie Leprince de Beaumont

The next day met Isabelle with an overcast sky and a wintry breeze. The cold winds had risen seemingly overnight, sweeping Demrov in an icy fist. Isabelle wandered the dirt pathway leading to her cottage at a brisk pace. She clutched a wicker basket against her chest, which she'd filled with the few blooms that had survived the winter. Softly she hummed a lullaby under her breath while a chilly breeze rustled her hair. The flowers' sweet aromas mingled with the crisp air and helped relieve her tumultuous thoughts.

Strange, she mused, caressing one of her roses as if it were a priceless treasure. *Usually all the flowers have died by this time so late in the season...*

Slipping into her inward fantasies, she turned her face to the frozen air and allowed her eyes to slide shut. The rustling of branches heightened her senses; winter had stripped the trees of their foliage, leaving behind only a smattering of colorful blooms.

Isabelle exhaled a long breath, opened her eyes, and

scanned the row of skeletal shrubs. A burst of color ensnared her attention; she secured the cloak about her shoulders, then halted in front of a rosebush. A single, crimson rose decorated its branches. Isabelle ran her fingertips over the delicate petals. Cupping it in her palm, she leaned forward and inhaled the honeyed fragrance.

"Whatcha doin' that for?"

Isabelle pulled away from the rose and smiled down at little Timmy. As usual, his red curls looked wild and unkempt, and mud and dreck splattered his clothes and freckled face. He really was too adorable for words. She'd imagined her family's circumstances were quite bleak, yet the sight of Timmy, whose father had died in a reckless duel and whose mother labored in factories almost fourteen hours a day, reminded Isabelle to count her blessings.

"Oh, *bonjour*, Monsieur Timmy!" Isabelle plucked the rose and held it out for Timmy to admire. "Isn't it lovely?"

He nodded, grinning from ear to ear.

Isabelle playfully propped a hand on her hip in mock scolding. Gaping and staring down at his muddy grin, she exclaimed, "Goodness! Now, aren't you a sight? Pray tell, what sort of mischief have you found this morning?"

Timmy straightened his posture, thoroughly pleased with himself. "I've been catchin' frogs!"

"Oh, were you now? And in such cold weather?"

Puffing out his chest like a surly warrior, he said, "I sure was! You oughtta see 'em for yourself." He swept back a step and positioned his stained hands wide apart. A prideful grin appeared on his face while his eyes sparkled with youthful fire and indignation. Isabelle swallowed back her laughter as warmth spread through her body. Indeed—she saw a bit of herself in the bright-eyed child. "They were *this* big!"

"That cannot be." Isabelle dramatically gasped and pressed her palm to her breast, feigning shock. "I simply don't believe it!"

Timmy gave a shy look as his mud-streaked cheeks visibly pinkened. Grasping his filthy coat, which was missing half its buttons, he wrung the material between blistered fingers and dirt-clogged nails. Eyes fixed on the path below his feet, he murmured, "You can come with me to catch 'em next time, ya know, if you wanna."

"Why, of course," she said with a curtsy, as if she'd been invited to a ball. "I would be most honored."

"Oh, boy!"

"So let me guess… that's why you're not bringin' any back home to your maman?" Isabelle held her hands wide apart. "Because they're *this* big?"

Timmy glanced down and kicked at the dirt path with his toe. "*Non.* See, Mama don't like 'em too much. Says 'they're ugly as sin.' And they 'spread warts like the devil's plague.' Well, I think they're jus' beauuutiful!"

Isabelle let go of her laughter. The release felt liberating, and a heavy weight lifted off her heart. "I would say so. Back when I was a girl, I used to kiss 'em, you know."

"Oh, gross! What'd you do that for?"

"Why, to find my prince, of course."

"Now that's just silly!"

"What's a young maid to do?" Isabelle's heart warmed from the exchange, and her worries briefly thawed. "Wait… wait a moment…" Narrowing her gaze, she crouched beside him and suspiciously glanced about. Then she signaled him near with a hooked index finger and lowered her voice to a conspicuous whisper. "Oh, no… it cannot be…"

"What is it? What is it, Mademoiselle Isabelle?"

"Now, I don't know for certain, but… I believe something's hiding inside your ear?"

She reached behind his head and revealed the rose by a clever sleight of hand. Papa had often played the trick on her when she was a girl. Timmy's eyes bugged out as she tucked the bloom behind his right ear.

"Goodness! How'd you do that?"

"Have I not told you? I have magical powers. Now, you'd better run along, sweeting." Isabelle came to her feet and glanced at the cloudy horizon. "Looks like a storm may be moving in."

Timmy tossed his arms around her legs, squeezed them in

a tender hug, then spouted heartfelt good-byes. Left alone with her worries again, Isabelle's thoughts darkened as she recalled last night's encounter with Raphael.

A storm *was* moving in.

And she and Papa had nowhere to hide.

PAPA LOUNGED IN HIS ROCKING CHAIR, looking anything but comfortable or at peace. Isabelle's heart stirred at the sight.

What madness.

She grasped her basket's handle until her knuckles grew white. Clarice and Elizabeth hovered on either side of his body and leaned against the rocking chair, causing it to sway back and forth like a wretched seesaw. Isabelle felt a migraine stir to life as they simultaneously shrieked incoherent, overlapping demands into his poor ears. Anguish and frustration were etched in Papa's brow, though he visibly lacked the energy to fight them off.

"You'll make certain it's silk, won't you, Daddy? And don't you dare rely on Isabelle! Ugh! All her taste is in her mouth!"

"Oh, and pearls! Real pearls. A strand of beautiful, *real* pearls!"

"You mustn't forget the ribbons! Maybe a pair of silver earrings, as well? Please, Papa? And I don't mean those tin pieces of junk!"

Isabelle set down her basket and hung the cloak on a suspended hook. She eyed the commotion in red-hot silence, her anger steadily mounting.

Finally noticing her entrance, Clarice and Elizabeth fell silent and whispered into each other's ears.

"Isabelle?" Papa called out, lifting his head from the back of the rocking chair. "Is that you, my dear?"

"*Bonjour*, Papa. Feeling better this morning?" Isabelle turned to her stepsisters with a pointed look. She allowed her silence to speak, knowing well that Papa needed quiet—not further commotion. Clarice and Elizabeth begrudgingly stepped away from the rocking chair and studied her with their scrutinizing glares.

"Oh, yes. Quite better."

She studied his labored breathing and trembling hands. He held his head up high, though she could see the effort exhausted him. "Hmm. Is that so? Perhaps I should be the one to judge that."

Suspicious of his hearty attitude, she crouched beside his rocking chair while Elizabeth and Clarice crossed the room to huddle around the basket. Giggling and trading whispers, they took turns removing the blooms and threading them through each other's mousy brown locks.

Good. Let them busy themselves with such nonsense.

"Tell me... when I came in, what was all that excitement about?"

Clarice and Elizabeth paused their movements and exchanged helpless glances.

"Nothing that concerns you," Clarice cut in.

"Oh, she's going to spoil everything. I just *know* it!"

"Of course she will. She'll do anything to make us unhappy."

Isabelle ignored her stepsisters' senseless remarks. Scooting closer to the rocking chair, she clutched Papa's hands and held on tight. His flesh was stretched over a delicate web of veins and nearly translucent. His palms trembled against her fingers, reminding Isabelle of his fragility. His hands had once been strong and sure; now, they were thin and splattered with brown spots. Even his eyes appeared deeper set and more distant, though an inner strength prevailed. She saw the determination in his gaze, could feel it surging through his fingertips.

"What, pray tell, is going on?"

"This Sunday... it's the annual Merchants' Fair. Isn't that grand?" An impish grin rearranged the wrinkles that embedded his face, making them appear deeper in some places and nonexistent in others.

The Merchants' Fair.

Those words hit her like a steel fist. She drew her hands away in stunned silence. Clarice and Elizabeth's smirks were visible from the corner of her eye—something that escalated Isabelle's frustration tenfold. "What? How... how can you even think of leaving? Especially when you've been feeling so ill! You've gone quite mad if you believe I—"

"Why, it's tradition! Your mother, God rest her soul, would never forgive us, should we miss a year." His grin melted away at her blatant disapproval. He released a long sigh. Then, in a hushed tone, he said, "It's our only chance, Isabelle. My last chance. Travelers come from all over Demrov... You know it's true. It could secure us for months. You might even find what your mother and I had." His voice dropped to a whisper; Isabelle had to lean forward to decipher the words. "Come now, *ma petite*. How happy does Raphael make you, really? Is this the life you truly want?"

That question, the seeming awareness in his voice, took Isabelle by surprise. Perhaps Papa wasn't as blind as she thought.

"No, it's not," she heard herself answer.

Her thoughts crawled back to the conversation they'd had the previous night. How much could Papa *really* see? Isabelle knew her unhappiness was quite apparent; with each passing day, disguising her tears with feigned smiles and empty laughter was becoming more difficult.

A hopeful thought wriggled in her mind—one she couldn't shake away.

This could mean our freedom. Her mind began to formulate a plan—to lay out the groundwork for an adventure that would sweep them away from here and Raphael's iron clasp.

"Where? How far this time?"

"Oh, just off the port, in Le Florin. The journey shouldn't take us more than three days."

A LIGHT RAIN DESCENDED from the dark horizon as Isabelle stood outside the Dumont Chateau. Unmoved by its grandiose beauty, she glared at the impressive monument, examining the ornate buttresses and curved arches.

The chateau was indeed beautiful, as grand as any palace or castle... and also cold, empty, and bleak. As always, the smooth, pristine stonework inspired no feelings of awe—and the French Baroque cathedral ceilings only roused a sense of claustrophobia. The pair of conservatory windows returned her stare, resembling black eye sockets in a death's skull.

Isabelle inhaled a steadying breath. Then she held on to her silver cross and murmured a silent prayer. After a moment, she reluctantly paced toward the massive front door. Every fiber of her being screamed to return home, to find another way to make this journey. But time was running short and her options shorter still.

The Merchants' Fair was the perfect excuse to land a carriage and the necessary funds; she would use Raphael, that cold-hearted fool, just as he meant to use her.

The brass knocker, which bore two roaring lion heads, seemed to echo her apprehensive stare. Summoning her courage, she grabbed hold of the ugly thing and banged on the hefty wooden door. The knock echoed ominously inside the chateau's walls.

A portly footman answered almost at once. He wore his taut expression with as much severity as his tied-back queue. There was no emotion in his strange ashen eyes; in fact, he appeared to stare straight through her.

She fought back the chill and forced a sweet smile to her face.

"*Bonsoir.*"

"*Bonsoir*, mademoiselle. Monsieur le Vicomte is presently entertaining company." The footman smoothed down his fine navy livery before finally meeting her gaze. The lack of warmth she encountered in those eyes sent another chill down her spine.

"Regardless—I must speak with him right away."

A brief silence took hold. The only sounds were the pattering rain and the wind's low moan as it whistled through the stripped trees.

"I don't believe he is expecting you this evening."

"I'm sure he shan't mind. In fact, he may be pleasantly surprised." The footman said nothing; he simply raised his winged brows and smoothed down his pristine livery again. Her frustration mounting, Isabelle vainly hugged her body and rubbed both shoulders. "If nothing else, surely you can see how cold and wet it is. Now, let me pass, or Raphael shall know the reason why."

Those words worked magic.

Quite defeated, the footman nodded, thrust the door open, and then gestured Isabelle inside the grand foyer. He eyed the medallion floor with blatant disapproval, his gaze tracking the puddles of water Isabelle had brought with her.

"Oh, my... I apologize for that."

He said nothing, merely sweeping forward with an upturned nose.

Like the chateau's facade, the ornate foyer was beautiful but hollow. The footman reached for her cloak's fastening; Isabelle took an unsteady step backward and clasped the material for dear life. "No—no, thank you. I am quite comfortable."

The footman's expression grew more sour if that was even possible, and his already taut skin pulled tighter. His thin lips creased into a disapproving frown. "Very well, then. I shall alert Monsieur le Vicomte of your calling."

"ISABELLE... WHY, HOW FINE IT IS TO SEE YOU AGAIN."

An hour later, Isabelle turned toward Vivian Brazin's light and airy voice. Raphael's mistress was a vision in lavender lace and billowing damask silks as she descended the winding stairwell like some immaculate goddess. Yet her green eyes appeared cold, sharp, calculating. An abundance of red hair was swept into an elegant coiffure, exposing the pale column of her neck. That hair glowed a vibrant shade of red, burning with cinnamon highlights.

"Vivian," Isabelle returned in greeting, if it could be called such a thing, simultaneously lowering her chin.

Vivian paused in midstride and gave a small, delicate shake of her head. "Madame Brazin," she said by way of correction. Clutching a lavish fur coat, the footman rushed back inside the foyer as Vivian reached the end of the stairwell. Isabelle bit her lip to stifle her amusement; the foolish man, who was normally so smooth and unaffected, almost tripped over his own feet while he helped Vivian into the ridiculous garment.

"How unfortunate." Vivian sighed, petting her coat's thick fur as if it were a prized feline. "Young ladies simply have no sense of etiquette anymore. Didn't your papa ever teach you how to address your betters?"

"Well stated, madame," the footman said with a sharp nod. "My sentiment precisely."

"Alas. He failed to teach you, didn't he?" Vivian asked with a huff. "A shame. From the sound of his condition, there isn't much time left for you to learn."

Isabelle held her tongue and forced back her boiling rage. Silence filled the opulent foyer. She felt the scrutinizing burn of Vivian's eyes as the woman visibly sized her up and down. Every fiber of Isabelle wanted to shout, *Be my guest. You can have your monstrous vicomte. Take him, and go back to France.* Instead, she flashed Vivian an achingly sweet smile and met her insipid gaze. Then the woman headed into the night, her challenge still hanging in the air.

ANOTHER HOUR CRAWLED by before the footman showed Isabelle inside a glittering withdrawing room. Finery surrounded her—an impressive grand pianoforte, a stone hearth, Persian rugs, immaculate wainscoting, gilded mirrors, and an opulent crystal chandelier—yet Isabelle felt like she'd been tossed into a dungeon. Indeed, the rich furnishings were nothing more than a mask, a facade, which disguised a source of evil she didn't dare contemplate. She eyed the regal Queen Anne secretary while her rebellious nature caught fire. She wondered how difficult it would be to rifle through those lacquered drawers... to uncover the Dumont's safely guarded secrets and expose them to the world...

Movement ensnared her peripheral vision and cut her fantasy short.

Raphael lounged in one of the sleek chaises, sipping on a glass of brandy, his wrinkled cravat loose and hanging. A cigar lay on the nearby end table and infused the room with hazy wisps and a smoky odor. If his appearance was any sign, it wasn't his first drink of the evening. With her luck, he was already deep in his cups.

Stonily he stared forward and locked gazes with a hanging portrait. Both men—Raphael and the painted one—looked remarkably similar. Isabelle immediately likened the heavy brows, slick, straight blond hair, and glittering eyes to his father, the comte. Raphael shook his head in silent contemplation before soothing himself with another swig of brandy.

Then two more.

At last the footman's voice split the silence. "Monsieur le Vicomte, may I present Mademoiselle Rose." The words sounded like a death sentence rather than a formal introduction.

Raphael took three more swigs.

Finally, he lifted his head, as if he'd noticed Isabelle's

presence for the first time since her entry. "Ah. Good. Leave us. Now. And do not disturb us for any reason." His voice sounded slurred, confirming Isabelle's suspicion about his drunken stupor.

The footman departed from the withdrawing room. Isabelle grew tense. Uneasy. And just a little panicked.

Coming here was a foolish mistake.

They no longer stood on equal ground. Not in Raphael's chateau; not in the Dumonts' domain. Isabelle's thoughts traveled to the safe cocoon that was her humble cottage. Anxiously smoothing her hands over her cloak, she eyed the hulking furniture and glittering finery—seeing nothing but obstacles and barricades to her freedom.

Raphael chuckled, apparently amused by her discomfort and vulnerability. *Am I that easy to read?* She glanced at him and resisted the urge to flee. They were all alone now. And Raphael looked more than a bit tipsy.

"Raphael, I—"

Remaining seated on the chaise, he drawled, "Sit. Don't be shy. We are to be married, after all."

So you think.

"I need a favor." The words left a bitter taste in her mouth. She felt Raphael's eyes sliding across her skin as if he were physically touching her.

He leaned back, reclining on the chaise like a spoiled feline, then took another drag of alcohol.

"Interesting, though not so unexpected. Pray tell, what's the nature of this favor?" His tone sounded sardonic and ice-cold as he visibly fought the brandy's haze. A certain bitterness laced those words together, which further garbled their meaning.

"My father and I... we're traveling. This weekend. It's the annual Merchants' Fair—"

"Wait, wait. Let me guess. You want a horse and means for traveling."

Two more hearty swigs.

"Yes. A simple brougham will do, and I shan't need a driver. It'll take three days. Two if we're lucky and can leave at first light."

"And you require funds."

Another liberal swig.

Isabelle tightened the cloak about her body and raised her chin several centimeters. She refused for those unfeeling eyes to intimidate her. And she refused to play the part of a victim. Steeling her nerves, she met his gaze and smoothed down the front of her cloak with shaking hands. *Quit trembling, you foolish girl.* She gripped the fabric to better hide her rattled nerves. "Yes. For food and shelter... and if we happen across an inn."

"And what's in this for me? Hmm? How do I benefit?" Silence hung between them, thick and palpable. Only the crackling fireplace breached the quiet. Raphael glanced into the flames, his cold, regal features set aglow. Then his gaze landed on the comte's portrait again. He tensed. His manicured fingernails burrowed into the fabric of his chaise, snagging the fine upholstery. "Ah. That's what I suspected. No matter—we shall make do."

Raphael signaled her forward in a slick come-hither motion. Examining her from head to toe, his eyes crept down her body as she moved with baby steps. He crossed his strong arms over his chest and captured her gaze. From the corner of her eye, she surveyed the grand pianoforte, searching for a barricade, for some form of shelter—knowing well the game Raphael played.

"Your cloak. Remove it."

Another suffocating silence infected the air. "No."

"No? *Now.*" When Isabelle remained quiet and took a step back, he slammed his fist onto the nearby end table. "I said now!"

The jarring crack of knuckles on wood made Isabelle's heart somersault. The movement caused his brandy to spill over the glass, drenching the table's polished surface. Her stomach turning, she mutely watched as the alcohol dripped off the end table and stained the regal Persian rug. Raphael paid it no measure. He merely kept his glower fixed on her with an unwavering intensity.

Maintaining her pride wasn't worth it. There was no telling what a drunken Raphael was capable of.

Her fingers trembled as they worked the cloak's clasp. So rattled were her nerves, it took a full minute to complete the dreadful task. All the while, Raphael watched in stony silence, his eyes fixed on her every breath, his ringed fingers drumming against the wet end table. A king's ransom of rubies and amethysts glittered in the fire's blaze.

"Good girl. Now, set it aside." She hesitated. "That was not a request."

Isabelle folded her cloak, placing it atop the grand pianoforte. She smoothed down the material of her dress and held his steel gaze. The material was torn and embarrassingly faded. Regardless, she squared both shoulders and took a measured step forward.

"What is this?" he asked, gesturing to her attire with a sloppy wave.

"I... I don't understand?"

"I sent gowns. Demrov and Paris's finest. Yet you stand before me looking like a fucking scullery maid. Well? What's your excuse?"

Isabelle felt as her eyes burned into Raphael's. "You know well. My father's medical care is expensive. I can hardly—"

"I don't want to hear it." Raphael violently chucked his brandy into the hearth. "Your excuses bore me." The fire exploded, fueled by the alcohol and his escalating anger. He shot onto his feet and paced over to Isabelle in a few decisive strides. She instinctively stepped away from him, though her burning glare refused to waver. "Indeed. Your excuses bore me nearly as much as your coldness." Isabelle sensed his composure unraveling. His hands began to shake, and his genteel facade was quickly slipping away.

"We have an agreement. One I fully intend to hold you to. Look at you, prancing about in peasant's garb, disgracing my family's name."

You disgrace your family's name every day, just by breathing the air. A profound loathing, unlike anything she'd ever experienced before, sparked an inferno inside her soul. The one thing that kept Isabelle's tongue in check was the thought of Papa and the Merchants' Fair. A promise of a new start.

And an opportunity for our freedom.

Raphael stormed closer still; she moved away, feeling trapped. Hunted. He tugged on the tattered fabric of her dress like a master might summon his hound. "Pitiful. I could have anyone. Anyone." Her bottom bumped into the grand pianoforte—and she found herself caged between Raphael and the wretched instrument.

"Then take someone else and be done with it." She fought to sound strong and capable, though a small quaver betrayed her. Something crossed his eyes—possibly affection—and the gentle emotion looked alarmingly out of place on his stern expression.

Body heat radiated as he towered over her body, staring down. Then he grabbed her shoulder blades and seized her in an iron grip. His fingers pinched her skin, caused a frisson of pain to shoot through her limbs. "Except I don't want someone else. I want *you*."

"You are hurting me. *Let go*." He said nothing. His nails dug through the fabric and embedded in her flesh. "I still don't understand. Why? Why me?" Her voice sounded firm, angry. She felt all that and more.

Raphael shook his head in contemplation. His fingers slid away. When he spoke, at last, the words were soft and barely audible, as if he was addressing a distant memory. "My late mother... you resemble her. Your hair," he said, raking his fingers through her tumbling curls. "Your eyes, your spirit..." His voice trailed off, and Isabelle gasped for air as he pulled her flush against his body.

"Don't... don't touch me. Get your filthy hands off me."

"I am lifting you from a life of poverty and denigration—you ought to show some gratitude, ungrateful *putain*. I am prepared to give you everything your heart could ever desire. The finest gowns and jeweled necklaces, more carriages than you'd ever have a use for. Even *power*." Isabelle doubted he could hear the irony of his own words. "Isabelle... let me make you worthy," he said, gesturing to the room, "of all this." Hot breaths wafted against her face. Then he reached out and traced the curve of her chin with a hooked index finger. "Beautiful. Tempting. Beautifully tempting..."

"You are drunk."

He merely chuckled. The sound echoed despairingly in the ornate withdrawing room, morphing the space into something ugly.

A jail cell.

He outstretched both arms and planted his palms on the pianoforte, imprisoning her between his limbs. The keys shuddered at the movement and quietly reverberated in the large room. The pungent stench of the brandy fanned against her cheeks in a repulsive assault on the senses. Glaring down, he pinned her to the instrument with every fraction of his body weight. She attempted to shove him away while he vulgarly ground against her.

His body came alive—the jut of his arousal painful against her stomach.

"Get off me, Raphael." Nothing. "I shall scream. I swear it. I shall—"

"I call your bluff." His hands slid down and over the sides of her body. Goose bumps rose on her skin, and a nauseous feeling coiled inside her gut. Whatever affection she once held for Raphael mutated into a blinding hatred. "And the only thing you shall scream is my name... as I take you again and again and again..."

"You wouldn't do it. You—you have far too much pride."

It was the wrong thing to say. His eyes sparked to life at the challenge, and his unwanted caresses grew more invasive, horribly intimate. Isabelle felt as though her heart smashed against her ribs, threatening to shatter through flesh and bone.

"Funny you mention such a thing. My father has much pride... In fact, he believes he's God's fucking gift to society. Indeed. He has much pride, to be certain, yet he used to... impose himself on my mother quite often. Why, if it wasn't for his forceful hands, I might not be standing before you today..." Cold, long fingers curled under Isabelle's chin and lifted her face. Raphael locked on to her stare as that queer, soft emotion surfaced once more. "Does that make you sad, *ma chérie*? Does that melt your fragile little heart? Shall you weep for me?"

A stab of pity impaled her; then she met his icy stare again, and any empathy she felt vanished as quickly as it'd come. A rough chuckle resonated from his chest. The harsh vibrations circulated through her body as he firmly pressed against her. "*Non*. You'd best not answer that. What was I saying? Oh, yes— my father is full of pride. And rather quick with his hands and tongue." A chilling smile curled his lips.

Isabelle exhaled a relieved breath as he stepped away and turned toward the painting of his father. "Allow me to share a little story with you. My mother was an exquisite beauty, much like yourself. Needless to say, she made a stunning bride. I used to stare at her wedding portrait for hours, completely transfixed. She looked like an angel..." Raphael spun toward her again and reached her position in one clumsy stride. "Much like you, in fact. Long chestnut curls, eyes that could drive a man to madness, a spirit that could rival even the most rebellious souls. She only met my father one time before the wedding. Young, shy... She wasn't too keen about consummating the marriage. Regardless, Father took what he wanted. What was rightfully *his*. That night, he held her in place, much like this," Raphael whispered, simultaneously reaching for her wrists and holding them captive. "Indeed. He told me all about it the night she died. He laughed as I wept over her dead body, which was still quite warm."

"Let go of me." Isabelle fought his iron grasp as his nails dug into her wrists. "Now!"

She kneed him in the groin. Hard. With all her power. He flinched and emitted a pained grunt, then shook his head and stepped back with a low chuckle. After a moment of collecting himself, he said, "The more she fought, the more he liked it. The more she tried to break free, the more he restrained her. It was a sweet little game they played." He smiled a most wicked smile, leaned close again, and breathed the taunt against her neck while she struggled. His nails dug deeper, drawing blood that curled around her suspended wrists. "Tsk-tsk, you disappoint me, mademoiselle. I took you for a faster learner."

He enjoyed the pain—both receiving and giving it.

A true hunter.

Isabelle felt queasy, *trapped*, sick to her stomach. Sure, Raphael had made his idle threats before... yet something warned her he'd push further tonight. Never had she seen him so deep in his cups—nor had she ever witnessed this strangely... *emotional* side. But she would not fight him; it only intensified his cruelty and kindled his fire. And she refused to fall further into his trap, to become his plaything.

Be brave. Be strong.

Air gushed from her lungs as he unclasped the topmost buttons of her dress. He parted the fabric with fumbling hands and muttered a slurred sentiment. Nestled against Isabelle's chest, the silver cross sparked to life and gleamed in the moonlight.

Maman... grant me strength. Help me find courage.

One of his cold, smooth hands slithered over her shoulder and skated beneath the material of her dress and chemise. For once in her life, she yearned for a corset and petticoats—anything to help keep Raphael out. He cupped her breast in his palm and mercilessly kneaded the flesh. Tears she refused to shed stung the back of her eyes. His thumb and forefinger pinched her bare nipple, twisting the tender skin, causing a jolt of pain to blast down her spine. Then he wedged his thigh between her legs and forced them apart with a coarse, drunken movement. A heartbeat later, he stood between her spread thighs.

Bile rose in her throat, hot and churning; she felt the wretched object of his desire swell and jerk against her. His hand slid out from her bodice and swept down her side. The opposite hand hiked up her skirts, leaving her completely vulnerable and exposed.

She couldn't stop it, couldn't stop her reaction, couldn't subdue her panicked breaths. Surely she would faint from the lack of oxygen. Indeed, her lungs battled for air as her own breathing betrayed her and quickened.

She peered down at her silver cross and whispered another silent prayer.

She tried to harness the tears, to detach herself from the reality of what was happening, but then he opened the slit in her pantalettes and touched her *there*. She shattered. Tears flowed down her cheeks, the bile rose in her throat, and the beat of her heart thundered in her ears. It drowned out her thoughts—muffled everything but the painful feel of his hooked finger *inside* her, the stench of his alcohol-laden breaths, the sound of his mocking voice in her ear...

"What are you trying to prove?" she managed to choke out. Her voice sounded distant and weary; she didn't recognize it as her own.

"That you are *mine*. And you belong to me."

"*Never.*"

Isabelle felt like she was on the verge of fainting. Her body grew limp, her mind drew blank, and all she perceived was the intrusive twisting of his finger and the musky scent of his breaths. His other hand moved back to her breast and squeezed the tender skin. Two more fingers invaded her, hooking deep inside her flesh. Then he retracted from her body, and his nails dragged across her thighs. Alas, there would be scars; they'd be branded on her heart if not her skin. She shook against the pianoforte with stunned disbelief and agony. Sharp, blistering pain shot through every centimeter of her body and constricted her pleas. He inserted three fingers this time; her dry inner walls strained and clenched, fighting to keep him out.

"You won't do it. You cannot."

Raphael withdrew his fingers—which were coated in her blood—and seized her gaze with his own. Isabelle felt some of her spirit returning, and a fire blazed inside her soul.

"Did you say something?"

"I said you cannot follow through with this vile act," she answered through a reed-thin voice. "*I* call your bluff. And this time, I know I'm right."

He chuckled low. The haunting sound made her skin tighten. "And how are you so certain?" He petted her face—a gesture that was at odds with his actions a moment ago—and streaked her cheek with warm blood. *Her* blood. Isabelle straightened her back and returned his stare with an unblinking, daring intensity.

That blood resembled war paint.

"I ask you again, *ma chérie*: How are you so certain, so very sure of yourself?"

"Because you could never face the mirror again without seeing your father." The words felt painful, though she pushed them out to prevent him from going any further. Yet, in her eyes and heart, Raphael had already raped and ruined her all the same.

He freed her from his clutches, and Isabelle gasped for air, clasping her pulsating throat. It was as if she'd been held under water and could finally draw breaths again.

"You play with fire." Raphael paced back and forth for several moments, running shaking hands through his disheveled hair. Sweat shone on his temples and tracked down the sides of his face. "Play with fire, and you get burned."

He is mad.

Isabelle pushed away from the pianoforte and crossed the room. Space. She needed room to breathe. Staring down at her discarded cloak, she hugged her body and willed herself to quit trembling. She swiped at her cheek, then gazed at the blood on her shaky fingers.

A flurry of emotions overwhelmed her. Anger. Revulsion. Pain. Disgust with her own foolishness.

And a blinding fury.

How could I have been so naive?

Because I was desperate to protect Papa and I, she thought. *And we've reached the end of our rope.*

They would leave at first light and never return. That thought—the irony that Raphael himself was handing her the tools for escape—saved Isabelle from breaking down completely.

"You are a *monster*, Raphael. A despicable waste of breath." Those were all the words she could manage. The venom in her voice shocked even herself.

She didn't know how and didn't know when; somehow, someway, she'd make Raphael pay for his unthinkable cruelty.

"Look at you. You think you're so pure, so untouchable.

The perfect little martyr," he said. "You think just because I wasn't born in a fucking prison cell or in the back of a tavern that I haven't known suffering? I guarantee you, mademoiselle, that you would be dead thrice over if you'd received half my beatings."

The disgust in his eyes was evident—but another emotion was also there. One Isabelle couldn't fully place. One that made him even more dangerous.

Then he harshly reeled away, cursed beneath a ragged breath, and refused to meet her gaze again. "Fine," he continued, visibly trying to gather his shattered composure. He paced the length of the drawing room, once, twice, three times—like a manic, caged beast. "Take a brougham, a horse, funds, whatever the hell you require. Be pacified for the time being." He stopped, then looked her up and down, the desire heavy in his stare, his fingers balled into two unyielding fists. He wanted to beat her; she saw it in his glare, in the merciless clenching of his long, bejeweled fingers, which were coated with her blood. "But we marry upon your return."

The words hung in the air long after he left—and Isabelle knew, with every beat of her heart, that he wasn't bluffing this time.

Chapter Three

THE NEXT MORNING dawned with indecent haste. Isabelle had tossed and turned all night, haunted by Raphael's vile words and touches. The memory of his hands on—and inside—her most intimate parts was a nightmare she'd never escape. His words and caresses... the pungent odor of his alcohol-laden breaths... the eerie sound of his laughter... they would forever echo in her mind.

She felt like her body was no longer her own... as if it had been contaminated and was something repulsive she longed to shed.

Isabelle stared into her coffee, contemplating the dark, bitter liquid with vacant eyes. She couldn't eat. Could barely hold a coherent conversation with Papa. Her soul felt raw and exposed... like an open wound that had no hope of healing.

She'd never recover from Raphael's assault should she live to see a thousand years. She still felt what he did to her—and not inside her poor heart where it pained her so. Where Raphael was concerned, her heart had turned to stone months ago. *Non*, she still felt it physically, inside the depths of her sore and bruised body. He'd ruined and scarred her, both inside and out.

She had underestimated Vicomte Raphael Dumont for the last time.

Never again.

Isabelle glanced at Papa, who was presently napping in his beloved rocking chair.

This shall be our freedom.

That thought fortified her, helped banish the gruesome turn of events from her mind. The muffled sound of an approaching carriage ensnared her attention. Papa stirred from his sleep and wearily lifted his head. "You hear that, *ma petite*?"

Inhaling a calming breath, Isabelle climbed to her feet and swept the tattered curtain aside. Beyond the small window, an elegant brougham sat in front of the cottage. She watched with swelling trepidation as the driver stowed a small crate of goods inside the carriage's boot—the few possessions she intended to transport. Raphael's engagement ring would be their greatest prize by far. Bringing too much of her and Papa's personal things could jeopardize the plan and give away her true intentions.

Escape. A new life—and a fresh beginning.

A stunning white mare headed the vehicle, and DUMONT decorated its lacquered door in fancy script. Isabelle lifted her gaze to the horizon; the sky was a deep blue-black shade, and a rough wind shook the bare trees and hedges. Her grasp tightened on the drapery while her nerves churned. Doubt reared its head.

This is wrong. Papa's too weak, too ill... yet we can no longer remain here.

We have no other choice.

The chance of achieving security—true security, without depending on Raphael Dumont a day more—surged through her like a breath of air.

Together, she and Papa would endure. Just as they always had.

A moment later, Clarice and Elizabeth burst into the room, rushing from their back bedchamber. They pushed Isabelle aside, then crowded the window and gawked at the parked brougham. Morning's light glinted off the slick door and set the Dumont coat of arms aglow. The pair of golden lions glinted in the sun's rays. Isabelle warily eyed them, feeling like she was being hunted.

"Let me see!" Clarice screeched into Isabelle's ear.

"Out of our way." Elizabeth moved square in front of her, sufficiently blocking her view. "It's such a lovely carriage. It could be from a fairy tale!" Isabelle couldn't have disagreed more. "Oh, what does Vicomte Dumont possibly see in her? It's so cruelly unfair."

Be my guest and take him. The both of you. Isabelle kept the retort to herself. Instead, she heard herself say, "Clarice, Elizabeth—listen to me, you foolish chits, and listen carefully. As I've said repeatedly, I don't know when Papa and I shall return. Come with us. We can—"

"You don't know when you'll return?" Elizabeth whined. "What about our presents?"

"Come with *you*?" Clarice said, understanding Isabelle's meaning and ignoring Elizabeth's daft remark. "Why, you're even more stupid than I thought. Good-bye and good riddance, I say."

"Oh, but I'd like to ride in the carriage!" Elizabeth complained.

"Shut up, Elizabeth."

Isabelle sighed and shook her downcast head. She chose her words with great care, cautious not to reveal her plan; they would likely run off and tell Raphael at first chance. "Fine, then. I've left sufficient funds. I'll be sending more when I find the opportunity. But you should really reconsider—"

"Just don't forget to send those funds."

Isabelle lost the heart and will to fight them. There were greater battles to brave. Greater storms to sail. Shoving away a nagging guilt, she returned to Papa's rocking chair, knelt before him, and grabbed his cold hands. She smoothed her fingertips over his swollen knuckles, caressing the raised veins. A protective instinct, a renewed resolve, flushed through her. "Papa... you are quite sure you want to do this? It's not too late. I could—"

"That is why we must do this. Why I must do this. If I don't, it shall *become* too late."

Isabelle briefly glanced at Clarice and Elizabeth, who were

chattering away again. Resentment pulsated her insides, squeezing them in an angry fist. Whatever guilt she'd felt moments ago rapidly vanished.

What silly, ridiculous girls, who know nothing of life. Nothing of love or compassion.

"But, Papa, we still have Raphael's aid." Those words pained her. "He—"

"Yes. And at what cost?"

Papa's inquiry tossed her into stunned silence.

How much could he see? *Is Papa really, truly blind?*

"My eyesight may be gone, but I assure you, my hearing is still quite good," he said beneath a rigid sigh, referring to her sobbing the night before.

"I—I didn't mean—"

"Quiet now. Quiet yourself, and listen to me carefully." He squeezed her hand with his fingers, his hold strong, reassuring—a true lifeline. "You have a pure heart, Isabelle. A truly good, kind heart. One you must protect. One that I must protect—my health be damned. As I said nights ago… you shall always be my little girl. *Ma petite.*" He exhaled a long-suffering breath and lifted her knuckles against his lips. "And I refuse to let anyone, vicomte or otherwise, spirit you away."

Those words sealed their fate.

NIGHTTIME GRASPED DEMROV in cold fingers. Dawn had brought winter's first snow; now that dusk had fallen, the snowfall came in heavy sheets. A strange haze rolled down the dirt pathway, which snaked through the vast forest in milky ribbons. Above, the sky appeared black, oily, slicker than ink.

Isabelle and Papa had ventured away from the heart of Demrov kilometers ago; the sight of bustling towns, cobblestone roadways, and lively marketplaces seemed to have become a distant memory. Untouched by the hands of men, the inland forests were dense and untamed; only the occasional dwelling reminded Isabelle that they'd not left civilization completely. The trees were massive silent sentries guarding the thick of Demrov, with gnarled limbs that wove through one another. Each breath of wind caused them to creak and sway, and every so often, the hoot of an owl joined their eerie song.

The brougham shuddered and squelched in the mud as they passed through a shallow river. Isabelle tugged at the reins and retrieved the map from inside her cloak; according to its faded pages, they'd just crossed the Layon River and were fast approaching the desolate province of Hartville.

Isabelle spared a moment to run a fingertip over the river's winding blue design; the pages were tinged a deep yellow and faded at the corners—a testament to the map's countless adventures.

She shut her eyes, remembering the travels she and Papa had taken during her childhood. He'd smile as she'd examine the map over his shoulder. Then, waving his gloved hand across the parchment, he'd proclaim, "Demrov is a true beauty, and you, my lady, are the queen of it all!"

The memory felt like a knife in her heart, and cold reality came rushing back. A blast of wind screamed through the towering trees and threw the cloak's hood from her head. The mare rose onto her back hooves and tossed her great mane with a disgruntled snort.

Yes, she and Papa would attend the Merchants' Fair, just like they had for fifteen years, selling whatever wares they could.

Then hopefully a new life shall begin for us.

"Easy, *chérie*, easy," she coaxed the mare—though her words were swept away by the hammering wind. "I'm confident you've endured worse than this wretched storm." *Such as your master, Vicomte Dumont,* she silently added. The mare nickered and pawed at the snowy ground before journeying forward again. She was truly a thing of beauty. Her white body looked ghostlike within the shadowy forest. Her hide was the color of fresh-fallen snow, the brilliant mane and tail a cascade of silver. Arabian blood showed in her elegant profile, her tapered ears, the strong, curved neck, and powerful chest.

Battling the wind and snow, Isabelle refolded the map, secured her hood, then glanced over her shoulder for the hundredth time. Her breath hung pale and cloudy in the frigid air. Behind the brougham's small viewing window, Papa safely lounged inside, resting against the velvet upholstery and cushions. A lantern dangled from a suspended hook and swayed with each jostling movement.

Safely? On the contrary—I have placed him in far greater danger.

A tattered blanket was sprawled across Papa's lap. Dressed in his fine tweed vest, frock coat, and matching top hat, he looked the part of the traveling merchant. Light from the lantern danced across his taut, sleeping expression and caused Isabelle's heart to give a painful jolt; he appeared impossibly pale, weak, as if he'd aged several years since they'd embarked that morning. A hard cough tore through his body, and he trembled from the bitter cold.

Alas, his illness had worsened.

This was a mistake. Perhaps a dire one.

Papa needed shelter—and quickly. Isabelle considered turning back. They'd traveled for nearly a day, and the occasional hovel and cottage was becoming more scarce with each kilometer. She fought the urge to cry, lest the tears freeze on her face.

This is my doing. Completely my fault.

Her heart knocked against her rib cage as she urged the mare to a steady trot. All around them, towering trees reached out of the darkness and groped for a moonless sky. Their skeletal limbs resembled claws, and she felt them grasping for her and Papa.

A half an hour later, the trees began to clear out, though the haze thickened. She could barely see ten meters in front of her.

Something caught Isabelle's gaze. Hardly believing her eyes, she tugged at the reins and brought the brougham to a jarring halt. The mare whinnied and pawed at the snowy ground. Then she shook her flowing, silver mane and glanced back at Isabelle.

In the clearing, jagged spires and intricate buttresses towered into a black eternity. They resembled swords perched upon an iron throne—a damning message to anyone who dared set eyes upon the fortress.

A crumbling castle, straight from the depths of a nightmare, rose before her like a waking monster. Its face was demented, Gothic—and it seemed an evil intent had laid each stone. The towers and battlements reached hundreds of meters into the oily sky. Courtyards and corridors tied the buildings together, and collectively, the fortress was as large as a city.

She shivered. The castle resembled a crouching beast.

Isabelle glanced over her shoulder as Papa surrendered to another brutal cough—then she ordered the mare forward and halted in front of the rusted front gate. A frigid gust of wind rattled the looming bars, causing them to sway. Wisps of haze curled around them like ghostly fingers. Isabelle crossed herself, leapt down from the box seat, and then thrust those colossal gates apart. They were partially entrenched in the snowy ground. It took an enormous effort to move them. Those gates seemed to dig their feet into the snow and mud—as if battling to keep out any potential trespasser.

Isabelle climbed into the box seat once more and began the long, winding journey toward the hulking castle. The mist gradually thinned, revealing a faint beam of light.

A sconce lantern.

Whoever occupied this dismal ruin was presently home. Hope bloomed inside Isabelle's chest as she tugged on the reins and parked the brougham. She spared a moment to pat the restless mare and toss Papa's blanket over her back.

Minutes later, Isabelle led Papa to the castle's massive front door. Gargoyles glared down from their perches on the flying buttresses. Their wings were fully spread, as if about to take flight, those black eye sockets returning her stare. Isabelle felt a resounding shiver course through her veins. And it wasn't from the stormy weather.

The archway appeared nearly black with age—a looming curve of imposing darkness. Isabelle froze before the threshold while another shudder blasted down her spine.

Maybe we ought to turn back.
No. This was their final hope.
Our last chance.
"Where—" A rough cough shattered Papa's words and shook his entire body.

Isabelle gently clasped his shoulder and pressed a warm kiss to his cheek. He felt colder than ice. "Shh. You mustn't speak. Just rest yourself."

Inhaling a taut breath, she balled her fingers into a fist and banged on the door. The splintered wood snagged her skin while the sound of her knocking echoed within. She recoiled her fist with a cry and spouted an unladylike curse.

"Isabelle, please, *ma petite*—what has—"

"We can find shelter here. Stay until the storm tempers and your cough settles."

But *had* they found shelter? Or just another dead-end, another false pathway, which would only lead them into a deeper despair? She glanced at the looming gargoyles while hope silently slipped away. Snow fell on her cheeks and clashed against the cloak's midnight hue, chilling her to the marrow of her bones. She refused to believe this was it. Heart thudding and determination rising, she lifted her hand again and prepared for another solid knock.

Someone answered her prayer.

Deep, unsettling clanking shook the night. Then the black door groaned open, and Isabelle had to remind herself to breathe.

Chapter Four

> *"Welcome, Beauty, banish fear,*
> *You are queen and mistress here."*
> —Jeanne-Marie Leprince de Beaumont

Isabelle's mouth went dry. She couldn't find her voice, let alone form a coherent sentence. Every fiber of her being drew quiet with cold, sudden fear.

A dark figure lurked beneath the castle's archway. He towered above her, impossibly tall, his long, lean body a flesh-and-blood barricade to her one chance for shelter. A tattered black cloak concealed him from head to toe, making him resemble Death. Indeed. From her vantage point, she couldn't see a centimeter of skin.

His gloved hand clutched a rusted lantern, which gave off a rather inadequate light. Manipulated by the wind's breath, it eerily bobbed in midair and threw shadows along the castle's walls.

She'd never witnessed someone so tall, so imposing… so strangely *regal*. In spite of the cloak, she noticed that his shoulders and chest were broad, likely corded with muscle; their immense width almost brushed against either side of the doorjamb. Standing like a king before his council, his head remained high and proud, his back straighter than an arrow. Hot breaths wafted from the folds on his hood, pale against the darkness, resembling smoke from a dragon's mouth.

But alas, this is no fairy tale. Only cold, harsh reality.

In spite of herself, Isabelle's eyes fell downward. She took a measured step back, noticing for the first time since he'd opened the door that a gigantic dog stood at his side. The thing was by far the tallest and most formidable canine she'd ever seen. It boasted a muscular, lithe body, a long neck, a gray rough-coat, and oddly soulful eyes. It reminded her more of a small horse than a dog.

The creature's lips curled back to flash his sharp teeth, his body arched, and he released a low warning growl. Papa trembled and pushed close to her body. Isabelle tightened her hold on his arm and whispered reassuring words into his ear. Her other hand rose to her throat in an unconscious, protective gesture. "It's fine, Papa. Don't be frightened." Despite her words, her heartbeat was a panicked staccato. She swallowed deeply, then exhaled a calming breath.

"*Non.* Stand down."

The dog obeyed at once and plopped onto the ground next to his master. Silence stretched between the three of them. So bizarre and surreal was this man and beast's presence, Isabelle wondered if she was dreaming. Or rather, perhaps, she was trapped in a lucid nightmare. Soon she'd awaken at her little cottage with a book sprawled across her lap. Papa would lounge in his beloved rocking chair, looking healthy and vibrant once more.

Her train of thought brutally shattered and whipped her back to reality. When the figure spoke again, his voice sounded low, raspy, morbidly sensual. "What do you want?" The decadent baritone surrounded her like liquid velvet—and Isabelle felt herself drowning beneath those sultry refrains.

She turned to Papa and saw he'd physically stiffened. There was an acute fear in those cloudy, hazel eyes.

Be strong. Be brave.

"I—we got caught in the storm... My father—he's very sick. The cold has weakened him greatly. I was hoping—"

"Not my concern."

"Wait. Please! We only need shelter, somewhere to stay for

the night until the storm calms. Please, monsieur. He's terribly ill. I only—"

A haunting chuckle resonated while the door slowly creaked shut. That sound was hollow, void of humor and joy. No one in their right mind would have called it laughter.

Non.

Isabelle wedged her foot in the door, lunging forward in a desperate movement, and latched on to the man's sweeping cloak. He spun around, agile and quick as lightning, his six-foot-three frame towering above her. She glanced at his hooded face and struggled to make out his features. That damnable hood obscured most of him, and darkness cloaked whatever details were left exposed. She could bear not knowing his face. Not seeing his eyes, however, disturbed her greatly; it felt as though she were pleading with Death, rather than a flesh-and-blood man.

Isabelle straightened her posture and fixed her gaze on what she assumed was his eye level. "Let us stay till morning. Please, monsieur. That's all I ask. He'll die out in the cold."

Pure silence. Only the howling wind shattered the quiet. The figure remained still, his immense form blocking her one hope for shelter. She refused to be frightened or intimidated by his callous attitude and demeanor. He'd answered her knock. Now, he would answer her request.

After a long silence, he said in a tone designed to strike terror in the boldest heart, "A pity. As I said, not my—"

"I heard what you said, monsieur, with resounding clarity." He visibly stiffened at her words, as if they were a slap to his face. If he thought such a menacing tone would frighten her off, he had another thing coming. "Now hear *me*. I refuse to be turned away." Indeed, she would die before he refused her again. Her papa's life depended on this beast's mercy—and, *Mon Dieu*, she would have it.

"Is that so?" Isabelle's skin tingled at the deep baritone. The man's voice blasted down her spine and made her skin prickle with gooseflesh. He sounded slightly amused, which increased her frustration tenfold.

Then he edged closer until he stood intimately close. After

Raphael, instinct taught her to move back, to resist a man's nearness. Each of his steps was slow and measured, as though testing her tolerance for his proximity. His hot breaths wafted against her cheeks in tantalizing caresses. She yearned to draw backward—even just a blessed centimeter—to release herself from his suffocating presence, yet she refused to show fear. Instead, she stood a little straighter, lifted her chin a little higher, and grasped Papa's arm with a firmer resolve.

At this nearness, the scents of sandalwood and pine reached her nose. The unique blend mixed with the winter air in a rather compelling way. Her heart pounded. Both palms grew hot and clammy in spite of the cold. All five of her senses felt overwhelmed, challenged, lifted. The man raised the lantern in a graceful motion and illuminated her face. Or rather, *scorched* her face. For such an inadequate candle, the thing gave off an intense and penetrating heat. Warmth from the flame burned her skin and assaulted her eyes. She squinted and turned away, needing refuge from that burning light.

"He is blind." It wasn't a question. The accent of the man's voice, morbidly husky and slightly cultured, spilled through her veins like wine.

Isabelle silently nodded, still turned away. She needed her resolve and couldn't bear the sight of that looming hooded figure another moment. If only he'd remove that damnable hood and let her meet his eyes, person to person...

Within that silence, an eternity seemed to crawl by. Then he shifted backward and gestured them inside the castle with a hauntingly elegant motion.

THE INSIDE OF THE CASTLE was barren and nearly pitch-black. Isabelle felt like she'd entered a tomb. Cracked flagstones covered the floor in irregular, imperfect patterns. Cobwebs hung from every corner, their eight-legged widows infesting the silk strands. The fortress rocked beneath her heels as the heavy oak door banged shut, sealing her and Papa inside its gut. All breaths vacated her lungs, and a feeling of hopelessness descended. For several moments, she stood in silent awe and shivered in the castle's wake. A vaulted ceiling loomed a hundred feet above, black, scarred and webbed with intricate hairline cracks. Countless stone arches and alcoves led in all directions. Two spiral staircases occupied the heart of the foyer. Their bodies twisted into blackness like a pair of fractured spines. Or two interlaced salamanders.

Dust particles floated in midair, illuminated by the swinging lantern and an occasional sconce. Beyond the walls, gusts of wind penetrated the castle and infused the rooms with a bone-chilling draft. Fighting to chase away the cold, Isabelle vainly massaged her arm.

No warmth was to be found.

She grasped Papa's quaking body and held tight, following the lantern's transitory glow. He stumbled on beside her, a look of confusion stretched across his pallid face. Isabelle fought to still her pounding heart, to be strong for him.

"Papa, are... are you all right?"

Some of the tension in his brow faded at the sound of her voice.

"I believe so."

"Good. I—" Isabelle's thoughts were cropped short as the hooded figure glanced over his shoulder; she shivered, feeling his eyes move back and forth between her and Papa. Then he continued to surge forward without another glance. The enormous dog stumbled along beside him—a silent guardian shadowing each of his steps. Their footfalls echoed despairingly, amplified by the room's colossal size.

"We traveled here from Ruillé," she said, needing to shatter the stillness. "It's... it's a rather small village, to be sure, about halfway between here and Lavoncourt—"

"I am aware of where Ruillé is," he scoffed, that deep voice lowering several octaves.

Isabelle snapped her mouth shut, not daring to utter another word. *I best not press my luck. A roof over our heads and food inside our bellies is more than we can hope for.* Her eyes remained fastened to the man's strong back while they strode deeper inside the castle.

She shuddered as she passed through an archway and became entangled in a spider web. The cloaked man hesitated—then reached out and gently helped her regain her footing. A heartbeat later, he and the massive dog continued onward through the shadows. Burdened by a damaged left hind leg, the canine struggled to keep pace. Both man and beast nearly camouflaged in the surrounding darkness. Isabelle felt chills slide through her body while the uneasy sensation expanded within. A small voice warned her to turn away now—to brave the weather and leave this desolate place.

It seemed she'd escaped one storm for an even greater one.

THE DRAWING ROOM was nearly as dim and uninviting as the main hall. Several large sconces provided wavering light, and the bodies of interlaced salamanders constructed their dusty, cobwebbed holders. A brass chandelier hung in the heart of the room. It looked tarnished; only half the candles were lit, imbuing the room with an eerie murmur. In a far corner lurked a fine rosewood chess board. If the strewn pieces were any indication, the thing had been abandoned mid-game. A moth-eaten chaise and faded wingback chairs surrounded the black hearth. The mantel appeared quite filthy; its chipped surface was bare of any sentiments or décor. In fact, all the furniture looked dusty and neglected, as if it had been rotting for an eternity.

Once upon a time, this room—the entire castle—had been a thing of beauty. Isabelle's imagination sparked to life, envisioning a crush of colorful frocks and billowing gowns as ladies and gentlemen conversed beside the hearth in intimate whispers. In her mind's eye, the tarnished chandelier flared to life—chasing away the shadows and illuminating the intricately carved mantel and polished furniture. She could almost smell the honeyed, floral perfumes and hear the tinkle of wine glasses as two gentlemen toasted each other's health and fortune...

I've been indulging in far too many novels.

Isabelle shook her head and chased away her romantic thoughts. Snapping back into the present, she led Papa to the chaise and gently arranged his shivering body. Both the dog and man mutely watched them from across the room. Indeed, Isabelle felt as they assessed her every movement. Every breath.

Minutes later, she sat in the darkness and watched the chandelier's inadequate glow, her small, strong hands resting loosely in her lap. The huge wingback chair dwarfed her slight frame and made her feel all the more overpowered and inferior.

She exhaled a weary sigh and listened to the stillness all around her. How could anyone live in such a desolate place? She sensed a sadness in her host, as well as great anger and resentment. From their brief conversation, she'd gotten the distinct feeling that he despised her. Well, perhaps not *her*... but he certainly loathed the world outside of these strange, drafty walls.

"Thank you for this kindness." The stranger gave a sharp nod, though he remained as quiet as the grave. "He's very cold," she said, gesturing toward Papa. "Could you light the fire?"

The man said nothing. His cloaked form visibly stiffened—the one telltale sign of his discomfort. She glanced across the room, feeling the burn of eyes on her. As their host silently watched her, Papa leaned forward and whispered, "I... I'm so sorry. I should have listened. I never—"

"Shh. Everything shall be fine. Just rest now. I know—"

"I'll see to your horse."

Have my ears deceived me? Taken aback, Isabelle jackknifed toward the deep lull of the man's voice. But the hooded figure and his canine companion were already gone from the room.

AN HOUR LATER, Isabelle lounged in the large chair and gazed into the black hearth. Cobwebs and dust infected the logs, attesting its negligence for some time. The great room was colder than ice; she rubbed her numb fingers together and exhaled a relieved breath.

For the time being, it appeared they were safe. How good it felt to relax, knowing countless kilometers separated her from Raphael Dumont. Papa was fast asleep on the chaise, fresh food and drink arranged on the end table. Indeed, like two starved peasants, she and Papa had devoured half a loaf of bread and an entire pot of mint tea since the cloaked man had set the items in front of them.

Now the stranger crouched before the hearth, kindling the fire in slow, oddly reluctant movements. He kept his face averted from her gaze, while that macabre hood veiled his profile. That cloak spilled across the stone floor in a pool of pitch-black. The massive dog clung to his heels like the most loyal of companions. Isabelle observed man and beast alike, dazed with a mixture of awe and apprehension.

Drafts of wind seeped through the cracks in the walls. Yawning, she tightened the cloak about herself and turned to Papa.

He'd grown so pale, and whatever semblance of peace she'd felt moments ago slipped away. She broke off a chunk of bread, then surveyed the wall decoration, which hung above the hearth's mantel. It was a handsome coat of arms, featuring interlinked salamanders twisted around a flaming shield. A piece of fabric covered the lower half of the decoration, hiding the house's words from sight.

Strange.

She'd seen the design before, of course, as had every other Demrovian. It was the royal coat of arms, which boasted the proud sigil of the country's ancestral family.

A million questions blazed through her mind, each one burning hotter than the last.

After a moment, the hearth sparked to life and cut Isabelle's thoughts in two. The hooded figure gracefully came to his feet; she felt his eyes on her from across the room and couldn't help but admire his height and strong stature. The dog also rose from his hind legs; he was suffering from acute arthritis or an injury of some kind. The back left leg dragged when he walked, and his foot was bent at an awkward angle.

The silence thickened; it pressed hard on her eardrums. Even the fire's ashes fell without a whisper. Isabelle rapped her fingernails against the arms of her chair simply to make noise and break that damming quiet. There was something about the way the man stood there, immobile and cloaked in mystery. The urge to cross the room and offer him comfort struck her without warning.

Instead, she swallowed and attempted a smile, though her nerves all but prevented the simple movement. "Thank... you." He and the dog vanished just as the words emerged, leaving Isabelle and Papa alone again, with only the crackling fire for company.

QUITE A WHILE LATER, as Isabelle relaxed and soaked in the hearth's warmth, she found herself nodding off to sleep. Her mind detached from the stress of the past few days and receded to another time and place. She recalled her journeys with Papa when she'd been little more than a girl. All the villages they'd passed through; all the faces they'd seen. She thought of reading storybooks beneath a bejeweled sky, of leaning against a mountain of crates as Papa pointed out the constellations and their eternal stories—

Rattling seized her attention and ruptured her thoughts. She peered at Papa, who was carefully examining his teacup.

Not with his eyes, of course—but with wandering fingertips. The same impressive coat of arms engraved the fine porcelain; Papa ran his weathered fingers over its surface, clearly in awe of the raised gold decorations and studded gems. The thing must have cost a small fortune. Indeed, she'd never beheld such finery. Even the wares Papa had once sold paled in comparison. The faded brim of his top hat hung low and covered his glassy eyes.

Then her mouth went dry as he slipped the teacup *inside* his coat.

Has he gone mad—or simply grown that desperate? It was completely unlike Papa to steal. *How could he—and after being shown hospitality?*

Her outcry startled him. He half leapt from the chair—and Isabelle watched in shock as the teacup tumbled out from the coat. It rattled and rolled onto the stone ground, shattering into numberless pieces.

A gloved hand broke through the darkness, quicker than a lightning strike. The hooded figure emerged from the shadows and seized Papa by his cravat. His other hand clasped a branch of flickering candles. The illumination flashed across the folds of his cloak, soaking him in a pool of light.

"Stealing from me, are you? Breaking my family's keepsakes?" A sharp jerk forced Papa to his feet. The rough movement sent the top hat tumbling from his head and onto the stone floor. Papa's waxen features melted into an expression of horror and confusion.

Her heart pounding, Isabelle lunged forward and frantically cried out, "Let him alone! It was an accident. Don't you see that you're frightening him?"

"Good." The simple declaration threw Isabelle into stunned silence. Papa called out for her as the man strode from the sitting room, his solid legs eating up the ground in swift, decisive strides. He was physically dragging Papa through the castle.

This isn't happening. It cannot be...

"Stop it! Stop it now—you monster!" Isabelle picked up her skirts and frantically chased after them. Parts of the castle were dark and unkempt, causing her to trip several times over wayward pieces of furniture. Her heart violently pounded in her ears. The man moved impressively fast; between his agile stride and sweeping cloak, he almost appeared to float through the corridors. Plopping onto the stone floor, his dog gave up trying to keep pace. Dust motes rose and fell in midair like ashes, obscuring her vision. She followed the branch's illumination, watching as the candlelight threw prisms along the walls and floor.

"Please, monsieur. Have mercy, I beg you! He didn't know any better. He's not in his right mind. He would never—"

"No one steals from me." His low voice echoed in the darkness, steady as a war drum.

Isabelle felt herself descending. She ducked as she crossed a low archway, where she was met with a steep flight of stairs. A mouth into Hell. The ceiling lurked unusually low and was strung with cobwebs. Isabelle hiked up her skirts, which were now a filthy mess, and raced down the decayed steps. The hooded figure kept a swift pace while she desperately pursued Papa's frightened cries.

Plagued by the darkness, Isabelle tripped and crashed down the stone steps. Pain cascaded through her body, knocking the breath from her lungs. Her skinned knees and elbows throbbed, her heart pounded, her head burned. She spared a moment to catch her breath as she struggled to her feet and resumed her vain quest. Papa's muffled pleas and the sound of *slamming bars* ripped at her very soul.

The dungeon was nearly black. She slowed her pace, moving toward a beam of light at the far end. Rats the size of kittens scurried across the stone floor and filled the space with their terrible squeaking. Her heart thudding, Isabelle rushed through the maze of cells, following Papa's voice and that flickering light. Chains and crude-looking objects littered the ground—torture devices from a past age, she realized with a shudder.

She found them.

Papa was grasping the rusted bars; disoriented and frightened, he was murmuring incoherent pleas. Tears fell from his sightless eyes, though Isabelle knew he fought to restrain them. The branch of candles sat in front of the cell, its wavering light illuminating his terrified expression.

"Forgive me. I have wronged you when you showed my daughter and me hospitality and mercy. Please, monsieur!"

The man towered before him, silent and still. His long arms remaining crossed, he stood with his lean torso straighter than a broadsword. His hood was drawn back, though Isabelle couldn't see his face from her angle.

"Papa, I'm here," she said beneath the weight of a strained breath.

"I-Isabelle?"

Not sparing a moment, she dashed over to the cell—and the man slowly rotated into sight.

Except he resembled more of a beast than any man she'd ever seen.

Isabelle clamped both hands over her mouth and forced her eyes away. The sight burned—and the inferno in his gaze only kindled that fire.

Half of his face looked monstrously twisted; charred mounds of puckered flesh distorted the features beyond any recognition, draining him of all traces of humanity. Those heaps of burned, leather-like skin gleamed and glistened in the candlelight. His hairline receded on the left side of his face and slanted high above a shriveled ear.

Under the severe scarring, his age was more or less indistinguishable—though Isabelle guessed he wasn't a day under thirty-five.

But his eyes were breathtaking. Two brilliant sapphires. There was also a great sadness and anger in those eyes, as if he'd suffered more than his share of original sin. As she gazed into his eyes, all she saw was blue ice—an endless, arctic landscape of cold desolation.

The man turned away, appearing greatly affected by her stare, and hastily rearranged the hood. His scarred hands trembled as he smoothed down the cloak's thick folds.

"Release him," she demanded. "He didn't mean any harm. I—"

"No one meddles with my family's possessions. He can rot

down here as my prisoner. He ought to count himself fortunate that I haven't taken his hand."

"Your prisoner? This... this is a mistake! You must believe me. He'd never—"

A deep, husky chuckle cut through her plea. "Even so."

"Please. Just let him out."

"It's too late for that." Those words seemed to speak volumes. He exhaled a long breath, and Isabelle watched as it unfurled against the darkness in a cloud.

Silence.

"Why... why are you so angry? Why must you be so hateful? So cruel?"

"If I let him go," he said at length, "what can you offer in return?" Isabelle couldn't find her tongue. She wandered directly in front of the cell, almost in a lucid trance, and clasped the cold bars. Papa was huddled in the corner now, coughing and shivering. Guilt, unlike anything she'd known before, pulsated through her.

I'm to blame for this. And if Papa stays here, he'll die well within a fortnight, likely much sooner...

"Get out of my sight." The man's voice jarred Isabelle from her inward stupor. She turned to him and stepped forward, raising her chin at a defiant angle.

I am not so easily broken or frightened.

I am a survivor.

She scanned her empty, dank surroundings: the cold stone walls, sweeping cobwebs, and blazing branch of candles. Despair encased her. Stark emptiness. She dared to step closer while a faint trace of pity bloomed inside her heart.

They stood centimeters apart. Heat radiated from the man's body, surrounding her, immersing her. Isabelle vainly searched for softness in him, but only a dark, embittered spirit reached her. She stared up at his towering frame and gestured for him to bow forward. He hesitated, then did as she commanded. Her hands shook, damn her, as she peeled back his hood and met that piercing gaze again.

Half of his face was handsome—devastatingly so. In her twenty-two years of life, she'd never beheld such haunting beauty.

Jet-black waves, rich and flowing, framed the chiseled lines of his startling features. Stubble peppered the strong curve of his jawline and shadowed a smooth, sculpted cheekbone. The right side of his face was striking, beautiful—a stark contrast to its wrecked counterpart. And within those patrician angles and intense eyes, she encountered his humanity.

His was a face of inconsistencies. Complex. Damaged. Predatory. And more than a bit intriguing.

"I will stay with you," she heard herself whisper. "In my father's place."

"Isabelle—no! I forbid it!"

The man folded long, strong arms across his broad chest. His gaze moved down her face and settled on the rise of her breasts—planting directly on her silver cross.

"I demand he's seen by the finest of physicians."

"Isabelle! Listen to me! I'm an old man. I'm dying. I—"

The man's dark, strangely erotic voice cut through the cellar, and his eyes whipped back to her own with a startling force. "As my mistress."

"What?"

"You must stay here as my mistress. For as long as I demand. Perhaps forever."

Forever.

The word rang with a note of finality.

"Please, Isabelle! I beg you. Don't do this!"

How could I endure it?

"Do as I say and your father shall safely return home." He waved his cloaked arms with a magician's delicate grace. "Your father—whatever family you may have—shall want for nothing. A house, clothing, anything they require. You only need to say the word. Your father will be under my protection—under the care of nurses and physicians—until his last breath."

Isabelle briefly recalled what—and who—was waiting for her back in Ruillé. This fate wouldn't be much worse. This desolate castle could serve as the perfect hideout. Papa would live in France, free from Raphael's clutches and in the hands of the world's greatest physicians...

"How… how can I trust you?" *And does he even have the wealth to uphold such a promise?*

"You cannot."

She had faith Papa would send help once his health recovered. Or she'd find a way out, means of escape. In the interim, she would survive this grim castle and whatever horrors it concealed.

Papa would not. The castle would crush him beneath its dark heel in a matter of days.

Isabelle glanced at Papa again, then stared into the man's brilliant eyes. There, lurking within those expressive depths, she found the softness she'd pursued minutes before.

She sucked in her breath and nodded her agreement.

"It is done." The man swept backward. "He's to remain down here till first light. Then our agreement shall be carried out. In the meantime, I will bring blankets and food—"

"But it's so cold! He—"

"Stole from me while he was a guest in my castle."

He would not compromise. That much was certain.

"I demand to stay with him."

"As you please." He unlocked the cell. "Beyond the dungeon lies a labyrinth. Try to escape, and you'll be lost forever."

He tapped the wall with his booted heel. It swiveled, spun, and rotated, sweeping her captor to the other side...

Chapter Five

Isabelle awoke several hours later to find sheepskin blankets draped over her and Papa. She wearily sat up, careful not to rouse him, her eyes darting across her macabre surroundings. Faint squeaking echoed through the dungeon—and in the corner of the cell a crude, rusted chain glinted in the sconce's illumination.

It took several minutes to remember where she was and how she came to be there. A brief flash of the hooded figure invaded her mind—an image of him standing in the far shadows and watching her sleep. Her skin tightened as she recalled him smoothing the blankets over her body in a ghostlike touch while he believed she slumbered on...

Perhaps I'm imagining things.

Exhaling a breath and tempering her overactive imagination, she clutched the blanket between her fingers. The fabric felt impressively thick and warm. She sank deeper into those welcoming skins as her eyelids grew heavy from sheer pleasure. Her errant thoughts dissolved into the memories of her childhood, when Papa had been energetic and full of spirit. Together they'd traveled all of Demrov, free as two birds, the entire world at their feet...

How long have we been here?

She couldn't tell whether it was night or day; within this despairing crypt, time seemed to vanish. Yet she felt momentarily safe and secure. Raphael was far away, and all that mattered was the warmth of these two blankets and the feeling of Papa's body pressed against her own.

We are safe for the time being. And that's all that matters. It's all that's ever mattered.

The wind wailed, and winter's cold breath seeped through the castle's cracks and crevices. Isabelle snuggled closer to her papa, brushed back his sparse hair strands, and then whispered in his ear, "Papa, are you warm enough?"

Silence.

Isabelle peeled the heavy blanket off her chest and sat up, carefully nudging Papa's body. Only two of the sconce lanterns had survived the night; she strained her eyes as they adjusted to the dark atmosphere.

Non.

Isabelle felt breathless. Like the air had been knocked from her lungs. Papa's sunken eyes were staring forward—unblinking, unmoving. Her hand trembled as she lifted it to his forehead and felt his temperature.

Ice-cold.

"N-no. No, *Dieu*, no."

A scream roared in her throat. She held on to his shoulders and shook his body with all her power, as if the movements might knock the life back into him. Her pulse hammered inside her chest, in her temples, in her neck. She wrung her hands in the tattered material of his tweed coat and crushed her forehead against his chest.

She struggled to hear the beat of his heart—but only silence answered.

"Please..."

A long while later, or perhaps in no time at all, the tears finally came. Alas, shattering tears of disbelief sprang to her eyes, blurring the world around her. Deep, soul-wrenching sobs convulsed her gut as she rocked Papa's body in her arms. Everything felt surreal... as if she'd plunged into the depths of a nightmare and would soon awake. Her body grew cold and numb, resembling an empty shell.

Yes, this must be a nightmare. A terrible dream. This cannot be... cannot be happening. Not after everything we've endured together.

But the truth radiated from Papa's immobile body and vacant stare. His hands were tinted blue, his purplish skin tight and waxy. This was reality at its darkest and most perverse.

"Please... Please come back to me... Please, Papa, I need you... Please don't leave me alone in this abyss where I cannot find you..."

Isabelle wrapped her arms around her body and physically held herself together.

He'd always been her hero, her best friend, her confidant, her anchor. He'd given her everything since her first breath; despite his ailing health, he had fought to continue giving her the world until his last. In return, Isabelle had sacrificed everything in her power to protect him, to keep their close-knit family safe—and now it was all for naught.

This journey should have been their chance at a new beginning.

Instead, they'd reached the end.

"I tried. I—" The words lodged in her throat, barricaded by her gasping sobs. Her gut had been clawed open, leaving her insides raw and exposed. She held Papa against the restless beat of her heart again and rocked him in her arms. It felt as if her small window of happiness had been shattered. All the darkness, heartache, and despair were spilling through in a crushing landslide. "I've failed us..."

Minutes later, Isabelle cowered against the dungeon wall, her chin pressed on top of her upright knees. Deeper and deeper, she sank into the miserable, trembling barricade of her own body.

She rocked on her heels, unable to behold her papa's lifeless pallor again. Muffling her sobs inside her hands, she slowly lifted her head and gazed at his strewn body. He looked like a stranger—and Isabelle felt utterly alone.

"I'm sorry. I'm so sorry..."

Her erratic movements gradually ceased, reality took hold, and a profound terror, a deep sadness unlike anything she'd ever known before, consumed her—body and soul.

PRINCE ADAM DELACROIX dreamt of warm summer nights that evening.

An endless garden of roses surrounded him and spread farther than the eye could see. Maman and Papa ran beside him, their mingled laughter riding the tepid breeze. The scents of ocean water and fresh blooms flavored the damp air and tugged at his imagination. Dusk had recently broken, sending luminous shafts of orange and red across a darkening horizon. Not so far in the distance, Castle Delacroix towered against the skyline.

Adam's emotions stirred to life as he experienced a resounding jolt of pride. Golden light fringed the buttresses and jutting towers, infusing the ancient stonework with a distinct personality. Adam felt as his childhood home spoke to him, and something deep inside his soul answered.

Prince Adam loved this immense garden most of all. Along with the kitchens and menagerie, it was his favorite area of the castle's thousand-acre property. Here, standing among the roses and swaying grass, his family was free. The kingdom's politics, propaganda, and stuffy ballrooms existed as nothing more than a distant memory. The French invaders and their wars imposed no threat—and all boded well in the prince's comfortable world.

Indeed, away from everything and everyone, Adam rejoiced in watching Maman and Papa, who were so proper and formal at court, let their guards slide away.

Nearby, a pair of servants conversed in low voices while they watered the horses. If the change in their king and queen's demeanors alarmed them, they dared not show it. They merely kept their eyes averted, their tones hushed, and all comments few and far between. Sébastien, one of the younger servants, looked distracted as he gazed at the castle's shimmering facade.

Still running, Adam sighed and shifted his eyes to the swaying roses and grass. Earthy, rustic fragrances ascended from the garden, from the rumbling ocean many kilometers off, from the new factories hard at work, and from the very dirt of the prince's beloved homeland. A great wall enclosed the garden—as well as the entirety of the castle—each stone shielding the kingdom's heart as they had for over a thousand years. Papa's voice echoed in his mind: *And we, the Delacroix house, shall stand for a thousand more, because we are the true pillars of Demrov. Always remember, my son: A kingdom is only as strong as her leader.*

Adam came to a panting stop and pointed at a distant cloud of smoke. He'd never seen such a thing. It gushed into the air, soaring above a cluster of tight-knit buildings, resembling smoke from a dragon's mouth. "Maman, Papa, look there!"

Papa shaded his blue eyes with his palm, blocking out the glinting sunrays. "Ah, yes, one of the new factories hard at work. Coal, if I'm not mistaken."

"Won't you take me to the village, Papa? Just once?"

Something dark eclipsed Papa's gaze. His hand trembled in midair, and an apprehensive note entered his normally clear voice. "*Non, mon fils.* Listen carefully," he said, meeting Adam's eyes. "You must stay here within the protection of the castle's walls. There's been much unrest as of late. We can't take chances—not after what happened in France."

Adam heaved a sigh and surveyed the stone wall, which suddenly resembled a jail cell.

Castle Delacroix stood along the coastline, encrusted with the cliffs' jagged faces; at this elevation, the kingdom could be seen and admired—the budding workshops, bustling towns, tight-knit villages, and the sprawling farms, which resembled green and brown patchwork on a quilt. Inland, dense forests infested Demrov—but here, along the coastline, open land and a wealth of possibilities surrounded them. Every wave was unique and brimming with character. Some crashed into the rocks with a vengeance while others kissed the earth. The ocean whispered a husky, forlorn lullaby—the music of the prince's homeland.

"Am I quite clear, Adam?" his father demanded, grasping his shoulder.

Adam nodded.

The three of them ran some more, dashing for the edge of the cliff. Maman clasped her swollen belly as she caught her breath. Laughing, she sank to her knees—right in the middle of an aromatic patch of grass—and pulled Adam and Papa down next to her. Unlike most other highborn ladies, she didn't mind the dirt or dreck, nor that her skirts would likely gather thorns and branches.

"Remember I am running for two now," she said, her voice as soft and warm as the summer breeze. Raven curls curtained her flushed cheeks and fell about her shoulders in dark waves—a stunning contrast to her porcelain skin.

Papa's love strong in his eyes, he wrapped an arm around her waist and observed her with an unwavering intensity. Maman sighed, then reached into a patch of flowers and plucked a single red rose. She turned it between her slender fingers while a small, almost secretive smile graced her lips. Then she laid her free hand on her belly and met Papa's gaze. "If it's a girl... well, I should like to name her Rosemary. After our rose garden. And after this moment."

Papa's deep-set eyes grew misty, though he held back his tears. Maman, however, permitted them to flow down her pinkened cheeks. She flung her arms about Papa's neck and embraced him, whispering words only he could hear. The red rose tumbled free and onto the navy silks of her skirts; Adam collected it with a content smile and inhaled its sugary scent. The music of chirping crickets and the birds' last calls of the evening mated in the air, creating a peaceful ambience.

Night gathered. A rush of cold air violently swept over the wall and across the garden; the roses trembled, manipulated by the sudden chill. The very atmosphere seemed to thicken, to hang in breathless suspense, while a pale mist blew across the garden and consumed everything in its path.

The Kingdom of Demrov was weeping for its fate.

Ice slowly coated everything; icicles hung from Adam's fingers like crystallized tears. Frantically he called out to his maman and papa, but the wind spirited his voice away.

I mustn't cry. I mustn't cry. I must be brave like Papa always says I should be. But hope was dying, and without hope, he lost his will to brave the coming storm. The roses withered and died as if icy fingers had strangled them, draining all color from the Kingdom of Demrov. Prince Adam wept silent tears while his maman and papa dissolved into ashes and rejoined the quiet earth.

As the tears froze on his cheeks, Adam remained crouched in the middle of the decrepit garden—that single red rose clasped between his fingers...

ADAM LOUNGED BEFORE the hearth as an avalanche of emotions crashed through him—guilt, resentment, sorrow, and, most prominent of all, an all-encompassing loneliness and despair.

He'd found no rest that night. Only vivid dreams and the lamentations of past ghosts. Remarkably he hadn't dreamt of that tragic eve; he'd dreamt of warm summer nights, a garden of roses, and the rush of a cold breath, which almost felt like a death rattle, as icy fingers seized the world.

The hearth seemed to reach out for him, to whisper his name, while the fire diabolically crackled and devoured the logs. And he saw everything within those unrelenting flames—his entire past identity and the horrors of that long-ago night.

He much preferred the nightmares over the dreams. They were somehow less painful. More one-note. They didn't leave him aching with a hope and wistfulness that threatened to conquer what remained of his heart. He draped his arm down the side of the wingback chair and absently stroked Stranger, his beloved wolfhound and one true companion.

Heaving a sigh, he comforted himself with a sip of brandy. Beyond the window, sleet thumped against the pane with the audacity of defiant fists. He much liked the gloom of winter; he found solace in the clotted shadows that helped conceal his secrets and monstrous appearance...

Here, within the muted darkness, he didn't have to remember.

Except for that woman. She was a reminder of what he'd become—the catalyst for his dream. And she was impossibly beautiful. Of course she would be immaculate, representing everything he was not.

God has a cruel sense of humor in that way, he mused, a flash of her silver cross racing through his thoughts.

He'd detected an admirable inner strength and compassion in her—one that had nearly stolen his breath away—one he'd believed no longer existed in the world.

Indeed. She'd sacrificed everything for her old man.

If only I could have done the same...

This decrepit castle would surely crush her spirit under its dark heel. For the first time in memory, something moved within Adam, something thawed and stirred to life. *A good man would free them both at first light. A good man would have never made such a twisted arrangement.*

Adam hadn't been a good man for many years.

She'd only ever see him as a monster—and her hatred would fester like an infection until it consumed both their souls. His deformity repulsed women, he knew well. Even the lowest base-born prostitutes fled in disgust at the sight of him. Adam had learned that truth during an especially lonely night. Over time, he'd taught himself not to care, to content himself with a solitary existence. A quiet life of reflection and the pursuit of simple pleasures.

Such as his music.

Then she'd arrived on his doorstep, armed with a willpower that rivaled his own.

That beauty had awakened him. In truth, he didn't know how much longer he could endure living in total seclusion. How long could he stand listening to the echo of loneliness and past ghosts? How many fortnights could he drown in this emptiness and the crush of memories?

He'd checked on her throughout the night; when the cold winds rose, he'd pulled the sheepskin blankets from his own chamber, covered her shivering body, and ensured her father remained warm. And when the sconces flickered out, he'd relit each one.

He'd stood and watched her sleep for nearly an hour. The gentle movements of her rising and falling chest held a strangely calming effect on him. Seconds had grown into minutes; a minute had blossomed into a full hour—and all the while, he'd observed her... completely taken away.

Yes, Adam knew she saw him as a hideous monster—and he was precisely that. The countless years of solitude, of reliving the terrors of that night over and over, had eaten away at his soul, leaving an ugly shell in its wake. And his outburst toward her father hadn't helped. Sighing, feeling a frisson of regret, Adam brought a scarred hand to his temple and ran his fingers over the distorted flesh.

He'd offered the girl and her father shelter from the cold, a place by his fire... and the old man had repaid his mercy with thievery. Adam fiddled with his signet ring, observing how the hearth's flames set the emblem afire. When he'd looked upon that shattered coat of arms, the very symbol of his family, he'd felt a fury unlike anything he'd known in years. Grief and anger had seized hold with iron manacles—and now, he found himself the captor of a sickly man and his stunning daughter.

And she'd agreed to stay here with *him*. As his *mistress*. Despite Adam's effort to combat the emotion, a touch of hope cut through his darkness. *A dangerous thing, hope.* Hope was a barb in his chest, a false horizon amid a sea of blackness. Surely its false light would lead him to destruction—much like a sailor lured by the siren's call.

He exhaled a deep sigh and lowered his head. The shattered teacup still sat at his heels, his family's coat of arms lying in a million unidentifiable pieces. It was like it never had existed. As if *they* never had existed.

Adam knelt to the ground, his heart pounding against his

ribs, and caressed one of the fragmented pieces. The ache in his chest expanded while he felt himself slipping into the memories once more.

Stranger's hot tongue splashed against his disfigurement, and Adam couldn't suppress his chuckle. The corner of the porcelain cut through his finger and ushered him back into the moment; his blood splattered onto the piece, blotting out a salamander. His family's words were crushed, unreadable—yet Adam didn't need them. He'd found his own words, his own personal mantra, long ago.

Never trust. Never forget.

And never forgive.

Knocking jarred Adam from his thoughts. He bolted to his feet and flung the hood into place with a harsh movement. Then he yanked open the door and exhaled a sigh of relief.

"Sébastien. You're late."

Sébastien, now fifty years old, was the reason he still lived. Whether he wanted to thank the fool or throw him into the hearth for that, he couldn't decide. He looked quite tired—not like his usual self. Sébastien had been handsome once, but now his hair was already more white than red. Strain and worry were embedded in his tan expression, and those pale eyes had witnessed far too much. Yet he wore his years with dignity, and he boasted a mischievous smile that never left his damn face.

As expected, an overstuffed satchel hung from Sébastien's shoulder. He thrust the door open and slid past Adam without apology. "Fine thing to see you, too, Adam." Then, lifting his hat, "Ah, why *bonsoir*, Stranger." Adam observed his old friend—for lack of a better word—with a mixture of annoyance and ill humor.

The fool strolled in, right at home. Indeed. He strode the length of the hall as if he owned it. Cracking his fingers, he flopped the satchel on a table with an annoyed grunt. "Damn heavy thing. The carriage outside. What in God's teeth—"

Intrusive questions were the last thing he needed right now. Adam locked on to Sébastien's gaze and threw him a warning glance. He tugged open the satchel and fished out a bottle of wine, some fresh vegetables and fruits, a jar of powdered soap, and a score of other goods. Stranger shoved his massive head inside the satchel; Adam gently pried him out, then broke off a chunk of bread and fed him a piece.

"You'd best be grateful. Traveled all the way to the coast, to the very tip of Demrov. Paid a small fortune at that damn Merchants' Fair. Le Florin was bustlin' like I've never seen her. You would have hated it, *mon ami*."

Adam scowled, not in the mood for Sébastien's silver tongue or clever japes. Usually they were the highlight of his month, but tonight, he held no such patience. His mind was on the two guests downstairs. And on how his entire world was about to change.

Adam dug a hand inside his cloak and retrieved a princely sum of francs. He tossed them on the table, next to the overflowing satchel. Sébastien eyed the loose change, a glint in those pale, sea-green eyes.

"Now, shall that keep you quiet?"

"It's a hell of a start, monsieur." Sébastien nodded his appreciation, then journeyed into the central drawing room. His footsteps echoed as he moved toward the hearth. Eyeing the wavering flames, he blew hot air into his hands and shook his head. "Strange. You've never lit a fire. Not once in twenty-five years." He outstretched both palms and warmed them above the fire. "Not since that night..." He turned back to Adam, a perplexed expression plastered to his face. Then he expelled a sigh and scratched the stubble on his chin. "Come now, Adam. Something's up. That brougham outside... It says 'Dumont.' Tell me, do you have... houseguests... at present?"

"I grow weary and tired." Adam tightened the cloak about his body. "Take a bedchamber for a couple of nights. You can return home after the storm settles. I shall need a favor."

Sébastien nodded, clearly bothered, his stare focused on the shattered teacup and fallen top hat.

AN HOUR LATER, Adam lit a lantern, rearranged his hood, and began the journey into the bowels of his castle.

Carefully he moved down the twisting steps, which plunged into the dungeon, while Stranger hung back at the top of the stairwell. Old age and his left hind leg had gotten the better of him, making the journey an impossible feat. Most nights Adam was forced to carry Stranger up the stairs leading to his bedchamber. Not that he ever minded the burden.

"Not today, old man, not today." He rubbed his palm over the dog's wiry ears, then raced into the dungeon, taking the steps two at a time. Cold air swelled his hood and rushed over his face like icy fingers.

Adam's heart gave an unexpected jerk at the sight of the woman. The beauty was curled up with the allure of a napping kitten, her head resting on her father's thin shoulder. Adam shifted forward, careful not to disturb their slumber. Her long curls slathered across the dank ground, appearing as dark and as tempting as melted drinking chocolate. Everything in him stirred to life at that vision. He imagined them spilled across his chest, damp from their lovemaking. He knelt to the ground, keeping several meters of air between them, and allowed his lantern to illuminate her sleeping expression and dark hair.

Her mouth appeared full, red, the color of fresh rose petals. Erratic hair strands fluttered about her pale face as deep and dreamy breaths manipulated them. He gazed down at her, filled with a startling awareness. She looked immaculate in her sedated state. Content. Almost childlike. A cluster of freckles dusted the bridge of her upturned nose. He balled his gnarled hands into fists while he fought the need to acquaint himself with each one.

He scooted a touch closer, hungry to discern more details but almost frightened to get too near. He hadn't been this close to another human being for over two decades. Not without being met with repulsion and disgust. He recalled the fear in her eyes when she'd beheld his deformity. She had tried to conceal it—but, all the same, he'd seen everything in her disbelieving gaze.

He looked away, disgusted, as the anger inside him

simmered into rage.

Her nearness frustrated him while her beauty filled him with a bitter resentment. Indeed, this slip of a woman had trespassed, had invaded his solitude. Her very presence was a mockery to his fate.

And per their arrangement, she belonged to him.

Throwing his hood back, his eyes shot to her delicate beauty again. His brow scrunched and a frown twisted his mouth; dried tears tracked the woman's cheeks, and the skin under her eyes looked puffy and irritated. A sheen of sweat also covered her forehead. Her body convulsed with slight tremors in spite of the heavy blankets. He shifted his gaze to her father—the thief who had dared to break one of the few keepsakes of his family...

The man lay silent and still beside his daughter, their bodies melded together.

It cannot be.

The revelation hit Adam in a violent torrent.

Adam knew the look of death—and alas, he was staring death straight in the face. His head bowed forward, and a rush of guilt consumed him. He whispered into the darkness, knowing no one was there to answer. "What have I done?"

Chapter Six

Isabelle was thrust into a world of coldness and pain. She'd laid awake shivering for the past hour—or at least what she perceived to be an hour. Cradling her papa's stiffening body, she'd sobbed until she'd had nothing left to give. Her eyes felt raw, her heart ached, and her head pounded with the force of a war drum.

She felt emotionally and physically broken. She reached out, forcing her hand to slide across the grimy stone floor, craving a drink of water from the nearby pitcher.

That terrible man must have left it there during the night. Why does he even care if I drink or eat?

Indeed, a basket of bread, fruit, and nuts sat beside the pitcher. Isabelle's hand stilled while a wave of agony crashed in her gut. The mundane task proved too much to bear. She surrendered with a pained groan and closed her eyes once more. When she opened them again, she thought she was surely dead.

As if in answer to her thoughts, Death arched above her, looming with a regal grace and darkness. Then she felt gentle hands prying her from the cold stones, felt herself being lifted in midair... and experienced the strange, surreal sensation of floating.

Is this dying? Is my spirit ascending from my body and

leaving this quiet earth?

She glanced down and idly watched as the ground moved beneath her. Firm, warm arms carried her. Embraced her. Isabelle murmured another pained groan and lolled the side of her face against the man's hard chest. The beat of his heart thundered in her ear, and for the first time, his humanity hit her at full force.

He tensed, then briefly paused in mid-step, as if the subtle movement had knocked the air from his lungs. A strong, large hand grazed her forehead in a tentative caress; the gesture reminded Isabelle of her youth, when she'd caught whooping cough and Papa had tended to her fever. For over a fortnight, he never once abandoned her side. The memory summoned a cry from her throat.

Non. *Don't think of such things.*

"Where... where are you taking me?" It hurt to breathe, to speak; the words felt hot, like molten lava, and each one seared her sore throat.

"To my bedchamber."

The statement summoned another wave of panic. Isabelle tried to fight him, to somehow wriggle free of his hold, but the pain kept her manacled in place. Everything spun in nauseating circles. Dejectedly she observed as sconce lanterns slid by her. The sound of the man's hollow footsteps echoed through the great rooms. Hulking furniture whirled past them and the shadows erratically wavered.

They seemed to travel for an eternity.

"Take me back. Please. I cannot... cannot leave Papa in the dungeon alone..." The ridiculous sentiment of her own words shook Isabelle back into reality. The tears came rushing to her eyes, and she buried her face in the folds of the man's cloak, loath for him to see her cry.

He momentarily paused. She felt as his arms gripped her a little tighter. Warmth blew across the top of her skull—his breath, she absently registered. "I... I'm so sorry."

Her papa was dead, and he was *sorry.*

If she'd had the energy, she would've shattered into self-deprecating laughter.

Anger pulsated through her body and set her heart aflame. Because of this man—this cruel beast—Papa had spent his final hours behind stone walls and cold bars. The sound of his cries and torn pleas would forever echo in her mind. Her hatred for the man burned like a fire.

But most of all, she hated herself.

I should have known. I shouldn't have been so selfish, thinking only of freeing myself from Raphael...

What have I done?

The weight of her guilt threatened to crush her.

"Let me go..." Her voice barely reached a whisper, and the words burned straight through her throat.

"You are sick. You would die."

"At least I'd be with my father again."

A ragged, deep sigh. "This was never my intention," he whispered, though Isabelle wasn't sure if she'd imagined the words.

"You are a monster."

He made a sound of amusement—a husky, dark chuckle. "If I'm a monster, mademoiselle, it's because man's cruelty has made me so." His cryptic words washed over her, cavernous and steady, each one overflowing with a lifetime of resentment.

Now they were ascending a winding stairwell. A blast of light assaulted her eyes. A chandelier blared overhead, its candles imbuing the room with a low, eerie hum. It sounded like the whisper of a thousand ghosts. Shuddering, Isabelle squinted against the illumination and glanced up—straight into the man's pristine eyes.

As much as she loathed to admit it, even in spite of the drugging haze, Isabelle knew those weren't the eyes of a true monster. They held far too much emotion, too much heartache, as if they bore all the world's sadness.

Those eyes belonged to a man. Nothing more, nothing less.

ISABELLE WAS NEITHER awake nor asleep. She fell through a cyclone of memories—emerging from the fabric of her dreams only for brief instances. Like before, there were also moments of great pain and coldness; she often felt dizzy, almost drunk with agony and fatigue.

She muttered under her breath, fighting to anchor herself, to connect with something... to connect with *somebody*.

Alas, no one can hear me.

"Where am I... Where is Papa... Please..."

He's gone. Forever. All because of my carelessness and stupidity...

Blacker than pitch, the darkness enveloped her. And within this windowless prison, she found no hope.

Then all was well again because Papa sat by her side. Their humble wagon lurched through the paved streets of Demrov. The despair and coldness lifted while the world passed by in a blur of bartering tradesmen, canopy-covered booths, and colorful frocks.

Isabelle watched with a mixture of fascination and pride as citizens from across Europe huddled before Papa's booth. Beautiful crystals and rare gems danced in the afternoon light, drawing people over with their lustrous shine.

Isabelle leaned against the booth's wooden table and stole a glance at Papa. How tall and confident he looked, standing before his immaculate wares, a flock of Demrov's finest at his fingertips. Ladies donning white silk gloves and lace hats clung to the arms of their suitors as they admired the glittering jewels and porcelain treasures from the farthest reaches of the island. Isabelle's heart swelled with pride again; on this afternoon, within this moment, the world belonged to her and Papa.

A stall several meters away, which displayed rows of porcelain dolls, snagged her attention. She fought the temptation as best she could—but when the delectable scent of a roasting turkey leg reached her nose, the urge to wander the marketplace conquered her. Indeed, her affinity for adventure sparked to life.

"Papa..." The overlapping chatter drowned her voice. Isabelle grasped the edge of his fine walking jacket and gave an insistent pull.

"Pardon me, madame," he said to a pretty lady. He dropped to his knee and smiled at Isabelle. "You've been so patient. Only another hour. Then we'll snag one of those turkey legs. What do you say, *ma petite*?"

Isabelle felt her smile grow. "May I look around? I promise not to wander far!"

Papa gave a hesitant off look, a protective glint in his brown gaze. Then he turned to Isabelle and nodded. Pressing a kiss to her forehead, he said, "Stay within eyesight. Now show me your hands." He dropped several francs into her outstretched palms.

And without another word, she rushed toward those beautiful dollies.

Then something shifted.

The air grew heavy and ice-cold. Isabelle hugged her body and massaged her arms in an attempt to warm herself. She glanced over at Papa, and her heart gave a violent turn. Just behind him, a shadowy figure crawled through the long grass. It had the distinct shape of a man—long arms and legs, a strong chest—but something warned Isabelle that it was every bit monster. Wisps of smoke, which were nearly transparent, rose from its body. Wherever the thing crawled, a trail of ashes followed in its wake.

It was Death—and he was coming straight for Papa.

Her heart pounding in her throat, Isabelle ran toward him and watched in horror as the beast slithered closer. Ashes littered the ground like macabre flower petals at a wedding ceremony.

The crush of ladies and gentlemen thickened around her. Sweeping top hats blocked her view, and dozens of bodies crowded her vision of Papa. She pocketed her francs, then attempted to elbow her way through the ever-growing horde of people.

"Oh, let me through! Let me through! Papa!" Isabelle screamed at the top of her lungs, but a cold gust of wind swept her voice away. "Papa!"

Then a low, slurred voice was in her ear, mocking her fate. "Go run to your papa. While you still can..."

She was slipping into the darkness again, fighting to hold on to something.

Within that endless night, she perceived a calm, mesmerizing voice... gentle touches and coolness along her brow. She grew steady, and some of the pain and coldness ebbed away.

"You are in my care now. Shh. You are fine, *ma belle*. You must stop exerting yourself and relax."

Relax? she thought in mild panic. How could she possibly relax? She felt a light pressure on her back, urging her forward. A cup touched her lips, and cool water trickled down her parched throat. She groaned as sudden relief flowed through her veins.

"There we are. Easy now." Long fingers pushed he hair aside. Someone wiped the sweat from her brow, and she felt herself falling backward once more. Isabelle frantically reached forward and grasped handfuls of thick fabric.

Papa's cloak.

"*Non.* Papa, don't leave me—"

"Shh. Lie back and relax..." That deep, melodic voice whispered in her ear—the one tangible thing left in her life. She seized hold as if it were a lifeline. And in many ways, it was.

"Please... don't leave me... Please. Don't let go of me..."

"Don't worry. I am here with you, *ma belle*. And I shan't let you go."

Chapter Seven

For over two nights, the beauty slid in and out of delirium and consciousness. Adam left her side only to refill the water basin; he applied cool linens to her arms and legs and fought to reverse her sweltering fever. He hand-fed her warm broth, whispered calming words in her ear, cleaned and disinfected her bloodied knees, and continually wiped the sweat from her hairline.

Indeed, the sound of his voice appeared to soothe her. Whenever he spoke, her breaths grew more regular, and she stopped fighting whatever darkness seemed to beckon her.

The illness had sprung so suddenly, so violently—Adam knew the storm hadn't been the sole catalyst. He recalled all too well the mental, emotional, and physical tolls of despair and shock. How your insides felt gutted. Raw. Exposed. How the distress could morph into a sick fatigue, how your entire body could shut down, as if to scream, *I give up. No more suffering. This is the end.*

But Adam would not let her surrender to such a fate. Perhaps it was his own guilt or selfishness, but from the moment he'd embraced her trembling body, he vowed she'd emerge from this stronger than before.

He glanced down at her beauty, and her final words echoed in his mind. *You are a monster.*

That declaration had affected him more than she could ever know. A small part of him wanted to prove her right—to leave her alone in the dungeon while the fever pulled her into the depths of madness.

She had good reason to loathe him. In her eyes, he'd killed her father and stolen her freedom.

A monster.

He shoved away her words, his attention riveted on rebuilding the mental walls that prevented his self-hatred from conquering him completely.

Adam gently cradled her back and softly whispered in her ear. The woman's face was a beautiful song of a lush mouth, velvety eyes, high cheekbones, and a smattering of freckles across the pert bridge of her nose. He urged her into an upright position, the nearness of her slender body filling him with an excruciating longing, and lifted a cup to her lips. "You must drink, *ma belle*," he said in a low, careful tone, as if he were coaxing a wild horse into submission.

They were connected now—fate had made certain of that—and, *Mon Dieu*, he wouldn't let her fade away. Not without a fight.

Adam hesitantly reached out and ran his fingertips through her hair. They felt like fresh-spun silk, though the scars on his hand dulled the sensation. Even through the thick material of her dress, it was clear that she wore no petticoats or corset. Just a chemise and pantalettes. He eyed the mud-streaked hem and considered changing her garment.

Non, *it wouldn't be proper. I couldn't possibly invade her virtue in such a way.*

A lost part of his humanity resurfaced, and for the first time in countless years, he felt like a man again. Not a reclusive monster. Not a shadow of the person he'd once been. A true, living and breathing man who had urges like any other—

Slender arms lashed out and encircled his neck; the jarring movement knocked the air from his lungs and flooded his body with that wretched feeling again.

Hope.

Calm yourself, you stupid fool. She doesn't even know what she's doing. Or who you are.

Regardless, Adam melted against her warm curves. Lost in her scent and feel, he gathered her body and echoed her embrace with trembling arms. His shoulders shook, his heart thundered, and sudden tears misted his gaze. He sighed, hardly believing what was happening, then tracked his palms over her slim shoulders and back.

Such a simple thing, a hug. Something most people took for granted, never stopping to savor the feel of another person's warmth and closeness.

Feeling her heartbeat thumping against his own, the wisps of her breaths fanning his shoulder... It was nearly his undoing.

The soft curves of her breasts rocked against his chest. Painfully aware of the hardness of his body and surging blood, he took several deep breaths as he fought to regain control of himself. He made himself remember the prostitute who'd fled at the sight of his disfigurement... made himself recall what he'd done to the beauty's ill, blind father.

Her words echoed in his mind again and helped alleviate that aching want.

You are a monster.

Cursing away his wretched arousal, he murmured in her ear, brushed back her damp curls, and returned her to a reclined position. Then he glanced at the floor—where a sparkling engagement ring drank in the lantern's illumination.

THE FOLLOWING NIGHT, the beauty's fever and delirium settled considerably. Whatever demon she'd battled the first few evenings appeared to have temporarily subsided. Now, she slept soundly and deeply, occasionally stirring awake and grasping for him to come closer.

"Where in God's teeth did you ever manage to find a pretty piece like that?"

Adam jerked his hand away from the woman and turned to Sébastien, who was standing in the doorway. Both arms were knotted over his chest, a defiant curl quirking his thin lips. With all his focus on tending to the woman's fever, he'd forgotten about Sébastien's arrival several nights before.

"She is no one's business but my own," Adam shot over his shoulder. Stranger, who was napping beside the bed, stirred awake and stretched his colossal paws.

"*Dumont*," Sébastien muttered as he slid into Adam's bedchamber without invitation. "The name on the carriage—I've heard it before. Seen the coat of arms, too. Many times, actually. A quite distinguished family in Demrov... A comte who settled here from Paris a decade past... not so long after the French monarchy lost their reign." Cracking his knuckles, Sébastien shifted his weight from heel to foot. "The young vicomte is rumored to be a rather pretty-looking fellow. Makes ladies simper behind their fans with only a glance. Or so I've heard."

Adam shrugged, pretending Sébastien's words didn't deter him. "Good for him." He applied a damp linen to the woman's upper face and brow. She stirred in her sleep, and Adam gently brushed the hair back from her forehead. His fingers remained longer than necessary while her eyes slid open for half a heartbeat, locking on to his own. Then she faded back into darkness again.

Sébastien towered above the four-poster canopied bed, standing far too close for Adam's comfort, and pushed the linen from her brow. "Beautiful, to be sure. But she doesn't look like nobility," he said, gesturing to her plain wool dress. "Not by the appearance of her clothing. More like a scullery maid or kitchen wench. I ask again: Where did she come from?"

"Thankfully for you, her social standing doesn't make a bit of difference. She's under my care now. She came here seeking shelter from the snowstorm. That's all you need to know. She's quite ill," he added, stating the obvious—annoyed with Sébastien's hovering body and nosy inquiries.

"Well, I gathered as much, her being unconscious and such." Adam felt the scrutinizing burn of Sébastien's green eyes.

He was suspicious of the girl's presence—that much was obvious. "A young lady stumbled upon your castle all alone? With no escort or chaperone to speak of, dressed in a servant's shift and driving the comte's brougham? Queer, to say the least..."

The same thought had haunted Adam for several nights. The comte's brougham and the engagement ring.

What is she running from? Or from whom?

"Perhaps she prefers to observe her comfort rather than fashion's high demands." A transient smile played across Adam's mouth as his consciousness trickled into the past. Indeed, Maman had cursed the tight-laced, elaborate French gowns, which were always worn by the ladies at court. She'd much preferred the flowing and earthy garb of the peasants and common people. A familiar ache settled in his heart; he pushed away the response and shrugged his broad shoulders. The ritual had become as natural as breathing. Pretending not to care, then convincing himself of the blatant lie. For a teasing moment, Adam was back in the rose garden, running beside his parents and gazing down at Demrov when it still had existed as a kingdom. "Or better yet, maybe she's a highway woman on the run," Adam mused. "Perhaps she took off with the old comte's brougham and is headed for France or Italy."

Sébastien laughed and shook his head. "Careful now, *mon ami*. You'd best stop creating fanciful stories for the poor girl. If not, I'm afraid you'll make yourself heartsick with love for her."

Adam scoffed. He could never love again. Love demanded a considerable degree of trust, and after his family had been betrayed all those years ago, he'd lost his faith in others. Although he sometimes had doubts about his loyalty, he placed a delicate trust in Sébastien. The man was often a pain in the ass, to be sure—but he'd never betrayed him or his family in over twenty-five years. *Sébastien and Stranger*, he sardonically mused, *my two loyal companions.*

"What is she to you? A ticket back to the land of the living, I suppose?"

Adam opted for silence as his anger and frustration heated

from a simmer to a steady boil. The sound of Sébastien's cracking knuckles shattered the ambience. *Mon Dieu*, Adam loathed that habit.

"And what of the gentleman's hat by the fireplace?" Sébastien asked. "It's quite worn and outdated—clearly not the comte's possession. I assume that belonged to your lady friend as well?"

"Perhaps it belongs to me. I'm still a gentleman of sorts."

Sébastien gave a bark of laughter that could have woken the dead. Adam was surprised it didn't rouse his sleeping beauty. "That, *mon ami*, couldn't be further from the truth, I'm afraid. And I distinctly recall bringing you such a hat once, which you threw into a heap of trash while stating, 'a handsome hat won't make my face any prettier.'" Sébastien sighed and scratched the stubble on his square jawline. "I have known you for a very long time, Adam—since you were a carefree boy; when you still believed the Kingdom of Demrov was woven from rose gardens and pretty bedtime stories. You were a terrible liar then. You're an even worse liar now."

Adam gritted his teeth while he repeatedly thrust a scarred hand through his hairline. "I haven't the slightest idea how Dumont's brougham came into her possession. As I said, she came here seeking shelter from the damnable storm."

"And discovered a much more pleasant atmosphere inside these wretched walls, I suppose," Sébastien murmured, his words dripping with dry sarcasm and something more. Something that threatened to destroy his equilibrium and their tentative friendship.

"You are supposed to be my servant. Not an inspector."

"Yes, yes—I am your humble servant, your friend, and I like to think I was your father's friend as well, God rest his soul... All the same, I shall not stand idly by while I smell foul play. Or sense that you're tampering with Dumont's property. You may lurk obliviously in the dark, Adam, but I have not. I'll have you know the comte has ruined people for far less a crime."

"Property? She's a woman—not a goat for trade or barter."

"Yes, a woman, and a most stunning prize of a woman, at that. Pray tell, what is this woman's name?"

Adam swallowed, swiping his fingers along his hairline. "I... We didn't exchange names."

"What sort of *gentleman* fails to inquire a lady's name? Your parents would be quite disappointed." It was meant to be a jab in the side, a rather harmless jest, yet it stung all the same.

"The kind who hasn't said more than a few fucking sentences to a woman in over twenty years."

"Tell me now," Sébastien demanded at length. "What was that favor you wished to ask me?"

Wiping the woman's brow, Adam paused his handiwork, not sure how to proceed. He damn well needed Sébastien out of his way before the girl awoke, yet he also required his aid. His questions and prodding were bad enough. He couldn't risk Sébastien's presence when the girl regained consciousness. *First things first,* he decided, making the woman's health his priority.

My priority—and somewhat of an obsession.

"Come back in a fortnight. I'll explain the favor then."

Sébastien stabbed him with a penetrating glance, then strode toward the door. He buried his hands in his trouser pockets and whistled under his breath. His devil-may-care attitude flared Adam's temper, escalating it to new heights. "Very well," Sébastien muttered with a crack of his knuckles. "I daresay she'll have plenty to say to me in two weeks."

RAPHAEL'S BREATH, *sharp with the scents of alcohol and sweat, scorches my skin as he restrains my wrists and holds me close. Intimately close. He whispers in my ear, and his words render me more immobile than his physical hold. I fight to break free of him—to emerge from this nightmare with a semblance of my virtue still intact—but my protests are in vain. His deep chuckle vibrates against me, his grasp tightens until my hands whiten, and his words grow darker still. His speech sounds slurred and guttural, his breath smells rancid. Each word is half-drowned in alcohol.*

He pushes my body against the edge of the grand pianoforte, keeping me pinned in place. My heart pounds as he slips a cold, smooth hand inside my bodice. Revulsion and hatred fill me. I squeeze my eyes shut, resenting his vile caresses and how those fingers run over my skin, leaving their taint.

Most of all, I resent myself for ever lowering myself to such disgrace. Then, in a slow and suggestive perusal, his gaze slithers down and over my heaving chest. He visibly drinks me in, undressing me with those hazy eyes. I feel consumed, vulnerable, helpless. Fear seizes my beating heart with the force of a steel fist. His erection strains against his trousers with each movement. I struggle, jerk, and plead—but nothing seems to reach him.

A hooked finger is deep inside me now—twisting, tearing—causing a jolt of pain to speed through my limbs. Then his hands wrap around either side of my head, and he pulls me forward, forcing his musky breath upon me. He slides his dry lips over my collarbone, branding me forever. "You are mine. You belong to me."

Isabelle fell back into reality like a babe taking its first breath of life. Her heart thudded while tears swam down her clammy cheeks. She panted, battling for the precious air; it felt as though a weight laid across her chest, causing her lungs to fold up and surrender. Her eyes came into focus, though the edge of her vision remained frayed and fuzzy. But she saw enough.

Large hands enclosed either side of her face, and a pair of startling sapphire eyes stared into her own. Everything came rushing back.

Raphael's vile assault. Journeying with Papa through Demrov's dense forest as the storm raged around them. Venturing inside the desolate province of Hartville—and straight into this man's clutches. Oddly she recalled his voice most of all—her one lifeline, a guiding light within an endless darkness...

Except he didn't save me from the darkness. He brought the darkness.

For a brief instant, she wondered where Papa was—then

her great loss returned at full force and spirited away her breaths. On the verge of descending into blackness again, Isabelle scooted backward as she held the man's powerful stare. His hands slid away, almost in slow motion, as if he was struggling not to frighten her any further.

A little too late for that.

Reality and the imagery from her nightmares melded together. They thundered through her mind and body in a violent storm. She felt herself drowning, gasping for air again. Her breaths grew shorter still, and the bedchamber appeared to physically spin.

How long have I been here?

Dieu, is this the beast's private quarters?

Isabelle clutched her chest as she caught herself slipping into darkness. Then a gentle hand grazed her shoulder, and an equally gentle voice murmured in her ear. "Take deep breaths." His fingers moved in slow, deliberate circles. Isabelle felt some of the agony ebb away. "Slowly breathe. Slowly. That's it. In. Out. In. Out. Good." She did as commanded. Unexpected relief swelled her mind and body. She turned to him and took in his hovering features. He wasn't wearing the hood, and his entire deformity was in sight. The sight of those puckered welts hit her hard; she lowered her lashes over her eyes and looked away.

His intimate proximity summoned a flash of that night. A flash of Raphael.

Vicomte Dumont's granite expression blazed through her mind, and her flight or fight instinct seized hold. She shoved the man's scarred hand away. Then she recalled the bargain they'd struck—the arrangement she'd halfheartedly agreed to when she thought Papa could still be saved. Her thoughts returned to Raphael's pungent breaths and painful caresses; she couldn't bear such an existence.

"Don't—don't you dare touch me. My father died at your hands!" she said, straightening her back against the headboard, capturing the man's gaze with her own. Tears threatened to resurface; she inhaled a calming breath to suppress them. "Any 'agreement' we might have made is undone now."

Mutely he stared at her. Some of her resolve slipped away

at the penetrating glint in those eyes. Then he exhaled, releasing a long-suffering sigh, and thrust scarred fingers through his hairline. "I've played nurse to you for several days and nights," he said, his voice a waterfall of dark wine. "You can hardly carry your own body weight—not to mention, you have insufficient funds on your person. I—"

"You—you searched through my belongings?"

"Yes," he said without apology. "And I've fed and watered your horse. Setting off into the snowstorm may be noble indeed—but it's also madness, suicide. You wouldn't last the night, *ma belle*. Give this place a chance," he whispered, his voice almost inaudible. The words weren't spoken, yet she heard them all the same: *Give me a chance.* "This castle shall be your home, just as it's mine. You may venture wherever you like, *except* the eastern tower. It's forbidden to you and any other person who steps foot inside this castle." Her curiosity piqued, she began to question this eastern tower—but Adam sufficiently cut her sentence short. "I won't hold you to... the other parts of our arrangement."

Isabelle couldn't argue with his logic—she was sick and in no shape to travel. The storm would kill her within hours. But she questioned his intentions.

"Why... why do you even want me here?"

Silence. Then he reached forward and tentatively brushed the side of her face with a featherlight touch. She instinctively recoiled.

Her head knocked against hard wood, preventing her from moving back any farther. When he spoke again, that deep, mesmerizing voice—the voice from her dreams—fell across her ears like black velvet.

Another heartfelt sigh.

Even his sighs sounded beautiful and expressive—almost like music. "I know you're confused and in pain. And I know you're hurting. But you don't have to fear me."

Isabelle finally found her voice. Inhaling deeply, she locked on to the man's wavering, blue gaze. Those eyes were deep. Penetrating. Dare she think even a bit thrilling. His was a face that impaled; his were eyes that burned. "How—how can you say such things? After what you did to my father? Throwing him inside that—"

"He was ill," he cut in, the tone of his voice smooth and controlled. "Deathly ill. And he stole from me while he stayed beneath my roof as a guest."

"Tell me, monsieur. What kind of monster imprisons a blind, ill man?"

The word *monster* rattled something inside him. He visibly tightened, and the mangled half of his face drew taut. Then his long, slender fingers coiled into tight fists. "What kind of daughter journeys into a snowstorm with their dying father?"

Isabelle couldn't find a reply. She'd been seeking the same answer ever since she and Papa had set off. Reality had found her within her nightmares, in that bottomless darkness, and now it spread through her heart like a poison.

"Are you always so polite to your 'guests'?"

Adam shrugged, then gestured toward his monstrous companion. Her gaze snapped to the huge dog, and she wondered how she hadn't noticed him until that moment. "Stranger and I aren't accustomed to guests, I'm afraid." He paused, adjusted his body, then ran his fingers through his dark hair. The raven waves glistened in the lantern's light, drinking in the illumination. Likewise, his eyes glittered like a pair of twin sapphires as they coolly fixed on her. "And besides... you are no longer a guest."

"You may soften the blow of your words with logic, but I hear what you're saying all the same. You intend to fully hold me to our agreement—despite everything that's happened since?"

Isabelle's eyes shifted from the beast and ran over Adam's seated form. The breadth of the man's shoulders was impossibly wide. The dark cloak dripped over his long body like water from an icicle. From this angle, the deformed, left side of his face was out of sight. Jet-black hair fell to his nape in thick waves. The right-side portion of his face, which did not suffer from ruin, was truly magnificent to behold. The jut of his chin was regal, chiseled, commanding. A strong, dark brow accented his right eye, and several days' worth of stubble shadowed his austere cheekbone. The overall effect was valiant and rugged, softened only by dark, sweeping lashes. But most arresting was that gaze. Soul-deep. Cutting. Then he turned his head—and Isabelle's throat plummeted into her gut.

Jarred by the warped flesh and raised welts, she emitted a startled sound and looked away. She felt him physically tense beside her.

"What I said before, about the... terms... of our arrangement," he whispered, "you can trust me."

"I thought you said I can't trust you."

Silence seized hold. Only the flickering lantern breached the quiet.

"My name is Adam," he finally said in a low, cautious tone, as if he wasn't used to sharing something as simple as his name.

"Adam..." He further stiffened as she tested the feel of his name on her lips. "You live here alone? Without any family or servants?"

He said nothing, though his eyes whispered a thousand unspoken words. A rush of sadness washed over her, shocking her to the very core. She battled the response—fought to perceive Adam as nothing more than a beast—but when he dipped a piece of linen into a basin and offered it to her, some of her fear and hatred melted.

She stared at him, dumbly, with a blend of mute dread and awe. When she failed to take the linen from his hands, he slid forward, his eyes never leaving hers, and carefully laid it across her brow. Relief came to her in a sweet, swift rush. Her eyes fell shut as the damp material absorbed some of the pain and allowed her thoughts to refocus.

Adam scooted backward, though they remained less than a meter apart. The warmth of his body wafted toward her, carrying with it the enticing scents of sandalwood, pine, and winter. "I believe your fever's almost broken."

Isabelle swallowed deeply before attempting a reply. "How long was I unconscious?" Silence weighed heavily in the air, a palpable current of tension. She adjusted her body with a pained groan while her head suffered a splintering migraine. "How... how long has it been?" *Since Papa was stolen from me,* she inwardly added.

Adam shifted on the bed, causing the mattress to dip inward. He appeared to be as wary and unsure as she was. "Tonight makes three nights."

Three nights. She had been under his care—completely vulnerable and unconscious—for three whole nights. The thought left her feeling violated but also strangely relieved. In spite of his unforgivable cruelty nights ago, she was in no immediate danger. He'd watched over her, tended to her illness with great tenderness and care...

Don't worry. I am here with you, ma belle. And I shan't let you go.

Indeed, for three nights, he'd never abandoned her. He'd kept her calm and anchored during those hours of darkness. Amid the nightmares and disorientation, she'd been aware of Adam caring for her with astonishing tenderness. Warring emotions clashed inside, draining her energy and focus.

I just want to rest. I want to rest and be with Papa again.

"How do you feel?"

The deep lull of his voice jerked Isabelle from her thoughts. The pain from her illness felt quite horrible—though the greatest discomfort lay in her heart, invisible and radiating where no one could see.

And something warned Isabelle that Adam's external scars weren't the worse of his pains; likewise, his true torment lay deep inside, seared across his soul. Yet she couldn't escape the echo of Papa's cries or the haunting image of Adam pulling him through the dark corridors.

"Let us see... my throat and ears feel like they're on fire, and my head resembles a godforsaken war drum... but I shall manage quite well. *Merci.*" Her voice sounded tense, an unstoppable anger fortifying the words.

Adam nodded, then absently fiddled with his ring. Isabelle strained forward and battled to decipher the emblem. *AFD* engraved the smooth, golden surface and glinted in the candlelight.

A signet ring?

"I admire your strength. Most would have broken in such

circumstances." Another lingering silence infected the air. Adam drummed his fingers and brought them together in the form of a steeple. The signet ring ensnared her gaze, shimmering like a beacon. "I understand how you feel. And I am so sorry."

Isabelle bit her bottom lip to stop the retort. She straightened against the headboard and met Adam's leveled stare. "Where is he? *Where?*" She battled to keep the emotion from her voice, but the quaver betrayed her.

"I laid him to rest. In the courtyard beneath a black ash tree."

The thought of Papa alone in the eternal dirt caused a wave of nausea to rise in her throat. It didn't matter that his spirit had gone to rest. He was still very much alive in her mind and heart.

"I suppose I shall let you sleep, then." Clearly uncomfortable with the turn of their conversation, Adam climbed to his feet and patted his strong, muscled thigh. Stranger limped to his side. They both strode toward the door, Adam moving with an impressive grace for a man his size. The chandelier flickered above him like a diva's spotlight, causing the black of his hair to shine with bluish highlights. She studied his face in its entirety—the deformed, mangled half and the handsome side. How exquisite he'd once been. All darkness and torn emotion, he glided through the chamber like a shadow.

Suddenly she recalled the faint sound of another person's voice. A second man had been here. She was certain of it.

"You live here all alone. This castle—it belongs to you?"

Adam turned to her in a slow, hauntingly elegant motion. "Everything inside these walls is mine." A not so idle threat—a sensual innuendo—laced those words together.

"'Everything is mine.'" She released a small, cynical laugh in spite of her better judgment. "Spoken like any other man. You disappoint me, monsieur." The faintest ghost of a smile appeared on the handsome side of his face. A gleam also entered his eyes—and she saw her tart retort had sparked something to life.

"Does anything else here disappoint you?" He gestured to himself with self-deprecating humor, his movements slick and suave. She stared at the distorted features and found she couldn't bring herself to reply. Isabelle had always prided herself on not being judgmental about outward appearances—unlike her stepsisters and late stepmother—yet the warped, leather-like skin sent a shiver down her backbone. When she offered no response, he dipped his head and swept closer to the door.

"Isabelle," she blurted out, stopping him in his tracks again. Rearranging the hood, he turned to her and stared down. She returned his gaze, breathless, overpowered by his very presence. "You never asked for my name. It's Isabelle. Isabelle Rose."

He paused in the doorway and released a long, rigid sigh. "You are safe here with me. I shall never harm you, Isabelle. You have my word."

Silence circulated between them. Pulsated through the air. That silence ate away at Isabelle and served as a grim reminder. Within the quiet, she remembered why she was here. She remembered what she had lost. And she remembered how and why.

Because of you.
And because of myself.
"You already have harmed me."

Chapter Eight

A MELODY SEDUCED Isabelle from her sleep. Enchanting music, unlike anything she'd ever heard, caressed her skin with the sensual pull of a thousand fingers. She'd only attended the opera once in her lifetime, so she had little to compare the music against—but the range of emotion it possessed sounded like genius. It stroked her, ignited her imagination, brought a splash of color to the darkness she'd known for several nights.

Has it been nights? Or weeks?

Her heart grew heavy as those chords sensually washed over her. The center of her body felt weak, hot, vulnerable; surely she'd collapse in on herself. The music pulsated through her veins and lit a fire inside her soul.

Shaken, she sat up in her bed—as if the spellbinding music had physically lifted her—and followed those passionate refrains with her lantern. Half sleepwalking, caught between dreams and reality, her insides turned hotter and heavier as she slipped on her boots and wandered down the spiral stairwell. The wooden railing slid under her palm—the one thing anchoring her mind and body in place. Only a few sconces lit her path and ruptured the endless darkness. She gave a sigh of relief when she reached the landing. Then the music grew louder and more commanding with each step. It beckoned her forward, closer, those chords sinking below her tingling skin...

Isabelle stopped outside a half-open door. Inside, a candle lightly flickered and cast a ring of light. Leaning against the doorway, her eyes focused on the tall figure hovering over the pianoforte.

Adam. Elegantly long and limber fingers flew across the keys as he caressed them like a lover's body. He swayed along with the soulful music, lost in his own melody; his mind and soul visibly transported to another time and place.

Much like when I read. Adam may be secluded within these decrepit walls... yet he is an escape artist, just like me.

Music was his freedom, Isabelle realized—his way of connecting to the world and finding peace and contentment. Only the handsome portion of his face was visible; candlelight flickered across the striking arch of his brow, the austere jut of his chin, and the strong column of his neck. In this light, he looked breathtakingly handsome. Powerful. Captivating. His hair's thick black waves brushed his collar—just barely. Isabelle ached to run her fingers through those shining locks, to feel their weight beneath her palms. A flowing linen shirt framed his muscular body, the deep V-neck granting a peek at his scarred torso.

He hummed low, seducing the decadent lull of his voice to mate with the music. It was a beautiful marriage of darkness and light, of melody and passion. Isabelle's breathing grew a little shallower, and she suddenly felt lightheaded all over again. Her eyes closed of their own accord while her heart beat an uneven tempo against her ribs. Then his humming melted into song; liquid heat flowed through her veins and carried her away. She felt suspended. Free. Much like when she lost herself within the pages of her books.

It was a lullaby, the somber whispers of a past life; he sang the words with such depth, such soul and agony. Beautiful. Terrible. Gut-wrenching. A crush of emotions stirred in each word, each chord, every breath. In spite of herself, Isabelle felt her heart shatter for him a little bit.

"*Sleep well, my little prince.*
Sleep true, my sweet prince.

Roses love sunshine, violets love dew.
All the angels in heaven wrap their wings over you.
Sleep well, my little prince.
Sleep true, my sweet prince.
The world lays at your feet.
Now let my love make you complete."

The music stopped without warning, and the final note rang despairingly in the air. Isabelle felt like she'd been released from a hook... like she'd been flung out of a dream, only to wake into cold reality. She shifted her body weight and attempted to discreetly edge away. The subtle sound echoed in the large, acoustical room and drew Adam's attention. His head jerked toward her, fast as lightning, and she felt his stare fix on her face.

Their gazes caught. For several weightless moments, those blue eyes held her spellbound. Immobile. Utterly breathless. An entire conversation seemed to explode between them—and the lamentations hummed inside her aching chest.

"I... Forgive me."

And without another word, she vanished down the dark hall.

SHE HAD BEEN WATCHING HIM.

Adam peeled his fingers away from the pianoforte's slick keys and swiped an unsteady hand through his hairline. He felt vulnerable, exposed—as if a window to his soul had been thrust opened and was now in danger of forever shattering. Every nerve and tendon resembled a violin string pulled too tight and on the verge of snapping.

How long had she stood there, silently observing him from the shadows? Unable to find rest, he'd come to his music room, searching for a reprieve from his tumultuous thoughts. It was no wonder she'd heard him; he'd played loudly, soulfully, pouring his whole self into the music, willing it to absorb his tangled mind.

But no rest was to be found. And certainly no peace or contentment.

Adam exhaled a long-suffering sigh and climbed to his feet. He tossed on his cloak, which rested beside him on the long bench. Then he blew out the lantern, well accustomed to the darkness, and deftly searched for any trace of that damnable beauty.

Women were too curious by far. And Adam had a strong feeling his hands would be full with this one.

The light scuffle of her boots echoed through the halls and cathedral ceilings, leading him straight to her location. Secretly observing her, he stayed close to the walls and stuck to the shadows.

She hugged her arms about her slender body, visibly shivering, as she paced through the castle's vast rooms and countless halls. Indeed, this fortress was a wilderness of stone— one she'd easily become lost in. Labyrinth-like corridors. Slim flights of stairs twisting into blackness. More rooms than one could keep track of. The castle was a wild beast that would swallow her whole at the slightest provocation. Shadows slid along the walls and ceiling as her lantern swayed in midair. First, she ventured mindlessly into the kitchens. An erratic turn to the left took her into the scullery, then the servants' quarter, which was, of course, empty.

Appearing on the verge of exhaustion, she wandered back into the halls and found herself in one of the dusty parlors. Gothic, demon-like figures were carved into the black stone walls. She raised her lantern and spun in place, her disorientation and fear visibly growing. Rusted suits of armor lined the corridor; they lurked within the clotted shadows like silent sentries. A look of desperation knotted her brow, and a palpable despair eclipsed her eyes.

Where is she going so urgently? She still appeared weak from the illness and fever, even a bit delirious; every few steps, she'd stop to catch her breath. Finally she made her way past the central drawing room and inside the main hall.

Adam's heart ground to a dead stop as she eased open the heavy door and wandered into the dark night.

Is she daring to run away? Anger and hurt blazed through him; she was clearly using this opportunity to sneak out of the castle, to escape the monster who held her prisoner. *But in the piercing cold, that foolish chit?* His heart thudding, he descended the entry stairs and paused beneath the Gothic archway, following Isabelle's figure and the eerie sway of her lantern with his gaze. Streams of moonlight trickled through the surrounding trees; the illumination shimmered in her locks and set the fabric of her dress aglow.

Her beauty struck him in the gut. She was stunning. A beacon of light. He was mesmerized. Barely able to draw breath. She resembled a flesh-and-blood angel, her pale complexion alive with the moonlight, her curls falling enticingly just past the curve of her pert bottom.

No wonder she thinks you're a monster, imagining such lustful thoughts.

A bang resounded, muffled by the snow-covered ground as she set down the lantern. She turned to the sky, and the illumination washed over her grief-stricken expression. Something remarkable stirred inside his chest. He leaned against the archway, lost in the sight of her, lost in her unearthly beauty.

What I wouldn't give to be worthy of you...

She looked brokenhearted, overcome with despair, disjointed. Adam fought the urge to sweep her into his arms. He'd gently rock her back and forth, whisper that she had no reason to be frightened—and that he'd never let harm come to her again.

But alas, she perceives me as a monster. A murderer.

The snowfall had lightened a bit, though the chill in the air was unshakable. Adam silently followed after her. Isabelle tightened her grasp on the night robe and wandered through the untamed maze of trees and bushes. Branches cradled wedges of ice in their skeletal arms and shuddered in the cold.

Her breaths misted the air while her gaze ran across the castle's overgrown courtyard, desperately searching for *something*. Nearby, the front gate rattled and moaned, manipulated by a powerful gust of wind.

It hit him—and the revelation knocked the remaining breath from his lungs. He knew what she was searching for.

She came to a stop, her eyes fixed on the snowy ground with an unwavering intensity.

Her father's grave, which sat beneath the branches of a black ash tree.

Blood drained from her face. She clasped her chest, the heartache visible in her eyes. The wind tossed her dark curls against her pale cheeks and unblinking gaze; she stood in front of her father's resting place, silent and still, resembling a porcelain doll. Then she slowly edged forward and knelt before the pile of stones.

Isabelle...

She heard her father's voice in the wind, felt his presence in the air. She gazed at the courtyard's snow-covered ground, studying the raised dirt and pile of stones that marked his resting spot.

Papa, you should not be here...

She reached out and grazed the cairn, caressing his memory. Her heart pounded, and the frigid wind numbed her all over.

My little Isabelle... ma petite...

"Papa... I'm so sorry..." Her words choked off. She clasped her chest, relieving the unseen ache. She felt lightheaded. Defeated. Lost. The initial despair had left her heartbroken, and the grief had exhausted her to the point of sickness. Now, that raw, shattered feeling gave way to anger and resentment.

"Sometimes, it hurts just to breathe. I don't know how I can go on without you. And *he* stole you from me. He—" Her words shattered into a choked sob.

Non. *I'm mainly to blame.*

She pressed her fist against her mouth while deep shudders wracked her body.

"Isabelle..."

That time, it was not her father's voice. Instead, a deep baritone shook the night, and she felt body heat radiating beside her. Adam knelt on the snowy ground, a riot of emotions etched into his irregular features.

"He didn't deserve this. He didn't deserve to die in such a cold, dark place." Isabelle lifted her face into the biting wind as snow struck her cheeks. "Before he'd fallen ill, Papa had been an adventurer, a free spirit. He does not belong here, imprisoned by these desolate walls." She felt the sting of tears, but she harnessed them back.

Adam gazed down at her, his long, dark lashes sweeping over his eyes, the material of his cloak fluttering like wings. "You are right." He exhaled a sigh, which misted against the air and unfurled in white coils. "He didn't deserve such a fate. Yet from what little I saw... I know he lived a life of love and warmth. And that's the most any of us can hope for." Cynicism imbued his words but also a sincere empathy and compassion.

"What do you know of how he lived? How can you say he 'led a life of love and warmth'?"

"He had you."

Isabelle icily nodded, then glanced at the front gate and swaying trees, whose long branches were naked of foliage and shivering in the night. She inhaled a steadying breath, allowing the winter air to fill her lungs. She stole another glance of Adam and ran her gaze over his formidable length—but all she could see was the terror in her father's glassy eyes, the terrible image of him clinging on to those iron bars...

"You shouldn't be out here, alone and in the cold."

No, I should not, she silently agreed, her resentment building as she glanced at the cairn. *We should not be here at all.*

Adam unclasped his cloak and swept it off his shoulders. Closing the distance between them, he draped the material over her body, then smoothed it down with gentle hands.

Heat from his slender, scarred fingers penetrated the fabric and helped ease the chill. His shirtsleeves fluttered against the hard planes of his chest, whipping with the grace of a high-flying flag. She swallowed deeply and cast a final glance at the pile of stones. How lonely they looked. So very lonely and disconnected from the world.

Adam climbed to his feet and stood before her. He held out his hand, the wind whipping jet-black strands over his eyes and ruffling the crème-colored shirt. Isabelle had thought his eyes were dark before; now they resembled the color of nightmares.

"You are still quite weak," he said, almost by way of explanation for his outheld hand. The memory of his enchanting music came rushing back; for a moment, the courtyard didn't seem so silent and still. She nodded and stared down at his mangled skin. The flesh was a light red, puckered, raised, bearing the same texture as the left side of his face. "Come back inside, *ma belle*. Have something warm to eat. I'll prepare you a plate of food, a hot cup of tea. Let this be your home."

Isabelle numbed herself to Adam, to the pile of stones that lay at her side... to everything. Detachment was her only chance for survival.

She took hold of his outstretched hand and followed him inside the castle.

My new home.

Chapter Nine

THE NEXT MORNING, Isabelle surprised herself and awoke with a new energy. Morning's light pried through the high, curved windows and set Adam's exquisite bedchamber aglow.

The room was beautiful, rich, robust. Dark panels and burgundy drapes covered the long walls, making the chamber seem unexpectedly cozy despite its size. Leather armchairs sat beside a black hearth, and a mahogany writing desk and mirrorless vanity lined the walls. A pile of parchment, books, musical compositions, and ink in glass-cut bottles cluttered the desk's surface.

Isabelle couldn't stifle her smile; the desk contained enough pigeonholes to appease even the most enthusiastic of scholars. On the opposite side of the chamber, arched windows reached up to the high ceiling, their panes touching a luxurious, velvet gold-and-burgundy seat.

A loud whine captured her attention. Isabelle glanced over the side of her canopied bed, where a large pair of soulful, almond-shaped eyes stared at her. Startled, she sat up and clutched a hand to her breast. Stranger—*was that the beast's name?*—barked, as if in greeting, then plopped his huge head onto the mattress. His tail whipped back and forth, smacking the end table, nearly causing a pitcher and plate of food to fly off the surface. Isabelle had never owned a pet—she and Papa had traveled far too much for that—and she couldn't help but feel threatened.

"You seem to have forgotten," she warily murmured, arching a fine brow, "that you growled at me and flashed your teeth when we first met." Isabelle shrunk farther against the headboard as a wet tongue swept across her knuckles. Laughter burst from her lips in spite of the circumstances. "Oh, now you want to make nice, do you?"

The creature responded with an insistent toss of his muzzle, urging her attention. "Guess we're no longer strangers, then, Stranger." His lithe body came alive at the sound of his name; his bottom wagged from side to side, smacking against the edge of her mattress. More laughter erupted from her lips; the sensation felt foreign. Thrilling. She recited his name several more times, delighting in the shimmy of his backside, then scratched the scruff below his chin. His pale, speckled tongue rolled out, spilling across the mattress like a royal carpet. He tilted his head on its side while his good hind leg thumped up and down.

The wooden planks boomed beneath the assault and seemed to make the entire bedchamber vibrate. Isabelle's eyes darted back to the end table, where the ceramic plate overflowed with fresh fruits and nuts.

She shot Stranger a suspicious glance, then snatched a handful of nuts and popped two in her mouth. "Ah-ha. You like me just for the food, don't you? You simply—"

Something caught her eye and stilled her words. Papa's top hat—sitting on an ottoman beside the mirrorless vanity.

Adam must have placed it there overnight.

Isabelle stumbled from the bed as her gut grew heavy. Grasping the rim of Papa's hat, she ran her fingers over the smooth, faded fabric with reverence. She edged onto the mattress again while her heart constricted into a tight ball. A thousand memories came rushing back, and tears stung her eyes. She lifted the brim to her nose, inhaling the scents that would forever permeate the well-loved material. Behind her shut eyes, she saw the colorful booths at the Merchants' Fair, heard the mingled chatter of princes and paupers as they admired his wares and negotiated offers—

Isabelle *felt* his very presence; lowering the top hat, she opened her eyes and mentally returned to the bedchamber.

Adam's broad form graced the doorway. Strong, wide shoulders tapered off to his slender waist, which flowed into legs that appeared to go on forever. Flakes of sleet and snow clashed against his wavy, thick hair, and a handsome pair of kidskin gloves covered his hands. She drank him in for several moments of silence, in awe of his formidable presence. A ruddy, endearing flush darkened his good cheek. He'd obviously ventured outside to labor. He wasn't wearing the cloak, leaving his disfigurement and strong stature in full view, though he kept his face turned at a precise angle, so the good-looking side remained in her sight.

The contrast of his handsome side and disfigured half struck her hard. Tousled by fingers of light, streaks of blue-black flashed within his silky hair and tugged at her imagination. She took an unexpected pleasure in every detail, every line, every imperfection.

Commanding. Regal. Proud yet unsure.

Stranger clambered to his feet with an old man's groan. Bellowing a low whine, he unceremoniously dragged his back left foot as he crossed the bedchamber. Arthritis had clearly weakened the hind leg; Isabelle's heart reached out to the poor creature. Adam knelt and ran long, graceful fingers over Stranger's coat. Studying those hands, she recalled how he'd seduced melodies from the pianoforte as if by magic... as if pulling sensual moans and cries from a lover's trembling depths. She eyed his caress while a strange, heavy sensation pooled in her stomach. Her fascination mixed with an underlying fear and uncertainty. Shifting against the headboard, her eyes ran over the broad curve of Adam's back; suddenly she felt like she was encaged with a poorly restrained beast.

Adam's gaze flickered over her, hotter than coals. "My

apologies for... this," he said, motioning to his bare face. "The cloak becomes tiresome."

"You... you have every right to be comfortable in your own home."

Isabelle battled her resentment and anxiety, inhaled a calming breath, and forced a smile to her lips. The simple motion pained her. But it was time to pull herself up and move forward. *I must do it for Papa, if not for myself.* That thought consoled her and acted as a guiding light.

"We were just getting acquainted," she went on, gesturing to Stranger. "I've never seen anything quite like him before." The creature padded over to her with an amiable bark. At first, the sound startled her—but then he licked the back of her knuckles, and her fear evaporated.

"I'm not surprised. Wolfhounds are rare in Demrov."

"Is it arthritis?" she asked, gesturing to the dog's crumpled hind leg.

"Only in part. I found him in a bear trap several years ago. His leg hasn't been the same since, and old age certainly has not made it easier."

"It never does."

Adam's lips quirked. An amused glint heated his blue eyes. Isabelle felt herself relax; the sight of his smile softened his rugged appearance and helped subdue her apprehension.

"He's quite gentle," she said, her tone cautious. "The first time I saw him... Well, I thought he'd tear my throat out."

"He's protective of his master. A loyal beast. And a good friend." The words weren't spoken, but Isabelle heard them all the same. *My only friend.*

He pulled his hand away from Stranger and marched toward her, reaching her position in a few swift strides. All of Isabelle's senses went on high alert. Suddenly trembling, needing to be away from the bed, she leapt to her feet as Adam towered above her. She swayed from the sudden movement. Indeed, she still felt woozy and sick with despair—and this man's formidable presence didn't help. He laid a hand on her shoulder to help stabilize her body. His fingers lingered for several seconds before he thrust his hand away. Then he curled his fingers into a tight ball, and she watched as he flexed them once, twice, three times...

Shifting backward, he glanced at Stranger again and rewarded his companion with a solid pat. "Come, Isabelle. I'll show you around the castle."

ADAM'S HEART SOMERSAULTED as he and Isabelle slipped down the twisting stairwell. He'd opened many of the draperies, flooding the castle with a rare light. Stranger plopped onto his stomach and promptly fell asleep in a golden patch. Typically Adam only opened one or two windows, so he was unused to such brightness.

Sunrays streamed through the arched windows and baroque stained glass, tangling in Isabelle's chocolate tresses and illuminating her complexion. Tearing his eyes away, he squinted against those dancing prisms and glanced out-of-doors. Beyond the large panes, snow descended from a bruised sky and encased Hartville in an icy shell. Every so often, a blast of wind shook the castle and infused the walls with a frigid draft.

The worst of the storm has yet to come.

Adam chanced a look at Isabelle and felt his soul clench at the hostility and fear in her eyes. She was attempting to be cordial, though he knew it was nothing more than a pretty act.

"This way." He signaled as they arrived at the stairwell's landing. Fractured rays of light seeped through the baroque stained glass window; the design's vibrant mosaic pattern drew colorful prisms along the flagstones. He'd cleaned up what he could manage, though the castle was still quite dirty. A nagging guilt churned in his gut; Isabelle didn't deserve to live in such ruin.

Minutes later, Adam entered a darkened room and pulled the heavy drapes aside, permitting the light to enter. He turned to Isabelle and watched as her hostile expression transformed into one of awe and naked appreciation.

Indeed. His music room was one of the most beautiful spaces in the castle. An ornate grand pianoforte functioned as the centerpiece. A golden harp and stringed instruments sat in the corner. Beside them lurked a gilded easel; it resided in front of the large curved window and overlooked the castle's lush gardens—Adam's other pride and joy. The canvas was blank, unloved, neglected, and slightly curled at the corners. The domed, vaulted ceiling loomed proudly overhead, allowing the music to amplify itself and swell the walls. A chandelier hung in the heart of the room; its evocative silhouette cast over the medallion flooring.

"Do you play an instrument?" he asked, gesturing around the room. "The pianoforte, perhaps?"

Isabelle burst into laughter. "Oh, heavens, no! And you'd best hope I shan't attempt to."

A chuckle rustled in his throat.

"My father," she continued, speaking more to herself, those intoxicating, hazel eyes dancing from one instrument to the next, "he used to play the fiddle while I'd dance. He was quite good." The rush of sadness that washed over her struck Adam like a knife. The reaction took him by surprise and left him momentarily void of speech. He knew that grief all too well. Guilt rippled through him as an image of her father surfaced.

Shaking away the thought, he paced over to the pianoforte, lifted the lid, and allowed his fingers to dance across the ivory keys. It was only a single chord—but it was clearly enough.

Isabelle paused in midstride and turned toward the melody. Appreciation shone in her beautiful eyes, causing his fingers to still. They lingered above the keys; the final note hung in the air and swirled around them, sweeter than honey from the comb.

She joined him at the pianoforte and ran a slender hand over the keys. They tinkled beneath her light touch and fractured the silence. Adam stood on the opposite side of the instrument, unable to tear his gaze away.

How would those hands feel upon his skin? Could she ever caress him with the same delicacy, the same wonder and appreciation? Or would she only recoil in horror?

"I know you heard me playing... I know you saw me." The words emerged before he could stop them. Her face jerked toward his own, and her brilliant eyes captured his from across the pianoforte.

"A part of me imagined that was a dream," she said, her lush hood of lashes lowering over her eyes. Adam had thought the same thing when he'd first beheld her. "You play beautifully. I could hardly believe it. So much emotion. So much feeling. I admit—your music had frightened me a little. I'd never heard anything like it..." The words trailed off. Adam knew she hadn't meant to speak them aloud.

"I shall consider that a compliment."

"You should. Who taught you to play like that?"

"I had a tutor as a boy. A handful of governesses, too. Monsieur Beaumont, my music tutor, had trained some of the world's finest composers." Ancient memories swept over him, and Adam felt his mouth tick into a smile. "He used to say that the greats—Grétry, Le Sueur, Beethoven—never die. They simply become their music. They earn immortality."

"You were a child prodigy." It wasn't a question. Just an acute observation she'd somehow unearthed. Adam gave a curt nod and felt a blush sear his cheeks.

A heartbeat later, he wheeled around the pianoforte, and his self-doubt slid away while he soaked up the power of his music room. Isabelle visibly stiffened as he towered above her. She shifted backward until her bottom bumped into the pianoforte. Then she stared up at him, clearly transfixed yet afraid, her red lips slightly parted. The warmth of her body and the sweet scent of her skin sailed toward him, whispering his name. White-hot desire flowed through his veins and stirred the man to life. "My mother was gifted on the harp and violin. Is that such a revelation, mademoiselle?"

"No, not at all..." She ached to press him further—he could see the inquiry dancing in her eyes, could practically hear the questions tumbling from those rosebud lips. Yet only silence prevailed.

He gazed down at her, his eyes slowly tracking over the

elegant column of her neck. "Once upon a time, I wasn't a monster..." He reached out—hesitated in midair for a heartbeat—then pressed his gloved fingertips to her collarbone. She leaned against the pianoforte and gazed up at him. Her breaths grew shallower, and a distinct fear surfaced in her eyes.

Alas, it was no great wonder. She loathed him—and he clearly repulsed her. He repulsed even himself.

Holding her gaze with his own, his fingertips danced lazy circles along the fine architecture of her collarbone. He cursed the gloves that covered his hands as he ached to feel her creamy skin free from barriers. "Once upon a time, I was just a man. But each passing year has changed that." He stepped behind her, aligning their bodies. Gliding his palms down and over her russet mane of curls, he watched in awe as the dark strands slipped through his fingers.

Much like everything else in my life.

She trembled against him; whether from revulsion or desire, he couldn't say. Her gaze appeared to peer inward—as if she were watching something unfold inside her mind.

I ought to leave her, to back away now...

Instead, he stepped closer, if that was even possible, and inhaled the sweet incense of her hair. Adam felt strangely alive... as if he'd awoken from a twenty-five-year slumber. He saw the war on her face, heard it in the ragged sound of her breathing. Torn between fear and something else, she wanted to pull away yet appeared quite mesmerized. He waited, expecting her to flee—to push past him and escape into the shadows.

But she did nothing of the sort.

Instead, her head tilted back in undeniable ecstasy. A shallow sigh escaped from those parted lips. Her breaths wafted against him in an erotic assault on the senses, causing his blood to burn and rush southward. She looked remarkably innocent, fragile, like a porcelain doll. He turned her body in a full circle and gently cupped the curve of her chin.

"What if I demanded that you fulfill our original terms? Right now, in this very room?"

Silence pressed between them and poisoned the air. He felt her swallow beneath his fingertips, saw as her eyes filled with a stark *terror* that overpowered all other emotions.

"It would break whatever is left of me."

Adam captured her gaze for several weightless moments. Then he released her chin, a bit harsher than he intended, and swept back. Isabelle exhaled deeply, as if his distancing had allowed her to breathe again.

You are a monster.

"As I said nights ago, I won't hold you to that part of our agreement. Now follow me, and I'll show you to your private quarters."

HEAT AND DARKNESS SEAL MY FATE.

Inside, I am weeping, screaming, cursing—yet my cheeks remain bone-dry, as I have nothing left to give. Flames flash before me, consuming everything that once mattered. Smoke infects my lungs and singes my insides into ashes. I fight to cry out, to scream for help... but my throat can't function. Even swallowing proves to be a monumental task as the walls of my throat swell and close. Hard coughs shake my body, rattling my brittle bones. Surely I'll choke to death. Vainly I battle the binds that tie my wrists together as I feel myself slipping into blackness.

As the world rapidly fades away, my family's ancient mantra echoes in my mind.

Nutrisco et extinguo. *I nourish the good and extinguish the evil.*

But I no longer find comfort in those words—only a painful despair.

BONE-CHILLING CRIES jarred Isabelle from her sleep. She awoke with a startled gasp, feeling disoriented and detached all over again. It took several moments to remember where she was and how she came to be there.

The candle on her nightstand had burned out hours ago, sentencing her private quarters to blackness. Moonlight trickled through the sole window and illuminated the hulking mahogany furniture; the towering bureau and armoire resembled crouching monsters. *Mon Dieu*, she felt ice-cold. Her breaths misted against the darkness and emerged in silver clouds. She massaged her arms and swept wayward curls from her eyes. Her skin seemed to physically crawl.

Those cries... They sounded guttural, heart-wrenching, almost inhuman in their despair. Her heart pounding, she caressed her silver pendant, then slipped out of bed and crossed herself in a clumsy movement. She relit her lantern as her feet sank into the Flemish carpet. Hesitantly she slipped into the winding corridor.

She followed Adam's choked sobs without conscious thought. They beckoned her forward, pulled at her heartstrings with the force of a puppet master. Caught in a disjointed reality, her feet seemed to bear a mind of their own as she wandered through the halls. The lantern swayed unsteadily in her grip and caused the shadows to lengthen and deepen. Its light glimmered along the peeling walls and ragged tapestries; the faded designs depicted muted biblical scenes. In stark contrast, demon-like creatures stared down at her, their horned heads and winged bodies carved into the cracked walls.

On nights such as these, the castle transformed into a living entity with a will of its own. She felt it pulsate and cycle through a complex range of emotions: sadness, grief, despair, and anger. All around her, stone and wood shifted and emitted a low grumbling noise. She sensed the dust motes settling as they glided through the air like snowflakes; she felt the wooden beams aging below her heels. Meanwhile, the sounds of Adam's sobs pulled her forward and punctuated the darkness.

Finally she reached the end of the corridor and stood outside his private bedchamber. The door was half-open, the room nearly pitch-black. She eased inside, knowing she'd curse her meddling and curiosity later, and lifted her lantern.

What she saw purged the air from her lungs. Adam was jerking in his bed like a wild beast, visibly fighting some unseen demon. She inhaled a breath for courage, then moved forward several meters. Stranger sat beside the huge four-poster bed, his tail tucked beneath trembling legs.

Overhead, the canopy filled with a draft of air and billowed like a pair of wings. A strange restlessness stirred the atmosphere, and Isabelle knew they weren't entirely alone. She trembled, feeling the whispers of ghosts on the back of her neck. Shivering, she swept her palm over the dog's head, whispered words of comfort, then turned her disbelieving gaze back to Adam.

The center of her chest grew heavy. Her pulse thundered in her ears. The lantern's illumination danced across his restless body and threw shadows along the dark-paneled walls. Isabelle couldn't restrain her gasp; fearful of waking him, she slapped a palm over her mouth to stifle the sound.

Adam was dressed in undergarments and not a shred more. His body was impressively large, strong, well-muscled—and warped by grotesque scars. Twisted mounds of flesh, deep trenches, and ridges distorted most of his upper body. Isabelle fought the urge to reach out and track her fingers down his torso... to help calm his anguish in whatever way she could. His frantic sobs sank under her skin, pulling her forward like a lasso.

She took a tentative step toward the bed, watching as the light illuminated his scarred, sweat-lined skin.

Heat from the lantern, which she held at eye level, caused sweat to bead on her forehead. She knuckled it away—and discovered that her cheeks were damp with tears.

Tears not for her beloved papa. Not for her fate. They were tears for Adam. *Whoever he is.*

Chapter Ten

Adam drove his axe in a precise arc, splitting an upright log down its middle. A crack rippled across the frozen courtyard and vibrated through his gloved hands. His movements were smooth and calculated—a vast contradiction to his tangled mind. He readjusted the long wooden handle, then swung the axe with another savage crash. Nearby, the mare wandered the length of the snow-covered courtyard; she flinched at the deafening bang before continuing to search for whatever greenery she could find amid the frost. Her silver tail swatted at the cold air, waving like a banner.

He dealt two more deathblows. Sweat poured from his brows, every muscle ached and trembled—and still, he soldiered on. Another deafening crash resounded. A small flock of birds volleyed out of a hedge and flew into the sky. Adam turned his gaze to the castle; the setting sun fringed the turrets and jutting towers in a blood-red cloak.

Wiping the perspiration from his brow and eyes, he repeated the ritual again and again, urging it to sedate his tumultuous mind, stacking the woodpile so high until it appeared no number of logs could ever comfort or warm him. Even before Isabelle stumbled upon his doorstep and he'd lit fires, Adam had wasted countless hours butchering logs; it kept his body strong, his mind sharp, and helped soothe his storming emotions.

Finally, when the sun tucked itself in for the night, he repeatedly stalked the length of his East Tower like a manic, caged beast. This section of the castle was a vault into his childhood. A variety of items he and Sébastien had recovered from the Delacroix ruins were haphazardly stashed here, lost amid the cavernous shadows and hulking furniture that had come with this castle.

Shortly after the siege, Sébastien had helped Adam recover his inheritance and purchase this decrepit castle (thanks to the aid of a shady banker or two) in the most desolate province of Hartville...

Away from everyone. Far from the memories. Yet the distance had never brought him peace of mind or contentment.

Ashamed of his monstrous appearance and overcome with despair, he'd hid himself away as the years crawled by and the shadows only deepened.

Adam inhaled the musty atmosphere and ran his gaze over the wreckage. The East Tower had once been a storage area, he supposed. Now, it served as a portal into another time and place—into a time when he'd been a different person and into a place he'd regarded as home.

Moonlight poured through the row of high, arched windows, which graced a lushly curved, domed ceiling. Precious keepsakes from his past life whirled by as he crossed the jumbled space again and again. Those remnants seemed to close in on him, to whisper things he'd refused to hear for over two decades. Expelling a breath, he stopped in front of a row of suspended cloths and jerked one down with a flick of his wrist.

His mind and body went quiet with cold agony. He could feel his mother's portrait staring directly at him—probing the turbulent depths of his soul.

What have you become, mon fils? *Is this truly all that's left of you? A selfish beast who's imprisoned a young woman and caused her papa's death?*

Adam didn't want to believe that. Not yet. He glanced around the ruins of his East Tower and observed a musical box from his childhood. Edging forward, he rotated the golden turnkey; the hoarse melody swelled through the tower and carried him back to his fourth birthday. *Non*, he surrendered nothing without a fight—including what remained of his frayed soul.

His hands trembling, the signet ring drank in the moonlight as Adam tentatively traced his mother's eternal profile.

You are better than that, my sweet son...

"But I don't know how to be," he replied, the tone of his voice rising in the air like a melancholy pianoforte refrain. The words twisted with the musical box's melody, uniting them as one. "There are so many things you never were able to teach me. Maman... I'm starting to care for her—and I don't know what to do, don't know how to act. She loathes me—sees nothing but a beast, a monster. I am lost. Without you, I am lost. And I've been lost for years..."

Adam was met with the sound of silence. Heaving another sigh, he leaned against the stone wall as a riot of emotions battled within. Clashing memories poured through him: Maman teaching him the waltz, picnics in the rose garden, standing beside Rosemary's bassinet—and the sight of flames consuming her...

Without warning, a vision of Isabelle materialized inside his mind, and he felt some of the agony trickle away.

An hour later, he eased inside Isabelle's bedchamber and contented himself with watching her sleep. When he merely spoke to her, he felt a brief connection with the world again. It was one as simple yet as intimate as taking a person's hand. Clasping it tight.

And how I ache to hold on a little longer...

Several nights had passed since their interlude in the music room. That connection he'd felt with the world had faded at the blatant repulsion and fear in her eyes. It reminded Adam of what he was, what he lost, and what he never could be.

He'd kept to himself since, sulking in the darkness, detaching himself from everything—including his own wretched longings. He'd stroke Stranger, butcher logs, tend to Isabelle's mare, compose, or sit in his garden... thinking how this night was only one of thousands of nights.

Yet she made him dream of a different time when he was still young and handsome. When the world had laid at his feet, and everything was beautiful. Pure. An ocean of possibilities as vast and endless as Lavoncourt's glittering coastline.

Now, he lurked in Isabelle's chamber against the farthest wall, just another shadow within the castle, until morning's golden light fringed the draperies. Stranger slumbered at the foot of her bed, his enormous paws twitching in time with his dreams. "Traitor," Adam muttered at the dog, who usually kept him company at night.

Damn him, he'd fought to stay away, to keep his distance—but Isabelle's mere presence drew him forward like a moth to a flame. For ten minutes longer, he watched with admiration as sunrays blared through the pane and highlighted her wealth of curls.

Mon Dieu, she's been here for a week and a half.

She stirred, as if the sun's warmth had reached out and physically touched her brow, then grew still again. Hardly thinking, Adam edged forward and listened to the melodic sound of her breathing, observed the graceful rise and fall of her chest. Both his body and soul ached with a painful longing—one that extended far beyond the pleasures of the flesh. He yearned to simply lie beside her, to take her curves in his arms and hold her against his body.

Then a damning voice invaded his thoughts. It was a voice he recognized straight away—a voice that had haunted him for years.

You are living the life you have earned—one of solitude and darkness.

It was his own voice.

A moment later, a second voice chimed in and echoed his self-doubt.

Careful now, mon ami. *I'm afraid you'll make yourself heartsick with love for her...*

RAPHAEL DEJECTEDLY OBSERVED as Vivian's heavy, pale breasts jiggled beneath his body. Her long nails dug into his back, and she bit her bottom lip in pleasure.

Focus, worthless fool.

He tried to anchor his focus, to concentrate on fucking her—but thoughts of Isabelle wove in and out of his skull, hissing for his attention like some malicious serpent.

She had played him for a fool. A quick correspondence with his acquaintances in Le Florin had confirmed his suspicions just that afternoon. No trace of his beloved fiancée or her decrepit old man had ever appeared at the Merchants' Fair. More than a week had passed since their foolhardy and desperate expedition; Raphael held little hope they'd be returning soon as scheduled.

Oh, no. Isabelle had made off with his funds, his brougham, and one of his exquisite Arabian mares. She'd stolen what was rightfully his. Disgraced his name in the worse way possible. And played him for a fucking fool.

Except he *would* get the last laugh. Him and Vivian, to be sure.

Father's damning words twisted inside his mind: *You are nothing but a stupid, sentimental fool, just like your whore of a mother.* Even now, over a decade later, he felt the sting of the buckle and the smoldering burns from Father's cigar butts. Mocking laughter rang in his head, drowning the world around him.

Bastard.

He gave a final, hard thrust, and spilled himself inside of Vivian's tight sheath. Her nails raked at his back as she lost herself in the throes of a pulsating climax. Then he stumbled off her, snatched a bottle of hard liquor from the vanity, and downed a liberal swallow. Behind him, Vivian stretched across the crumpled sheets with a satisfied sigh.

Raphael glanced at his bare arm, examining the welts and burns that would forever brand his skin. God's teeth, anger sizzled through every sinew, every muscle, every vein. He'd supped with his father just last night; as always, Philippe Dumont had no shortage of insults or scorn—and Raphael had felt a measure of joy at his father's disapproval.

Still chasing after that peasant wench, I see, like a lovesick pup? Despite my disdain—despite the fact she's sullied your name and made you a laughing stock? You're more pathetic than I'd imagined. No matter, it appears she's truly gone now, Raphael, I'm pleased to say.

Now *Father* would get the last laugh, should he fail to track her down.

Stupid chit. Raphael had intended to give her the world on a silver platter, to gift her with the happy ending his poor mother hadn't known. Vicomtesse Isabelle Rose would have lived in the lap of luxury and refinement—a far cry from that shabby little cottage or the back of her father's broken wagon. That was before she showed her treachery, her true colors— colors that were a different shade than his mother's, mind you—and made a joke of his generosity.

Like most women, she certainly lacked brains and the capacity for rational thought. Hunting was one of his most prized pastimes—and Isabelle Rose had simply set him up for the chase.

Yes. He and Vivian would indeed get the last laugh...

Raphael took another swig, then propped his palms on the vanity's edge and stared down at the various trinkets littering the surface. A solitary candle glowed, encircling his mother's keepsakes in a ring of light. Exotic perfumes from the far reaches of the world. Dazzling jewels of all shapes and sizes. Delicate combs carved from tortoiseshell and ivory. Raphael traced his finger over the comb's brittle teeth while his thoughts crept inward again.

Vivian sat up in bed and allowed the silk blanket to fall enticingly to her waist. Her breasts shone creamy and white, illuminated by the candle and shafts of moonlight that trickled through the oversized window. The lace curtains billowed within the dim chamber like the wings of a butterfly.

"You keep brooding over that lowborn whore." Vivian pouted—though the hurt in her voice sounded genuine. She fought to appear unaffected, but Raphael saw the flash of sorrow that entered her blazing eyes, heard the quaver in her husky voice, and noticed how a frown tugged at the corner of her wry smile. "Why, I'm beginning to think you may love her."

And there it was.

Raphael released a harsh, bitter laugh and shook his head. "Madame, you worry your pretty head for naught. I'm afraid I'm incapable of such a petty thing."

He locked gazes with her reflection. She tensed at his words, as if he'd slapped her across the face. Then she swallowed and glanced away, visibly gathering her nerves—something contrary to her character.

"Come now, Vivian. Chin up—"

"I have fucked my fair share of men," she interrupted, her eyes betraying the harshness of her words. She slipped out of bed, every step executed with a lustful grace as she wandered toward him. "And when we fuck, my love, it's more than fucking." Slender arms wrapped his naked torso, ran over his chest, and then lower still. The beat of his heart thundered below her long fingers and betrayed his outward composure.

Down her hands went, touching him in all the right places, her voice murmuring all the right things.

Raphael groaned and tensed at her intimate caresses. His manhood stirred to life once more, and a searing heat pumped through his veins. He half-melted against her, cursing his weakness all the while. It was a remarkable talent—how she could unravel his composure at will, reducing him to a mound of clay in those fair hands.

"You're right. I misspoke. I've loved another woman, once. My mother." Vivian's hands stilled, and he heard her breath catch. "And my worthless father stole her from me. His beatings put her into the ground. He never even had the decency to hide his outbursts. He rather boasted about them to me—like a hunter showcasing some prized buck. I would have followed

Mother into the dirt, had he not be so desperate for an heir."

Damn him. Raphael hadn't meant to spill his wretched soul, but years of bottled resentment suddenly poured out of him, like venom rushing from a snakebite. "He makes me sick, Vivian..." Gazing into the vanity's mirror, Raphael cupped his own cheek and caressed the skin, hearing Isabelle's words in his mind again and again. "His mere face makes me ill inside."

You could never face the mirror again without seeing your father.

The little witch had cursed him. Every time he looked at his own reflection, Raphael saw his father's cold, placid gaze glowering back. A rare, compassionate spark entered Vivian's jade-colored eyes. Even her voice softened; a note of empathy laced her words together. She rested her hand on top of his and gently peeled his fingers from his cheek. "You'd best hope your father and I never cross paths. I may very well put him into that dirt myself."

"I would rather enjoy seeing that." Raphael felt the corner of his mouth twitch. Then he sighed, propped his palms on the vanity, and stared at his reflection. "All of Demrov knows exactly what their noble comte is. My family has lived here for over a decade, yet we're still regarded as fucking outsiders." Raphael shook his downcast head. "Isabelle was supposed to change that. I've seen it myself in the villages—Demrov seems to be under her spell."

As am I, damn it all.

Vivian disregarded his last statement, her soft voice reaching out to him like a mother's embrace. "Except you're not an outsider, Raphael. Not to me." An answering emotion welled up inside him. He'd never known such gentleness and hardness all at once. Vivian's hands returned to his bare chest, and he ceased to think any further. Locking gazes with his reflection, she ran her fingers over his torso in sensual, leisurely strokes. Hot breaths wafted against his skin as she pressed her mouth down his back. Damp, sultry lips tracked a wet line over his flesh and roused something deep inside him.

"You're insatiable, *amour*. Doesn't your husband ever satisfy your desires?"

"What a good laugh. Why, my husband can't even satisfy himself with those gnarled old hands. Damn the world, I say. Damn your father. Damn my husband and his ancient cock." A deep moan vibrated through Raphael's body as Vivian's slender, strong hands worked their magic. She wrapped his manhood in an unyielding grip and slid her fingers up and down his turgid length. Up and down. Nursing him back into oblivion, she breathed against his nape, "Damn your little Isabelle and her worthless, rotting papa. Damn everyone who isn't us. When I was little more than a girl, my father shipped me off to Comte Brazin like some package mule. I have no great love for this world. Only you. My noble husband will soon vanish into the dirt where he belongs—*I promise you that*—then it shall be just you and me. Together, we'll find that little wide-eyed whore. And we'll make sure she never disgraces *our* names again."

ISABELLE LAY AWAKE within an infinite darkness, her thoughts and emotions swept up in a whirlwind. The window jostled against its pane, and a harsh draft volleyed through her private chamber.

She shivered and clasped the silk coverlet tighter, listening to the clamor of the fierce storm. Her lantern had burned out hours ago, tossing her into a world of pitch-black.

Nights like these proved to be the most difficult—and Adam's constant avoidance caused her to feel more alone with a deeper sense of detachment and unreality. Each day, he delivered meals to her room, behaving like a servant in his own castle, before vanishing into the shadows once more. Isabelle hugged her pillow tighter; the blistering storm and Adam's night terrors made her relive Papa's death again and again. In the solitude of her massive chamber, with only the storm for company, she sank into a black void. She relived Raphael's assault again and again... heard his haunting, sadistic voice in her ear... felt as he took what was never his, forever contaminating a piece or her mind and body.

The darkness only served as a twisted canvas for her thoughts. Floating above her, she envisioned Papa's lonely cairn in the courtyard. The pile of stones drifted within an inky sea of black, hanging in limbo, real enough to reach out and touch. Isabelle lifted her hand and groped at the imagery. She needed something tangible to hold, a way to anchor her grief and relieve her loneliness. The cold air nipped her skin and caused gooseflesh to rise on her extended arm.

Dejectedly she lowered her arm and listened to the storm. Heavy drafts penetrated the castle's ancient stones as the blizzard raged on, as fierce and unrelenting as a beast. The chill numbed her to the marrow of her bones, causing her insides to constrict and quiver. She clutched the coverlet firmly against her breast, watching as her breaths misted the air like smoke. Suddenly within the solitude of her bedchamber, alone and numb, terror crept up her spine.

Who is Adam really? And what dark secrets does he hide?

She had to know. She couldn't survive while being kept in such darkness—both within these walls, and within its master's mind.

Not sparing another thought, Isabelle relit her lantern with unsteady hands. It sparked to life, illuminating the intricately molded ceiling, wainscoting, and pale, silk-hung walls. Her chamber was a beautiful room—filled with exquisite, outdated dresses, stale perfumes, and more trinkets than a lady could ever wish for. Yet those delicate pearl necklaces and aged gowns only expanded her unease.

Who have they belonged to? What other woman has slept in these sheets and gazed out this window? A late wife or mistress?

The entire chamber was a twisted glimpse into the past.

Out. I need out.

Escape.

She set the lantern on her satinwood vanity, then rushed into the adjoining dressing room to change into a night rail, shoes, kidskin gloves, and a heavy robe; a claw-foot bathing tub and chamber pot also occupied the space. She shut the armoire's elegantly carved doors and rushed back inside the main chamber. Hugging both arms around her body, she paced to the window as the pane jostled, manipulated by a gust of wind. She exhaled a long breath and threw open the damask drapes.

The sun was just making its descent over Hartville's dense forest, fringing the trees in cloaks of gold. Wind rippled the skeletal branches, which were half-bare from the cold and assaulted by hammering snow. Her gaze passed over the castle's jagged architecture until it settled on the eastern wing. A pediment graced the tower and pierced the sky like one great needle. Isabelle absently thought of a fairy tale she adored, *The Sleeping Beauty in the Wood*. The spinning wheel came to mind—how it had seduced the princess, drawing her forward and to her doom...

Isabelle shook away her wayward thoughts. She often observed Adam standing on the tower's stone balcony, deep in thought, his gaze fixed on the sweeping gardens that lurked below his East Tower.

Gardens that appeared lush and in full bloom, as if removed from winter's grasp... As if removed from reality, much like herself...

She'd noticed them when she'd moved into her private quarters; at first, she'd blamed her fatigue and an overactive imagination. Yet there they lurked—sparkling amid a sea of untamed weeds and frozen earth.

I'm going mad here, lost within these queer, suffocating walls..

She recalled Adam's warning—she could venture anywhere inside the castle except that tower.

Why? What great secrets does it hold? What mystery could it unlock—what light could it bring to this darkness?

Her hot breaths fogged the pane as she stared out the window, quite transfixed as she absently watched the snow flurry by. Snow that didn't seem to affect the vibrant roses...

The East Tower stood silent and still within the night, beckoning her with its mysteries, tempting her curious nature...

She desperately needed to know what kind of man Adam *truly* was. In her mind, he'd become an enigma, a mystery, and the inability to grasp who he was as a human being numbed her with a deeper chill than the blizzard or unworldly rose garden.

She needed to uncover the truth.

Her mind decided, Isabelle relit the lantern beside her bed, tightened her robe's sash, and paced down the winding corridors. The lantern swayed in her grasp and tossed shadows along the dark walls and ceiling. The illumination flitted across the wooden floors, morphing into different shapes. She charged down the spiral stairwell as her palm slid over the banister. Dust motes glided in midair, illuminated by the large stained glass window that touched the cathedral ceiling. The sun had almost fully descended now, sentencing the castle to a familiar and unsettling blackness.

It took Isabelle well over an hour to find the tower's stairwell, and when it finally revealed itself, she felt her nerves cool and dampen. Chewing on her bottom lip, Isabelle lurked at the landing and lowered her lantern. The stairwell sat against the far wall, curving upward into an impenetrable void.

He's likely asleep or elsewhere. Surely he must be—or else it wouldn't be as dark as pitch up there.

Isabelle inhaled a calming breath, then shifted toward the steep flight of stairs. They seemed to call her name, to beckon her forward with the promise of answers...

Before she could change her mind again, she quickly ascended; her lantern's light shattered the darkness before her and chased away the shadows. They fled with each of her steps, receding like monsters slipping into hiding.

Even with the lantern, Isabelle could hardly see a meter in front of her. Her footsteps echoed despairingly as they slapped against the stone ground, each one amplified by the tall ceiling. How high it reached, she couldn't say for certain—it was far too dark. But as she ascended, the sound of her footfalls grew shallower, telling her the space was shrinking. Alas, she felt the walls closing in on her... felt them fast approaching. The blizzard roared beyond the walls and infused the stairwell with a merciless draft. The lantern's candle wavered, threatening to snuff out. In the back of her mind, Adam's broken sobs echoed, and she recalled his restless body thrashing in the sheets.

The key to Adam's anguish and hostility lies in the East Tower. I can sense it...

Up and up she climbed, listening as her footsteps became shallower still, watching as the top of the stairwell finally spiraled into view.

The eastern tower was a ruin in every sense of the word. Broken furniture littered the ground, and threadbare tapestries hung from the arched ceiling. A pair of French doors claimed the farthest wall, which led to a circular balcony. Moonlight shimmered through the frosted glass planes and danced over the wreckage. She eased inside, her breaths silver against the blackness, and set the lantern on a dusty table.

The wind hissed and whipped through the castle's cracks and crevices. Her skin prickled with gooseflesh, and an involuntary tremble shook her body.

She staggered forward, moving farther inside, her curiosity mounting. Shadows shifted. The silence pressed against her eardrums in a deafening roar. She hummed beneath her breath, needing to shatter that damning quiet. It wasn't until the lyrics graced her ears that she realized it was Adam's lullaby. Emotion constricted her voice and added a note of despair to the words. Together, Adam's genius and her own heartache wove a spell and brought tears to her eyes.

"Sleep well, my little prince.
Sleep true, my sweet prince.
Roses love sunshine, violets love dew.
All the angels in heaven wrap their wings over you..."

She'd heard those words in her dreams for the past few nights. Should she live a thousand years, she'd never escape them. Humming the forlorn melody, she searched the tower, knowing well she was trespassing, yet unable to tear herself away.

I've come too far—and now too close—to turn back.

Despair and the remnants of a broken soul engulfed her. Troubled by the sight, an unexpected weight descended upon her heart. She blinked back her burning tears, slipping through the torrent of memories and broken dreams. Shards of Adam's soul seemed to resurrect and whisper to her from the shadows. And within the wreckage, signs of beauty and life flurried by. Pull toys and strewn wooden blocks. An elegantly carved rocking horse, whose paint was peeling and whose black eyes tracked her every breath. Musical compositions. Pocket watches frozen in time. Fine silk coats from a past era. Glittering necklaces and enough jewels to satiate a king.

An ornate musical box in the shape of an oval birdcage.

She found herself paralyzed in front of the stunning, rusted trinket. Her fingertip caressed the wired bars as she examined the small porcelain figurine inside the metal prison. Inhaling a rigid breath, she carefully rotated the golden turnkey and felt her body respond to the soft, sorrowful melody that swelled the darkness. The porcelain bird fluttered his dusty wings and emitted a hypnotic whistle. It sounded hoarse from disuse—something that only enhanced the haunting quality. The little bird tinkled sad refrains, a morose and despairing song, which could only be compared to the weeping of a violin. The tone was different, yes, but the emotion felt one and the same.

As the sound of silence resumed, Isabelle moved toward a burlap sheet that hung from the wall. She brushed the heavy material aside where she met eyes with herself. Indeed, a mirror hung beyond the faded fabric—the one mirror she'd seen in the castle. A web of cracks marred the grimy surface, and a massive dent made up the epicenter, which was stained with dried blood. An image of Adam hurling his fist at his reflection flashed through her mind; she bit back a sob and drove the thought away.

She hardly recognized her own reflection; her eyes appeared several shades dimmer. Some of their light had been stolen, and when she attempted to smile, the gesture never rose to her gaze.

Isabelle staggered back, her stare still fixed on her reflection, her mind lost in a disjointed reality. Her body slammed into a table, causing debris and particles to form an explosive cloud. The musical box flew from the surface and tumbled to the ground with a resounding crash.

No... Mon Dieu, no...

She fell to her knees with a cry, her gaze darting over the broken pieces; the brittle bars had fractured on impact, leaving the bird uncaged and, thankfully, unharmed. *At least she's free now,* she dejectedly imagined, barely registering the absurdity of such a thought.

Hugging her arms around her body, she rose to her feet, covered the mirror again, and then moved toward the opposite side of the room. A row of suspended cloths hung against the black stone wall. As if moving through a dream, she ran her fingers over the ragged, sun-faded fabric. It swayed forward, manipulated by her searching hands, to reveal a veiled portrait. She tried to peek behind the hanging cloth, to see the design—but the room was far too dark. Isabelle glanced over her shoulder, knowing well that she ought to turn away now—that she was not welcome here and had already caused enough damage. Yet those portraits whispered her name, beckoning her curious nature, drawing her toward them like Bluebeard's secret room...

She pulled the first cloth down. It landed at her feet in a sun-washed puddle of faded crimson. Fairly holding her breath, she stepped closer and examined the portrait's uncloaked beauty. It depicted a stunning lady in her mid-twenties. Her skin glowed a porcelain white, contrasting against a wealth of hair that fell around her rosy cheeks. A small crown was half-buried in her hair. Striking amethysts, rubies, and emeralds decorated the fine metalwork. The woman's eyes appeared strangely alive... as if they were laughing at her. Isabelle couldn't help but return the portrait's smile. She took a step to the side, moving down the row and removing the next cloth.

A handsome king greeted her. His expression lacked the subtle smile of the queen's, yet his gaze exuded just as much warmth and spirit. Those eyes were a brilliant, pristine sapphire... *just like Adam's...*

The following cloth called out to her—yet Isabelle couldn't bring herself to take another step. She was half-paralyzed, the realization creeping up like an ice-cold wave. An image of her bedchamber and its numberless trinkets flashed through her mind.

I must see it. I must know.

Arms sprang out from the darkness. They spun her full circle and slammed her body against the king's portrait. Isabelle gasped, more in shock than from pain, as she stared into Adam's deformed face. The lantern flickered behind his massive form, casting his cloaked body in silhouette. But she saw enough to know he was far from pleased. Rage and frustration radiated from his body like a palpable force.

"I warned you to stay out of here," he said, his voice dangerously cold and deep. Those rugged vocals vibrated against her body and seeped into her marrow. "What part of *forbidden* didn't you comprehend?" His voice lashed out from the darkness like a hurtled knife, and the word "forbidden" seemed to whisper another meaning altogether. Isabelle tried to answer but failed to find her voice. Indeed, her vocal cords had turned to solid ice, as numb and cold as the blood rushing through her veins. She couldn't breathe; she felt like she was suffocating.

"My mother gave me that musical box on my fourth birthday," he said, the sensual lull of his voice causing the fine hairs on her nape to stand erect. "And now your recklessness has destroyed it. Have you nothing to say?"

"I—I'm sorry." He offered no reply; only the ragged sound of his breathing and the hammering blizzard broke the silence. "Please—I didn't mean any harm."

She struggled under the weight of Adam's colossal body and battled to free herself. He merely gave a low chuckle and pressed her firmly against the portrait. He looked otherworldly at that moment, like an angel of death seeking vengeance. Both beautiful and monstrous, his bright eyes overflowed with warring emotions. In spite of his harsh and ruthless exterior, she detected a quaver in his voice and saw that his large, cloaked shoulders trembled. The darkness in his soul cast a shadow that embraced her; as she peered up at him, she knew he was drowning in the turbulent waters of a past time.

"What a disappointment," he went on, his voice growing deeper still, mocking her words from so many days ago, "You're like any other woman."

"I—I'm sorry. Please, Adam. I—" Her gaze shot past his body and over the wreckage of a past life. She thought of her private chamber again—of the stale perfumes and outdated garments.

Her flight or fight instinct seized hold of her. She attempted to scramble free, but he merely grabbed her shoulder and whirled her back against the portrait. Gloves wrapped his hands; his long, silk-clad fingers grasped her shoulder and kept her firmly in place.

He stood intimately close.

Far too close.

As close as Raphael had been that night.

"Going somewhere, *ma belle*? After you've worked so hard to find my East Tower?"

Hands like two steel bands held her wrists in place. Hot breaths, which faintly smelled of wine, assaulted her senses. Her breasts flattened against the pressure of his strong chest, and she felt that same chest swell and deflate in perfect sync with her own. One large hand slipped down her elbow and glided across her extended arm. The lush material of his gloves drew a shudder from her heaving chest. His breathing grew more ragged, shallower, and the erratic beat of his heart thrashed against her own.

Anger and desire warred on his face, twisting his features into a mess of both monster and man. "Find anything of interest, aside from my musical box? Come, come. You went through such great trouble to get here," he asked, his voice now threaded with both anger and *something else*.

Yes, Isabelle recognized that something else. It was the same note that had entered Raphael's voice that night...

She attempted to duck under his arm, but he moved swiftly, capturing her in the crook of his elbow. Reeling her toward him, he emitted a low, haunting chuckle that swelled the eastern tower to its rafters. She was back where she'd started—pinned against the portrait, Adam's body serving as a flesh-and-blood blockade.

Hunger radiated from him, enfolding her in a current of sizzling power. His silk-clad hand grazed the curve of her breast as it moved down her body in a painfully slow caress. Even more alarming was her reaction to him. Her treacherous body responded with a crush of hot and cold waves. Then he whispered a taunt in her ear, and his liquid baritone slid down her backbone like honey; it swirled inside her, finding its home in her most intimate area.

He leaned closer still. His face's uneven skin brushed against her neck, the black waves of his hair tickled her chin...

His lips *almost* teased the base of her throat. Cursing her traitorous body, Isabelle gasped at the gentle scraping of his teeth. His tongue and lips tormented her throbbing pulse—just barely, stirring her skin in a mere ghost of a touch. She wondered if she'd imagined it.

"Let me go," she whispered, her halfhearted plea swallowed by the darkness. "You gave me your word. Please. I—"

Seeming to arrive at this senses, he loosened his hold and took a backward step. Powerful hands glided from her back to the front of her body, inadvertently brushing close to where Raphael had once assaulted her.

Too close—this entire twist of events.

Her mind drew parallels between Adam and Raphael's touches—the only other time she'd been held in such a way. The ripping sensation as Raphael's hooked finger had invaded her body rushed back. The incredible pain of him scraping her insides, the ugly words he'd uttered in her ear. Then the sight of the dried blood on her legs—not all of which was a product of her maidenhood. *Non*, his nails had drawn a separate blood, had torn her insides and the flesh of her thighs. She still bore the marks, like hateful brands forever seared across her skin.

Adam's wine-laden breaths intensified the connection as she recalled how deep in his cups Raphael had been that night. She doubted she could survive such pain and humiliation a second time. Nor did she intend to. She would rather die fighting for her integrity.

And so she fought.

With her free arm, she struck him on the side of the head with all her strength. He cursed from the blow and loosened his hold. She ducked below his muscular, outstretched arms... whirled around the table holding her lantern, her breaths rising in broken pants that misted the air. She stepped behind the overturned furniture, using the strewn pieces as a barricade—needing space between her and Adam. He followed her every move, slow and steady, stepping over the huge obstructions without a single misstep. The cloak swirled around his ankles in a ghostlike movement; he appeared to float in midair. She set down the lantern and continued to slip backward, into the shadows.

"Isabelle..." He sounded half-dazed, and agony warped his beautiful voice. "Forgive me. I—"

"Keep away from me! Just stay back! I—I should have never agreed to stay here."

She whirled on her heels and darted from the tower. Darkness enveloped her as she flew down the winding stairwell, gripping the curving wall for guidance. The moonlight cast a delicate glow, yet its illumination was inadequate for sight. She fumbled, blind and disoriented, just as Papa must have felt all those years. The thought of her beloved father amplified her panic. She hastened down the steps at an accelerated speed, not sure where she was going—only knowing she needed *out*, that she needed to feel the wind on her cheeks and to run far from here.

How mad I've been, not escaping this desolate castle sooner.

The torn sound of her breathing swelled the small corridor. She glanced over her shoulder—and felt a jolt of panic as the light from her lantern trailed after her.

Adam was fast approaching. Suddenly she regretted the blow she'd delivered and wished she could take everything back. She shouldn't have allowed her curiosity to claim the best of her... should have never poked around the East Tower or struck the side of his head. A blinding terror had claimed her;

she'd felt like prey cornered by a starved predator. But she couldn't take her rash behavior back now. And she wasn't planning to suffer the consequences or his rage.

Her own name echoed the stone walls as he called after her; a note of desperation rang in his voice and seeped below her tingling skin. The heavy clatter of his boots echoed, surrounding her and filling the darkness like a grim funeral march. Isabelle lost her footing and stumbled down the stone stairs, bloodying her knees and tearing the nightgown. Rising back onto her feet, she hiked up her skirts, mumbled a silent prayer, and pounded through the castle with a sense of disjointed reality.

ADAM CURSED UNDER HIS BREATH, the expletive forming a steamy cloud of the cold air. He could still sense Isabelle pressed against his body, could smell the enticing scent of her skin and feel the rush of her breaths against his face. He frantically called after her as he slipped down the winding stairwell and fled his eastern tower. He hadn't meant to frighten her so—but seeing her gaze upon those portraits had cut open a window to his past... one he couldn't bear having exposed.

He'd lost control himself, in truth—felt overwhelmed with an ever-growing longing for her. His anger had quickly transformed into a raw passion... a longing for something he could never have... a craving she'd ignited ever since she stumbled upon his doorway and insisted upon entry.

He deserved to lose her.

Except, you fool, you can't lose what was never yours.

Self-disgust twisted inside him. He was truly a beast, a monster, and in every sense of the word.

I must make it right—or at least try.

Isabelle's lantern swayed in his unsteady grasp, bobbing off the stone walls. The sight momentarily paralyzed him as his thoughts crept back to that long-ago night. For a moment, the world wavered. *Torchlight flickering across the walls... The heat of their fire as they approach my hiding spot and set the tapestry aglow... The sound of their taunting voices... "Little prince... come out, come out, wherever you are..."*

Meanwhile, Isabelle raced through the castle, apparently familiar with its colossal layout, and drew open the front door. Cold wind blasted inside as she charged through the courtyard and past her father's grave.

Running out of the castle, Adam made a hasty detour to the stables. The mare nervously stamped her hooves and bobbed her head as he burst inside. Moonlight slanted through the irregular panels and set her cascading silver mane aglow. He blew out the lantern and set it on the straw-covered floor.

"Shh, you must calm yourself, *ma belle*," he whispered in the mare's shifting ear. "Remember me? I've been caring for you every morning and night." After a moment, she settled down with a resigned nicker, as if she'd absorbed the sentiment of his words.

Adam didn't bother saddling the creature. He threw open the stall's latch, swept onto her back, and gripped her flowing mane. The stunning cascade of silver streamed through his gloved fingers like fresh-spun silk. With an urgent kick to her flank, the mare soared from her confinement and into the blackness of the night.

Branches rustled past Adam's body and scratched at his face while the mare cantered through the forest. The trees grew rather close together, making it difficult to dodge them in the darkness. Most of the branches were naked and bore no foliage; this permitted moonlight to stream through the trees' groping limbs and dapple the dark forest with glowing prisms.

Adam ducked low, laying his chest against the mare's silver mane, as he dodged a low-hanging branch. The sound of the blizzard pressed on his eardrums in a deafening wail; the snow had lightened considerably, though wet flakes still fell from the sky and further obstructed his vision. Freezing cold and wet, Adam backtracked toward the castle, knowing Isabelle couldn't have traveled so far in the storm and without a horse. He squinted his eyes to better make out his surroundings and watched as his breaths formed steamy clouds on the cold air.

His numb, silk-encased fingers twisted in the mare's mane as terror seized him; Isabelle wouldn't last out here more than a half an hour.

Should something happen to her... I shall never forgive myself.

A heartbeat late, he breathed a sigh of relief as he caught sight of her slender form; her white sleeping rail and robe glowed within the night, lending her with an otherworldly appearance. Battling the harsh blizzard and a chill that crept into his very veins, Adam tugged the mare's mane and commanded her to a halt. Isabelle stood in the thicket of trees and snowfall, looking lost, defeated, completely alone. Wet and shivering, she held her breast, visibly exhausted from the exertion and frigid cold. Pale flakes of snow clashed against her damp curls, and she swayed on her feet. Adam wheeled the mare around a fallen log and trotted forward. Isabelle spun in place with a wobbly movement, facing him and the mare while they approached. She warily backed away while a riot of emotions surfaced in her hazel eyes.

The vision mesmerized him, awakening something inside his soul.

"Just—leave me! I need to be alone." The wind almost carried her words away. "I... I need to breathe, to find myself."

Adam's dark chuckle fluttered between the trees. "In the forest? And in the middle of a blizzard? What are you, foolish? Or just plain mad? You'll catch your death within the hour. Pray tell, would your father have wished for that?"

She said nothing, drifting away from him, her gaze seeming to only look inward. Hugging her trembling body, she said, "Papa and I used to camp in the woods, snuggled beneath a single blanket..." She was speaking to herself, he knew, to ghosts that hadn't been laid to rest. "We would whisper stories to each other... scare each other with spectral legends and folklore. Now he's gone, and I can't find myself..." Her eyes returned to his, connecting. "I am lost, Adam. Lost and so very cold."

Adam exhaled a long-suffering breath and gently urged the mare forward. She resisted, her snow-white head swinging toward the dark crevices and shuddering branches.

"And now, I have found you. Come to me, Isabelle," he called down, the words reaching out to her, his voice soft and gentle. "I shouldn't have frightened you so. Shouldn't have touched you in such a way. This is your home now—you have every right to venture where you please. I lost control. I'm afraid my temper is one of my uglier facets, among other things." The self-deprecating note in his voice disgusted him; absently he twisted the mare's silver mane between his fingers and exhaled a rigid breath. They desperately needed to get back to the castle.

"You will fall ill again. And I shan't allow it. Please, Isabelle... allow me to make amends, to show you I'm not the monster you perceive me to be." The mare anxiously shuffled her hooves and swung her great head, agitated by the blizzard and rustling trees. Skeletal branches shuddered in the dark forest like trembling limbs. Snow flurried around her hooves as she restlessly shifted forward. Her body swayed beneath him, tottering like a ship in stormy waves. "Whatever you may think, you are not alone. I, too, feel so lost and cold."

An irresistible note of command crept into his voice as he held out a gloved hand; Isabelle drew toward him with that simple gesture. He observed her from his perch on the mare's back, aware that she was holding her breath and visibly overcome with a mixture of fascination and dull horror. Momentarily she lapsed into a semi-aware state; unsettled by her harsh surroundings, the mare fiercely thumped her hooves. Adam tugged on her mane and fought to regain his dominance.

"Move away. Get back, Isabelle. Now—" A heartbeat later, the mare slipped on a patch of ice. Her huge body wavered... She reared back onto her hindquarters and released a thunderous whinny that split the night. "Easy. Easy!"

Without a saddle or reins, Adam lost his balance and was flung into the night. Then everything fell black.

Chapter Eleven

It happened in an explosion of movement. The poor mare slipped and reeled, tossing Adam off her back and into a tree. His head slammed against the massive trunk, rendering him silent and still on the snow-covered ground. Nearby, the creature regained her footing and stomped her hooves dangerously close to his head. The deafening sound rippled across the forest floor and pulled Isabelle from her inward trance—propelling her back into the moment.

"Adam!" She rushed toward him without sparing a thought, hesitantly pushed the spooked mare aside, and knelt beside Adam's strewn body.

He was out cold, the side of his head bloodied from the impact. Illuminated by the moonlight, a crimson line streamed from his temple and slid down his face like one great tear. She glanced at the panicked mare, torn between fleeing on the creature's back and staying by Adam's side.

Strained breaths stormed inside her lungs. Shivering, she stared at his enormous unconscious body. Conflicting emotions stirred within and reached a fierce crescendo.

Recalling the caress of Adam's hands from minutes ago,

she shifted away. His words, the spellbinding lull of his voice, echoed in her mind and spiraled through her icy veins. Her skin still tingled from where he'd touched her.

Her hand trembling in midair, she reached out and gently urged the damp black forelock from his shut eyes. She compared his likeness to the king and queen in the portraits, and another shiver raced down her spine.

And then it hit her. She wasn't the only one who'd chosen to run away. Adam had been running as well.

Her discoveries in the East Tower warned Isabelle that he was far from an ordinary man. Clearly there was more to Adam than what met the eye.

I, too, feel lost and cold...

Of course she couldn't leave him. Not like this. Papa had raised her better, with greater compassion. She was quite accustomed to playing the role of caretaker—and care for Adam she would.

She forced the recent turn of events from her mind and focused on the moment. The whipping wind and harsh blizzard made it almost impossible to draw breaths, let alone formulate a coherent plan. She violently shivered, numb and soaked to the bone.

What can I possibly do?

A wave of adrenaline rushed through her veins, setting fire to her resolve and chasing away some of the cold. She resolutely rubbed her arms, urging heat back into her limbs. Then she shrugged Adam's immobile arm around her shoulder and tested his body weight. Indeed, there was no way she could ever bear his massive size by herself.

As if in answer to her predicament, Adam stirred awake and released a pained groan. Isabelle cradled the back of his head, lifting it from the frozen ground as snow flurried around them and her skin prickled. Meanwhile, the mare continued to toss her muzzle and stomp her hooves. Adam's eyes flashed open, momentarily jarring Isabelle with their surreal beauty.

"Isabelle? What... Where...?" Groaning, he strained his body and attempted to sit up. Isabelle seized hold of his muscled shoulders and gently urged him back on the ground.

"*Non*, you mustn't exert yourself so. You hit your head and blacked out for several minutes."

A ghost of a smile formed on his lips. His gloved hand lifted from the ground to cup her cheek, his gaze never parting from her own. Stroking the curve of her chin with his thumb, he whispered, "Sometimes, when I look at you, I can hardly believe that you are real, that you are here with me..."

His words sounded strained, almost dreamlike, spoken in a quiet voice that the wind half swept away. Isabelle returned his smile as a peculiar fluttering sensation formed in her chest. She curved her hand over his own, wrapping his thick wrist with her fingers. "Well, I am real. And I am here with you."

Isabelle felt tears form in the corners of her eyes as she stared down at his quaint expression. Her gaze tracked over the two sides of his face—the beautiful and the deformed one. He looked lost and defeated. Almost childlike.

It was quite remarkable. The sensation—the jarring and unexpected flush of emotions—took her by complete surprise, momentarily plunging her in stunned silence. Her limbs felt paralyzed, completely numb—and the cold wasn't to blame. Then Adam's eyes shuttered closed, causing his long, sooty lashes to cast shadows on his cheekbones. The warmth from his gloved palm and fingers melted away as his hand slid from her face.

They needed to get out of the storm—and quickly.

I must be mad to have ventured out here in the first place.

That thought scared her a little, though she forced it away. She needed total focus and full control of her faculties. Isabelle glanced at the mare, who seemed to have calmed, and wedged her arm under Adam's shoulder.

"Please, Adam... I need you to help me," she said in a gentle whisper. "Can you try to stand?" He strained his body while Isabelle gently wrapped her arms around his torso. His muscles bunched underneath her fingers, reminding her of his sheer strength and size. She guided him into a sitting position, panting from the exertion, and slowly caught his gaze as she pulled her arms free. She held out her hand, her breaths misting the night air. Adam seized hold of her lower arm with a pained groan, groggily stumbling onto his knees, and then finally to his feet. The dark forelock fluttered over his gaze, shielding his emotions from sight, as she carefully walked him to the mare.

She delved deep inside herself for courage she hoped she possessed. "I doubt you can ride in your state... but perhaps—"

"Yes, yes. Say no more, *ma belle*..." Adam swayed forward and leaned against the mare before climbing onto her body with a woozy groan. The energy visibly drained out of him; he fell motionless in moments, his body slung over the creature's side like some great deer. Isabelle drew close to them, checked that he was securely in place, then urged his draped body farther onto the mare's back. He stirred for a moment, mumbling some incoherent words, before he sunk back into whatever haze awaited his return.

Isabelle gently stroked the mare's curved neck. White clouds ascended from her nose and clashed against the darkness. She still looked quite restless, her eyes and ears dancing in time with the rustling branches and blistering wind.

"I don't know your name, pretty girl," she whispered, watching as the mare's ear turned toward her soft voice. "So I shall name you myself. You quite look like a *Spirit* to me." Isabelle pressed her lips against the velvety muzzle. The mare's nearness infused her with warmth and helped chase the chill from her bones. "Good girl, Spirit. Now stay nice and calm for me. We're going home."

Isabelle guided Spirit forward, wading through the dense copse of trees, one hand pressed against Adam's back. And as the castle's looming gates rose into sight again, a startling relief empowered her steps.

ADAM AWOKE TO WARMTH and a tender touch. Pain bonded his eyelids together as he fought to untangle his surroundings. A deep, penetrative throbbing weighed on his brain with a nauseating force. And what little he could see appeared to be tilted onto its axis. Indeed, everything spun in circles and wavered. He brought two fingertips against the side of his head, where he felt a raised welt and dampness.

Blood. Then he felt a gentle, exquisite touch, and some of the pain subsided. He strained his eyes and caught sight of a flesh-and-blood angel.

Isabelle.

She'd hastily fastened back her hair with a ribbon, exposing her lovely collarbone. A single wayward strand swirled in front of her eyes and clashed against the porcelain hue of her skin. She exhaled a puff of air, blowing the errant strand away. It merely fluttered against her cheek and obstructed her vision again. She chewed her bottom lip in contemplation, then stepped out of his line of sight. A heartbeat later, she returned with a damp piece of linen clasped between her slim fingers.

Their gazes merged. When she spoke, the airy melody of her voice seduced him, anchoring his senses and numbing the pain. "Oh, Adam. Thank God—you're finally awake. I feared for the worse."

"Awake, maybe, but daft after that blow." He was lounged on the chaise in the central drawing room, reclining on his back. The hearth blazed before him, infusing the room with heat and the soft murmur of burning embers. His rumpled coat lay beside the chaise—and Adam absently remembered staggering off the mare's back and through the castle. "What... what happened?"

Isabelle eased onto the Persian rug, seating herself a meter from his strewn body. Firelight shone in her hair, summoning brilliant copper highlights in her curls. She hesitated, then brushed away the wayward strand again. Darkness settled across her expression. Gazing into the fire, she said, "What can you remember? Anything at all?"

Adam squeezed both eyes shut and tried to recall the turn

of events. He'd delivered Isabelle's supper to her room, a plate of boiled rabbit and fresh vegetables, which she'd eaten alone like every other night. Then he'd attempted to compose a new piece... and had been drained of any inspiration.

Ah, yes. The East Tower.

His eyes tracked the pale column of her throat, and he suddenly recalled everything—holding her against the stone wall, the invigorating sensation of her body melded to his own... and all that followed...

From the shadows, he'd observed while she'd gazed upon his mother and father's portraits, watching as a tremor of wonder crossed her stunning face. She'd run her pale fingertips along his mother's painted cheek. Then she'd turned back to the ruin of his East Tower, her gaze flittering across the overturned pieces and dusty keepsakes from his childhood. She'd almost uncovered the last portrait—a part of himself that had died long ago. Humiliation and despair had flamed inside his heart, in every muscle and sinew. Indeed, Isabelle, in all her damned curiosity and willfulness, had wrenched open a dark passageway lined with restless ghosts.

He'd stopped her just before she'd unveiled everything. He recalled the terror in her eyes. Never had he beheld such a thing. She'd appeared frightened for her very life—and then she'd fled the castle as if the devil himself had been on her heels.

Perhaps that isn't so far from the truth, Adam sardonically mused.

A new admiration and respect for Isabelle ignited; she had brought him back from the forest—soaked to the bone, shivering, and without any aid. That alone was an astonishing feat. Add the fact that he'd chased her out of the castle and into the blizzard... His awe couldn't be put into words. Her strength and courage stole his voice.

She truly is an angel. And much too good-hearted for me.

"You don't remember anything?" she asked again from her spot on the floor.

Shaken by his emotions, he cleared his throat and glanced over the edge of the chaise where Stranger was obliviously sprawled across the warm floorboards. Absorbing the heat, he contently napped before the fire on a threadbare rug. Below his snout, a stream of drool leaked onto the rug where it formed an ever-growing puddle. Adam felt a stab of jealousy as he observed Stranger immersed in peaceful dreams. *How I envy you.* Even now, Adam felt the unquietness of his own mind. It pressed hard on his skull and flattened his thoughts. He slid his hand over his forehead and drove away the waking nightmare.

"I remember the terror in your eyes when I touched you in the East Tower," he finally answered. "I shouldn't have done so. It was wrong of me. But you... *you*, Isabelle, you make me want to be better..."

Adam captured her gaze. She inhaled an audible breath before leaning forward and tentatively pressing the wet cloth to his temple. "Then show me. Become better."

"You have my promise."

"I thought I couldn't trust you?" she replied in a half-teasing, half-accusatory voice.

Adam couldn't suppress his chuckle. Cool beads of water dripped down the side of his head and helped to temper his desire. Their faces were centimeters apart. Only a kiss away. Wisps of breath fanned against his disfigurement, caressing him in a sensual assault. They remained mute for several moments, their gazes interlocked and eyes searching.

His fingers itched to cup her cheeks and draw her forward to close the scant distance between them. At this close proximity, he could make out every freckle, every sweeping eyelash. He clenched his fingers and fought to combat the swelling tension in his loins. How he longed to pull her against his reclined body—to follow the intimate passage of her breaths... to inhale her exhales and lose himself in the warmth of her body. She swallowed deeply. He observed the muscles in her throat... the delicate beauty of her collarbone and the supple rise of her breasts. They strained against her white robe with their seductive fullness.

His errant thoughts whirled back to the East Tower—to the incredible feel of Isabelle in his arms, the sweet scent of her skin, the heat of her pushed against him. His body hardening and blood rushing, Adam lay in stunned silence from the memory, not believing he'd found the boldness to touch her. She'd recoiled at his nearness, of course, just as he'd expected.

Just as every other female has since that night.

How he ached to be *good*—to be worthy of Isabelle. The painful longing lodged in his chest and shadowed his thoughts.

"Why did you run off into the blizzard?" he asked as he simultaneously cleared his throat. "You might have died."

She gave a dejected sigh, then shook her head. "I admit it wasn't one of my brighter moments—certainly not something I'd want to be engraved on my epitaph. But you frightened me, Adam... and I suppose I felt the need to be free. This castle, these walls—they can be crushing."

Adam nodded and released a sigh. "I have a habit of doing that. Frightening people, I mean." He gently grasped her suspended wrist and lowered the dripping linen. She stiffened at his touch, and that terror surfaced in her gaze again. "What are you so afraid of? What happened to you?" Only silence. A rough draft whistled through the walls, and the castle shook in its wake. "I know your fear extends far beyond this," he said, gesturing to his own face. "I can see the darkness in your eyes. It's the same darkness I see each night..."

Her gaze dropped as she glanced at Stranger; lush hoods of lashes cast crescent moons upon her high cheekbones. The rebellious curl fell in front of her stare once more as she shook her downcast head. "It doesn't matter any longer. It is part of my past. And I never plan to return to it."

Adam drew off his gloves with his teeth, then slid his fingers down her wrist and seized her small hand.

Simple, human touch. The sensation of her slender fingers gliding through his own summoned a riot of unforeseen emotions and longings. Human contact was something he'd lived without for decades. Something he'd secretly craved with every fiber of his being and with every beat of his bruised heart.

She offered it to him, that simple thing he craved most, without revulsion or fear in her hazel eyes.

Just a mutual yearning—a longing for simple companionship and connection.

ISABELLE'S HEART FLIPPED as Adam's strong, gnarled fingers entwined with her own. Something drifted in the air between them, in the way his gaze searched hers and filled with empathy and red-hot desire.

Remarkably, her fears shrank away, and she momentarily felt safe and secure.

His eyes skimmed over her mouth, a stark longing in his blue stare. The hunger she'd witnessed in the East Tower visibly resurfaced. It swirled around them, alive and electric, crackling like lightning. She shifted back; his gaze flew to her eyes, as though her movement had whisked him out of a trance. Then a smile curled his lips as he turned away and stared into the flaming hearth.

"Funny thing, the past. No matter how hard you try to shut it from your mind, you always hear those whispers in your skull..." That low, masculine whisper curled around her like smoke. His eyes fastened shut, and he visibly shivered, reacting to lamentations only he could hear. Overwhelmed with the urge to reach out and touch him, she twisted her fingers in the sullied fabric of her robe. "It's inescapable; a true prison in every sense of the word. Almost like being chased by a predator. The faster you run away, the more it chases you, and the more it demands your surrender..."

Isabelle caught herself nodding. She studied Adam's profile, in awe of the handsome side of his face—the austere jut of his chin, the straight, strong nose, and dark, slightly winged brow. Her mind slipped back to the likeness in the portrait—then to his outburst in the eastern tower.

Long ago, she and Papa had traveled all the way to Lavoncourt—Demrov's glittering capital. Papa had pointed to Castle Delacroix's ruins, which stood as a mere shadow of the fortress it'd once been, and Isabelle had wept for the royal family.

Could he possibly be...?
No—he's dead. He's been dead for over two decades.

A million questions burned on the tip of her tongue. She held them back and expelled a tired sigh. "I suppose we aren't so different, after all." He turned to her, captured her gaze with his own. How she ached to unwrap his secrets—to understand how he'd come to live in complete solitude, burned outside and in, hiding so many kilometers away from civilization. The walls he'd erected around himself were as strong and sure as the castle itself.

"I don't understand," he said, splitting her thoughts in two. "Why did you help me? After everything I've done to you? After all the pain I've brought..."

Silently she shook her head. "I've seen glimpses of the good in you. Gentleness, a compassionate spirit. And besides... you helped me, stayed by my side. I couldn't have lived with myself had I left you lying in the snow to die. Papa taught me better than that." She paused to collect her nerves. "The beautiful trinkets and clothing in my chamber—did... did they belong to someone special?" She ached to press further about the eastern wing, but she stilled her tongue, knowing it was neither the time nor place.

"Yes," he murmured, fiddling with his signet ring. "They were my mother's."

Silence thrummed between them, as evocative and meaningful as a pianoforte refrain. Mutely she stared down at her robe and night rail and stroked the intricate lace detail with her free hand.

His mother's robe and night rail.

"Keeping her memory alive in that way... it's clear that you really loved her."

"Thank you," he whispered at length, "for giving me another chance." Tangible emotion laced the words together and reached out to her with a gentle, seductive caress. He leaned closer, and the pressure of his fingers intensified on her hand. His unique scents filled her nostrils in a compelling assault of the senses. Firelight danced in the dark waves of his hair, infusing those thick strands with flashes of navy blue. Her gaze tracked over the contrasting sides of his face, then became ensnared in the spell of his eyes. Once again, the king's portrait flared through her racing thoughts.

"You are mine now, Isabelle," he said, his voice a husky purr that brushed against her. "Mine to guard and protect."

Another powerful silence seized hold. She peered down at their intertwined fingers—studying how his much larger hand overpowered and dominated her own. "*Non*, Adam," she whispered, pulling her hand away. "That's where you are wrong. I shall never belong to another. Never again."

Chapter Twelve

"She warned him not to be deceived by appearances, for beauty is found within."
—Walt Disney, *Beauty and the Beast*

I'VE BEEN HERE two weeks now. Who would ever believe it? Gazing into the hearth, Isabelle placed her empty breakfast plate on the end table. Secretly she longed for Adam's company during her mealtimes, yet he rarely showed himself. And so she'd contented herself with Stranger and Spirit.

She'd spent the past few days exploring the twisting corridors and ancient rooms, where the castle's distractions had proved endless. Reading. Piecing wooden puzzles together. Uncovering treasures from a past age. Tidying the place and trying her luck at new recipes; she absently wondered where the food came from, since Adam never left the security of his castle.

Yes, the distractions were quite endless yet proved mundane and empty all the same. Except for Adam's music. She enjoyed that most of all; each night, he'd play a song of her choosing as she nodded off to sleep and into the lush fabric of a dream world. His melodies added color to her world and a stunning light to her days...

Sipping her tea, she heaved a weary sigh as the mantel's decorative coat of arms ensnared her focus. Light from the fireplace flashed across the intricate metalwork and jewel embellishments, illuminating the two intertwined salamanders and ignited shield. Stranger lay beside the wingback chair, silent and still. Isabelle draped her hand down the side of her chair and idly ran her fingers over his ragged fur.

The Delacroix royal coat of arms. She'd seen it in books before, where she'd read about the family's heart-wrenching tale countless times. Betrayal and deceit had sealed their dark fate.

But what sealed Adam's?

An hour later, donning one of the walking dresses from her quarters, Isabelle wandered through the castle's stunning gardens. The storm had cleared the previous morning, leaving the world revived and refreshed in its wake.

Her breath caught; her ears vibrated with her heartbeats. She felt like she'd stepped into the pages of a storybook. The roses, which were miraculously in full bloom, appeared perfect and undisturbed—unaffected by winter's touch or any other ailments. Here, right in the colorful heart of the rose garden, the mosaic hedges looked lush and healthy. No weeds were in sight, and the small fruit trees reached for the overcast sky as if embracing a summer sun. The courtyard, encased in an icy shell and overgrown with untamed foliage, materialized in Isabelle's mind. Every petal and blade of grass looked perfect, beautiful, polished—like a jeweler had handcrafted each one into an extraordinary gem.

She'd seen the gardens from her balcony before and had pushed their mystical quality from her mind. Now, standing in the aromatic garden and touching those flawless petals, she could no longer ignore its existence or power. The realization sent a tremor of mingled fright and awe through her.

Much like Adam does...

If she was completely honest with herself, she was beginning to fall in love with the castle's mysteries and darkness.

Morning's rays trickled through the pine trees like prying fingers and bathed the manicured hedges, flowers, and ponds with dappled light. How wonderful it felt to be out of the dark castle and one with nature again. Indeed, Isabelle had always held a great love for the outdoors. She suppressed the memories of her papa, knowing nothing good could come from immersing herself in further grief.

Turning into the aromatic, crisp breeze, she relished the caress of the wind on her cheeks.

Isabelle surrendered to an inward sigh, then collected several colorful blooms and placed them in her skirts. The dress was quite beautiful, and she couldn't help but stroke her fingers over the fine silks and lace. Flowing, crème-colored fabric spilled over her body in elegant lines. The waist was about one size too large and the chest one too small, but she felt like royalty all the same.

Crouched before a towering hedge, she stared at the massive castle, in awe of the intricate architecture and jutting buttresses. An unexpected emotion filled her and shook her to the very core.

Heartache for Adam.

It was all incredibly frustrating and confusing; a part of herself felt like she was betraying her papa.

Adam was a true enigma. Confident yet full of insecurities. Commanding yet strangely shy and withdrawn.

How long had he lived here, alone and in the shadow of this castle?

Isabelle felt his formidable presence before she saw him. Glancing over her shoulder, she stared into his penetrating blue eyes for a weightless moment. A breeze rustled his dark, wavy hair, causing the wayward strands to whip against his face. She inwardly chastened herself. It was no great wonder why he lived completely alone and cut off from society. Despite his callous demeanor and quick temper, Isabelle knew he had a sensitive, compassionate side. He preferred to keep that side hidden, but she'd witnessed it nonetheless. She recalled their interaction when she'd tended to his head wound, and a resounding warmth spread through her limbs.

His brilliant gaze tracked over her dress in a slow perusal.

She cleared her throat, then glanced at the cluster of flowers lying in her skirts. "I feel like I'm going mad. Your garden—it's thriving in the middle of winter. How? How is such a thing possible?"

Adam's lips quirked. A note of cold steel carried in his voice, blending with his cultured accent in a rather compelling way. "I've seen this garden outlive winter so many times that I hardly notice it anymore. Indeed, after all these years, it's come to look as normal as anything else. That first season, when I planted the flowers, I watched them with a morbid anticipation—waiting for winter to choke them like it does everything else, waiting for their petals to fall away and rejoin the earth. But they endured. They survived that harsh winter, unchanged, beautiful, complete... I thought I was living in a dream of sorts..." His voice trailed off, and a shadow eclipsed his blue eyes.

"And now?"

His lips quirked again—this time with a humorless mirth. "I wouldn't call my life a dream."

She felt his eyes on her as she stroked one of the silken petals. Clearing her throat again, she whispered, "Papa always loved asters. I thought I'd brighten his grave."

Isabelle inwardly cursed herself as a tear escaped her eye. She swatted it away and inhaled a long breath.

Then Adam knelt beside her, intimately close. The heat of his body radiated and brushed against her own. Hardly thinking, Isabelle urged his hair aside, leaned closer to him, and gently ran her fingertip over the wound. The skin was scabbed and slightly raised. Her thoughts traveled back to the East Tower—to the feel of his body against hers, the sensation of his lips brushing her pulse—

He shuddered at her touch; she retracted her hand and scooted back a few centimeters. "Oh, I—I'm sorry. I thought I'd check on your wound. I didn't mean to cause you any pain."

"You didn't. You couldn't." He repeatedly swept a hand through his silky hair before speaking again. The unconscious movement urged the heavy locks off his face and exposed his shriveled ear. Isabelle dropped her eyes and focused on the darkly hypnotic lull of his voice. It wrapped around her thoughts, cloaking her mind and body in a dangerous oblivion.

"I understand how you feel. The hurt, that vacant feeling inside your heart... I lost my parents when I was just a boy." That haunted look entered his eyes again, and Isabelle felt an undeniable pull toward him. "Some nights, it feels like it happened only yesterday."

Isabelle swallowed and glanced at the vivid blooms in her lap. The East Tower portraits materialized in her mind. "I suppose this sort of wound never fully heals. But does it get easier?" she asked in a whisper, half speaking to herself.

A long silence seized hold. Isabelle inhaled the cool winter air, inviting it inside her lungs. It had a strange, purifying effect, and she felt some of her grief subside. Then Adam reached out and gently clasped her hand. She watched in admiration as his large, scarred fingers swallowed her own. Breathless, her heart thudding, she stared at their untied grips for several iridescent moments. He unfurled his fingers and massaged her palm with his thumb pad. The rough, uneven skin grated against hers in a tender caress.

Dieu, she wanted to continue to hate him—to spit curses at him and condemn him for the tragedy that had befallen her father... but she could not. The remorse was evident in his touches and words, in how he'd cared for her during her hours of darkness and every day since—and she was coming to realize they needed each other.

Since the East Tower incident, her heart had lightened several shades—yet the sadness lurked like a transient shadow. She supposed it would always exist—a dark void that could never be filled or made complete. And when she imagined her papa, the way he'd looked that night—the sadness seized her soul in an iron grip, and an avalanche of despair came rushing back.

Searching Adam's gaze, a tremor raced through her as she recalled his night terrors. Alas, the nights brought a separate agony and darkness altogether. Almost every evening, she'd lie in bed, her face crushed in her pillow, bearing witness to Adam's cries as they echoed through the castle's corridors. Truly it felt like a form of torture—and with each passing day, it was becoming harder to stomach. Within the darkness, she'd listen to those heart-wrenching sobs while her mind ventured through the East Tower and all its secrets again and again...

"No," he finally answered, his voice a broken and husky whisper. So faint were his words, the wind nearly carried them away. Body heat and the scent of his skin radiated, urged her trust. He continued to massage her palm, drawing invisible half circles and carefully tracing her lifeline. She swallowed and shut her eyes, savoring the simple feel of human contact.

How she'd missed it.

"The wound never fully heals. The loss and pain are always there, like a raw sore, reminding you of what once was... of what should have been." Her eyes whipped open as his body heat moved away. He smoothed down his cloak, climbed back to his feet, and held out his hand for her taking. "But you grow stronger. You move forward as best you can. And you learn to endure."

You survive the winter.

ADAM OBSERVED AS ISABELLE approached her father's resting spot. Overhead, the black ash bowed as a gust of wind manipulated it. A wooden cross, assembled from two slabs of pine, jutted out from the heart of the cairn.

Restless and unable to sleep, he'd constructed it the previous evening. He'd collected the wood from the surrounding forest, sanded it to a shine, and carefully etched the date of the man's death. He'd laid awake for hours, afraid to sleep—anxious of what would be waiting in his nightmares. Now, he felt a little calmer, and the world appeared brighter with Isabelle close by.

"I... I didn't know his name," Adam whispered, gesturing to the wooden cross.

"Bernard." Her eyes captured his, those hazel depths

inflamed with a naked curiosity and wonder. He stole a glance at her features—her small, upturned, freckled nose, the deep red of her lips, and her whirlwind of dark curls.

His gaze dropped lower, to the rise of her full breasts; they strained against the dress's silks and lace, as if beckoning his touch. "It's lovely," she said, cropping his erotic thoughts in two. "Thank you. Your parents—how did they die?" When his answer never came, she shook her head and whispered, "I shouldn't have asked. You don't have to share such things with me."

Adam felt his blood run cold. He gazed at her papa's resting place, then reached out and tracked his scarred fingers over the cross. "They were killed." As he spoke, he extracted a small, gem-studded folding knife from his cloak's pocket and engraved the man's name above the date. Isabelle visibly flinched at the sight of the blade and inconspicuously scooted backward. He fought to ignore her reaction and continued to engrave the cross. "They were brutally murdered when I was just a boy." *And I was forced to witness everything.* A deep shudder rocked his body. His hand stilled in midair, and the knife shook in his grip.

Suddenly a featherlight touch graced his arm. Fairly holding his breath, he glanced over to find Isabelle's slender hand grasping his bicep. Her eyes captured his own again, and for several moments, he had to remind himself to so much as breathe.

"I'm so sorry, Adam. *Dieu...* I can't imagine the pain you must have endured all these years."

Her eyes lifted to the cross. A vacant, faraway look entered her beautiful gaze.

"Your scars—" Adam heard the cautious and wary note in her voice, as if she were traveling from one stepping-stone to the next, hopping with care across a tumultuous stream. A dark shadow had also crossed her lovely eyes—one that drew him in and whispered to the most intimate caverns of his soul. "Did they happen on the night of your parents' deaths?"

"Yes," he said as he carved the final letter of her father's name. "These scars and others." She was asking too many questions. Spinning the knife between his thumb and forefinger, he mutely shook his head and inhaled a rigid breath. If he didn't tread with caution, he'd fall into those tumultuous waters and bring Isabelle down with him.

Silence took hold with the force of an iron fist. She met his eyes again, then slowly shifted her gaze over his deformity. *Mon Dieu*, how he ached to run and hide. Shame and resentment twisted inside him like a knife. "Men have endured worse in the wars. You don't have to shut yourself away, to—"

"Men fighting in the wars are *heroes*. Soldiers," he harshly spat, tossing the knife point first into the snow-covered ground. "Their scars are badges of honor." Adam waved toward his deformity while the resentment reached a steady boil. "These bring me no honor, and I am certainly no hero."

I watched as my mother and father were massacred in cold blood, he thought, simultaneously cringing at the hypocrisy of his words from moments ago. He'd never grown stronger. He'd never moved forward. And he never had endured. Instead, he'd shut himself up and hid from humanity, like a grotesque beetle scuttling beneath a rock. "And besides... I'm afraid most people don't have your compassion. Or stomach."

"Forgive me, but those are rather cynical words from a man who's kept himself hidden away. You haven't seen the world. You don't know what—"

"I've seen enough."

She said nothing—merely returned her gaze to the wooden cross and exhaled a weary breath. "The storm killed him." She shook her head, physically battling her own revelation. "You frightened him—you frightened us both, there's no doubting that. And you frightened me in your eastern tower. But the storm stole Papa from me. That and his illness." She swallowed deeply, and Adam found himself mesmerized by the slender muscles in her throat, the way her pale breaths misted the air. "I should have known better. Disregarding the truth and hating you won't bring him back. It won't change anything."

"And neither shall blaming yourself." He hesitated, then plucked the blade from the ground and pocketed it. "Do you have any other relatives? A sister or brother, perhaps? Even a cousin?"

Isabelle mutely stared forward while her fine brows knotted in concentration. The simple question appeared to puzzle her. "Two stepsisters. Though I'd hardly call them family..." She shook her head in defeat, as if arriving at an unpleasant decision. "My father never turned his cheek to Clarice and Elizabeth—and God knows they often deserved that and worse. My stepsisters have always despised me. Their mother made certain of that..." Her voice trailed off, and she swatted the air like swishing away a horsefly. "Never mind. It doesn't matter now. They are probably grateful to be rid of me. And I certainly shan't miss their scowling faces. But you would... provide them with funds? Security?"

"Of course. If that's what you wish."

"It's what Papa would have wanted, anyway. Thank you, Adam."

"It is the least I can do."

The atmosphere shifted between them. He outstretched his hand and gently cupped her chin, turning her face from the cross and forcing her gaze to meet his own. A smile curved her lips, and something primitive stirred to life inside him. He studied the lush shape of her mouth... those sensual curves, the deep, exotic hue...

She was pure temptation. Unlike anything he'd known before. And her loyalty to her family unnerved him far more than her beauty. It forced him to glance inward, to witness the full measure of the beast he'd become.

Half of him wanted to send her away, while the other half ached to hold her close. Never had he felt so torn, so inferior—and all because of a slip of a girl. Resentment curdled inside him, morphing his apprehension into a cold, silent despair.

Non, she's far from a slip of a girl, you fool. She's strong. Courageous. Beautiful, inside and out. And loyal to her core. Aside from the East Tower, she's never even tried to escape me.

Adam wrenched his hand away and silently cursed himself. He brushed unsteady fingers through his hairline and forced his thoughts into another territory.

That was when it hit him. Sébastien would be arriving this

afternoon, should the fool stick to their arrangement.

"There's a village not so far from here. It's small but has all the basic necessities." His eyes fixed on her mouth again before sliding down her body. "You can purchase your own clothing there... whatever other things you may require. It's quite close—not over half an hour on horseback if you know the path. You can ride?" She silently nodded. "I thought as much." Adam imagined Isabelle unleashing her adventurous spirit—riding through a field of flowers and swaying grass. Her long curls would wave behind her like a banner while her robust laughter floated on the breeze...

Snapping out of his fantasy, he withdrew a handful of francs from inside his cloak. He pressed them into her small, delicate palm, then curled her fingers closed.

When he at last spoke, a painful longing filled his voice—one he no longer could hide. "Return to me, Isabelle."

Chapter Thirteen

THE DAMNABLE BROUGHAM hadn't budged a bit. Sébastien's eyes fixed on its ice-locked wheels and emblazoned letters, then darted back to his own modest phaeton. Adjusting his satchel, he pounded on the castle's monstrous wooden door and waited.

And waited.

No answer.

That brougham had occupied his mind ever since his last visit—nagging at his thoughts with an unsettling intensity. The brougham, Adam's beautiful lady guest (or perhaps hostage), and that gentleman's top hat. They had become somewhat of an obsession, and in their wake, a hostility toward Adam took flight.

That damnable brougham and top hat had sent him racing across the country. Indeed, he'd fled his comfortable apartment, which lay far enough from Ruillé not to bear its stain, yet close enough not to suffer the ghastly cost of the nearby provinces. Even the Dumonts lived quite near to him in Laché, Demrov—less than a brisk carriage ride away.

He'd known Adam since he was a green lad—but did he truly know the *man* he'd become? After all, a person could only endure so much for so long...

Another knock; more silence.

Living in such a filthy, drafty castle in complete solitude for so many years... it could drive even the sanest man to desperation. It was a true wonder Adam hadn't snapped before now, especially with that scalding temper of his. But then again, he'd never encountered anything quite like that beauty...

Sébastien found it quite unbelievable she'd ever stay of her own volition. She'd have to be mad. Or threatened. Something had to be *keeping* her here. There was no other explanation. And Sébastien had a feeling that something was Adam.

Shoving away the torrential thoughts, he smoothed down his coat and banged against the door again. The sound echoed inside the castle like a beast's deep bellow. He adjusted the overstuffed satchel and cursed Adam for making him wait so damn long.

Minutes later, the door wrenched open, and Sébastien found himself staring into Adam's naked face. It was a darkly tragic sight, to be sure, and some of Sébastien's hostility evaporated. Twenty-five years did little to soften the uneven ridges of skin or that shriveled ear. He donned no hood, no cloak. The sight only nursed the uneasy feeling in his gut. Adam almost always wore that hideous cloak—oftentimes even in his wretched solitude.

What, in God's teeth, has lured him out from his rock?

Adam turned away, clearly bothered by Sébastien's long perusal.

"You don't have to scowl at me," he said as he pushed past Adam's towering form. "You're already unsightly enough without twisting your face like that."

"Let's make our meeting quick this time, shall we?" His face contorted even more, and Sébastien couldn't help but turn away.

"Ah, you wound me, *mon ami*." Adam tried to hide his grin but failed miserably. It was a welcomed sight, and Sébastien felt his mood brighten.

Stranger greeted him with a low, friendly bark. He ran his palm over the dog's bristly coat and gently patted his bad leg, then followed him and his master inside the castle.

Even the atmosphere felt somehow different, less

oppressive. Cleaner, too. Once again, a fire burned low in the hearth, and a fresh pot of tea sat on the chipped end table. Two cups had been poured, Sébastien took note.

Who is he entertaining?

His beauty?

It was all very peculiar and unlike Adam. Red flags shot into place while his suspicions grew.

"Ah. Your lady friend is still with us, I suspect?" Sébastien asked, gesturing toward one of the empty teacups. Silently Adam stood in front of the hearth and stared into the flames with a vacant expression. Sébastien's chest constricted as the memories surfaced on his scarred face. Indeed, he'd never stop reliving that fateful night. Even Sébastien often awoke in a sweat, those tragic images blazing through his mind like a wild inferno.

And that's precisely why Adam is such a danger—and in many ways unknowable.

"She comes and goes," he finally replied, breaking the heavy silence.

Sébastien couldn't restrain his laughter. He'd spoken those words with such a casual tone. For a moment, Sébastien might have mistaken Adam for any other suitor... or even the boy he used to be. But alas, he knew better.

Adam Delacroix was far from an ordinary man.

Adam whipped toward his laughter. Sébastien instantly fell silent. Then he shrugged his shoulders and poured a cup of tea. "I don't claim it's impossible for you to have a female companion. Quite honestly, this whole affair—the lit fire, the carriage, the hat—"

"Would you forget about the damn hat? You are obsessed!"

"—they all stink of shit, of foul play." Sébastien sighed before he downed a sip of the tea. Nodding his head in appreciation, he murmured, "It's quite good. You harvested the leaves from your gardens?"

Adam mutely nodded, then rubbed behind Stranger's long ears. The dog had shoved his massive skull under his palm, demanding his master's affection.

"I ask you again, Adam, as your friend. Is the woman still here? Every sign indicates that she is indeed. And likely her father, as well. Although, I imagine that would be a bit awkward—her father staggering about—"

"Yes, yes, she is still here," Adam spat. Sébastien knew he'd only come clean to quiet him. And he'd made no mention of the girl's father. A gust of wind wailed and wriggled its way through the castle's cracks. Sébastien shivered at the draft and tightened the fastenings on his coat. That quiet grew until he could hardly stand the silence.

Then Adam whirled toward him and locked on to his gaze. The intensity in his blue eyes gave him a start, nearly causing him to spill his tea. "I'm ready for you to fulfill that favor. It's to the girl's benefit."

Nausea infected his body. He straightened his posture and held his friend's penetrating glare. "I see. Fine, then, *mon ami*. I shall do what you ask—for the girl's sake and hers alone. But consider this the final time and my last favor. I shan't return again."

HOW WONDERFUL IT FELT to be one with the world again. The snowfall had mostly cleared, though a heavy frost still encapsulated Demrov. Isabelle inhaled the cool air as Spirit cantered down the simple dirt pathway and returned her to the castle. Various odds and ends made her riding saddlebag burst at the seams. Her trip to Hartville's marketplace, however, had left her feeling empty and homesick for Ruillé. She had missed Monsieur Lafitte's cheerful greetings and warm bread rolls; she'd yearned for the dusty bookshop and its humble collection. And she'd missed strolling down the bustling walkways with Papa... though it had been years since his health had permitted trips to their modest village.

Soon, Hartville's marketplace fell out of sight, and the trees thickened into a dense forest. With each step the mare took, hesitation crept into Isabelle's heart and chipped at her resolve.

Her mind grew quiet and still. She tugged on the reins, bringing Spirit to a sudden halt. Isabelle observed as her breaths shone in the air. What was she doing?

Have I gone mad, returning to Adam's castle in a sort of trance? She gazed at the winding dirt path that lay ahead—a true crossroad.

This is my chance to leave this behind. My chance for freedom... to start a new life, away from Raphael and this nightmare.

But had her time with Adam *truly* been a nightmare?

Her heartbeat was a manic staccato. The urge to turn back to the village and flee Demrov overwhelmed her... as did the desire to see Adam again. It was madness. Insanity. He'd imprisoned her beloved father, had likely frightened him half to death...

And he'd held me in my hour of darkness. Stood by my bedside for three nights straight. He cooled my brow, fed me soup, and whispered comforting words into my ear.

Adam's broken plea echoed in her mind.

I am here with you, ma belle. *And I shan't let you go.*

Something about Adam touched her deeply. It couldn't be put into words. It lacked reason and logic. Isabelle gripped the reins tighter until the leather cut into her fingers.

Turn away, her mind screamed.

Return to Adam, her heart chimed with its characteristic stubbornness. Last time she'd listened to her heart, things had ended in disaster.

Strangely enough, the garden flashed through her thoughts and solidified her tenacity: beautiful, immaculate, and untouched by winter's grasp.

You grow stronger. You move forward as best you can. And you learn to endure.

Yes, she stood at a true crossroad—yet she didn't think twice as she edged into the forest and lost herself in the great copse of trees. Indeed, with each step, a singular thought rang in her mind, as clear and as powerful as Notre Dame's eternal bells: *Home.*

ADAM ANSWERED HER knock almost at once. His face was bare, the brutal scarring fully exposed. But what took her breath away were his eyes. They softened and overflowed with emotion at the mere sight of her.

He thought I wasn't going to return.

Worry etched his thick brows; he looked a bit panicked... like he had something important to say but couldn't quite find the words.

He took the saddlebag from her clutches, then gracefully stepped aside. She silently followed him through the rooms until they reached the main hearth.

A man sat in Adam's favored wingback chair. His muddy boots were propped on a footstool as he lazily ran a gloved hand down Stranger's back. Isabelle threw Adam a questioning look. Before he could respond, however, the man's voice echoed in the large drawing room. "Ah, glad to see you finally on your feet again, mademoiselle." A light humor laced the words together.

The man rose from the chair, stepped in front of the hearth, and rubbed his hands. The flames shone in his wavy red locks and enhanced the mischievous glint in his eyes. She instantly took a liking to him. And Isabelle knew, without a doubt, that Adam's hands were full with this one.

Whoever he is.

"Good to meet you, monsieur. And you are...?" She found herself tongue-tied, completely taken off guard.

Adam does have a connection to the outside world.

Stranger followed alongside the man's heels as he crossed

the room in three swift strides. "Name's Sébastien." Dipping into a bow, he collected Isabelle's hand and kissed her knuckles. From the corner of her eye, she noticed that Adam tensed and threw Sébastien something along the lines of a warning glance.

"I believe you were just leaving," Adam cut in while he gently seized hold of Isabelle's elbow. "Come."

"Ah, *mon ami*, I was just acquainting myself with your lovely lady friend. Pray tell, what's your name?"

Isabelle returned his smile and shooed away Adam's insistent groping. "Isabelle. Isabelle Rose."

"Fitting. A beautiful name for a beautiful woman."

"*Merci.* You're too kind. Before—you said you were 'glad to see me on my feet again.' You were here while I was ill?"

"I was indeed. Didn't Adam tell you about me?" He turned away from Adam, then leaned against a hulking chair.

"No," she replied, throwing Adam an accusatory glance. "He said nothing."

"Ah, you mustn't be offended, mademoiselle. He's said very little about you. But that must be quite a story, how you came to be in Adam's caretaking. You were traveling with your father, were you not?"

Adam's fingers returned to Isabelle's elbow again; she nodded, though the color flushed from her cheeks at the mention of her father, and her heart gave a painful twist.

"Is he here now?" Sébastien asked in a careful tone.

Isabelle staggered back. She wrung her hands while everything welled up inside her at once. She swallowed deeply as the words escaped her. "No. No, he's not, monsieur. He's no longer here." Emotion constricted her words into a heavy silence. "Forgive me. I'm quite tired." Was it just her, or did her voice sound breathless? "I think... I think I'll rest before lunch. It was a pleasure to meet you, Sébastien." And without another word or backward glance, Isabelle wheeled away and rushed for her private quarters.

SÉBASTIEN RETURNED Adam's glare as Isabelle paced out of the room. Her cordial demeanor did little to smooth his feathers or ease his mind. Adam's intervention waved like a stark-red flag, and he'd likely commanded her silence and obedience with a single word. Even still, she hadn't been able to conceal her anxiety or grief. How she'd reacted to the simple *mention* of her father was evidence enough. And in Sébastien's mind, that spoke volumes. Not to mention, he'd recognized that gown—a garment he'd rescued from the Delacroix ruins... one Adam's mother had worn decades ago...

The very thought shook him to the core and fortified his resolve. That sweet girl—that Isabelle Rose—didn't belong here, trapped in the shadow of Adam's unfortunate past.

Sébastien shook his head while silence infected the air. Once the girl had vanished completely, he strode over to Adam until they stood less than a meter apart. He said in a low warning voice, "I'll ask you once and only more. What became of that girl's father?" Nothing. Not a single utterance. *Come now, Adam*, he silently pleaded. "Your silence says everything."

Adam hooked both hands behind his back and paced the length of the drawing room. Only the sound of his boots hitting the floor shattered the quiet. Sébastien stole a glance at the flaming hearth and felt those red flags raised into place once more.

"He died," Adam finally whispered, his gaze also fixed on the fire. "In the dungeon." He raked unsteady fingers through his hairline—a clear telltale of his discomfort. Sébastien caught a glimpse of the signet ring; he glared into the fire again, unable to bear the sight. "He was very ill—"

The dungeon. Mon Dieu...

"A suitable coincidence, wouldn't you agree? Him dying so shortly after their arrival?"

Not to mention the shattered teacup and strewn top hat—evidence of a struggle.

Another silence took hold. Adam stopped pacing the room, stepped in front of him, and met his unwavering gaze. Sébastien fought to detect a trace of softness or remorse in those eyes, but only an embittered spirit radiated.

"Are you implying that I murdered him?" Adam's tone dropped several octaves, and a shudder raced down Sébastien's spine. "To keep the girl for myself?"

"You said the words, not I."

Adam's eyes darkened. "You call me 'friend,' yet you regard me as little more than a savage beast. It's because of people like you that I've shut myself away."

"It's because of *me* that you even breathe the air, you ungrateful fool. Perhaps I've done the world a great disservice, dragging your wretched skin from your parents' chamber. Yes, I should have risen up with the other servants—I should have watched your home and family burn—"

It happened in a flash. Adam lunged forward and grabbed Sébastien's cravat. *Thwap!* Air whooshed from his lungs as Adam slammed his back, full force, against the wall. Adam's face contorted, transformed—morphing into something truly frightening to behold. Even the handsome side lost its beauty. He stared daggers, his blue eyes flashing fire, the raven waves of his hair wildly tousled. He grasped the material of Sébastien's frock coat with steel fists and actually lifted him off the ground a few centimeters.

Adam's violent outburst had confirmed the inevitable.

He is mad—he's truly become a monster.

"You might not have killed him directly. I'll allow you that—but you caused his death all the same. Didn't you, Adam?"

"I never want to see your face again," he replied, lowering him back onto the ground. "Get out of my house, Sébastien." Adam's words struck him like a hurtled knife. "Get the fuck out and never return. I don't have a purpose for you anymore."

He tried not to let those words affect him—yet inside, he was weeping. Forcing a poker face, he broke out of Adam's hold and smoothed down his frock coat with trembling hands. He gazed at that man he now knew, searching to find any trace of the boy he'd once been.

"Gladly, monsieur. After all, *your* face never was the highlight of my month." Those words were a lie—but he forced them out all the same.

Moving through the drawing room and toward the main hall, he fought to steady his tone and emotions, but twenty-five years of unspoken feelings stirred to life. "I've known you since you were a babe in your mother's arms. I was there that night— I saw everything. Or have you forgotten? You're not the only one who suffers from the nightmares."

As much as you believed it to be true... you were never truly alone.

But now you will be.

His heart aching, Sébastien departed without another word, leaving Adam in stunned silence. As he walked at a brisk pace toward the stable to collect his horse and phaeton, a peculiar sight ensnared his focus. How he'd missed the grave upon his arrival was beyond him. But there it stood, glinting in the moonlight, swaying back and forth as the crisp winter breeze cradled it.

A wooden cross, jutting from a pile of stones. Holding his breath, Sébastien lowered to one knee while his gaze danced across the fresh aster flowers and engraved lettering, which he recognized as Adam's neat script:

Bernard Rose
February 7, 1833

Chapter Fourteen

THE NEXT MORNING a peaceful calm settled over the castle. Isabelle wandered down the spiral stairwell, her belly full from a breakfast of fresh nuts and fruit. She tightened the cloak about her body and headed for the main drawing room. Indeed, the castle was becoming quite familiar to her... almost like it truly was her home.

Isabelle paused in the archway and secretly watched as Adam lounged before the black hearth; his long legs were crossed knee high, and a book was cradled in his lap. A branch of candles sat on the end table. It shed a faint ring of light that mated with the sunrays.

The illuminations shone in his hair, kissing the strands with opulent shades of navy blue. Only the handsome side of his face was in sight. Never had she beheld such devastating features. In this light, they appeared regal. Aristocratic. Even a touch arrogant.

Stranger climbed onto his legs. He gave a massive stretch before greeting her with an amiable bark. Isabelle instantly shrank into the shadows as Adam's gaze captured her own and held it from across the room. Slowly he lowered his book, then placed his hand on Stranger's hind leg and rewarded the creature with a gentle massage.

His back leg thumped up and down, rocking the panels beneath his heavy paws. Isabelle's eyes whipped to those long, agile fingers, and she found herself wondering how they'd feel upon her skin. The erotic musing caught her off guard; Adam's lip tipped at the corner, as if he'd read her wretched mind. Shooing away the swarm of butterflies in her stomach, she stepped forward and broke the silence.

"Sorry. I... I didn't mean to disturb you."

A playful look had also entered his gaze—a distinct challenge. He straightened against the high back of his chair and swept a hand through his glinting hairline. The signet ring glittered as it drank in the candlelight. "You've disturbed nothing, *ma belle*." The endearment sounded like liquid velvet sliding from his tongue. His voice was deep and rich, laced with an emotion she couldn't comprehend. "Come and join Stranger and me."

Isabelle's heart thundered as she eased into the parallel chair. Adam's very presence set her pulse on fire. They stared at each other for a long stretch of silence; at the close proximity, she noticed that his eyes were a bit puffy and dark circles rimmed each one. Clearly he hadn't slept, and a palpable agony radiated from him. Isabelle finally said, "I... I quite liked Sébastien. How long have you known him?"

She immediately regretted asking the question. Adam's eyes darkened even more while storming emotions flashed across his face. He continued running his hands over Stranger's back, visibly searching for the right words and suffering from a silent agony.

"Since forever. Since I was a boy. Since I can first remember," he said, his deep voice little more than a whisper. A great sadness was evident in his tone—one that called out to Isabelle and echoed her own despair. He looked broken. Defeated. Lost. He ran a shaky hand through his hair and sunk deeper into the wingback chair. Beneath a reverent, pained sigh, he added, "He knew my father and mother quite well. Worked for them, actually."

Isabelle eased onto the edge of her chair, waiting in suspense for him to reveal more. Adam's desire for solitude extended far beyond the castle's desolate walls; he was incredibly withdrawn and secretive, his heart encased by a protective barrier. She yearned to tear those barriers down, to understand a man who could act so resentful and gentle by turns. Her eyes ascended to the coat of arms hanging above the mantel and the piece of fabric that covered the house's words. "Sébastien... was he a servant of some kind?"

"You might say that." Adam's gaze briefly traveled to the coat of arms. He exhaled another sigh and adjusted his strong back against the chair. "I owe him my life. He can be a real pebble in my shoe, to be sure. I didn't believe in much anymore. Strangely enough, I still believed in our friendship..." An uneasy sensation filled her as Adam spoke of their friendship in the past tense. "He was—" His words broke off, as if he'd caught himself mid-sentence. He swallowed deeply while painful emotions churned in his blue eyes. They even misted over with tears. A heartbeat later, he visibly fortified those inner walls; he cleared his throat, sat up a little straighter, and harnessed the tears back. "Never mind," he said in a clipped tone that poorly disguised the depth of his despair. "It doesn't matter any longer."

What was causing this new isolation and anguish? There had been clear tension between Adam and Sébastien. What had transpired after she'd escaped to her quarters and into the pages of a book? She wondered if she was the source of the unrest—if Adam had been hiding something from his old friend. Had she done something to drive Sébastien away? The very thought filled her with an unshakable guilt and remorse; Adam already had so little contact with humanity and the world outside of these somber walls.

"You grew up in Ruillé?" he asked, breaking the silence and her train of thoughts. "I remember you mentioning it when you first arrived."

Isabelle felt a grin appear on her lips. "I must say I'm surprised you remember. That night, you didn't seem to have the slightest interest in where I came from or where I might end up."

Adam bowed his head while an endearing blush spread

across the handsome side of his face. The effect nearly stole Isabelle's breath away. For a moment, a cloud appeared to lift, and Adam's rugged countenance held an almost youthful appeal. The wavy forelock tumbled over his right eyebrow; he tossed it aside in a boyish gesture that contradicted his formidable presence. Unexpected heat sped through her limbs and pooled down below. "Yes, well... as I said before, Stranger and I aren't accustomed to receiving houseguests. And certainly not beautiful women."

Isabelle's chest heated at the compliment, and a reciprocal blush burned her cheekbones. "What about Sébastien?"

Adam chuckled—a husky, deeply masculine sound—then shook his downcast head. The subtle movement sent the forelock spiraling across his blue eyes again. Isabelle's hands twisted in the material of her dress as the urge to sweep it away overcame her. Her gaze drank in the mesmerizing sight of him. His muscular, solid body seemed to dwarf the huge wingback chair. "I must say—I've seen fairer maids than Sébastien."

"You know well what I meant, monsieur." Isabelle leaned forward and playfully slapped his shoulder; he grabbed where she'd struck him and feigned injury.

Then he lifted his own hand and pressed two fingers against his thick brow; her eyes drew to the signet ring's golden face and engraved initials.

AFD.

A thousand questions burned on her tongue. But when he flashed her another smile, all coherent thoughts fell from her mind. She could only focus on the man before her—this strange man who both frightened and excited her, who cried out in the night, who could touch her with an impossible gentleness, and who knew the depths of a darkness she couldn't comprehend.

Stranger rose onto his feet, coolly limped toward the black hearth, lifted his good back leg, and urinated on the pile of logs.

"Stranger," Adam exclaimed, his lush mouth falling slack. "Why, there is a lady present."

Laughter erupted from Isabelle's lips. The sensation felt liberating, freeing. When was the last time she'd laughed? She couldn't recall. The revelation both thrilled and saddened her.

Adam's eyes flickered with amusement as he released a thunderous chuckle. Stranger padded back to his side, then flopped onto the ground with an apathetic groan and promptly dozed off to sleep.

"As I said, Stranger and I aren't accustomed to receiving houseguests," Adam murmured, shaking his head at the mischievous creature. "You have no shame at all."

Isabelle was mesmerized, unable to tear her gaze from Adam. Indeed, he seemed to transform before her very eyes.

"When you smile—when you laugh—you are beautiful." The words took Isabelle by surprise. She hadn't meant to speak them aloud. She swallowed deeply, then continued in a careful, clear voice. "I mean, when you smile, you are no different from any of us. I hate to inform you, Monsieur Adam, but you're not the formidable beast you make yourself out to be. Sometimes, I think you act difficult just for the sake of being difficult."

His grin widened, then the smile fell away completely. "And you... I think there's much more to you as well. When I look into your eyes, I see strength and perseverance... but also a great sadness. A certain darkness. I encountered it the moment we met."

Taken aback by his sensitivity, Isabelle clasped the arms of her chair as Adam rose to his feet. He reached her spot in a swift stride. His eyes hooked on to her own, intense and searching. Then he lowered to his knees as his head bowed forward. She admired his sleek black hair; the thick waves combed back over the tips of his ears, barely grazing the edge of his white collar. Then he gently caressed her palms, her knuckles, each of her fingers. His bare skin felt rough beneath her palm, every ridge sliding against her. His hand was shaking. "What's your story, Isabelle? What great secrets are *you* hiding?" She felt the refrains of his voice, the enticing wisp of his breath, with every part of her body.

She gave a nervous laugh, then wriggled free of his grasp. "Pardon me, monsieur, but you are hardly one to talk. I don't even know your surname."

He shook his downcast head and half whispered the words, "*I* hardly know who I am anymore." His gaze planted on the stone floor, he withdrew from Isabelle and returned to his own chair. The agony in his brilliant blue eyes was tangible—and Isabelle longed for his nearness again.

She silently observed as he ran his fingertips down Stranger's long, lean back, then idly scratched behind each ear. Needing to ease the tension, she asked at length, "Do you read often? It's... it's one of my favorite pastimes by far." She gestured to the closed book, which he'd set on the end table. In Isabelle's mind, few things were as romantic as the feel of a book in her hands. The smooth, slightly embossed face of its cover. The scent of words and parchment that wafted toward her with each flip of the page. And the countless possibilities and adventures that lay between the covers.

"Since I was a girl, all I've ever wanted were books. I used to wish I could live inside them, that I would fall asleep and wake up somewhere else as somebody else. It was my escape, my personal haven. Papa used to say that so long as I had my books, I'd always be free."

Her question lightened the mood and brought a smile to Adam's mouth. The handsome side of his face glowed, illuminated by the shaft of light that poured through the window. Those rays softened the rugged lines that burdened his brow and equipped him with a quite boyish appeal again. He came to his feet again and towered above her. Holding out his hand, he murmured, "Then come with me and prepare to be swept away."

MINUTES LATER, Adam strode through the castle with Stranger hugging close to his side. Morning's light trickled through the large stained glass windows, which faced the courtyard and displayed a frosty February morning. Prisms of light filtered through the colorful glass panels and splintered into rainbow shafts. Those shimmering colors gave the illusion of being inside a jewel box; a mosaic of red, gold, and green swirled around them and painted the normally somber walls and floor with shifting, tinted lights. Red rubies. Fresh-forged golds. And rare emeralds.

A jewel box, indeed.

Isabelle's stomach fluttered, her suspense building with each step. Ten minutes later, he paused outside a closed door, threw her a sly glance, and then pushed it open.

Inside, the room appeared to be pitch-black—completely sealed off to the sunshine. Adam gently took hold of her elbow and guided her across the archway. She stumbled blindly while the giddy sensation grew in her belly.

The door shut behind her with an echoing click. Isabelle's heartbeat rose inside her throat as she stood in the darkness with only her erratic breaths piercing the silence.

"Close your eyes, *ma belle*."

Strong hands cupped either side of her face. She felt as Adam's thumbs tentatively brushed back and forth, stroking her cheeks in reverent caresses. Isabelle shut her eyes and slipped beneath his spell... leaned closer in the darkness until they stood heartbeat to heartbeat. The warmth of his breaths teased her hairline, bringing with them a minty scent. His thumbs descended to just below her chin. She lowered her face... felt a featherlight kiss land on her brow. It happened so subtly and gently—Isabelle wasn't sure whether she'd imagined it.

She was allowing herself to feel too much. A stab of guilt penetrated her chest as her thoughts crept inward. Yet instincts told her to trust in her gut—to allow her heart to speak over her tumultuous thoughts. So she forced away her guilt and allowed herself to simply feel.

Pounding footfalls echoed in the room, attesting to its sheer size. Isabelle waited in anticipation under the veil of darkness, her small hands knotted in Stranger's wiry coat. The steady beat of Adam's boot moved away from her. A loud whipping noise and a burst of light illuminated the room as he tugged a heavy damask curtain aside.

"Open your eyes, Isabelle."

She did as he commanded. Shafts of sunlight tore inside, dancing across the marble floor in blaring prisms—though the darkness still obstructed the room's contents. Isabelle's imagination soared as she fantasized about what lay in those clotted shadows. Pale light fringed Adam's formidable shape, contrasting his silhouette against the dim atmosphere.

He paused in front of the opened window and folded both arms behind his ramrod-straight back. Isabelle gazed at the line of his body, unable to tear her eyes away. Indeed, light from the window set him aglow, shrouding him in a cloak of gold. He wore black trousers and a white silk shirt, which fluttered lightly when he moved. Over the past several days, he'd made a habit of abandoning the cloak and hood. Isabelle had become accustomed to the mismatched sides of his face; where she once felt horror and revulsion, she now tingled with curiosity and budding admiration. Alas, the only true revulsion that remained was the memory of that night...

Adam was an undeniably prideful man, and she knew he'd only scorn her pity. Even his stance exuded a sense of importance and authority. Strange, how he was so often shy and almost childlike; then, as if by a flip of a coin, he'd turn regal, confident. It was as though he was battling two separate halves... as if an intricate part of himself kept fighting to emerge.

Not unlike the two contrasting sides of his face, Isabelle mused.

For a suspended moment, he stood in front of the conservatory window, his scarred hands planted on his lean hips as he surveyed the distant gardens. Then he crossed the room, his footfalls amplified by the medallion flooring, and thrust open another curtain.

Whoosh. Light flooded the space and chased away the shadows, and the room's contents were ushered into view.

Isabelle nearly lost her breath at the sight.

It was a beautiful library—the most stunning sight she'd ever beheld. Ornate, intricately carved shelves towered against the painted walls and reached for a gilded ceiling. A baroque chandelier hung in the heart of the room; its crystals sparkled like diamonds as they drank in morning's light. Isabelle fought to temper her racing heart as she gaped at the sweeping shelves. An intimate reading nook lined a curved window; lush pillows decorated the chaise, and a brass candelabra towered beside it.

In all her life, she'd never seen so many books. There were far too many to count. Too many books to read in one lifetime. Isabelle couldn't help but think of the little storekeeper from Ruillé's bookshop; she imagined his astonishment, how his bushy white brows would rise at the sight of Adam's vast library. He'd run his wrinkled fingertips over the bindings and spines, reverently caressing each one. Her heart twisted with nostalgia at the thought of her former home. Once Raphael had entered her life, however, Ruillé had transformed into a prison.

The castle should have been just that. A jail cell. Yet she'd never felt more free than in that moment.

The library was larger than her whole cottage; several book-filled rooms connected to it, each one built with floor-to-ceiling shelves. Three sliding ladders were nestled against the circular walls, ascending to the very top of the domed ceiling.

She spun on her heels, twirling in place—watching as the immense collection flurried by in a mosaic of colorful spines and intricate woodwork.

Her eyes planted on Adam, who stood in front of the row of glowing, arched windows. His arms were still folded behind his body, his sleek back straighter than an arrow. She couldn't find her voice, couldn't move forward, although she ached to reach out and embrace his solid body.

How would it feel to be enveloped inside that commanding strength?

A devastating smile spread across his misshapen features and cut her thought short. He ran a shaky hand through his hair, which was highlighted by the sun's rays, and then hesitantly strode toward her. His boots rapped against the floor, and the sound swelled through the library. Stranger barked as he approached, the loud noise echoing in the room and jarring Isabelle from her trance.

"Do... do you like it?"

Finally he stood before her, silent and still. Isabelle inhaled a long breath, then laid her palm on the left side of his face. Her fingertips danced over the raised ridges and welts, the reddish scars and shriveled ear. His eyes shuttered closed, and she felt a shudder rake through his tense body.

"Yes. I love it..." *And I'm starting to fall for you, too...* Her fingers fell away. Adam's blue eyes flew open and captured her own. "It's astonishing, incredible... beyond anything I could have ever imagined. It's like a dream."

A boyish grin returned to his face. He ran his hand across Stranger's back as the dog pushed against his legs and urged his affection. "A reader's paradise, to be sure. And now it's yours."

"It's wonderful. Where on earth did you ever acquire so many books?"

"Most of them were already here when I moved in. The rest I added over the years, and each one is like a child. Sometimes, I like to imagine a wise philosopher used to study here, unraveling the mysteries of the world in this very room."

Smiling at his sentimental words, Isabelle slipped past him and approached the shelves. She ran her fingertips across the dusty spines, watching as streaks emerged wherever she touched. Then she glanced over her shoulder and met Adam's steady gaze again. Desire burned in those eyes, hot as a fire. "Over how many years?"

The question had been sweltering inside her ever since her first night in the castle. Adam returned her stare, though she knew he wasn't truly seeing her. He was peering *through* her—inwardly reliving the terrors he suffered each night. Indeed, almost every evening, after the sun fell behind the trees and darkness enveloped the castle, she and Adam would depart their separate ways. Yet a part of herself remained linked to him—even when they were doors apart. His shattered cries and sobs would echo through the halls in an eerie requiem. Each night, she crushed her face against her pillow, needing to muffle those heartrending sounds... craving a way to relieve his pain, yet too paralyzed by fear and her warring emotions to so much as stir a limb.

She heard his breath catch. Then he finally spoke in a low, wary tone. "Twenty-five years."

He'd holed himself up in this desolate castle for twenty-five years. Over two decades. Since he was little more than a boy, a child..."

Isabelle struggled to find her voice. "And... and you've been alone all this time. Apart from Sébastien's visits?"

Quite suddenly all the books and stories surrounding her held little significance. She ached to know *Adam's story*.

Slowly he nodded, then turned to the arched windows. The glass panes were cloaked in a light film, causing the outside world to look slightly distorted. Dust motes floated in midair, illuminated by gleaming shafts of light. "As I said before, I owe Sébastien my life."

Isabelle stepped forward, her feet carried by her soul. Lightly she placed her hand upon his strong shoulder. He didn't shrink from her touch, though she felt his muscles grow taut beneath her squeezing fingertips.

"I'd very much like you to find happiness here," he said at length, staring out the window, his beautiful voice barely above a whisper. "I know these walls are filled with shadows. But that doesn't mean you have to live in darkness."

A riot of emotions crossed the opposing sides of his face. "What happened?" Isabelle asked. "I—I need to understand. If I am ever to find happiness here, if I'm ever to know light, I need to see through the shadows first." Only silence. "Adam... I know we haven't been acquainted very long. But you can share with me."

ADAM FELT EVERY muscle tighten as Isabelle placed her tiny hand on the center of his chest. He gazed down at her slender figure and upturned face, admiring how the sunlight danced in her curls, how the airy fabric of the dress accentuated her curves. When she walked, he detected the movement of her breasts below that fabric. Her unique scent drifted toward him and made his insides grow tense and heavy. He desperately ached to feel the texture of her porcelain skin, to taste her lips and track his mouth over that cluster of freckles.

Her words from days ago echoed in his mind and fueled his resolve. *Show me. Become better.* They acted as a guiding light and summoned a flash of hope inside his heart. Then he thought of his near-fight with Sébastien, and his chest contracted at the loss of his old friend. *My only friend, my one connection to the outside world—aside from Isabelle.* Grief gathered overhead like a dark storm cloud; Adam pushed away the painful ache and focused his attention on Isabelle.

A small smile stretched her mouth. It took every gram of his willpower not to kiss her senseless. Then the impossible happened. As if in answer to his silent longing, her arms coiled around his torso in a tentative embrace. The gentle pressure of her hands drew a ragged breath from his lungs and rendered him immobile.

Adam hesitantly returned her hug. Time came to a standstill and suspended itself. Her forehead slouched forward, and she rested the side of her face against his thundering heart. His senses reeled in delight while a calming sensation flushed through him.

The realization blasted through him, awakening every nerve ending.

With every breath, every touch, I am falling hopelessly in love with her.

Emotion pressed hard on his throat, constricting his speech and robbing the air from his lungs. He couldn't stop himself—could not let go. Not yet.

He bowed forward, ever so carefully, and pressed his lips against her hairline. His hands came to life, moving of their own accord and with a will of their own. They slipped down and over the petite bend of her waist... over the luscious curve of her backside... then dared to venture back up again. They ran through her mass of curls and cupped her chin. He drew invisible circles along her skin, worshipping everything that was Isabelle, tracing down the smooth bend of each cheek and back up again. His hands ached to travel everywhere at once—to bring her closer and never let her go again. Hot blood violently rushed through his veins while a painful yearning weighed on his soul.

She's so close yet still so far away...

Heaving a sigh, he urged her neck back, stared down, and captured her gaze with his own. Her lips parted, and another smile crept across her rosebud lips. She was swept in the moment, seduced by some enchantment, just as he was—yet he sensed a distinct fear, saw an uncertainty flash in her beautiful eyes. He'd encountered the same terror that night in the East Tower.

That thought sobered him, stilling his hands.

"Close your eyes again, Isabelle."

She did as commanded, the fabric of her dress straining with her deep breaths.

I should lean forward and kiss her.

Would she give me my first kiss?

Uncertainty and nerves paralyzed Adam's limbs. His pulse raced in his ears and mated with the ragged sound of his own breathing.

Would my kiss repulse her? Adam doubted he could bear her rejection and disgust. He inhaled her sweet scent, allowing it to soak him in fantasies and false hopes.

He couldn't bring himself to move, to close the distance between them and claim her lips. And within that stretch of silence and painful longing, a storm of darkness eclipsed his thoughts.

Mon Dieu—*the East Tower.*

I don't deserve her. I don't deserve any of this.

Adam forced himself to let go. "How can I share with you?" he finally replied, his voice a hoarse whisper. Isabelle's eyes shot open, and the enchantment seemed to fall away. "When I can't even face it myself?"

Sébastien's words rang in his mind, drowning out the world around him. *Perhaps I've done the world a great disservice, dragging your wretched skin from your parents' chamber. Yes, I should have risen up with the other servants—I should have watched your home and family burn—*

"Adam. Don't speak like that. Please. I—"

"I hope this library can be your freedom. A light to help you see through the shadows." Without another word or backward glimpse, he whisked past her and vanished from the room.

Chapter Fifteen

"I love you dearly, and in making me happy, Beauty, you will find your own happiness. Be as true-hearted as you are beautiful, and we shall have nothing left to wish for."
—Madame de Villeneuve, *Beauty and the Beast*

MUSIC COMPOSED THE FOLLOWING DAYS, and Adam's grief over the loss of Sébastien's friendship tempered into a dull ache. He experienced an intense and unexpected jolt of inspiration—one unlike any he'd ever known; music flowed from the tips of his fingers with ease and grace while memories unfurled and manifested into decadent melodies. His heart pounded along with the chords as his mind turned to thoughts of Isabelle.

He reflected on their interlude in the library—how she'd twirled in place while a flush of happiness had washed over her smiling face. The desire to bring her happiness and contentment struck him hard; her smiles and the sound of her laughter brought an unforeseen, reciprocal joy to his soul.

How close I'd come to kissing her... The pressure and pace of his fingers eased. The deep, dark melody shifted and lightened. His entire body burned, and an aching desire swam through his veins.

Every time Isabelle came near him, he experienced surging emotions and a jarring connection. Admiration. Respect.

Gratitude for her friendship. And a blossoming love for both her inner and outer beauty. He feared his own desire for her—a desire that expanded far beyond sexual need. He ached to simply hear her voice and the robust melody of her laughter. He yearned for her touches and the sight of her delicate face. He anticipated the soft breeze of her breaths upon his skin. He tingled for the sweet aroma of her hair. He relished how her eyes always seemed to bear deeply into his own, as if she were truly seeing him and not his appearance. He ached for *her*—with every fiber of his soul.

Even more, he was starting to trust Isabelle completely.

Trust is a first stepping-stone to love.

Closing his eyes, he imagined how it would feel to hold her slender, naked body against him... to experience her head resting on his shoulder and the warmth of her breaths on his marred skin. He imagined the weight of her soft, supple breasts in his scarred hands... the feel of her erect nipple rolling between his thumb and forefinger... He'd apply a gentle, teasing pressure... then he'd lean forward and cup his lips over the taut peak... He'd draw that mound inside the cavern of his mouth with careful tugs... Meanwhile, his hands would glide over the velvety skin of her thighs, slip inside her pantalettes, and gently fondle the wet crease of her womanhood. He imagined the sweet flavor of her mouth and tongue... the music of her breathing and torn pleas as he brought her to climax again and again and again...

His body tightened and surged to life, reacting to the fantasy—

A gentle touch graced his shoulder. His fingers were paralyzed in midair, hanging above the keys. The last chord lingered for several moments, riding a tension that consumed the room. Exhaling a rigid breath, he adjusted his legs to better conceal his turgid arousal.

"It's beautiful, Adam. I've never heard it before. No sheet music?" He stiffened as Isabelle's hand slid across his back, moving from one shoulder to the other. The desire he'd felt moments ago reached a steady boil. A crescendo. He clenched his hands over the keys and squeezed both eyes shut. The soft melody of her voice reached out to him—more beautiful and tempting than any musical piece. He clenched his fingers numerous times, inspired and overwhelmed with the need to touch every bit of her. "Who's the composer?"

"I am."

"What? That's... that's incredible!" The awe and appreciation in her tone ignited his desire. "I had no idea." She shook her head, causing an errant curl to flurry against her flushed cheeks. "You are quite full of surprises... aren't you, Adam?"

He said nothing; merely scooted over on the bench, then seized her gaze. Her stunning hazel eyes softened to a velvety hue. He swallowed, then drank in the rest of her in a leisurely perusal.

She looked like a damn angel. A simple cotton walking dress graced her figure to perfection—an outfit she'd purchased in the village. Small embroidered swags and silk flowers decorated the cropped sleeves and modest neckline. The dress was humble yet brimmed with an alluring charm and beauty— much like Isabelle herself. A silk bow fastened her chocolate ringlets, exposing the pale shaft of her neck. A delicate smattering of freckles decorated her lower neck.

How he burned to slide his lips across that creamy skin... to taste the thundering beat of her pulse and free those lush curls from the bow. He ached to scoop her in his arms and thrust her on top of the pianoforte's keys... to listen as they softly chimed under the weight of her body.

He burned to claim her, right here and now, on top of his beloved instrument.

Her dark eyes appeared impossibly large—a beautiful contrast against her porcelain complexion. She clasped a hefty book in the crook of her arm; a smile tugging at her lips, she set it on the sideboard, then returned beside the pianoforte.

Unable to find his voice, he patted the wooden bench and gestured her to sit. She hesitated, slowly lowering onto the surface. The sweet aromas of her skin and hair sailed toward him; he made out the heady scent of roses on the cool, rising air. She sat intimately close—mere centimeters away. The heat of her body set his blood on fire and kindled his soul.

"You are incredibly talented, Adam."

Adam bowed his head, then adjusted his body, causing her leg to brush against his in a teasing caress. A knot of heat gathered and coiled down below. Blood rushed past his ears as he felt his groin stir to life and jerk against his trousers. He inhaled a calming breath and inwardly counted backward from five. "Music has become a kind of escape over the years," he said, almost trembling from the sheer force of his need. He couldn't bring himself to meet her eyes; surely she'd see the wretched desire in his stare and etched into every line of his face. Damn him, even his hands were lightly trembling. "It was a way to speak when no one was there to listen."

Conflicting emotions crossed her exquisite features. "I have been listening every night. Even when you don't play... I still hear your music." Her voice sounded husky, half-whispered, and laced with wonder. "And I feel it."

He needed to feel *her*—to reassure himself she wasn't a phantom carved from his mind. Adam released a withheld breath, then reached out and grasped one of her tiny hands. Soft. Delicate. Smoother than silk. Pure temptation. He set her hand on top of the keys, covering her knuckles with his palm and fingers. The enticing scent of her skin and hair whisked toward him like some whimsical perfume. "Here... I'll direct you."

ISABELLE'S HEART POUNDED against her ribs as Adam's large, scarred hand covered her own. His long fingers aligned with hers, and before she knew what was happening, her hands were dancing across the ivory keys. The gentle pressure of his fingers brought forth a rich melody, which ushered from her own hand. She fairly held her breath while the musical vibrations tremored through her fingers and dripped into the dimly lit room. She felt a foreign thrill, an exhilaration she'd never known before that moment. She'd glimpsed a taste of it whenever she'd read and embarked on adventures during her childhood—but this shared ecstasy overshadowed all prior experiences.

It was foreign. Exhilarating. An enchanted path into a world she'd never known or thought she could reach.

The music was beautiful, decadent—though it didn't convey the same emotional spectrum as when Adam himself played. Indeed. He played with total feeling and adoration; he dwelled inside the music, became one with the refrains, drawing it out of the pianoforte as if by magic. Now his melodies surged through *her*, like breaths leaving her own lungs.

She'd felt a budding connection with him for a while now, ever since she'd tended to his head wound. Now, it hit her straight on, undeniable and poignant, striking her deep within. They were united through this melancholy music... as if a pair of wings had unfurled within the darkness and arched above them in a protective dome. A myriad of emotions wrestled inside her—guilt, compassion, and something else. Something that left her breathless and made her feel strangely hot.

He hummed softly, deeply, the notes vibrating against her back like a dark hymn. His husky voice mated with the melody in a most intimate way. It was as though he was making love to her through his music.

All the while, his strong hand guided her own, causing strings of liquid gold to pour from her trembling fingertips. A familiar melody swelled the room as Adam guided her through well-loved pieces, flowing from one composer to the next. Mozart's opera *The Marriage of Figaro* took over—and he sang the libretto against the side of her face.

> "What I am experiencing I will tell you,
> It is new to me and I do not understand it.
> I have a feeling full of desire,
> That now, is both pleasure and suffering.
> At first frost, then I feel the soul burning,
> And in a moment I'm freezing again."

Isabelle crumpled under the enchantment of his voice. Then he wrapped a strong arm around her back and reached into her lap. He took her other hand in his own, enveloping her tingling skin with his strong, lithe fingers. She felt her breath catch at his nearness, overcome with the desire to both melt against his body and run away. The beautiful side of his face hovered mere centimeters from her own, his lips sharing the same breaths of air. She took in Adam's face as he whispered the lyrics—half achingly handsome, half a testament to a torment she couldn't begin to imagine.

> *"I do not know how to hold it; I do not know what it is.*
> *I sigh and moan without meaning to,*
> *Throb and tremble without knowing,*
> *I find no peace both night or day..."*

Suddenly his beautiful voice faded into silence. Memories of that horrible night—the burn of Raphael's touch, the stench of his alcohol-laden breaths—seared her thoughts. But then Adam tentatively removed one of his hands and brushed away a wayward curl; the gentleness of his touch fiercely contrasted against Raphael's, and Isabelle found herself relaxing in his arms. Indeed, she ached to get closer... *closer...*

His lips drew against her ear, answering her silent plea. He whispered the husky words upon her skin, then allowed his mouth to gently brush her temple. "During my childhood... I was very selective about whom I'd perform for. Music is an intimate affair, see... akin to making love..."

Isabelle's fingers turned limp and fell away from the ivory keys. Silence momentarily seized them. Adam responded to her flustered state with a deviant, low chuckle that sent her nerves spinning. Then he reclaimed her hands in his own and pressed her fingers, one by one, down onto the keys. His—*their*—beautiful music flooded the room once more with the lushness of a thundering waterfall. The light melody darkened to a Gothic shade—and Isabelle knew Adam had settled back into his own composition. Each note washed over her senses, revived her, even strengthened her.

"Have you always lived in Hartville?" Isabelle breathlessly asked as she fought to temper the quaver in her voice. His body seemed to engulf her, to draw her in, to seduce her with its strength and warmth. She ached to melt against the strong planes of his chest, to lay her cheek against the beat of his heart, to run her fingers through his hair. Nights ago, in the library, she'd thought he was going to kiss her.

Will he kiss me now? she thought with a trembling wonder.

He hesitated. "*Non.* I was born in Lavoncourt. Stayed there until I was eleven years old."

Isabelle nodded in understanding. Although the province lay on the edge of Demrov, Lavoncourt was truly the country's heart. *So that's where his cultured accent and regal demeanor emerged.* He was a product of little Paris—and somehow, through a tragedy she couldn't comprehend, he'd been flung into this desolate ruin. But how? And why? Her mind returned to the keepsakes and portraits in the eastern tower. The questions sang on her tongue, though she dared not ask them so boldly.

Adam was an enigma, a beautiful mystery that she ached to unravel. His music was enough to leave her breathless—and his refined mannerisms and the innate way he held and asserted himself reaffirmed that cultured upbringing.

Just as she battled for the proper phrasing, he broke her thoughts with his own inquiry. "And you? Have you always lived in Ruillé?" The music loudened, growing in power to slowly climax into a crescendo of emotion and genius.

Some of the magic in the air dissipated, and Isabelle slipped into an ocean of memories. "Yes... though my father and I traveled the country quite a bit when I was a girl."

The mood of the music darkened to a melancholy tune. Whether conscious or a mere byproduct of his sensitivity and skill, Adam had amended his music to echo her stirring emotions. Indeed, it was like an internal mirror—the only mirror inside the castle, apart from the broken one in the East Tower.

Something was growing between them, as deep and dark

as the forest. He was a dangerous man to tangle with; his fantastic hold on her reached further than she'd first imagined. She wasn't merely awestruck and intrigued. She was emotionally rocked, connected, under the enchantment of a carefully woven spell. Adam overwhelmed her in a way that surpassed physical influence.

The first time they met blazed through her thoughts. He'd resembled Death hiding beneath the dark folds of his cloak; his darkness had implored her with grasping arms.

The music's somber refrains seemed to reach inside her throat and pull the words out by sleight of hand. "Papa and I went everywhere together, as if the entire world laid at our feet. After he had married Theresa, everything changed overnight. The illness slowly took hold of him... and I can't help but think she stole whatever energy remained."

"You and your father were exceptionally close." It wasn't a question.

Isabelle's fingers faltered on the keys. "As close as any two people could ever be. The best of friends. Though we grew apart somewhat after he married Theresa. She died several years ago."

"I'm sorry for that."

"Don't be. I feel wicked saying so, but it was truly a blessing in disguise. Not even in disguise, actually. Theresa was an envious, petty woman who took advantage of an unwell merchant. Her dislike of me influenced her daughters and forever tainted our relationship."

"Forgive me for asking, but how could he love such a woman? Why did he allow such treatment, especially when you two had been so dear to each other?"

Isabelle sighed. "Love is a strong sentiment. Did my father love Theresa? Perhaps. Though, I believe he loved the *idea* of her more."

The melody intensified. Took full command. Her lips curled into a whimsical smile while Adam's music pulled her beneath its dark wing, urging her into a trancelike state. She felt like she was floating. "Maman made me vow to only marry for love, because then everything would be beautiful. Papa loved her so deeply—sometimes, I felt rather left out, as if they were enveloped in only each other. And so I became a dreamer, a bit of an escape artist. Storybooks transformed into magical portals, and the heroic knights and fine ladies became dear friends. He would waste the days away with Maman. I'd look at the pictures... make up stories for them before I learned to read the letters."

Adam's guiding hands came to a standstill, and the music faded away. Thrust back into the moment, her words trailed off only to be swallowed by the silence.

Isabelle felt like she'd been released from a dream. She met Adam's steady gaze—and the desire in his eyes flattened her. Overwhelmed and growing hotter all over, she rose from the pianoforte's bench in an unsteady motion. "Forgive me. I... I think I'll go relax for a bit."

MUSIC AND DARKNESS swirled around Isabelle, reaching for her with a thousand hands.

Cavernous chords resonated beneath her skin, pounding with each beat of her heart. A moan slid from her throat as she felt herself falling into a dark abyss. *Non*, she wasn't falling. She was being carried, cradled, caressed with rich melodies and mesmerizing touches.

A harmony quivered through every bone and muscle, causing her insides to turn hot and heavy. Isabelle groped blindly within the night. Her hands behaved of their own accord, as if pulled by an unseen puppet master. Trembling fingertips glided over the fabric of her nightgown... sank below the material and kneaded the tender skin. Her cupped hand moved in time to the melody, seduced into a strange erotic dance.

She arched into the touch. Another moan wriggled free of her throat. The music grew louder still; it vibrated her bones and pressed hard on her moving hands. Then it lightened and ebbed away, unfurling within the darkness in an alluring, slow melody. She reached for it, urging it to return to her at full force. Her opposite hand stirred over her damp thighs and sank below the hem of her nightgown.

Her fingers stopped *there*—right on top of the wet, hot mass of curls. She hesitated for a moment, and the spell almost broke. Then a pounding chord ripped through the room and pressed down on her knuckles. Hard. Resolutely. She gasped aloud, felt as her index finger pried through the curls and found the bundle of nerves buried underneath. She massaged it in tentative, slow circles while the music reached a pounding crescendo. Adam's rich, velvety voice whispered down her backbone and flooded her very soul.

*"What I am experiencing I will tell you,
It is new to me and I do not understand it..."*

A tall, formidable figure emerged within her thoughts. It was Adam, standing on the East Tower's circular balcony, his broad back turned to her. The cloak filled with air and waved around him like a pair of dark wings. He stared down at the gardens below, as stiff and unmovable as a shadow. Snow fell from the sky, tumbling around his body like ashes. She saw herself in third-person perspective, wandering toward him, the light from a sconce casting them both in a wavering shaft. Overhead, the moon shone bone white against a black sky, larger than a queen's dinner plate.

*"I have a feeling full of desire,
That now, is both pleasure and suffering..."*

The pressure on her core increased while she gazed up at Adam. Powerful. Regal. As dark and mysterious as the surrounding night. His features were silhouetted, not visible, and a delicate golden light shimmered along his cloak. She reached out to him, her movements empowered by the music, completely transfixed. Slowly he turned toward her, a great shadow looming above, and set his hands on her chin. She trembled beneath his touch, felt her insides caving inward. Scarred hands glided down her face, her neck...

> "*I sigh and moan without meaning to,
> Throb and tremble without knowing...*"

He crept closer, lowered his hand... traced his fingers over her aching womanhood. Just barely. She strained her body toward his touch, needing *more*. His head bowed forward, so that warm wafts of his breaths tickled her face and swelled her senses. Then his hands joined together and settled on her backside. She shut both eyes and inhaled a steadying breath. Soft, gentle lips ghosted over her cheek... down the side of her throbbing neck...

Kiss me. Consume me. Make me yours.

"Adam." Her voice sounded distant, faded, twisted by a blossoming passion. "Adam... what is happening?"

He leaned impossibly closer, his scents of pine, sandalwood, and winter swelling her senses, the heat of his body enveloping her own. The deep baritone of his voice caused her body to tremble; she felt his words vibrate through her bones, echo in each beat of her heart with the same power as his music. "Does it even matter? It has already happened..."

Take me.

"But I—" His desperate kiss smothered her words. At first, she hesitated—then her body surrendered, limb by limb. Every bit of her melted under the tender exploration of his tongue and hands. She reveled in his daring caress, molding herself to it. A peculiar, tingling sensation mounted inside her core. She rode the music's throbbing melody and suspended all further thoughts and feelings.

"That's it, *ma belle*... Let yourself go... Let my music fill you..."

The silky caress of his words pushed her over the edge. The melody splintered through her and melted any resistance. A heartbeat later, she reached a tingling, red-hot crescendo; mind-numbing pleasure swept through her body—shooting from the tips of her hair, down to her very toes. She shuddered, thrashing against the mattress.

The unbelievable sensation thrummed on and on, bringing forth a deep, penetrative wave of pleasure.

She let it crash down, wash over her, and soak her to the marrow of her bones. Every nerve ending buzzed and pulsed. A moan fluttered from her throat as her womanhood contracted in time to Adam's music and touches. On and on the release went, drawing torn moans and cries from her lips. Isabelle shifted her wet, slick thighs while her body descended from that exquisite peak.

In her mind's eye, her small hands frantically wove around Adam's torso, smoothed up and down his muscular back, and bunched in the folds of his cloak. He groaned low in his throat, and the husky sound shuddered through her entire body.

She threaded her fingers in the thick strands of his hair, relishing their silky weight. Absently she felt the left side of his face, bald and burned, his ear a shriveled mass, the skin leather-like and raised into interwoven ridges...

The spell shattered.

Isabelle broke off their kiss and opened her eyes. Her mind departed from the fantasy and returned to her private chamber. Darkness filled her vision—as if her eyes still remained shut. She blindly staggered against her bed's headboard, realizing the music had fallen into silence minutes ago.

Chapter Sixteen

PISTOL IN HAND, Rosemary's burned and shriveled body flashing through my mind, I huddle outside Maman and Papa's bedchamber while my home rocks beneath my naked heels. I fight to silence my own ragged breathing, struggle to decipher the voices behind the walls. My burned arms and hands pulsate with mind-bending pain, robbing the air from my lungs.

I must be brave, just like Papa...

The door is ajar; I adjust my posture a few centimeters and peek inside. My heart leaps in my throat, and my pulse races, threatening to shatter through each rib. Maman and Papa are standing in front of their large four-poster bed dressed in night rails. Red and blue scarves gag their mouths, and their hands are tied behind their backs. A group of men engulfs them, several clasping flickering torches. The illuminations toss eerie shadows against the damask walls and hulking furniture.

The leader holds a long, curved blade in his hand. His arms are tucked behind a broad, muscled back, and the crude blade drinks in the surrounding torchlight.

He tears the scarf from Papa's mouth in a harsh movement. A scar, which extends from the corner of his lip to his ear, twists as he surrenders to a cruel smile. "Care to say any words?" The leader looks formidable and severe with that scar and a thick black beard slashing across his face.

Hollering voices and stampeding footfalls echo from below. The castle shudders beneath my feet as more cannon fire blasts through the walls.

"Have you no fear of God?" Papa asks in a steady voice. The leader says nothing; he merely drags the point of his blade across Papa's neck, engraving his skin with a thin line of blood. I tremble from my hiding spot, overcome with nausea and rage. My heart races so fast... I'm convinced it'll give me away. Papa meets the man's leveled stare, refusing to show fear. Refusing to be bullied. Blood beads down his throat as he holds his head up with an unwavering pride and dignity. "What... what is this? A revolt?"

"Non, sire. A revolution."

It's now or never.

I tear inside the bedchamber and aim the pistol. Agony and sheer terror cause my hand to tremble in midair; severe burns cover my arms and hand, though a rush of adrenaline prevents me from succumbing to the pain. I find myself in a state of detachment and unreality—almost as if I'd died alongside Rosemary minutes ago.

The leader wheels toward me and bends into a mocking bow. "My prince. My men have been searching for you."

"Adam!" Papa cries out, struggling against his restraints, his cool composure from moments ago quickly unraveling. "Leave! Leave now! Don't defy me, *mon fils!*"

The leader signals to his men—who storm after me.

"Stay back!"

Bang! I fire the pistol without thinking, shooting the leader in the shoulder. He curses, and the curved blade tumbles from his hand. "Get him, you fools!" he orders, his voice a fierce rasp, his hand grasping his seething shoulder. "And keep him alive."

One of the men punches me straight in the stomach. The blow ripples through my entire body. I crumple to my knees, coughing and struggling for precious air. It feels like a stone has been laid across my breast. Maman cries out—her words muffled by the scarf—but then a sound punch to the gut silences her.

A second man latches on to the back of my night rail and drags me to my feet. I turn to him and encounter a pair of eyes I know well; the eyes of a servant, someone I'd known all my life and believed was my friend.

"William... please, I beg you... You, who taught me how to fish. Help us..." He glances away, shame embedded in his gaze, and focuses on a random spot on the wall.

"Do what you must," Papa whispers, his voice barely audible above the clamor and chaos. "Only spare my son. I beg you. Please."

The leader shoves the scarf between his teeth again. He signals the men, who hold my body upright like a puppet. "Now... you watch Maman and Papa die."

My pulse beats against my eardrums as I'm thrust in front of Maman and Papa. I lock on to their gazes while an entire conversation floats between the three of us.

Endure, my dear son. Be strong, be brave...

We, the Delacroix house, shall stand for a thousand more years, because we are the true pillars of Demrov...

The men hold me in place, their grips akin to iron manacles. I try to look away—to keep from witnessing the horror that's about to unfold—but William's callused hand grips my chin and keeps me staring forward.

"Don't you dare close your eyes, little prince."

The torch's heat flashes across my burning face. Sweat and tears and more vomit track down my neck and splatter onto the parquet floorboards.

It happens in a flash—though I perceive the moment as a weightless eternity. And in that suspended instant, my life, and everything that makes me who I am, vanishes like a phantom.

The blade's thrust back—then it's swung, full force, directly at Papa's neck. I fall faint...

My legs give out; William grips my shoulder and holds me up like a fish on a hook.

The leader seizes a torch from one his men and points the flame straight at me. His deep, steady voice slices through the bedchamber like a hurtled knife: "Nutrisco et extinguo..."

Then darkness swallows everything, and my house's words sardonically echo in that abyss.

ADAM AWOKE WITH A START, his entire body drenched in sweat. Tangled in his coverlet, he lurched upright and willed his breathing to return to normal.

He still felt the heat of the flames wafting toward him, still smelled the rancid scent of his burning skin while Rosemary's cries blasted in his ears...

His gaze shot to the end table; the lantern had fallen over, and a small fire blazed several meters from his bed. The drapes, which fell around the window in thick folds, were aflame.

Panic seized him. The room physically spun and rolled. Not thinking, unable to draw breaths, he stumbled away from those flames and rolled off the opposite side of the mattress.

Thwap.

The back of his head slammed against the wall, knocking the breaths from his lungs and causing blackness to fringe his consciousness.

He felt himself slipping away—felt the memories crashing down in a brutal avalanche.

Non, sire. A revolution.

That deep, dark voice hissed inside his skull with the cruelty of a serpent; twenty-five years had dulled neither the menacing tone nor the horror it summoned in Adam's mind and body.

Darkness and fear enveloped him. His heart reached a breakneck speed. His hands grew hot and clammy. Pain speared through his chest and weighed heavily on his straining lungs. The scent of the smoke burned his nostrils and caused bile to climb into his throat. All logic faded from his thoughts; he cried out and grasped either side of his head, blocking out the diabolic crackle of the flames. Alas, he was eleven years old again—and the horrors of that eve returned at full force. His pulse thundered in his temples and violently beat against his palms...

Now... you watch Maman and Papa die...

The thick scent of the smoke continued to drift toward him, swelling his lungs. Rosemary's cries blasted in his mind until he perceived nothing else. He pushed his palms harder against his ears, fought to muffle her sobs, struggled to cave inside the barricade of his shuddering body...

Nutrisco et extinguo.

In his mind's eye, he saw the blade slicing at the air—cutting straight through Papa's neck...

"Adam?" He perceived Isabelle's voice through a hazy filter; it seemed to emerge from many kilometers away. "Adam!"

His eyes flashed open. Somehow he grabbed hold of the bed's poster and pulled himself up. The entire chamber tilted and swayed as she yanked the cover off the mattress and suffocated those roaring flames.

Her gaze captured his from across the bed, and Adam felt the shame twist inside his chest. Stranger stood at her heels; Isabelle grabbed the scruff of his neck, directing him away from the rising smoke.

Adam's entire body trembled. He wobbled onto his feet and shrank against the wall. Isabelle wheeled around the bed, a shared anguish etched into her fine brows. She covered her mouth and nose with her sleeve and coughed into the fabric.

"I have to help her," he rasped, lulling toward the rising cloud of smoke and shriveled drapes. "Can't you hear her crying? She's still alive—she's suffering. Please..."

Be brave, my dear boy. Endure and be strong...

"Adam... You are safe." Soft, gentle fingers grazed his shoulders. He watched beneath heavy lids as Isabelle blocked his pathway and gazed up at him. She applied a careful pressure to his arms and guided him onto the mattress. "Shh..." She sank down next to him, her body pressed against his own. Stranger also dropped to the floor a meter away from the bed; clearly affected by Adam's anguish, he released a low whine and stared up at him with large, soulful eyes.

Isabelle's slim arms enclosed him, and Adam melted in her hold. Her hands tentatively rubbed his back in slow strokes, soothing his quaking limbs. His disjointed mind traveled back to their embrace in the library... to the tentative kiss he'd bestowed upon her brow.

The soft whisper of her breath fanned against his cheeks. He tightened his hold on her slender body, welcoming her gentle curves, soaking in the warmth and comfort she freely offered. Then her calming voice was in his ear, chasing away the shadows and memories. "Adam... share with me. You are not alone anymore. Let me help you. Let me inside..."

She scooted backward a centimeter or two, pulled away from his body, and captured his eyes with her own. Compassion swam in her gaze... one that stole his breath away and severed his defenses. "I'm here with you, here for you. And I shan't let you go..."

ISABELLE'S HEART CLENCHED as she gathered Adam against her chest again. His body madly shook beneath her fingers, and his gaze held a distant, faraway look. He seemed to watch something terrible unfold inside his mind.

The pounding of his heart thumped against her torso, echoing his despair and an unspoken torment. One of her hands glided up his nude, muscled back, tracing over the uneven flesh and raised welts. Her heart beat faster, and tears stung the corner of her eyes. Her fingertips slid down and up his strong back as she attempted to relieve his fear in the only way she knew how.

Her thoughts returned to how Papa used to comfort her in this way.

"I... I can still hear her..."

"It's only in your mind. Come back to me, Adam." Laying a hand on the center of his chest, she applied a light pressure and massaged his thundering heart. Her fingers moved in slow, deliberate circles while his breathing returned to normal. A moment later, he completely surrendered to her touch; his head fell across her shoulder, and his steady breaths filled her eardrums. Strong, blemished arms snaked around her torso as he returned her embrace.

They held each other for several minutes.

Isabelle swayed back and forth and murmured reassuring words against his marred cheek. Wetness seeped through the fabric of her nightgown.

Adam's tears.

"You are not alone. You don't have to be afraid any longer."

He inhaled a fortifying breath, as if gathering the courage to speak.

She lifted her fingers in midair, so they hung centimeters away from his face. Then she carefully traced the puckered skin. Adam's chest rattled, and he sucked in a taut breath. She watched in awe as his eyes fell shut and he dipped into the gentle, featherlight caress of her fingers. Her palm cupped his scarred, tear-tracked face; he turned into her outstretched fingers and pressed a kiss against the center of her palm.

Isabelle glanced over her shoulder and surveyed the crumpled, burned coverlet. She'd never encountered such fear in another person's eyes. How lost he'd looked—almost like a young child amid disaster, abandoned and with no one to turn to. Once, when she had been a girl, she'd witnessed as a stable caught fire. She'd never forgotten the look of terror in the horses' eyes as Papa had bravely guided them from the burning building.

That same terror flamed in Adam's gaze. He looked wild, unkempt, in a state of utter panic. His appearance and shattered composure were a stark contradiction to his demeanor in the music room. Every piece of her softened to him.

"Your scars..." she began, her voice a tentative whisper. "Your burns. How—how did they happen?" Her fingers slipped away from his cheek and seized hold of his trembling hand. She smoothed her thumb over his knuckles, cherishing the simple feel of his skin. Despite the scarring, his hands were elegantly carved and masterful. They were the hands of an artist—hands that any musician would envy... a flesh-and-blood testament to an abstract, powerful beauty.

She imagined how they'd feel against the planes of her body. Would he be rough? Would he force himself upon her as Raphael had done so many nights ago? Or would he be gentle, playing her body with the care of a well-loved instrument?

"You don't have to suffer alone any more. Let me take away some of your pain."

When he gave no answers, Isabelle wrapped her arms around his body and simply held him again. She rocked him in the circle of her arms, humming beneath her breath, soaking up the anguish that radiated from his quivering muscles.

She ached to lose herself in his tentative yet arresting touches... to crawl in his lap, hook both arms around his strong neck, and seize his mouth in a tender kiss. Instead, she nuzzled against his shoulder and inhaled the unique aroma of his skin. It swelled her senses and carried her back into the erotic throes of her dream...

"I'm here with you, for you. And I won't let you go."

Isabelle kept true to her word. She stayed with him throughout the night, reciting fanciful stories to distract him, stroking the hair from his eyes, and reading from the pages of books. A dreamy haze settled over them; together, they fell asleep, heartbeat to heartbeat. And she remained that way until morning's golden light trickled through the window and set his bedchamber aglow.

As warm light bathed her features and awoke her like a lover's caress, a single thought occupied her mind: It was the start of a new day.

SÉBASTIEN HESITATED OUTSIDE the cottage's peeling door and

spared a moment to gather his thoughts.

Stuck in an obsessive loop, his mind continually slid back to his final interaction with Adam. Only the night of the Delacroix siege compared to the anguish and unrest he felt; every time he reflected on Adam's final words, his resolve slipped away, and he considered dropping this plan altogether. Then he'd remember the lonely pile of stones, the wooden cross, and the sight of Isabelle wearing that gown... Adam's violent outburst replayed in his mind, and Sébastien's tenacity sparked to life again.

What kind of man would I be if I stood idly by, watching as that castle snuffs out the girl's spirit?

He'd fulfill Adam's request—and he would get to the bottom of the mystery and the comte's brougham.

Clarice and Elizabeth. Clarice and Elizabeth. Elizabeth and Clarice. He inwardly repeated the names of the girl's stepsisters, then banged against the cracked door panel with his fist. Several moments slipped by with no response. Sébastien sighed and turned back to the unpaved dirt pathway, which was encased in a light frost. Afternoon light shimmered through the rows of tight-knit homes and dappled the ground with dancing prisms. The sun was halfway hidden by a blanket of low-hanging clouds. Ruillé's province was small and its buildings equally so; nearly erected on top of one another, countless homes crowded the walkway, their walls splintered and windswept. Clotheslines and ropes of lanterns webbed the structures as one. From what he could make out, the streets appeared poorly tended.

A whiny voice echoed from within the cottage and captured Sébastien's focus. "What do you know, Elizabeth? I suppose they have returned, after all."

A heartbeat later, the front door cracked open. Sébastien peered inside, his gaze running over the girl's severe expression. Her face appeared quite thin, her small eyes narrowed with suspicion, and a long, tightly plaited braid draped over one shoulder. She might have been pretty if she smiled. But she offered no smile—only a shrewd glance and a huffy greeting. Her reedy shoulders and collarbone reminded Sébastien of a bird's. And that hawkish nose didn't temper the likening.

Stifling an inappropriate, chortled laugh, he bowed his chin and said, "*Bonjour*, mademoiselle. I'm looking for Clarice and Elizabeth."

A spark of interest flared in her eyes. Sébastien examined her unpleasant face for another moment, noting that she held little resemblance to Isabelle. It was rather apparent they didn't share the same bloodline.

"*I am* Clarice," she finally said, edging the door open a fraction more. "And who, pray tell, are you?"

A second girl crowded behind her and peeked past the chipped door. From what Sébastien could see, they looked quite similar; both women bore thin, angular faces, silver eyes, and wiry, stick-straight hair fastened into too-tight plaits. "Who is that? Oh, tell me now, Clarice, tell me straight away!"

"Quiet," Clarice snapped at her sister. Fixing her cool eyes on Sébastien again, she said, "What do *you* want?" Her gaze traveled down his fine walking coat, volleyed over his shoulder, then studied the parked phaeton before coming full circle again.

"Glad to make your acquaintances, mademoiselles," Sébastien replied with a small bow, ignoring her brashness. "I come on behalf of your sister Isabelle."

This caught the interest of both women. Clarice peered over her shoulder and met her sister's wide eyes.

"Might I come inside for a moment? I bring some important news."

Whispering ensued. The door emitted a creak as Clarice hesitantly pulled it open. Sébastien stepped inside the cottage, following the two women.

Mon Dieu, the room was tiny—the walls seemed to physically close in on him. His eyes drew to a nearly black hearth and a pair of rocking chairs. A stack of books sat on the floor beside the mantel, towering halfway up the peeling hearth. A small fire burned and imbued the room with a pleasant warmth.

The second sister swooped in front of him like the bird she so well resembled. "So what's your purpose here? Isabelle and her father left us here almost a month ago, just like every other year!"

"But why?" Sébastien asked, sensing jealousy and hurt in the girl's tone.

"That wretched Merchants' Fair, *of course!*" She plopped down in one of the rocking chairs while her sister claimed the other. Affected by the chit's dramatic flair, he was half tempted to run for some smelling salts.

"Forgive my younger sister," Clarice said with a huff and an air of importance. "She's prone to melodrama like our mother was."

"I am *not!*"

"Mademoiselle Isabelle never reached the fair," Sébastien said in a slow, cautious tone, turning the conversation back to the reason for his visit.

"Why? Where did she and Papa run off to?"

Sébastien searched for the right words. *Mention as little as you can,* Adam had warned. *See to the girls' needs and whatever they might require—but disclose little more.*

"She is safe and well, I assure you." He glanced around, struggling for a way to lighten the atmosphere. "I daresay she won't be lacking for comfort in my master's castle."

Silence swept over the cottage while the girls exchanged a look. "C-castle? Your master? What—"

A sudden thought crossed Sébastien's mind. "Do either of you two lovely ladies happen to know Vicomte Dumont?"

Elizabeth's eyes widened at the name, and he could have sworn a blush swept across her thin cheeks. "What, are you mad? Why, of course, we do! He used to call upon our home quite frequently."

Clarice, whom Adam pinned as the more level-headed of the two, tossed her hand in the air to silence her sister's words. She gave Sébastien a small smile, then rose and moved toward the cramped kitchen nook. "Coffee, monsieur? It's a rather cold afternoon."

"Ah, yes, *merci.* I'd be most grateful."

She shuffled with a rusted kettle and two ceramic cups. Then she rekindled the fire, hung said kettle in the hearth, and reclaimed her seat at the round table.

"Yes," Clarice continued, rewarding Sébastien with a

small grin, "my sweet sister and her vicomte are quite besotted with each other."

"Oh, yes!" the younger sister chimed in. "He was very kind to her! Treated her like a true queen." She covered her mouth with her palm and stifled a giggle. "Dear Isabelle used to sit at the window for hours at a time, just waiting for the vicomte's return. Isn't that right, sister?"

Clarice's smile grew as she gave a sharp nod. The hissing kettle broke the following silence. Clarice rose from her chair, wandered over to the hearth, and prepared Sébastien's cup of coffee with stiff movements and a vacant stare.

He nodded his gratitude as she slid the chipped cup across the table and into his hand. Then she reached across the surface and laid her palm on top of Sébastien's. "Isabelle was on the cusp of a bright new life... one full of love and fortune. Why, the vicomte was so kind, he intended to aid *all* of us," she said, lifting her hands and gesturing to the room for emphasis. She heaved a deep sigh and stared into her coffee's black depths. Tangible sorrow lined her deep-set eyes. Sébastien felt himself soften to both girls. "Now who knows what shall become of us..." She hid her face behind her palms and expelled another sigh. "I'm so sorry, monsieur. It's selfish and weak of me to cry. Why, all that matters now is Isabelle's happiness... not our own."

"On that first note," Sébastien said, pulling a handsome sum of bank notes from his coat's pocket. "This should ensure your comfort for a while."

Elizabeth burst across the table and grabbed for the notes; Clarice swatted her hand away, hissing something incoherent in her sister's ear.

"When shall we be seeing more?" Clarice asked, pocketing the notes as quickly as he'd retrieved them.

"Next month, most likely. I believe that's Adam's plan."

"Adam? Who is—" Elizabeth began—but Clarice set her hand upon her sister's shoulder, urging her to hush in a matronly gesture.

The realization crashed into Sébastien, and unstoppable pity swelled his chest.

They are really just children... abandoned, orphaned children, who are all alone in this world. Indeed, they may be simple and prone to dramatics—but what young ladies are not?

Heaving a long-suffering sigh, Clarice shook her head. "It's so very tragic. I know Raphael would do everything in his power to have his little Isabelle back in his arms."

Sébastien's insides clenched. He absently cracked his knuckles, then downed a generous sip of his coffee. "Well. I'm certainly not one to tear apart two lovers."

"We know where he lives! We went once to his beautiful chateau—oh, it's simply charming!" Elizabeth sprang to her feet and waltzed about the small room with a dreamy expression.

"Please, monsieur. Allow us to help you and our darling sister," Clarice murmured as she sipped her drink.

No more backward glances. Now, I shall set things right.

After a moment of hesitation, Sébastien nodded.

Chapter Seventeen

"Here is my secret. It is very simple: It is only with the heart that one can see rightly; what is essential is invisible to the eye."
—Antoine de Saint-Exupéry

THE FOLLOWING MORNING dawned in a burst of sunshine. Winter was at last fading for the season, giving birth to spring. Adam stood on his balcony and admired his gardens. A gentle breeze ruffled his hair and shirtsleeves, sending with it the honeyed scent of his roses. For the first time in longer than he could recall, he felt free, liberated, even happy.

His mind traveled back to evenings ago—to how Isabelle had chased away his shadows and stayed with him throughout the night. Something powerful stirred in his chest and sent his emotions spinning. He lifted a hand to his heart and massaged the tender ache. Day by day, moment by moment, Isabelle was easing her way inside and hounding away the shadows that had so long eclipsed his world.

He used to suffer from the gaping hole inside of him with every sunrise. It was where his heart had once been, and now where the memory of his family lived on. For years, grief and self-resentment had filled the rest of that inner void. But now, with each passing moment, those feelings were fading—and Isabelle was claiming their place.

As he studied the lush forest that lay beyond his thousand-acre property, a spectacular idea took shape. Smiling to himself, he rushed inside his bedchamber and set off to prepare for the day.

He found his beauty reading in the library an hour later. Seated beside a curved conservatory window, she was sprawled across the luxurious chaise. Stranger sat beside her, loyal to the core, snoring lazily within a patch of warm, shifting light. One of Isabelle's legs hung off the seat and dangled in midair. Adam watched as the slipper threatened to fall off her delicate foot, which was swinging back and forth, as if dancing to a melody only she could perceive.

Sunlight wove through her long and loose curls, infusing them with golden highlights. Leaning against the doorway and transfixed by the vision, Adam observed while varying emotions crossed her face. She gasped aloud and shook her head, totally immersed in the story—then eagerly flipped the page and read on.

Adam couldn't suppress his chuckle. The book nearly tumbled out of her hands as her face jerked toward the noise. Stranger rose from the floor and gave a talkative, *protective* bark, the cheeky bastard. When he realized his master stood in the doorway, he limped toward Adam, his thin tail slicing the air with erratic wags. He groaned with each step, favoring his right leg more than he ever had before. "Stand down," Adam ordered. Stranger plopped onto his bottom and stared up at him expectantly.

"Oh, Adam!" Isabelle exclaimed, pressing the book to her heaving breasts. "You gave me quite a start. How long have you been standing there?"

"Only a couple of minutes," Adam replied with a sly grin. He knelt to the floor, dropped the large satchel he'd been holding, and gently rubbed Stranger's left leg.

Isabelle surrendered to a smile that lit up both her face and the entire library. Then she set her book on the chaise, stretched her slender arms, and lounged her body against the lush throne of pillows. A mountain of books towered beside the yellow, damask chaise; Adam couldn't harness his grin.

The encounter was perfectly ordinary—mundane, even. Yet he relished the simple pleasure of watching Isabelle relax and read, the ease of their small talk, how morning's light wriggled through the lace curtains and set her tranquil expression aglow. They were modest pleasures—ones he'd believed he would never experience. Even more, she gazed upon his naked face without fear or revulsion. Instead, a soft emotion appeared in her stunning gaze, and she seemed to rather *enjoy* his company.

Swallowing the knot in his throat, Adam returned her smile as a distinct warmth spread through his limbs. He climbed back on his feet—to Stranger's groaned dismay—and stepped toward her cozy nook. She straightened her posture and played with one of her loose curls. Her velvety brown eyes traveled over his body in an admiring perusal, visibly drinking him in from head to toe.

How he wished her eyes were hands.

Yawning and stretching like an elegant feline, she gestured to the satchel with a wave of her fair hands.

"It's such a perfect day," he said, his voice a low whisper that forced her to lean forward to hear. "I thought we'd venture outside. Experience the world a bit. Maybe have some lunch."

Isabelle jumped to her feet without warning, her smile growing indefinitely. "Oh, really, Adam? I would love that!"

Nodding, he bridged the space between them and held out his gloved hand. His heart gave an eager jolt as she grabbed hold, not showing the slightest trace of hesitation or revulsion. On the contrary, she appeared elated and flooded with anticipation and excitement. Adam's fingers closed over her delicate hand. "Go and change, Isabelle. Meet me in the stable." Then he tapped his thigh and called out to Stranger, "And you—come along, ol' grump."

A half an hour later, Isabelle stood with her back firmly against the stable's wooden panels. Adam set down the satchel as he saddled Spirit, who was quite restless from her confinement.

He tensed while Isabelle drew near, his body perfectly in tune with her invigorating presence. She reached out and ran her fingertips over the mare's silky head.

Adam paused as he examined Isabelle, his heart in his throat. He stood beside her and placed his hand on top of the mare's muzzle. His and Isabelle's fingers nearly brushed against each other. Then Spirit dipped her stark-white nose, and Adam's palm slid downward until his thumb and forefinger collided with Isabelle's.

She cleared her throat, ceased petting the creature, then stepped back with a small blush. Adam wrestled not to take offense to the gesture, though a lifetime of insecurities reared in his gut and eclipsed his thoughts.

He recalled the prostitute's disbelieving stare as she'd lit a branch of candles and studied his scarred face. Adam had immediately veered into the shadows like some wounded beast. Her mouth had fallen open in a silent scream while she'd scrambled for her cloak. Crossing herself, she'd cried out, "The devil take you! Leave me and go! No—don't touch me! Keep away... Loathsome monster—"

Adam swallowed against the lump in his throat. *Isabelle is different,* he reassured himself, remembering how she'd comforted him in his bedchamber. Tightening the satchel and saddle around Spirit's powerful girth, he whispered, "Fits her well, if I may say so." Isabelle flashed him a warm smile. She ventured to the corner of the stall, where a wooden trough sat. She retrieved a handful of hay, and then offered some to Spirit, who gave a talkative nicker before devouring the treat.

"I assume she's not your horse," Adam said in a cautious, low tone, as an image of the Dumont carriage blazed through his mind. "Nor the brougham." Silence swelled the musky stable, pressing between them like a tangible force. "Do you know the Dumonts very well?"

Isabelle's smile melted away. A harsh darkness flitted across her hazel eyes, and her posture stiffened. Haphazardly she dropped the remaining hay onto the straw and dirt covered floor. Then she shook her head and exhaled a long-suffering sigh. "Too well. And hopefully, I shall never have to cross paths with him again."

Adam ached to ask a thousand questions, yet he knew it

was neither the time nor place. This afternoon would be a day of beautiful memories, a day of light and adventure. He slid behind Isabelle in a smooth movement and planted his hands on either side of her small body. She emitted an audible gasp, then glanced over her shoulder and met his gaze. He stood intimately close. Close enough to fully embrace Isabelle. Close enough to kiss her. The front of his body grazed her own from shoulder to bottom, and his staccato heartbeat thundered against her. Adam glanced down, observing how his large hands covered the entire span of her waist. His eyes closed against the surge of arousal.

Then he urged her forward with his shaking hands, directing her inside Spirit's dusty stall. The wooden door swung open and released a soft creak. "You ready, mademoiselle?"

It was a loaded question.

She hesitated. When she finally answered, her reply sounded quite breathless. "Absolutely."

His eyes held on Isabelle... on the pale column of her throat, on the way her lush hair tumbled down her slender back in spirals. His fingers slid away from her waist and coiled in those silken curls.

Without another thought, he gently lifted her in midair and placed her onto Spirit's back. Then he led them across the straw-covered floor by the leather reins. Adam took a moment to fill his lungs with fresh air, to concentrate on nature's sweet scents and the gentle feel of the wind blowing through his hair and against his nude face.

Adam swung onto Spirit's back in a swift movement, positioning himself in front of Isabelle.

"Hold on to me, and don't let go."

Isabelle hesitated, wrapping her arms around his midsection. He felt his pulse at the base of his throat, in his wrists, even behind each eye. His heart thundering, he gently kicked Spirit's side, and she trotted past the castle's looming front gate and into the thicket of trees.

Riding tandem with his beauty seduced his thoughts into a dangerously erotic territory. Warm, supple hips rocked against him, causing his groin to harden and wicked ideas to invade his mind. A gentle breeze swam through Isabelle's waving curls, bringing with them the delectable scent of the fresh roses she'd used in her bathing water. Long, slender legs brushed against him and made his entire body ignite with desire. The whisper of her breaths tickled his nape and nearly pushed him over that edge...

Adam wrestled his emotions and battled to focus on his surroundings. Brilliant shafts of light splintered through the trees, reaching for him and Isabelle like beckoning fingers. A light foliage covered the branches, which had been all but bare not long ago. The only sounds that breached the quiet were the crunch of fallen leaves beneath Spirit's hooves and the alluring melody of Isabelle's breathing. It continued to waft against his neck and send shivers racing through his granite-hard body.

With a slight quaver in her voice, she asked, "Do you often venture out-of-doors?"

"No. Hardly ever, in fact. But when I do... I go to a very special place."

ADAM URGED THE MARE into a gallop, and Isabelle rejoiced at the liberating sensation. She felt like she was flying. Cool air struck her flushed cheeks, and the wind caused her hair to dance behind her like a banner. She held tight to Adam's solid waist while Spirit's surging body moved under her. She gazed down, watching in breathless fascination as the frosty forest floor zoomed below the thundering hooves. Isabelle feared she'd fall and break her neck—yet, holding Adam's strong body, she felt safe. Secure. Enthralled. Within this enchanted moment, he was her pillar of strength.

Soon Adam tugged on Spirit's reins, slowing her to a brisk canter. The sound of rushing water washed over Isabelle. Patches of sunlight dabbled the pathway in bright splotches as they rode through the forest at a leisurely stride. Eventually they arrived at a clearing; Isabelle felt the breaths empty from her lungs while Adam urged Spirit to a halt.

This small corner of the world might have been stolen from a storybook. A glittering waterfall pooled into a small lake, and a prism of light danced across its restless surface.

Adam slid off Spirit's back, then pulled Isabelle down after him and removed the satchel. She stared at the sparkling waterfall, mesmerized, entranced, unable to bring a coherent word to mind. Slowly she turned to Adam and captured his soulful gaze. He reached out and grazed her cheeks with his fingertips, drawing a shudder from deep inside her.

"It's like from a dream."

Isabelle listened to the melodic sound of the thundering waterfall and allowed her eyes to drift shut.

"For so long, I've lived as if I'd died. I've forgotten how it feels to be alive, to breathe fresh air and feel the sun on my face." Isabelle's eyes snapped open. She watched beneath hooded lids as the sunrays shimmered across his tranquil expression and set his dark hair aglow. An echoed peace flushed through her and summoned a feeling of true contentment. "I even avoided this spot," Adam murmured, "I suppose as self-punishment."

Silence wrapped around them. But it wasn't quiet. The hammering of their heartbeats and heated breaths filled the atmosphere. The faint melody of the waterfall. The tempo of their pulses. The sensual crackle in the air.

Then he clasped her hand, which was trembling, and brought her to the foot of the lake. A smile sprung to Isabelle's face as heat wafted from the water; indeed, it wasn't a lake at all.

"A hot spring! Oh, Adam! I've read about these."

She dropped to her knees without further thought as the heat circulated below. It swirled into her face and caressed her, causing wayward strands of hair to dampen and curl against her nape. Seduced by the promising warmth, she unsheathed both hands, set her kidskin gloves aside, and reached down.

A moan slid from her throat. The water encircled her fingertips and summoned delicious waves through her body. It was much hotter than she'd imagined. The contrast of the crisp air and tepid liquid felt invigorating. Thrilling. Delicious. All the while, she felt Adam standing beside her, towering above her like some dark, solemn angel. Shaking her head, she laughed aloud at the dramatic comparison.

I've indulged in one too many Gothic novels.

"Incredible. At first glance, I would have never guessed it was a hot spring."

"Things aren't always as they appear to be, I suppose." The richness in his tone demanded her attention. She glanced up at him, her heart in her throat. A gust of wind whispered through his dark hair, sweeping the forelock from those mesmerizing eyes. His gaze held her own, and the smile faded from his mouth. In its place, an intense emotion surfaced—and she felt a resounding chill trickle down her spine. That stare was penetrative. Thrilling. Seductive.

Things aren't always as they appear to be.

Truer words were never spoken.

A MISCHIEVOUS GLINT sparkled in Isabelle's eyes. She sprang up from the ground, quick as a lightning strike, and spun away from Adam. He admired her slender back and swanlike neck, how those thick curls swirled down her body and kissed the pert rise of her bottom. He clenched his gloved hands as he battled the urge to sweep forward, to clasp his arms around her waist and press a deep, sensuous kiss to her neck. He longed to turn her slender body, to drag his mouth down the elegant column of her neck...

He relished watching Isabelle in her element—out-of-doors, the sun shining on her face and weaving through her loose hair. Indeed. Her adventurous spirit unfurled like a rose opening to morning's light.

The sound of rustling fabric cut his thoughts in two—and Adam realized she was *undoing the fastenings* on her cloak and dress.

"Why, shame on you! No peeking, monsieur." A smile curled her mouth, and laughter warmed her hazel eyes.

He couldn't tear his gaze away. He hardened as she shrugged off the dress, allowing the fabric to drop in a muslin puddle around her feet. Then she stepped over the heap of material, bent down, and unlaced her high boots. Her hair tumbled down across the ground like a velvet shawl. Sunlight limned her body, lending her a classic beauty that made his breath catch. She scooped the mass of curls into her hands and pushed them over one shoulder. Adam saw her pale nape flush a bright red, and he felt his wretched body stir to life. He ached to press his mouth against the creamy patch of skin... to slide the dress down her body and worship every centimeter of her with his tongue and fingers...

"You are mad, *ma belle*. Have you any idea how cold it is?"

"Not inside that water." She glanced up at him and arched a fine brow. "Don't tell me you've never taken a dip in this spring?"

"Never." The single word lodged inside his throat. He ran a shaky hand through his hairline while his gaze roamed over the white fabric of her chemise. Sunrays flittered across the material and silhouetted the lush curves of her body. The outline of her slim back and bottom made his blood rush southward and burn hot. Her lush hair acted as a curtain, which half veiled her body from his sight. Those strands pooled behind her body in a cascade of silk. He raked at his hairline some more, fidgeted with the damn signet ring, even counted backward from five. None of the rituals sedated his nerves or helped to temper his searing desire.

Isabelle kicked her boots aside, then glanced over her shoulder. Her mouth curved into an alluring smile. "Why, you are peeking again!"

Adam felt as a blush seared his cheeks. He tried to respond with some clever quip, but no coherent sentence came to mind.

Dressed only in her chemise, Isabelle scooted to the edge of the spring and slid into the water. She rotated toward him and sank neck-deep, hiding her body beneath the rippling surface.

Suddenly she looked quite shy and speechless.

"Join me, Adam. Today is supposed to be our grand adventure... remember?"

Adam almost refused her offer—felt the words pierce the edge of his tongue. But his body betrayed him; he glanced down to find his fingers working the clasps of his cloak and shirt.

Surely the sight will repulse her.

She'd seen his burned body before—but never in broad daylight. Never like this.

Shame welled inside him. He shrugged away the garments as fast as he could. His boots, gloves, and socks followed. Cold gusts of air blasted against his newly exposed skin and took him by surprise. He shuddered, caught between Isabelle's steady gaze and the crisp atmosphere.

"You made it look so easy, stripping down in winter," he muttered, his hands working faster still.

"Actually, it's nearly springtime, monsieur."

"And still damn cold."

Yet his body was on fire. He gave Spirit a quick glance, who was grazing at the frost-covered grass. Then he hesitantly joined Isabelle in the water. He half expected her to leap from the spring and run from him; instead, she gifted him another alluring grin.

Time stood still as she waded toward him, and the white fabric of her underclothes billowed behind her. The waterfall thundered in back of her, feeding into the spring and transforming her into a mythical water nymph. Adam held his breath. Arranging her body beside him, she leaned against the back of the spring, heaved a deep sigh, and shut her eyes. Dark lashes fanned against her velvety skin, casting crescent moons upon her cheekbones.

She sighed again and sank a little deeper into the water. "I could stay in here forever."

Isabelle's eyes flew open. Her own words seemed to jolt something profound inside her. Emotions warred on her sunlit face; Adam knew she was reliving the arrangement they'd struck almost a month earlier.

You must stay here as my mistress. For as long as I demand.

Maybe forever...

Water dripped from Adam's fingers as he lifted them from the water and grazed her chin. She clasped her slender fingers around his suspended wrist, her eyes fixed on his own. Their gazes clung. Searched. The chemistry between them was electric... far beyond anything he'd ever imagined. Even his darkest fantasies had paled in comparison.

His heart burst with emotion; it took every bit of his willpower not to scoop Isabelle in his arms and devour her lush, crimson lips. Blood rushed to his groin as perspiration and beads of water trickled down her neck and into the creamy valley between her breasts. He both cursed and thanked the rippling water, which prevented him from seeing her luscious curves and concealed his rock-hard arousal.

Her hand moved away from his wrist, and she tentatively slid her fingers across his jawline... over the normal side of his face... then across his disfigurement.

How can she bear it?

Her lips parted, and she elicited a sensual sigh. The sound stirred the blood in his veins, heating it to a steady boil.

He had to touch her. Adam waded forward, closing the scant distance between them, then slid his palm over Isabelle's abdomen. Steam rose from the spring and plastered the curls against her flushed cheeks. He felt her ribs beneath his palm, felt as her stomach contracted with each labored breath. Her skin was silky soft. Smooth. He heard her quick intake of air. Adam pulled his hand away and swallowed deeply. Every bit of him burned. Hummed. Throbbed. Once more, he ached to thrust her against the side of the spring and devour her lips in a soul-searing kiss.

"Tell me more about your adolescence," she whispered while her fingers resumed their daring exploration across the two sides of his face. She pushed back his hair, exposing his withered left ear. "Tell me everything..."

At that moment, Adam could deny her nothing. Relishing the feel of her damp fingertips, he spoke about his past while veiling his true identity. Her laughter sounded like pure music as he recalled the mischief he'd gotten into; the adventures

Sébastien had helped him achieve. He even spoke of his mother and father—of the love they shared and little Rosemary. She reminisced about her own childhood in turn; he savored each word, every tiny detail, as he caught himself falling in love with her again and again. Seconds slipped into minutes, and the minutes blossomed into a full hour.

I am losing myself to her.

Isabelle's fingers slid down his neck and over his fluttering pulse... down his sternum and the rapid beat of his heart. His head swam. Every nerve ending sizzled. She made him frantic with passion. Below the water's moving surface, she caressed his skin, each scar, the tops of his thighs and biceps.

At such close proximity, Adam detected a honeyed scent at the base of her throat. Roses. She'd clearly gathered some from his garden and garnished her bath water with their sweet petals. He inhaled the intoxicating fragrance, which mated flawlessly with the natural aroma of her skin. Delectable. Mouthwatering. He yearned to press his lips against the center of her throat... to drag his mouth and tongue all the way to the tips of her toes. How easy it'd be to nudge her slender thighs apart, to bridge the distance between them and bring his body flush against her feminine core.

What would it feel like to lose myself in such beauty and softness?

He yearned to bend his head, to kiss her shoulder, her neck, her chest. He'd tangle his fingers in her silky hair and whisper endearments against her skin. Ever so lightly, he'd catch her earlobe between his teeth... He'd move lower and tease her pulse point with his lips and mouth... move down to the lush rise of her breasts... He'd give her nipples the same attention as her earlobe; he'd gently take them between his teeth and lips... swirl his tongue around that taut peak and bundle of nerves... He'd pull both Isabelle and himself into oblivion with loving tugs and slow, sweeping licks—

Insecurities be damned; he couldn't fight off his desire any longer. Passion and blazing want caused his muscles to tremble. He needed to touch her, just as he needed air to breathe.

His quaking hand broke through the tepid water. Dragging a slow, deliberate caress down her smooth stomach, he traced the small dip of her belly button, circled around it... touched her hips and legs through the wet, billowing chemise, relishing how the material swished against his palm. Isabelle's audible moan encouraged his caresses and increased the beat of his heart. His fingers skated across the wavering fabric in a daring stroke, and he felt her muscles contract beneath his touch. Hardly thinking or able to breathe, he cupped his palm around her slender thigh and coaxed her legs apart. She visibly shuddered as he rested his fingers between her soft, parted thighs; the chemise's material barricaded his caress and whispered against his fingers. Below the fabric, he felt a dense spring of curls—just barely...

His soul felt close to bursting. He strived for sanity, for rational thought; the scent of her skin and hair overwhelmed him, while the feel of her silky-smooth thighs wound erotic imagery inside his mind. He dipped one finger past the pantalettes's slit and gently grazed her opening. She emitted a trembling moan as his thumb joined in the caress and grazed her feminine cleft. Back and forth. Up and down. He applied a little more pressure... watched with a shared ecstasy while her eyes closed and her thighs shifted farther apart in an erotic invitation...

"Adam..." She sighed his name, releasing the word on a husky exhale. Then she drew in a long breath, regarded him through hooded eyelids, and rested her head on the shelf of rock.

A heartbeat later, he forced his hand away and fought to breathe normally. Blood rushed past his eardrums and set his veins ablaze. Her eyes seized his in an intimate perusal. Whatever she encountered in his own expression appeared to captivate her.

"How can you allow me to touch you? How can you touch *me*?" he whispered, gesturing toward the marred skin of his face and neck. "How could you bare to touch this?"

Sighing, Isabelle merely smiled and shook her head. "Things aren't always as they appear to be, I suppose.

THAT NIGHT, Adam observed as Isabelle read a book before the hearth. She was snuggled up like a quaint kitten with a secretive smile curving her red lips. A whirlwind of hair cushioned her porcelain face and tumbled over her shoulders. Her mouth stirred with incantations as she mutely read from the page. A riot of emotions battled inside him while he studied her graceful movements... how her slender fingers eagerly flipped the pages and her fine brows scrunched together. She was utterly absorbed in her story; the rest of the world seemed to have fallen from her notice.

Stranger pushed past his legs and limped into the drawing room. Adam silently cursed the beast as Isabelle flipped her book shut, then greeted the dog with inaudible endearments. Her eyes rose to where he stood—and their gazes crashed together. A vision of her in the hot spring flashed through his mind: damp hair plastered to her glistening skin, morning's light illuminating her flushed cheeks, the feel of her abdomen rising and falling beneath his palm...

Adam shoved away the imagery and eased into the drawing room. His eyes flickered to the Delacroix coat of arms and his house's unveiled words; he'd removed the fabric the previous night.

Nutrisco et extinguo.

"Adam... come sit with me," she urged, her voice musical and airy. He did as she commanded, again finding he could refuse her nothing. Idly she scratched Stranger behind his long ears. Captivated by the sight, he nearly felt Isabelle's fingers sliding across his naked skin in a slow, passionate exploration...

"Glad to see you're making use of the library. The book," he murmured, gesturing to the volume and adjusting his body in the chair. "What are you reading?"

She gave another thoughtful smile, then flipped the cover

shut and recited the title aloud. "*Frankenstein*. One of my absolute favorites." Her eyes came to life, and Adam found a reflective joy spark inside his own heart. The reaction caught him off guard. He cleared his throat and fought to disguise the ever-growing power she held over him. *Dieu*, his nerves were in tatters, and he feared she could hear the wretched pounding of his heart. "Have you read it before?" she asked.

Silently he shook his head, not trusting himself to speak. Isabelle's smile grew as she tossed the cover open again. "Well, it's very good! It touches upon many of France's enlightened ideas."

She gazed down at the book, her intelligent eyes sharpening. Adam battled the urge to cup either side of her face and draw her into a slow, sensual kiss. He'd toss the book from her fair hands, climb onto the wingback chair, and encase her body with his arms...

The temperature seemed to increase by one hundred degrees. His heart thundered. Both palms grew hot and clammy. He held tight to the arms of his chair while his nails embedded in the faded fabric.

Looking quite flustered, she flipped the book open and scanned the page. "'You will rejoice to hear that no disaster has accompanied the commencement of an enterprise which you have regarded with such evil forebodings. I—'"

"What, pray tell, are you doing?"

"Why, reading to you, of course," she said, flashing him a playful look that heated his blood again. "Now, no interruptions, monsieur." Adam's grip on the arms of his chair loosened, and he felt his grin expand into a full-blown smile. "Just relax and close your eyes," she fairly purred, her soft voice washing over him like the waterfall. He did as commanded—falling fast and completely under her spell. The horrors of his past life lifted, leaving only the two of them in the world.

The hours flew by while the gentle lull of her voice carried him into a lush dream world. And for once in so many years, the nightmares never came.

Chapter Eighteen

SÉBASTIEN STOOD BEFORE Chateau de Dumont, staring up at the sweeping buttresses and intricate carvings in a state of disbelief. The family's noble coat of arms, which boasted a pair of roaring lion heads, was carved into the wooden door. A shiver coursed down his backbone as those shining, golden predators echoed his apprehensive glare.

Perhaps this is a mistake. Maybe I should forget this folly and turn back.

Sébastien dumbly scratched the stubble on his chin, then reached for the lion heads and gave the knocker a solid thrust. The sound reverberated despairingly inside the chateau's walls.

Almost immediately the front door wrenched open, exposing a rather pinch-faced looking footman. Sébastien guessed he was quite younger than he appeared, though judging by the leather-like skin and deep wrinkles, the man could have been anywhere from thirty to sixty-five. Sébastien yanked the bowler cap from his head and bowed his face in what he hoped was a proper formality.

"*Bonsoir*, monsieur. I am Monsieur Villeneuve. If it's not too much trouble, I would be honored to make the vicomte's acquaintance."

The footman raised sparse, tightly knit brows, the one telltale sign of his alarm, then spouted, "And what, precisely, shall I say this is in regards to?"

Sébastien hesitated for a moment, wishing he'd come armed with a better plan in place. Finally he opted for the truth. "Why, I have information regarding his charming fiancée—Mademoiselle Rose."

This piqued the footman's interest. He nodded and even showed a ghost of a smile, exposing a gap between his two front teeth. Smoothing down his livery, he stiffly swept aside and ushered Sébastien into the grand foyer. Sébastien scrunched his shoulders as the footman pried away his coat and tucked it inside a closet that was larger than a small drawing room.

Indeed, he wasn't used to such formality or grandeur. Not for several decades.

"Monsieur le Vicomte is presently consumed with a business affair. I shall alert him of your arrival and collect you when he is through." Sébastien nodded and nervously scrubbed his hand over his face. "In the meantime, shall I show you to the receiving room? Perhaps bring you a fresh pot of tea?"

"Oh, I'm quite comfortable here. *Merci*, monsieur."

The footman gave him a scrutinizing look. "Very well, monsieur."

As the footman made a quick bow and slipped down a long, connecting corridor, Sébastien found himself in awe of the chateau's looming and ornate beauty again. Overhead, twin chandeliers shone brightly, drinking in the sunrays that burst through rows of large arched windows. A glorious, flowered wall mural covered a portion of the wall, and elegant, gold-gilded scrollwork rimmed the ceiling.

The marble flooring echoed as he tracked forward, each of his steps amplified in the colossal room. The hollow sound of his footfalls seemed to reiterate his heartbeats. With each step, a nagging guilt and regret seeped into his marrow; the grand foyer reminded him of another fortress—one that had housed a line of kings and queens through the ages, and now stood in a lonely, desolate ruin in the middle of Demrov's most picturesque province.

Sébastien held his breath, half-expecting to see Adam, just emerging from his clumsy toddler years, bounding down the long hall, his youthful laughter ringing like a bell...

Desperately needing a distraction, Sébastien turned his gaze to an impressive display of portraits. The countless framed paintings were strategically grouped together in the popular salon wall fashion. Sébastien craned his neck back and examined the stern faces that seemed to glare down at him. Those fine ladies and gentlemen were clearly from the same bloodline; they all boasted the same placid expression, and their hair color typically ranged from a light brown to an almost stark-white blond. Sébastien drew closer in spite of himself as King and Queen Delacroix's faces materialized in his torrential mind; he blocked out the queen's wretched expression and the disappointed, disapproving look in her gaze.

Sébastien strained his eyes, noticing that a tiny inscription lined the bottom of each gilded frame. One showcased a beautiful young woman in the prime of life; she couldn't have been older than twenty years, and her hair was much darker than the surrounding ladies and gents. Her delicate features, creamy complexion, and chestnut curls seduced Sébastien's thoughts to those of another young woman... one he'd briefly met nearly a month earlier...

She's the reason for my visit. That thought set fire to his resolve and helped bar ancient memories from his mind.

Sébastien turned away from the portraits, needing to escape their collective gaze, and stole down the long foyer. His reflection shone in the medallion-patterned flooring. Despite being surrounded by beauty and elegance, he felt strangely cold. Hollow. As if he was being led down a dangerous path and desperately needed to find a way back.

I've already come too far to turn back now. I must think of the girl—I must focus on what's right.

Alas, since he was an adolescent, he'd made it a nauseating and tiresome habit... doing the right thing. Or at least what he perceived to be the right thing.

Muffled talking ensnared his attention. Sébastien glanced over his shoulder at the empty corridor, then followed the distant voices. Drawing toward the distinct sound of a heated conversation, he was careful to be lighter on his feet as he approached. Sébastien came to a dead standstill outside an arched doorway, whose door was slightly ajar.

"I cannot even bear to look at you, Raphael. You are a constant disgrace." He spoke the words in a deep, condemning tone that contained a slur. "Ever since your first breath, you have brought nothing but shame and disappointment upon our name! To think I expected greater from you this time around."

Silence seized hold like an iron fist. Sébastien edged closer to the archway and attempted to peer inside the withdrawing room.

After a minute had slipped by at a painfully slow crawl, a second voice joined in the conversation. "How dare you? Mother would turn in her very grave at your words." There was a distinct sadness in that voice. Sorrow. Hurt. And a powerful desperation. "Alas, she's turning in the grave you put her in," the man spat with a slight tremor. He was bursting with emotion, though visibly battling to remain tempered and in control of his wits. Yet with each word, Sébastien detected that the young man slipped further away—as if he were drowning in the waters of a past misery. "I grow weary of your condemnation, of your attempts to make me feel inferior to you and your precious fucking title."

Another silence prevailed. Tension rose in the air; it poisoned the atmosphere with an ominous taint. He slipped forward, his curiosity overwhelming all good sense, and peered inside the exquisite withdrawing room.

It was as magnificent and regally decorated as the rest of the chateau—and equally cold and hollow despite the blazing hearth and flickering sconces. Two men sat in adjacent wingback chairs. They looked remarkably similar, though one was at least two decades the other's senior. An unspoken challenge churned between them, and Sébastien felt his spine stiffen at the hatred in the younger man's eyes.

"Mother always—"

"Your mother was a whore. Just like that low-class wench who's somehow vanished into thin air. At first, I was rather glad about the turn of events. But the wagging tongues have changed all that."

Sébastien observed with a tinge of empathy as the vicomte scrubbed a trembling hand up and down his face. His other hand grasped a glass of liquor; he brought it to his lips and downed a swig, and the sound of tinkling ice cubes penetrated the quiet. "I have told you again and again. She shall return soon. I know—"

"You know nothing. You never have." The comte shot to his feet and stepped toward his son, towering over him. Cast in his father's shadow, the vicomte looked like a little boy. "But know this: Should this disgrace continue, I shall rid you of your allowance. The title will remain yours, as your whore of a mother provided me with no other heir."

The vicomte glared at his father's looming face as his grasp on the glass visibly tightened. "You have always disobeyed me, Raphael. No matter how hard I tried to teach you respect, to turn you into a man from a sniveling brat, you never learned. Now you've dragged our name through the mud once again. If only your wretched mother had given me another son, I would disown your inheritance *and* title completely."

The silence stretched on as the vicomte unraveled before Sébastien's eyes. His hands shook more fiercely than ever before, and Sébastien saw the revulsion in his stare even from where he stood. Then the young man lurched to his feet and closed the distance between him and his father. They stood mere centimeters apart, their chests nearly brushing. Sébastien caught himself holding his breath, so thick was the suspense. He felt like he was watching some melodramatic farce from a box seat.

The vicomte is going to strike him. Or worse.

But the vicomte simply shook his head, almost in defeat. Then he shouldered past the blockage of his father's husky body. He chucked the liquor into the hearth; the sound of the splitting glass fractured the quiet, followed by the fierce roar of the fire as the alcohol fueled it. The vicomte propped his hands on the intricately carved mantel while his broad back rose and fell with labored breaths. His gaze lifted, planting on the Dumont coat of arms, which was engraved into that wooden mantel.

Sébastien watched the smug look of satisfaction spread across the comte's face—and a part of himself broke for the vicomte. Raphael had clearly dwelled in his father's shadow all his life, bearing the taint of the comte's corrupt ways. He empathized with the young man—and it took every gram of his willpower not to strut inside the withdrawing room and voice that very thought.

"You aren't crying, are you? You haven't changed at all. Weakling! I—"

"Get out!" the young man screamed, whirling toward his father. "Get out of my life!"

The comte bowed his head in a mock display of formality, downed the rest of his liquor, and then slapped the empty glass onto a table. "I have business to attend to, anyhow. Though if I had half a mind, I'd throw you into those flames for presuming to toss me out of my own home. Without me, you'd be nothing more than an urchin on the streets. Remember that, Raphael. And remember I can take away everything you hold dear. Disgrace me again, and I'll make your life misery. On my word, you'll curse your *putain* mother for ever birthing you." And without another word or backward glance, the man wheeled away in a flurry of navy brocade and fine silks and stormed toward the archway.

Sébastien bolted down the corridor and returned to the foyer.

Nearly an hour had passed before the footman swept inside. Sébastien cringed at the man's sour expression and emotionless facade. "Vicomte de Dumont is ready to receive you now, monsieur."

The footman led Sébastien back to the same withdrawing room he'd spied on only an hour before. The vicomte lounged by the fire, wearing the same expression as when he'd battled with his father, staring blankly into the flames. They'd perished into glowing embers, and each one fought for breath.

"Monsieur le Vicomte. Sébastien Villeneuve."

Raphael swirled his glass of alcohol, took a drag, then tracked his gaze over the footman's stiff posture. "The hearth is nearly black." Silence. "Must I instruct your every move, your every breath? Do your job, you good for nothing fool!" Then, under bated breath, he added, "I can't even hire proper help. No wonder Father questions my worth."

The footman stumbled toward the hearth and immediately set off to work. Raphael shook his head in annoyance, then lifted his glass toward Sébastien. The tinkling of ice cubes resounded again and drew Sébastien's attention. "You—what do you want?"

Sébastien slinked forward, not sure of how to even breach the subject. He fought to keep the imagery and words from moments ago from his mind, but alas, he heard the comte's scorn and disdain clearly.

"Since you're good enough to ask... a couple thousand francs and a willing lady in my bed would be a decent start," he replied, hoping his wit would lighten the air and win the vicomte over. Indeed, most people wouldn't dream of speaking to a nobleman in such a tone—but past experiences had taught Sébastien better. King or queen, prince or pauper, all men enjoyed good-natured banter.

Raphael's lips quirked in amusement while his strained features loosened several notches.

"Your home is stunning, monsieur," Sébastien said with a note of sincerity, gesturing around the withdrawing room. "A true testament—"

"To all the good sense and high fashion of Paris and Lavoncourt," he finished, taking another generous sip of the alcohol. He polished off the drink in a single swallow, then harshly signaled toward the footman for a refill. "Yes, I've heard it a thousand times before. My father would love you," he mumbled. Then directing his words to the fumbling footman, he snapped his fingers. "Another glass for my guest here. And be quick about it." The footman gave a clumsy bow before darting to the far end of the room, where a mahogany bar was located.

"Ah, thank you, Monsieur le Vicomte." Sébastien warily took the adjacent seat as the footman placed a glass of brandy in his hand. He downed a swallow and relished the sharp burn as the liquor trickled down his throat.

"I like you," Raphael said with blunt frankness, his cool gaze sliding over Sébastien's face. "I can't say precisely why—but something about you is quite amiable. Honest and genuine. Now, cut the sentiments like I know you want to, and get on with it. What's the purpose of your visit?"

Sébastien felt the familiar war kick off inside his gut. He briefly shut his eyes and visualized Adam's face. Half as handsome as it'd been in his youth—half marred by a tragedy that still gave even Sébastien nightmares.

Have I gone mad? How can I do this?

He shook away the image, and the pile of stones quickly took its place. The wooden cross, the gentleman's top hat, and the girl's weariness...

What is right?

He felt Adam's clenched fingers in his cravat... felt as his back slammed into the wall and Adam's wild gaze cut through him—

Raphael cleared his throat, jarring Sébastien back into the moment. "My apologies. I have information." Silence prevailed. A silence that Sébastien hesitated to fill with words. The vicomte seemed kind enough, in spite of the disdain he suffered from his father, and Isabelle's stepsisters' words echoed in his mind. Together, these elements fueled his resolve and brought the truth to his lips. "Information regarding your fiancée—Mademoiselle Rose."

Raphael grunted and downed a swallow of his alcohol. He swirled the glass, his gaze fixed on the amber liquid. "My footman said as much. Which is why I permitted an audience with you." He set down the glass and leaned forward, his gaze narrowed with interest, the alcohol's haze fading from his eyes. "What can you tell me? I haven't seen her or received word in over a month."

Sébastien exhaled a long breath, downed a mouthful of brandy for courage, and then started at the beginning.

BONE-CHILLING CRIES jarred Isabelle from her dreams. Breathlessly she awoke in the darkness like so many nights before. Stranger, who was sprawled at the foot of her bed, also stirred awake and stretched his long legs with a groan.

The candle on her nightstand had burned out hours ago, plunging her chamber into blackness. Broken sobs and incoherent speech flowed through her partially open door. Her heart twisted into a thousand knots—and before she knew what she was doing, Isabelle commanded Stranger to follow her. Then she felt the rosewood floorboards sliding below her feet, felt the castle's frigid drafts whispering through her curls.

She hugged both arms about her body and massaged her arms. Goose bumps prickled her skin and caused every hair to stand on end. The nightdress offered little warmth against the castle's frigid atmosphere and drafts—and Adam's echoing cries chilled her into a deeper coldness. Her bare feet whispered against the panels as they eerily creaked under her heels. Stranger loyally followed her like a silent guardian, shadowing her every movement.

With each step, the sound of his cries grew louder and louder until they seemed to fill not just her hearing but all her senses too. Those sobs throbbed in her lips and fingers, in the flesh of her temples, in every vein and along with each heartbeat.

She froze outside his ajar door, observing as light from a candle bathed the intricate floorboards; a book rested beside it, attesting that he'd likely fallen asleep while reading. For a long stretch of time, she stood perfectly still, allowing Adam's cries to affect the deepest recesses of her soul, watching the illumination flutter within the dim chamber.

"Stay here, boy," she whispered to Stranger, simultaneously rewarding his head with an amiable pat. Inhaling a fortifying breath, she pushed the door open, shivering as it emitted an unsettling creak. This certainly wasn't the first time she'd heard Adam's night terrors.

Though he hasn't had an episode for several nights, she mused with a frown. *Not since I read to him.*

Normally she'd bury her face in her pillow and force herself back to sleep. But now everything had changed. Isabelle could no longer bear the thought of Adam's suffering, nor could she idly stand by.

Like the first time she'd entered his room, he was tossing and turning within the sheets. Sweat streamed from his hairline and down his quivering muscles. He wore nothing but his underclothes—leaving every scar, every sinew, painfully visible.

Isabelle knelt on his bed, her feet carried by her soul, a tender ache consuming her from the inside out. Agony warped his brow as he violently jerked and fought a horde of unseen demons. Isabelle's breath hung in the air, clashing against the coldness of the night. She reached out with a trembling hand and wove her fingers through his slick hairline. He stilled at her touch, and his incoherent cries faded into silence.

The sound of the howling wind surrounded them, filling the chamber with its forlorn song.

Isabelle's heart pounded against her ribs, threatening to burst through flesh and bone. Her palms cradled either side of his face. All her senses soared and heightened, taking on a life of their own. She felt the stubble scrape against her skin... smelled the unique scents that clung to Adam's hair and flesh— pinecones and winter... felt the dampness of his sweat and tears swimming against her fingers... listened as the ragged sound of his breathing tempered into a placid melody.

The effect she held over him touched something deep inside her soul. She inhaled a shuddered breath and harnessed back the tears that pierced the corners of her eyes. Hesitantly her thumb and forefinger stroked the sides of his face. She leaned forward, drew his head toward her own, her torn breathing rupturing the quiet...

It happened without conscious thought—just feeling. Her lips pressed against his in a whisper-soft caress. She felt as his body stiffened, then loosened on a long exhale. She tentatively pulled away, her palms still cupping his cheeks, hardly believing what she'd done.

Adam's eyes flashed open and captured her own. In a rush of movement, he closed the space between them and seized her mouth in a blistering kiss. It burned. Claimed her soul. Whispered a thousand unspoken secrets. His lips slid against her own, and he murmured something inside her mouth—something that sounded halfway between a groan and an expletive. She responded with a defeated whimper, and he chased the sound with his smooth tongue. He shifted his large body and propped onto one elbow; the other hand settled against her neck, drawing her nearer still, those long, masterful fingers caressing the sensitive skin below her ears.

Their lips worked in harmony—almost in a dance. The smooth tip of his tongue toyed inside her mouth and drew a shudder from her chest. He explored the tops of her teeth, then ventured into the warm silkiness that lay beyond. She met those gentle thrusts with an aching curiosity and passion, relishing as his moan vibrated against her and filled her own throat with a smoldering sensuality.

Then he sat up altogether and enfolded his arms around her. A feeling of weightlessness came over her as he urged her forward, upon the mattress and on top of his strewn body. Indeed, he descended into a reclined position, his mouth working against her own in that ageless dance as old as time itself. His blemished hands slid up and down her slender back, pressing her more firmly against his granite-hard body and thick arousal... Strong, trembling fingers dove into her hair, released the ribbon, and urged her curls over both their bodies like a secretive curtain. The irregular scarring and puckered skin grated against her nightgown as their chests melded together.

His body came alive—she felt his manhood jut and jerk against her stomach, surging with strength and vitality. She shuddered, half from that returning fear and half from a flood of desire. Adam unhinged his mouth from her own. He gazed up and into her eyes, a ghost of a smile on his lips, the two sides of his face for once not at war.

A rare peace softened his features and brought the conflicting halves of his face together.

Her heart pounded, yet the urge to flee never came. Though her fears remained ever-present, the yearning to lie in Adam's arms and lose herself in his tentative touches eclipsed everything else. A veil descended over them, closing the rest of the world off and blinding Isabelle to everything outside of Adam.

A swarm of emotions swam in his blue eyes—despair, uncertainty, searing desire. He looked dangerous. Rugged. Haunted. Powerful, long fingers coiled in her hair and gave a tender pull, reeling her closer. Her body responded without further encouragement. Tentatively she pressed against his straining erection and undulated her hips back and forth, up and down, side to side, moving purely by instinct...

His head bowed forward, bridging the space of air between them, and his mouth claimed hers in a slow, intense kiss. She welcomed his tongue inside. Rubbed it with her own. His beautiful, husky moan vibrated against her lips and stiffened her spine. He ground against her, his strong body arching toward her own, begging for a deeper connection and respite.

"Isabelle..." That enchanting voice swelled the darkness, surrounding her, gripping her senses with a thousand beckoning fingers. They held her captive—and she readily surrendered her freedom. The sensations from her erotic dream broke into her thoughts; in the recesses of her mind, she heard the refrains of his music, felt it surging through her body in a powerful rush. Her feminine core grew hot and damp, and she felt wetness slipping down her restless thighs.

She tracked her hands over his scarred muscles... listened to the ragged sound of his breaths as they filled her eardrums and mated with her own.

The scars on her thighs burned like so many brands. Fear won out as he tracked his hands over her trembling body and came dangerously close to touching her *there*. She grew immobile in his arms and whispered four shaky words. "Please... it's too much."

Warm lips brushed against her temple. She listened as

Adam's torn breathing turned regular, calming. He released a long sigh and embraced her in the circle of his arms, holding her snugly against his chest. Strong, capable hands trailed up and down her back in reassuring, slow strokes. She felt safe and secure. At peace. And momentarily complete.

"Of course," he whispered against her hairline, his long fingers stroking up and down her back. "This is more than enough. More than I could have ever hoped for."

Indeed, Isabelle thought, harnessing back her tears and tempering her breathing. *You, Adam, are more than I could have ever hoped for.*

Chapter Nineteen

THE FOLLOWING WEEK SOARED BY. Adam had surprised Isabelle with a tray of delicious fruits and a heavenly herbal tea just before the crack of dawn. Relishing the meal together, they'd watched from his bedchamber's window as the sun perched itself in a clear sky, streaking the horizon with brilliant swathes of red and orange.

They'd sat in companionable, comfortable silence—and Isabelle had realized just how much she cherished his company. Really, it was incredible what they could communicate without words. Even the unspoken interactions brought an unparalleled joy to her heart—the way he secured his cloak over her shoulders when she gave a small shudder... how he swept errant curls from her eyes and deftly tucked them behind her ears.

She could feel the gentle, tentative caress of his fingers even now. The scarred pads of his fingertips gliding across her temple... his penetrating gaze hooking into her own... how his breaths often grew shorter in her presence, echoing the beat of her own heart. For a passing moment, as they watched the sun ascend, Isabelle thought he would kiss her. And, *Mon Dieu*, she'd ached for it with every fiber of her being. The sensation, the painful want and desire, nearly stole her breaths away.

After she'd polished off her first helping of tea, she'd turned to Adam and asked to hear a story. "I want to hear more about you. More about your life before Hartville."

Silence had been his initial response. Then as the sky brightened and the clouds parted like a pair of lush opera curtains, he began. Isabelle's eyes had shuttered closed while the deep lull of his voice pulled at her thoughts. Her insides grew heavy, her core dampened; every syllable fluttered across the landscape of her imagination and stoked an inner fire to life.

He recalled the birth of Rosemary, his baby sister; emotion shook his deep voice as he spoke of the love in his mother and father's eyes... the feel of her tiny finger clasped in his palm. He'd lost all of them in an unthinkable tragedy, she knew—one she burned to understand. Yet she held her tongue while her eyes moistened with tears; she couldn't bring the words to her lips... couldn't ask him to recount the painful story of their deaths.

He already relives it in his nightmares. Although he hasn't had an episode for a week...

They spent the rest of the day riding Spirit through the dense forest and along the jagged coastline. Isabelle had never felt so free—and with every meter they traveled, Adam's hardened facade crumbled away, revealing the man underneath. Together, sitting side by side on the outskirts of the forest, they'd watched where the sea and sky coupled as one. The forest, which lurked behind them, soon came to life with night sounds.

They listened to the gentle rush of the sea, which resembled the breaths of a sleeping creature. Isabelle slipped into the fabric of a dream world and allowed nature's beauty to wash over her. They'd picnicked, then flown a small kite; how free she'd felt, her soul unleashed, as if she herself were riding the breeze. Within that moment, as Adam's large body encased her own, her fears had faded away, and her spirit took wing along with the fluttering kite.

Hours later, he clasped her hand as they lay on an enormous smooth rock. He set their untied grips over his heart, and the entire world seemed to fall away. Hardly thinking, she shifted closer to his strong body and rested her cheek on his chest. Her eyes fell shut as he repeatedly swept his fingers through her hair and combed the curls from her face. Then he bowed his head, so the wisps of his breaths tickled her scalp. A soothing, hypnotic humming swelled the growing night. His voice wrapped around her soul with the force of a lasso. She tingled all over, battling the temptation to turn her face those last centimeters and press her lips to his.

She burned to taste him, to mold her body against the hard planes of his chest... to run her palms over his scars and chase the shadows from his eyes—

Without warning, the clouds slashed open. A sudden rain curtained the world around them, drenching Isabelle and Adam to the marrow of their bones. Laughing, the heavy fabric of her cloak plastered to her tingling skin, Isabelle yelped and scrambled off the stone. Cocking a dark brow, Adam stared into the dark sky and shook his head. Isabelle watched in a state of silent awe and appreciation. His raven locks were glued to his temples and the sides of his face, resembling melted drinking chocolate.

"Island weather," he murmured as the rain assaulted them both, mimicking the sound of a thousand echoing heartbeats. "Completely and utterly unpredictable."

"Yes." Isabelle lifted her hands to the heavens and twirled in place. "And I love it." She felt cleansed... as if the disgrace of her former life was being washed away. Here she stood, at the edge of a new path with the dark, enigmatic man at her side behaving as her guiding light.

"Yes, well," Adam drawled, a smile in his voice, "even so, you shall catch your death. And I'm afraid I can't allow that." He moved forward with that mesmerizing, panther-like grace and caught her around the waist. Tossing her over his shoulder as if she were no heavier than a ragdoll, he strode over to Spirit while the rain beat down in unrelenting sheets.

Minutes later, Isabelle felt the stinging bite of the air and rain whip against her face. She clutched Adam's strong torso as Spirit galloped through the dense forest. Their wet bodies moved as one with each thrust. A chill seeped into her bones— one that had nothing to do with the rain and everything to do with her blossoming feelings.

Her heart hammered at a fierce rhythm as she glanced up

at the towering thicket of trees. The moon's glow faintly trickled through the dense wood and bathed her wet cheeks. The chill extended and spread through her veins as the sight of the castle's jutting towers broke through the forest.

Once they reached the castle, Adam leapt off Spirit's back with that awe-inspiring grace, then pulled her down after him. Grasping her hand, he tore inside the stable and led Spirit into her stall.

Listening to the melodic pitter-patter of the rain, Isabelle leaned against the panel, her gaze planted on Adam's solid back. She watched in wonder as he stroked Spirit's velvet muzzle and whispered sweet nothings into her shifting ear. After filling her troughs with hay and fresh water, he turned to Isabelle, and the very air crackled with an unspoken tension. Visibly holding his breath, Adam drew toward her, slow and steady, the moonbeams fluttering across the clashing sides of his face. In a few swift strides, he was upon her, his massive body enclosing her against the firm wooden panels.

"Adam..." she breathed more than whispered, reaching out to cup the marred half of his face. He stepped backward, as if her simple touch had caused him physical pain, and stared at the damp straw flooring beneath his boots.

He shook his downcast head and remained in silence for several moments. Only the driving rain broke the quiet. Isabelle listened to the melody and awaited Adam's next words on bated breath. Moonlight shimmered through the stable's panels and fluttered across his uneasy expression. Desire swam in his brilliant blue eyes—desire and a lifetime of self-doubt. When he at last spoke, his voice was a whisper, and a distinct heartache laced each syllable together.

"Before you came, Sébastien was my only tie to the outside world. I held a deep hatred for everyone—for no one more than myself. But you being here—simply seeing your beautiful face and hearing your voice—it has changed me. *You* have changed me. You have made me better."

Her own request echoed in her mind: *Show me. Become better.*

"Come closer," she whispered, hardly knowing she'd

spoken the words. Adam tentatively stepped forward, eliminating some of the space between them. Beyond the stable, the moon shifted in the sky and caused the light to move away from Adam's face. There he stood, cast in shadows as dark as night, the ragged sound of his breathing coupling with her own. His unique scents filled her nostrils in a compelling drift of pine and winter. Rivulets of water dripped from the dark strands of his hair and tracked down the sides of his face; they resembled the tears he refused to shed.

"You, Isabelle, have reminded me that goodness and beauty still exist in the world." His sheer height cast a shadow over her; his breaths stirred her curls, moving over her skin like a satin ribbon. A ribbon she ached to grab on to and reel him closer with. "I hardly know if I should send you away or bring you... *closer*."

"Closer." Again, Isabelle breathed the word into the darkness. He tugged her closer—much closer—until they stood heartbeat to heartbeat. Warm breaths drifted against her skin as every sinew, every muscle pressed against her.

She was falling in love with him. And she didn't understand how to deal with her conflicting emotions.

"Adam... I am frightened." She sagged against him, welcoming the strong knot of his arms around her waist. Her flesh seemed to catch fire in spite of the cold and the dampness of their bodies. He tentatively rubbed his large, strong hands up and down her back, easing the tension in her muscles. She sighed into his cloak and inhaled his scent, committing this moment to eternal memory.

"Of me? I frighten you?" There was a catch in his voice, a palpable grief to the question. He lifted his hands to her cheeks, inadvertently stroking his knuckles over her breasts on the way up.

Isabelle shook her head and stepped back, needing air between them. She inhaled the scents that flavored the air—the musk of the mare, the crisp night air, the damp twigs, and the dirt that crunched below her feet. "*Non*. I'm not frightened of you. Not any longer." The words clogged her throat, and emotion seized hold of her mind and body. She turned away and knotted both arms around herself. The cold circulated from within. It was inescapable—a brand that would forever taint her memories. "It... it was my fiancé."

And I'm frightened of my feelings for you.

Adam's blue eyes flashed in the darkness. "Dumont." A gentle hand grasped her shoulder and turned her full circle, almost in a graceful dance. He gazed down at her, a spectacular clash of anger and desire flashing in those piercing blue eyes.

She wanted to tell him everything, but the words froze on the edge of her tongue. Adam clasped either side of her face and stepped *closer*. "He shall never come near you again." He paused, allowing the sound of the driving rain to imbue the stable. "I am also afraid, Isabelle. Terrified, even. Ever since I was a boy, I contented myself with a life of solitude. Now, I crave so much more..." His hands were on her again, sliding down her neck in a sensual caress. "You possess an immaculate beauty, Isabelle," he whispered, placing his palm atop her frantic heartbeat, "*here*."

Isabelle shuddered as she sank into his decadent touch. Then she stepped nearer still until their mouths were mere centimeters away, sharing the same breaths. She followed the warm path of his exhales while her mouth tingled for his kiss. "Closer, Adam."

It happened in a blur. Adam's final defense visibly broke. He'd no longer deny himself. She collided into the wooden panels as he thrust her backward in a jarring motion. He was upon her. He extended his arms and propped them on either side of her head, encasing her between sinewy muscles.

She felt his resolve slip away; an all-consuming longing took its place... a molten desire that wouldn't be denied. Those wondrous, blue eyes—eyes that haunted her every dream—glittered in the darkness. His breathing grew strained and irregular, as if caught amid a heated session of lovemaking. It came in erratic pants, sweat beaded across his forehead, and those enticing eyes flashed like an inferno. He battled his passion and fought to drive it away. She could see it etched in every line of his face, could feel it in every tendon, every muscle, every fiber of his body. But over two decades of loneliness and emotional exile won out, and he stood defeated.

Adam half-pinned her against the panels. She felt him grow taut with his pent-up desire. His lips seized her throat's pulse point. His tongue joined in the dance, teasing her, sweeping up and down her throat...

Isabelle's thoughts trailed. She fantasized about a rather scandalous book she'd once gotten her hands on—Polidori's *Vampyre*—the notorious tale of a lord who delighted in seducing maidens and drinking their lifeblood from their very necks. She gasped aloud, weak at the knees, shamelessly leaning against the wall for support. His lips slid up her neck, pausing only to tease her thundering pulse. She squirmed against him, hissing between clenched teeth, the melodic sound of the rain flooding her ears. Her hands sank into his damp hair and drove through the thick mass.

Carefully she took his face in her palms. The left side felt bumpy and ragged under her hand, the right side smooth and warm. A hint of stubble prickled her palm and fingers. Expelling a breath as her heart beat erratically, she brought her mouth against his and molded their lips together. Deliberately. Softly. She poured all her longing, all her loneliness, into the intimate movement. The kiss began as a featherlight caress, a whisper of a butterfly's wing, that left her throbbing for more.

Much more.

As if in answer to her silent plea, Adam tilted his head and opened his mouth to her, welcoming her inside with a rugged groan that filled the stable and mated with the rain. He uttered incoherent words into her mouth, and Isabelle knew they were endearments.

She felt his desperation echo inside her; it set fire to her hands and sensual thoughts. Every bit of her burned. Ached. She yearned to strip away his cloak and run her hands over his muscles, to feel the weight of his thick locks sliding through her fingers...

Her trembling palms slid from his hair and down his back while their mouths worked in perfect unison, the kiss growing more desperate. More commanding. He pressed her firmly against the panels, cupped her backside, and lifted her in midair a few centimeters. His manhood jutted against her belly, its hardness easily felt through the thick layers of damp clothing.

Isabelle's fears slowly trickled back. She fought to focus on the moment, on the enticing feel of Adam's body moving against her own, how his hands securely held her in place...

"No, Isabelle," he finally said in a hoarse whisper, sounding like he was in physical pain. Yet she knew he only felt pleasure. He lowered her onto the ground, and her shoes touched the straw with a muffled sound. "Not here, not like this. Not in the cold dark. You deserve more. You deserve better... to know everything first. In so many ways, I'm still just a stranger..." Resting his forehead against hers, Adam lifted her hand and pressed a kiss to the center of her palm. Her skin tingled as she itched to slide her palms under his cloak and down the hardness of his chest. "Tomorrow night... after I've shown you everything."

The silent plea shone in his gaze, laced her every touch, his every word.

Love me for me. Nothing more, and nothing less.

THE NEXT DAY, Adam didn't touch Isabelle again—much to her disappointment—and his words from the previous evening repeatedly rang in her mind.

Tomorrow night... after I've shown you everything.

As nighttime fell upon the castle, they devoured a supper of vegetables and fresh caught rabbit while Isabelle read to Adam beside the roaring hearth. Afterward, they immersed themselves in deep conversation. They fought. They debated. They discussed a variety of topics—from philosophy to religion to the deep and deadly waters of politics. While they often clashed on the subtleties, Isabelle discovered their core values remained one and the same.

They shared their passion for literature and poetry and

challenged each other at chess over glasses of dark wine. All the while, Stranger lay between their two chairs and contently slept. Then she and Adam bickered some more as an old married couple might. Indeed, Adam's short fuse and Isabelle's fiery spirit ignited in a spectacular inferno. An inferno they both thoroughly enjoyed, though neither Isabelle nor Adam admitted such a thing. After supper and their verbal battle, a silence stretched between them, and they'd naturally turned to a different subject, like jumping to a new rock when hopping across a tumultuous river.

"Meet me in the ballroom in an hour," he said hours later, tracing a fingertip across her chin. "Now go and change, *ma belle*."

Upon returning to her chamber, the gown she'd discovered sprawled over the bed had nearly stolen her breath away. Three different layers composed the dress: a bonded bodice of blue silk damask, an ivory silk faille skirt, and a matching damask overskirt. Isabelle reverently ran her fingertips over the cornflower blue material and fine silk detail. She lifted it from the mattress with shaking hands, held it up to her body, and then stepped in front of the large gold-gilded mirror, which Adam had placed in her chamber just nights ago.

Smoothing the material over her breasts and torso, a smile grew on her lips as she admired her reflection. The ball gown was several centimeters too short—her ankles would show quite scandalously, no doubt of it—yet she'd never beheld a more beautiful garment. Breathless and feeling a bit fuzzy from the wine, she turned toward her vanity, where she discovered a sparkling tiara and a pair of satin gloves.

Isabelle entered the ballroom at precisely eight o'clock. Moonlight, bone white and lustrous, threaded through the grand windows like prying fingers. The illumination set the medallion flooring aglow. Columns lined the oval-shaped room and graced a domed ceiling. A handsome grandfather clock towered in the corner, ticking off the seconds with a pulsating drone. Candelabras reached around the edge of the circular room and lurked like quiet sentries. Their wavering candles mated with the moonbeams and threw golden patches across the intricate marble floor.

Incredible silence surrounded Isabelle, pressed into her very being, as she slipped into the heart of the ballroom. She could almost hear the gay whispers of ladies and the delicate swishing of their lace fans. She smelled the sweet scents of their exotic perfumes and could hear the distant, ghostly echo of a pianoforte. And she knew that, despite the castle's neglected state, it had once been a place of unrivaled beauty and glamour.

Much like Adam himself.

Isabelle spun around full circle, her mind transporting to a past era that brimmed with elegance and luxury. She felt the darkly romantic pull of the castle and its numberless mysteries... felt herself falling in love with its shadows and secrets. Dust motes danced in the shafts of moonbeams and wavering candles. Faintly she hummed beneath her breath, testing the acoustics in the spacious room. Her voice carried, swirling around her in an echoing cyclone. Then she came to a standstill as a soft touch grazed her bare shoulder. Large, silk-clad hands rotated her body with a startling gentleness. A breath escaped her lips as she drank in Adam's proud, towering form. Her mind slipped back to the previous day and night—to their sensual kiss in the stables.

A navy, double-breasted coat hugged the muscular curves of his body, offset by shimmering golden buttons. They looked like small glowing suns floating against a sky of rustic blue.

He resembled a prince. Proud. Formidable. In full command of everything and everyone in the room. Even a hint arrogant. Her heart hammered, threatening to burst. Suddenly she felt like she'd been thrust into a world of magic and romantic hushed secrets. *The scars look out of place on his smirking features,* she mused with a pang of sadness. And dressed in a cascade of cornflower damask and lace, the sparkling tiara half-buried in her hair, she felt like a princess.

Then it began.

Adam took a deft step backward, sank into a shallow bow, and outstretched his gloved hand. Isabelle grasped her flowing skirts and dipped into a curtsy, her heart madly pitter-pattering. Feeling like a young girl during her first ball, she accepted the invitation and abandoned her silk-encased palm in his own. Strength surged through his fingers, sending chords of awareness thrumming through her body.

Am I dreaming? If so, then let me sleep forever.

A muscled arm snaked around her torso and tugged her intimately close. Everything seemed to fade away while the heat of their bodies mingled as one. Her heart fluttered against her ribs as she sought the depths of his eyes. At this range, flicks of gold contrasted against his sky-blue irises. Much of the sadness seemed to have vanished, leaving an almost boyish delight in its wake. The right side of his face was devastatingly handsome, his hair so black it drank the twinkling candles.

Keeping her body pressed to his own, he swung her into the scandalous waltz dance. Her small fingers curled around his bicep as he lifted the other hand in midair. He swept her across the smooth marble floor, twirling her body, his large hand securely on the center of her back, his footwork extravagant and exact. Cords of muscle bunched and slid beneath her fingers, and light from the candelabras flashed over the mismatched sides of his face.

Isabelle felt clumsy—as if she had sprouted two left feet. She'd spent her youth traveling the countryside and coastline with Papa—not blushing behind a lace fan or dancing in lavish ballrooms. Adam, however, danced with a haunting grace; his movements executed with a fine, cultured polish. *He clearly hadn't been raised in the back of a wagon*, she mused. Prince-like and regal, he'd danced this dance many times before; maybe it had been in another place and another life, but his confident, masterful steps gave the truth away.

Isabelle struggled to keep up with his graceful strides, though she knew she was making a fool of herself. She stumbled as Adam swept her into an unexpected twirl again; he reeled her back to his side, so they stood intimately close, then chuckled in her ear with a pirate's boldness. The decadent sound rippled through her veins and mingled with the wine. His lips pressed against the shell of her ear, and the whisper of his warm breaths sent chills thrumming down her backbone.

I am falling for him—falling fast and hard.

Indeed. She'd been falling for him for some time.

"You're a dreadful dancer," he murmured against her ear. Paired with the husky baritone of his voice, the insult sounded rather like an endearment.

Regardless, she returned the blight with a swift and playful vengeance. "Perhaps my partner is to blame."

She cocked her head back and captured his bright gaze. He offered no retort aside from the arch in his thick brow.

Her face reached the height of his shoulder and not a centimeter more. She curled her head against the security of his chest and inhaled his essence with a reverent breath. A tangle of emotions welled in her gut, blurring everything but the moment... everything but the exquisite feel of Adam holding her. As he swept her across the smooth marble floor, the world whirled by in a dreamlike mosaic.

She felt like she'd fallen into one of her fairy tales.

"Oh, Adam... I never want this moment to end," she heard herself whisper against his coat.

"It doesn't have to."

Adam shifted back and forth in a tantalizing rocking motion, slow dancing to a melody only he could hear. As she melted into his embrace, the candelabras crackled and seductively flashed, accompanying each of their steps. Desperate to learn the feel of him free from barriers, she marveled at hard contours of his skin below the coat. Then he bowed his chin and hummed a beautiful tune against her forehead. It sounded achingly sweet, like a tender lullaby from the depths of a dream world. The force of his vocals resonated deep inside her, massaging Isabelle's body with delicious caresses. Her heart resembled a drum—and she trembled in time with its beat. That immaculate baritone stoked her imagination, igniting an inferno deep within her soul.

Closing her eyes, she rubbed her cheek against his coat's rugged material and sparkling buttons, abandoning herself to his rhythmic sways and husky baritone. Drawing her into its sultry, comforting depths, his voice surrounded her like liquid velvet. With increasing pressure, his palm swept up the length of her back, down and up, tickling her spine with each soothing movement. Heated breaths wafted against her hairline, stirring the curls about her shoulders. His every gesture felt numbingly gentle, executed with a startling grace. Isabelle had to remind herself to breathe, lest she faint from the pleasure of it all.

Emotion claimed the best of her. Isabelle exhaled a shaky breath as tears singed the corners of her eyes.

They danced like that for close to an hour, moving in perfect unison to the calming melody of Adam's voice, the slick medallion floor sliding beneath their feet like some magical carpet. The marble ground reflected their waltzing images with the ease of a looking glass.

Indeed, everything felt dreamlike. Peaceful. Beautiful.

A rare contentment—a true happiness—swelled inside her and drew the tears from her eyes. Something stirred in her heart... an emotion that felt remarkably like true love.

The grandfather clock struck the new hour and pulled Adam from the magic floating between them. He pressed his lips against her hairline, whispering the words against her flushed skin, "Do you trust me, Isabelle?" She nodded, unable to find her voice. "Good. Then follow me."

ADAM SLIPPED INTO the darkness of his East Tower as he'd done for twenty-five years. For the first time, however, he was no longer alone.

Isabelle stood beside him, her small, pale hand clasped in his own. Her skin felt soft, supple, reassuring. Shafts of moonlight twisted through the sweeping windows and set her wonder-struck expression aglow. His heart beat a manic staccato; never had he beheld such beauty, such gentleness, such goodness—and his soul burned with affection for her. The blue silks of her gown appeared to drink in the moonbeams, and the glittering tiara caught fire. Tonight, she resembled a flesh-and-blood princess. And how he ached to worship every part of her body. He watched, transfixed, as a memory of his mother in that same gown materialized and caused a shudder to tear through his body.

Isabelle had changed everything; she'd pulled him from the unquiet waters of his past and resurrected his belief in humanity. In goodness and love. Second chances and the beauty of hope.

Adam held tighter to her delicate hand, his thoughts reliving the last few hours again and again.

He hesitantly surveyed his East Tower. A scene of total devastation burned his eyes and severed his trancelike state. Dark reality surrounded him, filling his vision. Broken furniture and torn tapestries littered every corner; a coat of dust cloaked the hulking pieces like ashes from a past life. His thoughts traveled back to that night so long before, when he'd frightened Isabelle half to death.

How far I've come since then... and all because of her.

Adam exhaled a long breath and stared at the vaulted ceiling looming overhead. Dust motes drifted through the moon's iridescent light. From this perspective, they resembled small fairies fluttering amid a sea of black. A howling wind swept through the cracks in the castle's walls, filling the room with a bone-chilling draft.

Isabelle's hand slipped free of his own; she hugged her body while her teeth audibly chattered. Adam's reaction was automatic. He removed the coat from his shoulders and swept the material over her body. The fabric appeared to swallow her whole. It was more than several sizes too large, and the bottom of the coat fell past her slender knees. She clutched the material with her gloved hand, sealing it against the castle's drafts.

A small smile lit her face. Every fiber of his being softened at the vision. She gazed at him from beneath a lush curtain of lashes, her lips parted in imminent speech, the diamond-studded tiara sparkling like crystallized tears. Before she could utter a word, however, he wheeled in front of her body and pressed a finger to her mouth. Her lips felt softer than rose petals, and he burned to devour their honeyed taste. He inhaled a steadying breath and willed himself to quit shaking like a damn fool.

Adam paused, wandered farther inside the circular room. "Come *closer*... I want you to see. I want you to know..." He observed Isabelle from the corner of his eye, watching as she froze in front of a hanging portrait. The dusty frame was askew, and a deep dent marred the image. She stole a glance at Adam, then gently righted the tilted frame.

The painting depicted a bright-eyed adolescent of eleven years.

The boy he'd once been.

"Is... is this you?"

Adam hesitated. Then he stepped forward until he stood behind her. "It was. Many years ago."

Isabelle's hand trembled in midair as her two silk-clad fingers swept over the portrait; Adam could almost feel that touch upon his skin. He observed her in stony silence, watching as she shook her head and her eyes glinted with unshed tears.

The sight unnerved him, even filled him with a tinge of anger. He wanted nothing of her pity.

I want only her love, he realized in the unquietness of his own mind. *Mon Dieu, how I love her. Look around yourself, you fool: You're nothing more than a beast. A beast who's drowning in the waters of a past life...*

Adam stormed away from the portrait and shoved open the pair of French doors, which led to the circular balcony. The crisp night air wafted against his face and swelled his lungs.

"You're the crown prince," she breathlessly said, following him onto the balcony, half speaking to herself. "A part of me already knew. You're the son of King and Queen Delacroix. The revolt—the siege, the fire... you *survived*."

"That's questionable, I'm afraid. I'm not the boy in that portrait. Not any longer."

"But you are, Adam. I saw that boy—that man—in the ballroom. I danced with him, felt as he held me close and embraced me against his heart."

Adam released a long-suffering sigh and stared at the enormous moon. "When you first came here, and I saw you with your father... saw your connection, how close you were...

it tore at me. A part of me yearned to rip you two apart, to sentence you to the same fate I've known for twenty-five years. Your father died that night because of my jealousy and resentment."

"No, Adam, you mustn't say that. I—"

"I should have never kept you here with me. Not after you lost your father. I never fulfilled my end of the bargain. A decent man would have admitted that fact."

"But, Adam. I know—"

"You know nothing," he murmured, standing at the edge of the balcony, his gloved hands resting on the banister. "I am not a good man. I wasn't a good child, a good son... a good brother. I watched as traitors, servants whom I believed were my friends, massacred my entire family. I watched—and I lived." Adam spread his arms wide, gesturing to the contents of the East Tower. "Don't you see, Isabelle? This is my reminder, my constant purgatory. This pain... it's all I have left of them."

Isabelle stood in between the two French doors. The tears that had glazed her eyes minutes ago now streamed down her snow-white cheeks. They glistened in the moonlight, and Adam fought the urge to wipe them away and draw her against his chest. "I refuse to sentence you to my despair any longer." He turned away again, unable to bear the sight of her sorrow. He looked down at the sweeping gardens and swaying roses. Overhead, the clouds opened without warning, and a light drizzle curtained the world. "I care for you too much. I love you, Isabelle. More than anything in this world. And so I must let you go."

HER HEART CLOSE TO BURSTING, Isabelle slipped forward as his beautiful words washed over her.

I love you, Isabelle. More than anything in this world...

Half in a trance, she moved past the French doors and

near the edge of the balcony. Standing beside Adam's silent and still form, her breath hitched at the sight of the lush gardens below. She gently laid her hand over his own and entwined their fingers.

"Yes... I admit you were cruel and hostile when my papa and I first came here. I could see the hatred in your eyes, hear it in your voice. But you changed when I lost everything that mattered. Your true spirit emerged. Your gentleness and compassion. You were there for me, Adam, when I had no one else." She squeezed his fingers to help emphasize her declaration. "Now listen to me: I've known real monsters. You are not a bad person. You must believe that. But you've had bad things happen to you. As have I..." She hesitated and inhaled a breath for courage. "I haven't been completely honest. When I stumbled upon your castle, I was running."

"From what?" Adam's voice was a cropped whisper, nearly swept away by the wind and puttering rain.

"I know you saw the ring," she said, her words slow and cautious. "You must have. I... I was engaged to Vicomte Dumont. Still am, I suppose."

Isabelle tore her gaze from the gardens and locked on to Adam's stunning blue eyes. She grasped his scarred hand tighter still, then drew his knuckles against her lips. He edged closer until their bodies nearly touched. His warmth enveloped her, wrapped around her soul, and solidified her affection for him. Her *love*. "Listen, Adam... Raphael Dumont—he is a monster. A true monster."

"He assaulted you. Molested you." Rage laced Adam's words together. He visibly shook from his fury, and a terrifying anger flamed in his eyes. She felt more than a little startled—and *protected*.

"As I said, Raphael is a real monster. Someone to fear. Someone who deserves to live alone and in shadow. Not you, Adam Delacroix," she whispered, drawing her mouth against his own. "Please... make me not afraid any longer..."

The air shifted.

He grasped her waist, turned her full circle, and pushed her body against the stone banister. The rush of movement caused his coat to fall from her shoulders and onto the ground. Between soul-deep kisses, he murmured into her mouth, "I want to. I burn for you... more than anything. But I don't know if I can."

She paused, digesting his words, relishing the feel of his hands in her hair, on her hips, riding over her breasts. "Have... have you been with a woman before?" He stiffened, and his hands momentarily stilled in midair. The heat from his gloves caressed her bare shoulders and made her skin tingle for his touches. "Forgive me. I should not have—"

"Don't—no, you have every right." Adam sighed. His tentative hands returned to her skin, those large palms cupping each of her cheeks. Smooth, satiny silk brushed across her flesh and drew a shudder from her chest. His heated stare joined with hers, whispering a thousand unspoken secrets. "As you can see, I am not a handsome man. I haven't been handsome since I was an adolescent."

Isabelle swallowed the lump in her throat. Thinking of the East Tower's portraits, she reached out and gently caressed the scarred half of his face. Adam dipped into her touch as his eyes shuttered closed. "But you are, Adam. You are to me. I need you to believe that... to believe in yourself again." Her hand slid from his cheek and came to rest on the center of his chest. His heart thumped against her palm, strong and sure.

"I am trying, *ma belle*. I am trying."

Isabelle felt a smile grow on her lips. Her hand glided up his chest... over his throat, where she grasped his neck and pulled him *closer*.

His throat worked beneath her searching fingers, and she felt a sharp intake of breath pass his lips.

"You don't even realize your own allure, do you? The enticing beauty of your voice... the wondrous, seductive way you move..." Her hand continued its ascent, slipping through his dark, thick hair... descending back down his neck, over the curve of his shoulder and arm. She grasped his hand in her own, entwining their gloved fingers. "Many nights, I've laid awake, restless and aching... At the time, I didn't know what I craved. Now I know. I crave *you*."

Isabelle's words faltered while a burning flush crept across her cheeks. Adam responded with his touch. He seized either side of her body and hurled her forward.

Their lips collided once more and resumed that erotic, age-old dance. She gasped inside his mouth, and he chased the sound with his tongue, filling her with slick, promising heat.

"Wait, Isabelle," Adam choked out. "Let me tell you everything."

ADAM'S VOICE CUT OFF MID-SENTENCE. Emotion constricted his throat, making it difficult to speak, to think, to draw breath. How he ached to no longer hide within himself... to no longer live alone and ruled by the shadows of his past. He'd known this moment would come. But was he ready?

"Your past doesn't frighten me. Please... I want to fight it *with* you."

Isabelle's gentle words and caresses empowered him. Her grip on his hand was a simple gesture, though infinitely powerful. The comfort and acceptance she offered sent his heart racing. And how beautiful she looked, the moonlight kissing her curls, the tiara glinting within the night.

Adam drew on her strength.

I am ready.

Seated beside her on a long stone bench, he tensed, tightened his hold on her hand, and squeezed both eyes shut. Her exquisite touch counterbalanced the pain in his heart. She was his anchor, his light, his hope.

The memories blazed behind his eyes. He swallowed and focused on Isabelle's reassuring caresses, the music of the falling rain, the caress of the moonbeams, and the sound of the wind's low hum. Silk gloves wrapped her slender hands, yet the heat of her skin radiated just the same. Promising warmth seeped through the luscious material and inflamed his soul. Long fingers caressed his flesh, drawing invisible shapes along his knuckles. He felt himself grow stronger from her touch, felt the icy barrier he'd forged around his heart thaw and melt away. With a deep inhale, he opened his eyes and forced the words.

He revealed everything over the next hour—waking to the sound of the cannons, sneaking through the castle's halls as rebels stormed his home, his vain attempt to save his baby sister... witnessing his mother and father's executions...

Everything.

Isabelle drew off his gloves, then removed her own pair. With each word, she wept silent tears, clasped his scarred hands, and encouraged him with sensitive touches and warm embraces.

He brushed a fallen curl away. His fingertips lingered against her skin for several weightless moments. The need to consume her was almost too great; it took every gram of his restraint not to sweep her into his arms and kiss her senseless. Instead, he leaned forward, reached out, and caressed her silver cross. The metal felt cool beneath his touch as it drank in the shifting moonbeams.

He lifted his gaze and studied her exquisite, heart-shaped face. Shafts of moonlight bathed her cheeks, and a subtle smile tugged at those rosebud lips. Loose curls cushioned her face, awarding her with an ethereal quality. She pressed their palms together so their pulses united; his callused hand was much larger than hers, and when he curled his fingers they covered her own completely.

Heaving a deep sigh, he pulled his other hand away from the cross and toyed with his signet ring. "If you have changed your mind—if you want to leave after everything I've—"

"Leave? Change my mind?" She lifted her hands and cupped his face. Stroking his cheeks, her velvety brown eyes bearing into his own, she said, "Everything you've told me only solidifies my love for you. You are the bravest... the most caring, the strongest *man* I've ever known." A small, teasing smile quirked her lips. "Well, second only to my father."

"Naturally, *ma belle.*"

Her smile grew. She scooted forward and drew him into a

searing kiss.

Breathing the words inside his mouth, tears running down her cheeks, she went on, "This is my home now. I love you, Prince Adam Delacroix—heart, body, and soul. Wherever you go, that is my home."

Chapter Twenty

ADAM FELT LIKE he was floating through a beautiful, lucid dream. Isabelle's hand rested in his own, her slender fingers entwining with his in a poignant touch. He glanced down at her hand, admiring how it fit so perfectly in his much larger one. Indeed, he couldn't help but feel like she'd been created for him—a flawless foil to his darkness. He held tighter to her palm and fingers, overwhelmed with emotion—afraid this was nothing more than a dream and he'd soon awake.

She followed him down the East Tower's winding stairwell, a small smile tugging at her lips. He clasped a lantern in midair, casting a ring of light that punctured the castle's endless black belly.

They seemed to travel for a lifetime, and the dark halls and rooms drifted by without his notice. He was completely transfixed. Breathless. Caught in a powerful enchantment. He couldn't tear his eyes away from Isabelle; her beauty consumed him, swam through his very veins. She was breathtaking, a true flesh-and-blood angel. His passion intensified at the way the diamond tiara drank in the moonbeams and came to life with a brilliant sparkle. The billowing, cornflower silks of her gown trailed across the dark floor; the hem caressed the stones like a lover's embrace and emitted a soft swishing noise. Isabelle's rich, velvety gaze remained fixed on his face with each step, and an enticing blush brightened her cheeks.

Anxiety and anticipation clamored inside him, and his gut quivered. Yet on the outside, he held himself up with a confidence he didn't feel.

Finally he hesitated outside his bedchamber and turned to Isabelle. The lantern bathed her features in a warm light and underlined the riot of emotions in her eyes. She was as nervous as he was; he saw it in her gaze, felt it in her trembling fingertips and the ragged wafts of her breaths.

"Isabelle... you can still change your mind. Because once we enter my chamber, once we cross that threshold, I fear I won't be able to let you go again."

"Good," she replied without hesitation, drawing nearer, her breath a soft breeze against his face. Willing his heart to quit pounding, he inhaled the intoxicating aromas of her hair and skin, allowing her essence to wash over him, to fill his soul and help satiate his hunger. To cleanse him. "I don't want you to let me go. I want you to bring me *closer*." She edged nearer still; light from the lantern shifted against the peeling damask wallcovering as his hand shook in midair. *Get a hold of yourself. You're a grown man.* "And I've never felt so free," she went on, her voice a sensual and heartfelt waterfall that he felt against his cheeks, "not since I was a young girl traveling the countryside with my father. You are my freedom, Adam."

"And you are mine. I'd give you the whole world, *ma belle*, if only such a gift were in my power."

A wry smile curved her rosebud lips. "The whole world had laid at my feet—or at least its superficialities." Those beautiful eyes darkened, and she seemed to peer inward. Silently she shook her head and seized his gaze again. Her fingertips clasped either side of his face. Adam's stare swept over the smattering of freckles across her nose and the long wings of her dark lashes. "I don't desire the whole world. I don't care about pretty dresses, glittering jewels, or fancy balls. I've never wanted any of that. Just true love. Just you. Just *us*."

True love.

Heat coiled in his body and settled down below. She swept past him, a flush brightening her cheeks as she opened the door to his private chamber. Adam placed the lantern on his mirrorless vanity. He lit a branch of candles, imbuing the room with a soft, alluring glow. Moonbeams slanted through his window, mating with the candlelight and casting golden rings in the chamber. Together, they bathed Isabelle's dark curls and the dress's cornflower silks like a diva's spotlight.

Adam stepped toward her, his feet moving of their own accord, the cloak swishing around his ankles. He gently laid his hand upon her shoulder and exhaled a taut breath. She softened beneath his touch as her eyes fixed on the formidable bed lurking before them. Its four posts reached into the darkness with the force of groping arms. Dust motes glided in midair, the intimate candlelight transforming the debris into twinkling fairies.

"You showed me kindness," she whispered, her stare flitting across his chamber—the carved and mirrorless vanity, the crimson coverlet, the mahogany writing desk and a pile of books of every kind. Her eyes skimmed over their aged spines and faded covers with appreciation. "You cared for me in my hour of darkness, in this very room..." Her words trailed off. Mutely she shook her head, then turned her gaze back to his own. "And I called you a monster. I... I don't know if I can ever forgive myself."

Adam couldn't suppress his chuckle. He wheeled behind her without thought, molding his much larger body to her warm curves. The lace and satins of her dress fluttered enticingly against him and audibly rustled. One of his hands entwined in her long hair; the other hand carefully removed the tiara. He slipped it free of those luscious locks, then placed it on the vanity. His heart in his throat, he smoothed a lush section of hair over one shoulder, watching as the spirals grazed her back in a delectable chocolate waterfall. He idly combed his fingers through the curls, relishing how they slipped through them like fresh-spun silk.

"I was precisely that. A monster. A beast. I had no right to keep you here with me or to demand your freedom. I've done things I don't expect forgiveness for, Isabelle. But being with you... It makes me yearn to be a greater man."

Isabelle smiled, rotating in his arms. He dipped into her

tentative, healing touch as she trailed her fingertips over the blemished side of his face. He watched in silent reverence while tears formed in the corners of her eyes, listened as her voice quavered with empathy and compassion.

Compassion for him.

"And who has been here for you in your hours of darkness?"

Sébastien came to mind. He had been his sole link to the outside world—maybe even a companion. But he hadn't given Adam what he truly needed, the thing he'd craved for so many years with every beat of his heart.

"You have been here for me," he finally replied. His gaze darted to the tiara, whose diamonds glittered like stars within the dim chamber. His heart racing again, he brought his knuckles against her cheek in a shy caress and traced the curve of her chin.

Their stares connected with a force that flattened him.

Adam couldn't move. He could barely draw breaths. Held captive by the enchantment of her hazel eyes, he was powerless, overwhelmed with emotion and mounting anticipation. Quite suddenly, he felt like a green lad—the wide-eyed, ignorant prince he'd once been. His heart banged against his ribs and nerves swelled his belly; it felt like a swarm of butterflies had been released and were tickling his stomach with their lacy wings.

As if she could read his thoughts, an endearing blush rose on Isabelle's cheeks. Demurely she lowered her gaze and stared at the intricate parquet flooring. They were both out of their element.

But when Adam met her eyes again, his anxieties melted away. A soul-searing passion took their place, infusing his mind and body with a new confidence.

This was his element. Isabelle Rose *was* his element.

Silence took command. Adam dared not even breathe as he anticipated her next move. Her tiny, slender hand slid down his neck and grabbed his bicep. She drew him toward the canopied bed; her steps took on a renewed purpose, her eyes set aglow with a light he'd never witnessed before.

Ever so carefully, she guided him onto the mattress as a hesitant smile spread across her lips. "Let me be here for you now, *tonight*." Her hands rested on either side of his face, and she drew him into a drugging, hypnotic kiss. Her fingers shook against his skin, and her entire body grew stiff. Adam allowed primal instinct to take command. His hands lifted from the mattress and landed on the curves of her hips.

The voluptuous, thick folds of the gown swished against his palm, whooshing through his fingers and rustling in the hushed din. He unconsciously stroked the fine materials, felt as the damask details and laces slid under his palms. He filled her sweet mouth with his tongue, exploring the heat and gently nipping at her bottom lip. His hands moved on their own, sliding down her hips and around her body to rest on the curve of her backside. He reeled her closer still, urging her warmth flush against his hardening body.

He'd never felt more alive, more like a flesh-and-blood man.

"Are you still frightened?" he asked in a hoarse voice, suggestively trailing his fingers up and down her slim back, feeling as the silk fabric glided beneath his restless palms. "Does this frighten you?" He knew she'd suffered great pain and degradation at the vicomte's hands; he prayed she was ready— but he'd sooner wait an entire lifetime before causing her any more discomfort.

"No. Not when it's your hands," she said, drawing him into another soul-searing kiss. She countered the movements of his lips, mouth, and tongue, engaging him in an erotic waltz, a delectable feast of the senses that sent his mind and heart reeling with pleasure. "Not when it's your lips, your gentle touches... your beautiful voice in my ear."

I don't know what I'm doing...

And so he allowed a primitive instinct to guide him; his adoration and passion for Isabelle steered his hands and mouth, directing his every move, his every thought. He enclosed her face with his palms, tipped his head, and parted her soft lips again. She tasted sweeter than honey from the comb. His tongue dipped inside her mouth and stole a sensual whimper from the depths of her throat.

Gently he suckled on her bottom lip and dipped past the wet seam. He searched the intimate cavern of her mouth and ran his tongue over her smooth teeth and lips swollen from his kisses. "Not when it's *you*, my Adam," she breathed between their deep kisses, her voice growing throatier with each passing second.

They were both starved, feasting off each other with equal fervor.

Adam slipped a single fingertip along the length of her spine—up, up, up—all the way to the base of her neck. His palm coiled around the delicate shaft while her mouth moved in sync with his own. She moaned and rocked her hips against him, returning that age-old dance with a heated intensity.

His heart gave a quick somersault, spun by the sweet sounds that fluttered from her throat and swelled the room. The sputtering candles and whistling wind added to the ambience and heightened his senses.

Seconds transformed into minutes, and both Adam and Isabelle were left entirely spent and breathless.

Her cheekbones turned rosy while her lips darkened to a sensuous red. Defeated and at her mercy, he curved his neck until their foreheads joined together in a tentative touch.

Resting his temple against her own, his ragged breaths vibrating his entire body, he murmured, "This is new for me, too." He was so lost in Isabelle—he barely perceived his own whisper. "Together, we shall learn. Together…"

Anticipation burned through him, a need such as he had never known. He feared this was all a dream—one he sorely didn't want to end.

"Together…" Isabelle echoed the word, almost in a trance. Then her small, fair hands rose from her sides to cup his face. "Always together…"

EVERYTHING SHIFTED. Isabelle felt as Adam's resolve slipped away; all-consuming longing replaced it... a molten desire that would not be denied.

The way he looked at her, his stare overflowing with desire and appreciation... it set something wild and fearless free inside.

Adam shot forward, embraced her waist, and crushed her body to his own in a possessive, unyielding grasp. The lush fabrics of her dress bunched between their bodies and ruptured the ambience with a swishing noise. She gasped aloud as a great whoosh of air vacated her lungs at the sudden impact. His lips descended on her throat in a movement he seemed unable to control. His tongue teased her pulse, swept up and down her throbbing throat, and traced the fine architecture of her collarbone. Meanwhile, his masterful hands worked the ties of her dress with a new urgency.

Cool air nipped at her nape and back as he parted the back of her dress. The uneven texture of his lips ground against her flesh. She attempted to move away a centimeter or two—but his grasp possessively tightened... Strong, marred hands slid up and down her back and clasped her in a protective embrace.

"I shall never hurt you, Isabelle," he murmured between kisses. "I would sooner hurt myself."

Her neck grew limp, and her eyes drew shut in ecstasy. His delectable scents—pine and winter—swirled in the air and washed over her senses.

"I know, Adam Delacroix. I trust you..." Her voice sounded distant, like her soul had detached from her body and loomed several kilometers away.

Cool fingers traced her jaw, soothing, stroking, and turning her toward his lips. She shuddered as he moved his hot mouth down the column of her throat and teased her pulse with his tongue.

"Keep speaking, Adam," she moaned, her words laced with a mounting desire. "Your voice is an instrument of pleasure."

His husky vocals resonated against her flushed skin as he spoke, setting fire to her very soul. "You have opened my eyes. For so long, I had closed them to the world, shutting myself inside an impenetrable prison. A prison that was built from guilt and despair..." His lips moved over her covered chest, dampening the fine damask fabric to her flushed skin. His tongue darted out from his lips and traced over her veiled nipple. She felt hot, her breasts heavy and aching. "You tore down those walls, Isabelle... allowed me to see again... allowed me to feel... You are my light, my love, my life."

Suddenly she wanted this man more than she'd ever wanted anything else. She wanted his body, his spirit, his healing touches, and reassuring words. She wanted his playful side, his transitory smile, and those skillful musician's hands.

He pushed the dress down her body in an urgent movement; it fell to her feet, landing around her ankles in a cloud of billowed silk and lace. Adam's breaths shortened while his eyes roamed over her chemise—the final barrier that shielded her. Desire and an unmasked longing deepened his penetrating stare. She felt his passion echo inside her.

Carefully she stepped out from the dress's fabric and worked on his coat buttons. Frantically she slid them through the eyeholes, her fingers trembling in midair. The buttons clashed and sparkled against the navy fabric as the candlelight set them aglow.

Her breaths coming fast and hard, she brushed the handsome material aside and urged it from his broad shoulders. It joined her gown on the floor, forming an ever-growing heap of garments. His crème-colored shirtsleeves came next; she swished the silky fabric aside, watching as the muscles of his throat contracted and grew taut. She leaned forward and pressed her lips to his throat, relishing the feel of his thundering pulse against her lips. Then she moved back again and drank her fill.

Her breath hitched at the sight of his muscular, burned torso. His body wielded a raw, corded strength. The intricate valleys and puckered, leather-like flesh hit her hard. She inhaled a steadying breath before pressing her lips against a raised ridge—making her love unmistakable. His heart thundered below her mouth, strong and sure. When she gazed up at him, his eyes shimmered with a storm of unshed tears.

"To think you have suffered so..." Emotions constricted her words into silence.

He reached out and cupped her cheek, stroking her skin with his thumb and forefinger in a mesmerizing touch. "Being here with you, Isabelle... It feels like everything in my life has led to this moment—to you. All of my losses and heartaches. Everything. They have all shown me you—the light of my life. And for that, I can regret nothing."

My beautiful, dear Adam. My prince...

Isabelle's eyes misted over with shared tears. She tried to speak—but emotion constricted the words and dried her throat. She silently lifted her head, aligning it with his own, and set her palm on the center of his scarred chest. She caressed his skin, feeling the web of elevated ridges and irregular flesh below her palm. A shudder raked through his body and vibrated against her fingertips as she traced his sternum.

He swooped forward and claimed her mouth in a sweltering kiss. Passion made up for all inexperience. His hands cupped either side of her face, the rough skin of his palms tickling her neck and chin in an invigorating caress.

Their mouths momentarily broke apart. She felt the hot rush of his breaths against her neck. Candlelight illuminating his scarred arms and torso, he reached forward and took her hand, enveloping it completely. Time seemed to stand still. Her heart thundered as she felt herself falling backward. The sensation left her breathless. She seemed to float through time and space, as if she were disconnected from her body and only her spirit remained.

In an instant, he was right beside her, naked from the waist up and staring down, his eyes glazed with poignant emotion. Lush sheepskin and silk surrounded her like clouds. She withered against the luxurious fabrics as a painful longing surged through her body. Indeed, her desire for Adam rushed from her mind, down to her aching breasts, and to the tips of her naked toes, settling in her most intimate place. Her womanhood grew hot and wet, soaking through the pantalettes.

Heat coiled around her spine like twin salamanders. She arched into his touch, overwhelmed by the enticing pressure of his exploring hands. Then two fingertips dipped below the chemise's neckline. Isabelle worried her bottom lip as she bit back a moan. The marred pads of his fingers whispered against her bare flesh, kindling flames everywhere they touched. He strained his body, shifting closer, as his hands moved lower in a restless, intimate perusal. Then he bowed forward and ghosted kisses down the column of her throat—down, down, down—swirling his tongue over the creamy swells of her breasts, which spilled over her chemise. Both of her nipples grew painfully erect, echoing the very state of his swollen manhood. Indeed, she felt as his thick, hardening arousal pushed and jerked against her belly.

"You are immaculate..."

She glanced down as a blush seared her cheeks. The thin layer of silk clung to her like a second skin, and the flashing candles left very little to Adam's imagination. His dark head inclined, he latched on to a hardened bud and tugged the coated flesh between his lips—suckling her straight through the thin chemise. His tongue joined in the dance, darting out between his lips and sweeping across her tender, erect nipple. Sensation built to a steady, throbbing hum.

His hand kneaded her opposite breast, caressing and fondling—cupping the weight in his scarred palm. Gently he rolled the heavy flesh between his long fingers... caressed her nipple... stroked his thumb pad across the taut fabric. All the while, his tongue swirled around her veiled nipple, and the gentle scrape of his teeth drew a choked gasp from her throat.

Then he pushed the fabric down her body and stripped the material away. The pantalettes came next. They fell to the floor, and a cool breeze kissed her naked skin. She attempted to shield herself with crossed arms; Adam prevented the movement, his eyes blazing like a fire.

"Don't hide from me, *ma belle*. I've never seen such beauty," he whispered. Closing in on her again, he settled his strong body over hers like a coverlet. "Never believed it could exist in this world..."

He kissed the center of her chest, then moved his mouth and tongue over her nude breasts and pebbled nipples. Damp, wet lips crawled across the undersides of her breasts in a featherlight touch. The wisps of his hair tickled her flesh, and she felt the burned side of his face grate against her. He nibbled lightly on the swollen peak, branding her with tender love bites, and then soothed the ache with his swirling tongue.

His hands reached up as his lips quested lower... skimming across her clenched stomach, leaving hot lines wherever they touched. Her breasts filled his palms and spilled over those long fingers. Her insides constricted in anticipation. It took every gram of her willpower not to cry out and beg for more.

How she wanted more. She wanted it all. She wanted *everything*.

His penetrating blue eyes raked down and over her entire body in a slow perusal. Then that gaze darkened as they fixed on her inner thighs. She followed the path of his unwavering stare—and a wave of humiliation and grief crashed down at the sight of the scarring.

"They were from him. From Raphael." Her words choked off mid-sentence. She swallowed the lump in her throat as shameful tears pricked her eyes. "He—"

"Shh. Don't speak of it. Don't think. Simply feel... Abandon yourself to my touches, to the music of my voice."

Anger flashed in Adam's eyes—a searing rage that left Isabelle speechless and immobile. The sound of rustling sheets breached the silence as he slid down the length of her body and settled his head between her thighs. "My sweet Isabelle..." She inhaled a long breath as his lips pressed against those shameful scars. Indeed, his mouth tracked across her flesh, not leaving a single red line unloved. His kisses behaved like a healing balm. Those visceral memories of Raphael faded away... faded... until only she and Adam remained.

Within the beauty of that moment, only the two of them existed. Then she felt a splash of wetness on her upper thigh and realized he was weeping. For her. She reached down and tentatively ran her fingers through his tousled hair, needing to express her gratitude.

Her heart burned with love and adoration. He glanced at her and captured her eyes. The air grew thick with anticipation.

Isabelle sucked in a breath, readying herself for what was to come.

"I want to kiss you..." he breathed, his molten breath fanning against her wet thighs. "I want to kiss you... here."

Sultry breaths wafted against her very core. Adam blew lightly, and an exquisite tingling sensation roared through her veins. Her thighs grew slick and wet as his mouth hovered centimeters away—barely grazing her sensitive flesh. It was pure torture. A groan of frustration rattled her body as she instinctively grasped his neck and forced his mouth where she needed it most.

When his lips met her skin, at last, the effect was mind-blowing. Hot waves crashed through her, and that small bundle of nerves tingled as his warm breaths bathed it. Her knees and bottom instinctively tightened while ripples of pleasure melted her insides into a quivering, hot mass. His stubbly chin and uneven flesh grazed her inner thighs, creating a delicious friction that added to the blend of mounting sensations. One hand fisted in the sheepskin blanket; the other entwined in the thick locks of his hair. His gaze crept down her body and settled between the creamy, glistening flesh of her thighs. He murmured some words in a foreign tongue. Then followed suit in two more languages. Deaf to their meanings, Isabelle wished she was more cultured.

His wildly seductive voice and the mystery of his words washed over her, intensifying all five of her senses.

"Please... kiss me *there*, Adam."

"As you command, *ma reine*." His mouth slid over her wet opening—just barely—and a jolt of electricity surged within. She felt wetness seep from her nether lips and slide down her taut thighs. Tremors rattled her body—a testament to the pleasure to come.

She hadn't the slightest idea if this was a normal interaction between a man and woman—yet it didn't matter. A primitive, deep-rooted longing made up for their inexperience, urging both Isabelle and Adam to act on basal desire. Indeed. It seemed a perfectly natural thing for Adam to do... kissing her *there*, healing her own scars with his adoring tongue and mouth...

His tongue dipped halfway inside, past the damp, quivering folds—then retracted and swirled around the tingling bundle of her nerves several times. He withdrew completely, and her palm unconsciously applied pressure to his scalp, urging him back to where she needed him most. Two scarred fingertips gently pried her folds apart, and his tongue snaked across the sensitive bundle again with a flurry of wet, firm strokes.

Mon Dieu, she never wanted him to stop. Instinct guided each of their movements, acting like a third hand that pried open a door they'd never ventured through. One she doubted Adam ever hoped of crossing.

He played her body like an instrument, his masterful fingers and tongue seducing her to sing for him, to bend to his will and hand. The point of his tongue flirted with the tight bundle of nerves again—

He hesitated. "Adam, don't stop."

"I want to ensure I'm pleasing you."

"You are. You're doing everything right, *mon amour*. Believe me, I never imagined—"

Her thoughts ricocheted against each other as two thick fingertips burrowed inside her body. Then three. Sweet, sweet agony. They moved in and out, in and out... circled the tingling bundle of nerves... rocked deep, deep within... then spread her open before seizing the swollen, aching mound between two fingertips. He rolled the aching flesh between his thumb and forefinger... gently tugged... massaged the swollen ridge...

"Yes, Adam... there. Yes—"

An exquisite sensation mounted within as he angled his lips and drew the tip inside the hot cavern of his mouth. He latched on. Gently suckled. Her body unconsciously jerked upward, and Adam drank from her. *Mon Dieu*, he drank his fill. She arched against the mind-bending sensation while his tongue swirled around the swollen cleft. He blew softly, cupping her buttocks in his scarred palms... His teeth gently grazed her skin, eliciting a soft moan from deep inside her. Long, firm sweeps fell across the hardened nub as he applied delicate pressure... a little more... He gave a gentle nibble, sucked on the throbbing peak... then granted just enough pressure to drive her over that edge...

"Oh, don't... don't stop... Adam..."

Hard moans rocked Isabelle's body, shattering all coherent thoughts into breathless fragments. Her mind spun like an erratic toy top. Guided by her hand in his hair and torn pleas, he steadied her hips as he sucked on the swollen mound, drinking her deeper, deeper, consuming her. She heard him moan—and the erotic, masculine sound vibrated through her burning flesh. Colors burst in front of her eyes and spilled through every cell, every fiber of her being. Then she shattered irrevocably. And she knew, without a doubt, she'd never be whole again apart from Prince Adam Delacroix.

Adam returned to an upright position and seated himself on the mattress. Isabelle spared a moment to catch her breath, to gather her thoughts, to allow her humming body to return to equilibrium. Not knowing what she was doing—only knowing she wanted to return the favor and kiss him *there*—she leaned forward and reached for the front of Adam's trousers.

A choked groan issued from his throat. As she grazed the thick bulge through the fabric, his head lolled backward as if in agony—yet she knew he felt only desire. Burning, raging desire. She increased the pressure of her touch and swept his inner thighs, fondling him straight through the rugged material. He was large, his massive size spilling over her palm and fingers. He jerked against her and released a guttural moan, shifting inside the confines of his trousers.

"Undo them." The commanding note that entered his voice sent a delicious shiver through Isabelle.

Her hands shook as she unfastened the clasps, then slowly tugged the fabric down and over his smooth thighs. His underclothes came next; Isabelle's gaze ran over the firm curves of his thighs, which were corded with muscle and free from any scarring.

Her breath hitched at the sight of his swollen manhood, and she tentatively reached out, running her fingers over the velvety flesh in an experimental touch. Hot. Thick. Silky smooth. Her small hand barely fit around his girth. He jerked in her grasp and released a strangled moan. Isabelle drew her hand away and met his glassy eyes. The muscles in his throat worked as he swallowed deeply. One of his hands clasped the sheepskin blanket. He twisted the material between long, tapered fingers and sweat beaded down his forehead. Breaths hissed from between his gritted teeth as he stared down at her through smoke-filled eyes.

"I'm sorry. Did... does my touch cause you pain?"

His dark, sultry chuckle swelled the room and set Isabelle's insides on fire. Then he blew out a strained breath, shook his head, and raked a hand through his damp waves. Kissed by wavering candlelight, the signet ring flashed in the dim room. *AFD*. Absently she wondered what his middle name was and made a mental note to ask him later. Indeed, she wanted to know everything about him—every last detail, no matter how minute or seemingly mundane.

"*Non*. Not pain, *ma belle*. Please," he finally whispered, cupping her cheek with his large hand. Passion kindled within his blue eyes and set his irregular features aglow. That dark gaze glittered with mounting arousal and a primal hunger.

"Now *I* am going to kiss *you* there..." His breath audibly shivered in his throat. She wrapped her fingers around his shaft and scooted forward, then planted a kiss on its glistening crown. Clear liquid ran from the swollen flesh and tracked down the thick length. She was rewarded with another rich moan, and his fingers tangled in her curls with an insistent pull. Every centimeter of his body felt rock-hard and inflamed, resembling newly forged steel. A fierce confidence surged through her veins and set fire to her spirit.

"Please..."

"Lie back, Adam. Lie back and relax. Don't think... Just lose yourself in my touch," she crooned, parroting his words from minutes ago. He obliged with a choked moan. Isabelle leaned forward, crouched between his thighs, and shadowed his sensual ministrations. She ran her tongue over the silken flesh in long slow swipes, then cupped her mouth along the side of his stiff manhood and gently suckled, drawing the thick shaft between her gliding lips. Up and down. Down and up. A little more pressure. A gentle sweep of her tongue. Then two more. He drew in a sharp breath—and the sound fell upon her ears like music.

She gazed up at him. He threw his head back, one hand clenched in her hair, the other grasping the coverlet. She felt his thighs under her palms, hard as stone and taut. Cords of muscles clenched, convulsed, and tightened beneath her restless fingertips. The grip on her hair constricted. He surged his hips upward in a slight arch. She took the cue—positioning her lips around the swollen head and slit, taking him inside her mouth and, after a heartbeat, partway into her throat. His groans clipped off into hard, sharp grunts.

She felt his pleasure mounting like a palpable force, felt him swelling within the cavern of her mouth. Hearing his groans and seeing his need, she quickened her movements; his grip on the coverlet tightened. Her hands joined in the erotic dance, wrapping him in the empty space below her mouth and suckling lips. Then she wrapped her lips around the gleaming crown, welcoming the salty tang and his fullness inside her throat again—

"Ah... No more, *ma belle*," he breathed in a hoarse voice. "I can't bear it any longer. It shall be the end of me." Adam realigned their quivering bodies. His muscular arms trembled in the candlelight, and a deep, endearing blush covered the handsome side of his face. He looked consumed. Wild. Beast-like. Deliciously disheveled and lost to passion. Exhaling a rigid breath, he leaned forward and pressed a gentle kiss to the center of her forehead. "Are you certain?" he asked, his voice a delectable waterfall of dark wine. That enchanting, rich tone coursed through her veins and reawakened her passion. "This is what you want?"

She nodded, unable to speak, her voice tangled in her throat.

"Good," he sensually murmured, "because I've never wanted anything more. You, Isabelle Rose, are all I've ever needed or wanted. Exquisite. Honest. Courageous. Intelligent. Stubborn. Resolute. Beautiful inside and out. And loyal to your core. Every time I look at you, I'm in awe, and I find myself falling in love with you all over again. I want you now, tonight, tomorrow, and every moment after. I need you *always*."

Isabelle fought to speak, to say something—anything at all—but only a tearful, disbelieving gasp emerged. His fingertips glided down her cheeks, her neck, her shoulders, both her arms. Silence coiled around them like twin salamanders. Only the hammering of their heartbeats, the erotic crackle in the air, ruptured that quiet.

Then his warm, ragged breaths wafted against her hairline as he urged his manhood to part her womanly folds. He slid inside her in slow, measured movements. His thickness filled her, applying a delicious pressure against the peak of her womanhood. Centimeter by aching centimeter he pushed inside her tight, wet walls and made her feel complete. She couldn't think, completely swept away and transported by sensation. A moan tore from her throat and echoed through the chamber; she shut her eyes, listening to the crackling candles and whispering wind. Adam's knuckles skimmed her cheeks. She drew her eyes open and studied his concerned expression.

"Am I hurting you?" He leaned back on his elbows, capturing her eyes with his own. His words were broken into breathy fragments, and a hoarse moan laced them together.

"No. No, never," she said while tears streamed down her cheeks. "These are good tears. Ones of happiness. Tears of happiness."

He smiled down at her, his own eyes heavy with emotion and a reciprocated adoration. Then his lips grazed her forehead again, and he whispered the declaration against her sweat-lined skin. "I love you, Isabelle. And that shall never change. Always you."

The tears streamed ever harder, and her heart felt full, quite near to bursting. "I love you, my Adam. Always us."

His sparkling eyes said it all. He'd waited a lifetime to hear those words.

He buried himself to the hilt in a delicious rush of movement. There was no space between them, no more barriers or thresholds to cross. Thanks to Raphael's vile assault, the pain didn't come. Only a dull ache and an exquisite sensation of fullness. Total completion.

She knotted her arms around the strong column of his neck and lifted her hips, arching into him, urging him to move against her, deep within her. He met her silent command with a gentle, tentative rocking motion that reminded her of waves lapping against the coastline. Or of the shimmering waterfall feeding into Adam's hot spring. She joined in the dance with an equal vigor and passion while his breathing grew shallower and his thrusts faster and more urgent. Nothing filled her mind except the sound of their tangled moans and rigid breaths, the feel of Adam's essence entwining with her own. Then he hooked an arm below her undulating bottom, leaned back, and raised her body partway into the air.

Strong, muscled arms snaked around her midsection and held her tight. Perspiration covered their bodies and dampened the coverlet. Remaining connected in the most intimate of ways, he sat on his haunches and lifted her against his scarred chest. She ground against him in instinctive and intuitive movements... brushing back and forth... swiveling her hips full circle—in one direction then the other.

Adam trailed a single fingertip down her body, igniting her skin from breast to belly button. She varied her tempo in a soulful waltz. Adam angled his chin back and propped both hands onto the mattress, lost to pure ecstasy. Encouraged by his deep moans and even deeper thrusts, she gained a steady momentum as she made love to Adam Delacroix with her heart, her body, her soul.

She trembled against him and held tighter to his neck. Heartbeat to heartbeat, Adam gently maneuvered in and out of her slick walls. His hot, torn breaths wafted against her face, beating across her cheeks. The sound of the sputtering candle crescendoed and elevated every sensation.

She clung to his back, grasping him like a lifeline. With each thrust, her body gripped on to him in an unyielding clasp and forced them back as one. She arched her neck, and his lips came to the throbbing base of her throat. Their heartbeats slammed together, connecting their spirits in a profound and inseparable way. Little tremors escalated to a pounding rush of liquid heat and blistering pleasure.

Isabelle let everything go. Everything except for Prince Adam Delacroix.

Exquisite shocks rippled through her, overwhelming every pore, every nerve, and every fiber of her being.

She cried out as she rode the spine-tingling climax, shivering and quaking in the security of Adam's arms.

Joining in her release, he buried himself deep inside her body and threw his head back with a guttural moan.

The mingled sounds of their shared ecstasy came together.

He held her soundly against his chest—and Isabelle abandoned herself to a feeling of oneness and true love.

Always us. Always together.

Chapter Twenty-One

WINTER MELTED INTO SPRING, and along with it, the icicles that had clung to Adam's heart deftly fell away like shackles. Seasoned by fresh blooms, the morning air felt crisp and cool against his naked cheeks. From the premature flower buds up to the noisy nest of sparrows which was cradled by a tree's bough, the world whispered of birth and new beginnings.

Golden rays oozed between the shuddering branches while shafts of light illuminated their dew-covered leaves. A sea of tall grass swayed in the wind's breath, moving like an ocean tide. Exhaling a long breath, he thought of Lavoncourt's coastline—the sight of the waves crashing against the jagged rocks in a repetitive, forlorn melody...

Adam watched as Isabelle rode past the garden's climbing roses, which reached for the heavens.

Luminous shafts of orange and red streaked the horizon like colors in an oil painting. Standing on his East Tower balcony, Adam inhaled the cool air as true contentment and happiness flooded his entire being. He'd never thought it possible to feel such hope, to gaze at the world beyond his castle and perceive only beauty. Each evening, he fell asleep to the sweet melody of Isabelle's voice while she read to him. They'd only known each other for a couple of months, yet it felt like an entire lifetime.

The nights were woven from music and reciprocated stories, of shared dreams and the comfort of each other's embrace. They'd often make love until morning's light wriggled through the drapes, and then contently fall asleep in each other's arms. Isabelle felt so much a part of himself now... It was a wonder he'd ever lived without her.

Survived, maybe. But not lived.

Not before her.

Down below, Isabelle slid off Spirit's back and gently stroked the mare's muzzle. Then she shielded her gaze and glanced at the balcony. Adam watched in breathless wonder as a smile brightened her features and reached out to him from the gardens. She waved, her smile growing greater still—and an unspoken conversation passed between them.

Minutes later, shafts of sunlight shimmered through the windows as Adam headed for his music room. The draperies were thrown open, welcoming the outside world in. The melody of clicking heels echoed somewhere in the castle as a handful of servants tended to the rooms and cleared away a lifetime of dust. Indeed, Isabelle had returned from her last trip to the village with some unexpected inventory.

Adam lowered his face in an unconscious gesture while a maidservant whizzed by. He saw the way she kept sufficient space between their bodies as they crossed paths... heard the audible gasp that fled her lips and the look of repulsion and disbelief that shadowed her gaze. And when she believed he no longer watched, she made a clumsy sign of the cross and muttered an incoherent prayer. Adam shook his head and exhaled a sigh; her disgust and fear slid off him. Nothing mattered now with Isabelle at his side. Stranger found Adam in the corridor and greeted him with a good-natured bark. They entered his music room, and Adam sat before his pianoforte.

He felt himself unravel as his scarred hands danced across the ivory keys and filled the room with a soft, hypnotic melody. He quickly spiraled into his music, crafting a decadent piece without conscious thought. It consumed him and took on a life of its own as the notes slowly melted into a wedding requiem.

Adam's hands froze in midair. Sweetly tender notes

vibrated around him and dissolved into an introspective silence. He fished a trembling hand inside his coat pocket and withdrew one of his family's great heirlooms—an immaculate diamond engagement ring.

Memories surged through him as he clasped the gem in his palm. Exhaling a rigid breath, he unfurled his fingers and studied the crystal-clear diamond. Morning's light set the encircling rubies aglow as Adam rotated it between his thumb and forefinger...

Always together.

Indeed, Adam knew, with every beat of his heart, that he couldn't bear ever being separated from his Isabelle.

ISABELLE TURNED HER face to the morning sun, allowing its rays to caress her cheeks like warm fingers. She inhaled deeply, filling her lungs with the roses' sweet nectar and the scent of fresh dew. Her heart hammered against her ribs as her thoughts trailed to Adam. She'd lived in a sort of dream the past few weeks; Adam had become her lover, her best friend, and greatest confidant. Layer by layer, his stony demeanor had fallen away to reveal the kindhearted, gentle man beneath. In many ways, he was still that boy lying in bed, listening as his home was torn apart, stone by stone...

Isabelle clasped Spirit's reins and directed her through the lush gardens, around the castle's curved facade, and inside the stable. After she returned Spirit to her stall and filled her trough with a bundle of fresh hay, Isabelle found herself standing in front of her papa's gravesite. Breathlessly she knelt before the cross and pile of stones. Her words were soft, burdened by emotion; the breeze nearly carried them away.

"I miss you, Papa. I miss you every day..." Blinking back tears, she traced a fingertip over the engraved letters. "I have found happiness, true love... I have found what you and Maman had." She leaned forward with a strained breath and pressed her lips against the wooden cross. "You shall always have my love, Papa."

A half an hour later, Isabelle turned toward the castle and made the journey through the winding courtyard. Isabelle felt a smile spread across her face while each step brought her closer to Adam. She ached for his touch, the gentle brush of his breaths, the deep lull of his voice, the two wonderfully imperfect halves of his face—

Something shifted in the atmosphere. Each hair on the back of her neck prickled. Silence hung in the air like a bad omen. Even the wind held its breath. Isabelle stopped dead in her tracks while a dark premonition eclipsed her thoughts. Her flight or fight instinct kicked into place. She was being watched... hunted. Overcome with a prickling dread, she gathered her skirts and took off at a fierce sprint.

The breaths were half-knocked from her lungs as a pair of arms shot out and grabbed the middle of her body. A gloved hand clamped over her mouth and nose, muffling her screams. Then Raphael's voice was in her ear, filling her gut with hot bile as he dragged her against the side of the castle.

She gasped in pain and despair while her back slammed against the wall. The rough stones snagged her dress and tore at her skin. Raphael hovered above her, anger unlike she'd ever seen etched into every line of his handsome, aristocratic face.

"Not so much as a word. Understood? Don't underestimate me this time, *ma chérie*. I shall take great pleasure in sending you into the dirt alongside your beloved papa."

A faint *click* pierced the silence. Isabelle felt her legs grow numb and weak as the cool tip of Raphael's pistol nestled against her skull. Indeed, he held it against her sweat-lined temple none too gently; the metal scraped her flesh, echoing the warning in his stone-cold gaze.

"Another word and I'll blow your pretty brains halfway to hell."

How, in God's teeth, did he find her? Isabelle fought to recover her breathing, to cloak her fear beneath a show of apathy. She locked on to that unwavering stare and lifted her chin several centimeters.

Could she somehow wrestle the gun from him? Could she use her feminine wiles to turn the tables?

"Raphael... thank God. I... I feared you'd never find me. I have been hoping against hope that—"

Isabelle cringed as the nozzle dug a little deeper into her skull. "You're a terrible little liar, my love. Do you take me for a fucking fool?"

A tart reply rushed from her lips before she could stop it. Months of anger welled inside her; it crushed her composure beneath an avalanche of unbridled fury and revulsion. "A fool, no. A monster? A coward? *Yes.* You fight to thwart your father, to not be like him—yet you're nothing but a precise reflection. And you can't even see it. It's ironic, really, and so very pathetic."

Raphael's left hand squeezed her throat in a lightning-quick movement. His fingers constricted, clasping her vocal cords, causing the remaining breaths to smother inside her lungs.

"Say that again, *chérie*." Isabelle couldn't have spoken even if she wanted to; she felt herself choking, growing faint and slipping into a black void. His manicured nails dug into her flesh and drew blood; she felt it beading down her pulsating throat. Raphael muttered something under his breath, appeased for the moment, and then loosened his hold. "That's what I thought. I see your silver tongue has lost some of its bite. Now you'd best obey me."

He released her in a harsh movement. Coughs erupted from Isabelle's throat. She clasped her vocal cords, massaging the tender flesh, panting for precious air. Blood stained the tips of her fingers and smeared across her throat. She felt like she was drowning. Raphael took a calculated step back, crossed his brawny arms, and observed her with a disturbing intensity. His silent contemplation frightened her far more than his outburst.

"Are you quite finished?" he asked in a cold, nonchalant tone while her coughs subsided.

"What do you want from me, Raphael? *What?*" She knew

she shouldn't yell, not with Raphael's gun pointed in her direction—yet she couldn't control the frustration she felt. The tears slipped down her flushed cheeks, and she cursed herself for such weakness. "When we first met, I trusted you, I cared for you. I even believed myself in love with you! Now I can see what a naive, stupid girl I was. I shall never forgive myself for being so blind."

The distant sound of barking rushed toward them. Panic seized Isabelle in an iron grasp. Stranger must have heard her cries.

What if Adam comes with him—unarmed and unaware? Or one of the new servants? Isabelle squeezed both eyes shut as the thunderous sound of Stranger's barking reverberated off the stone walls and closed in on their location.

Raphael cursed under his breath; Isabelle's eyes shot open. Stranger lurked a meter away, his thin back curved into a menacing arch. His lips pulled back to show an impressive set of teeth. Isabelle's thoughts drifted to the evening she and Papa had stumbled upon the castle and implored Adam for refuge...

Her eyes fell shut while mounting horror flooded her mind and soul.

Run from here, my dear friend, she silently called out to the creature. Then Adam's words from a month ago echoed in her mind: *He's protective of his master. A loyal beast. And a good friend.*

The sound of a gunshot impaled the air; Stranger's barking fell silent. She slowly opened her eyes, her heart and nerves in tatters. *Non...* Stranger's crumpled body lay a meter away, an unholy sea of red spreading below his mottled gray fur. Isabelle felt lightheaded, woozy... like she was suffocating all over again. She leaned against the stone wall for support as she seemed to cave inward. Indeed, she was collapsing in on herself.

"I shall make this simple for you. Come with me now, submit to my will without a fight, without the melodrama, and you and your beloved monster shall remain unharmed." He stepped forward, his voice sinking to a diabolical whisper that sent tremors down her spine. "Make any more fuss, and Adam shall suffer the same fate as his wretched mongrel." His boot slammed against Stranger's motionless body, making his intentions clear. Isabelle cringed at the vulgar gesture, anger and hatred twisting inside her. "Am I quite clear?" Raphael snatched her wrist and reeled her forward. She cried out as his nails sank into her skin and drew blood.

"Without so much as a farewell? At—at the very least let me say good-bye! I—"

His grip tightening, he scoffed and shook his blond head in visible disbelief. "Unbelievable. You really think me daft, don't you?"

Minutes later, Raphael threw Isabelle in the back of his carriage and locked her inside with the turn of a small brass key. She shoved the burgundy curtain aside, watching as the forest swallowed up her prince's castle and her home receded into the horizon.

ADAM KNEW SOMETHING was amiss when Isabelle didn't show for lunch. He felt it inside his gut, within the core of his body. Brooding at the large, circular dining table, he shoved a full plate of roasted chicken and fresh vegetables aside, which the new cook had prepared only an hour before, and stormed through the castle.

He checked all her usual spots—the nook in the library, the gardens, her bedchamber, and her father's resting place.

Something's happened to her.

Panic seized Adam.

He raced through the winding halls, his body shaking all over, that uneasy sensation rising with every step. He crossed paths with a servant, who was carrying a bundle of fresh linens, and grasped her thin forearm. She released a pitiful cry—which was more from the sight of his naked face than his grip on her arm—and jackknifed against the wall. She cried out again while the linens tumbled from her hands. The sharp scents of soap and starch filled his nostrils and made him feel queasy. As if fighting off a sudden chill, she grasped her servant's garb and fisted the material between quivering fingertips.

Ignorant chit. She behaved like she'd seen a monster.

Adam scoffed and tore an unsteady hand through his hairline. "Have you seen her? Isabelle—when is the last time you saw her?" The girl shrank farther against the wall, if that was even possible, then knelt and haphazardly collected the strewn linens. Adam noticed the way her hands trembled—and he despised her for it. "Speak up, daft child! Tell me all you know or I shall make you suffer for such insolence."

The girl stared at him from her spot on the ground, a bright flush quickly spreading across her sallow cheeks. "Forgive me, master!" She stumbled onto her feet, though she kept her face halfway hidden behind the tower of freshly washed linens. "I—I saw her just this morning."

"In the garden. Yes, I know this," he mumbled, waving her words away. "Have you seen her since?"

"*Oui.* In the courtyard, if I'm not mistaken. I—"

Adam fled before she could finish the sentence. He backtracked to Bernard's grave, then searched the entire premises while calling out Isabelle's name like some reverent prayer. The choked sound of his voice rode the crisp breeze and echoed despairingly off the stone walls. He rounded the castle, growing strangely disoriented, breathless, and drenched with sweat. His hands trembled like those of an addict as he battled to shove the fierce thoughts from his mind.

Perhaps she has simply left me. Maybe her affection was nothing more than a ruse. A farce. He knew such thoughts were far from logical, yet it took only a glance in a mirror for them to surface again.

Adam was so distracted that he overlooked the great bundle of fur on the ground. Instead, he felt it. He glanced down at the blood-soaked fur and the crimson ring that surrounded Stranger's motionless body.

"*Non.* Stranger..."

Barely breathing, Adam dropped to his knees and stroked a trembling hand over the dog's lean back. His heart plummeted while a new grief seeped into his veins. Hardly thinking, he bowed forward and laid his cheek across Stranger's coarse body. He felt as a warm rush of blood stained the disfigured side of his face. Shaking fingers continued to run across the dog's motionless back in repetitive strokes.

"My friend… I'm so sorry… I—" Emotion constricted the words. Adam swallowed the lump in his throat and pressed his lips against Stranger's molted coat. "Be at peace," he whispered, staggering onto his feet and running his palm over Stranger's side one last time.

Adam cursed under his breath, the expletive forming a cloud on the air. Meters away, fresh tracks from a carriage were embedded in the dirt.

Mon Dieu, she's been taken. Vicomte Dumont has found her.

He knew it with every beat of his heart.

An hour later, as a plan formed inside Adam's mind, he stood before a gaping hole in the earth. His mind and heart overflowed with thoughts of Isabelle, and that despair he'd known for so long returned full circle.

Sébastien's betrayal—yes, he knew Sébastien was to blame for this—cut through his soul with the sharp edge of a blade. *I should have never trusted him. I should have never believed in his friendship, his apparent loyalty…* Adam twisted his fingers in Stranger's wiry coat as his eyes squeezed shut. He swept his palm up and down the dog's motionless back… affectionately stroked his fingers over each rib like striking the strings of a harp. Stranger had been a constant companion, a much-needed light within a world of darkness and solitude. Because of Sébastien, he'd lost Stranger—and possibly Isabelle as well.

Never.

Adam's sorrow quickly warped. It mutated into a throbbing anger and a hunger for vengeance. Sébastien would pay for his role in this disaster, even if he was forced to rip the world apart to hunt him down.

Adam gently lowered Stranger into the hole, mere meters away from Bernard's resting spot, and swiped the mound of dirt over the dog's bloodied fur.

He reflected on the night Isabelle had stumbled upon his doorstep, on how his humanity had resurrected when he'd buried her father under the black ash tree... and on everything they'd endured since.

No prayers were muttered. No requiems passed his lips.

Alas, he'd abandoned his faith long ago.

Once Stranger had rejoined the quiet earth, Adam lay on top of the fresh grave and gazed up at the heavens he'd for so long forsaken.

Chapter Twenty-Two

Isabelle dwelled in the depths of a living nightmare. She held back her tears and tried not to think about this cruel stroke of fate—how Raphael had torn the world out from her and Adam. Positioned on aching hands and knees, she ran an oiled cloth over the medallion-style marble floor.

Memories of Adam rained down on her thoughts. In his absence, a black void filled her chest. Rising in the morning was a battle. All stimulus fled from her world, abandoning her to a hollow existence. Food had no taste. Colors were depthless and bland. The art hanging in the Dumont Chateau was without form or beauty. And with each passing day, the precious light slipped from her world a little more. Only her love for Adam kept her sane and functioning.

He shall find me. I know it in my heart...

Or maybe I shall poison them both and take back my freedom myself. I don't need rescuing, she thought, glancing down at her silver cross. *Only courage and strength. And a semblance of a plan...*

One way or another, she would reclaim her happiness. These walls would not hold her.

In the interim, as a scheme took shape in her mind, she found it difficult to breathe. Impossible to stay anchored. The world seemed to move around her while she remained stationary, cold, alone. Her heart throbbed with a pain and emptiness she hadn't known to exist.

Blinking back tears, she paused in her handiwork and rocked onto her sore knees. Anger and frustration churned inside her gut. She gave her silver cross a squeeze and prayed for strength.

Then she felt the silky caress of Vivian Brazin's skirts. The woman's voice echoed in the empty hallway, amplified by the marble flooring and cathedral ceiling. At first, when Raphael had spirited her from Adam's castle, she'd thought he meant to force her into marriage—among other things. But she'd quickly learned that he had other, less noble plans in store. She was to be his and Vivian's plaything—and Raphael had every intention to make her pay for trying to escape him. Isabelle clasped the center of her chest as grief incapacitated her; she missed Adam so deeply it physically pained her.

"Why, you truly are as useless as Raphael says you are." Vivian bent forward and tilted her head. "I can hardly see my reflection."

Isabelle twisted the rag between her fingertips and inhaled a calming breath. It did nothing to soothe her nerves or mounting fury. "Then you should count yourself blessed. The very sight of your—"

Vivian's knuckles collided with Isabelle's jaw in a jarring crash. The impact of her large diamond ring sliced her cheek, tearing her flesh open. Isabelle lowered her head between her hands and watched as her blood puddled on the well-oiled marble. And indeed, she saw Vivian's smirking features in that shiny surface—and the sight made her insides curdle.

"Why, you are dirtying the floor again," Vivian said in a flat whisper. "Go on now, *ma chérie*... Clean up your mess like a good little girl." Using her dainty foot, Vivian kicked the rag toward Isabelle. Isabelle released a long breath, then rocked onto her knees and glared at Vivian's hovering face.

Beautiful. Cold. Callous.

She felt as blood trickled down her chin like one great tear. The words tumbled out of her mouth without warning, spilling from a very dark corner of her soul. "You may look down at me all you want. Your unimaginable capacity for cruelty doesn't change the fact that Raphael preferred me over you. Even now, your engagement is nothing more than a hushed secret, a farce." Vivian's porcelain complexion grew even paler, if that was at all possible, and a riot of emotions flickered in her stare. "Neither does it—"

"Now, now, Isabelle..." Raphael's slow drawl punctured Isabelle's thoughts. "Is that any way to speak to your soon-to-be mistress?" She shivered in spite of herself; nights ago, Vivian's husband had died in his sleep—yet Isabelle knew well Vivian had played a hand in the timely death. Now she and Raphael were secretly engaged—something that clearly rattled Vivian and for a good reason. Isabelle had overheard their argument—and the subsequent "lovemaking"—early that morning. *Why must it be a secret, Raphael? Tell me why! What are you so ashamed of? It's your wretched father again, the fucking comte! Or is because of that low-born whore?*

Raphael drew closer. The clink of polished boots echoed through the hallway in an eerie requiem; each of his steps parroted Isabelle's thundering heartbeat and ragged breaths. He sank to his knees with a condescending smile, regarding Isabelle as if she were a naughty child. Then he licked the pad of his thumb and wiped away the stream of blood. It took every bit of her willpower not to seize his thumb and shatter the bone in two.

"What an enchanting couple the two of you make," she spat, straightening her back so as not to be dwarfed by his presence. "You do your mother's memory a great honor, Raphael."

The flicker in his glare was unmistakable; his mute anger lashed out with the force of a whip.

Curb your tongue, foolish chit. Every word you utter only harms yourself and possibly Adam.

Calmly she waited, her eyes never leaving his own, preparing for the blow to her face.

It never came. Instead, he cupped her chin in a gesture of mock affection. Isabelle's glare slid to Vivian, who had staggered back several meters. Her small, pale hands balled into fists, and her lips tightened into a somber line. Those blazing eyes hit Isabelle like a hurtled knife, daring her to speak.

Take him from me, Isabelle silently pleaded to the damnable woman. *Take him and let me be.*

Bile rose in her throat as Raphael's caressing fingers ran through her curls in repetitive motions. Her eyes shuttered; within the sanctuary of her own thoughts, she saw Adam's face, heard the husky, drugging baritone of his voice...

My heart is breaking without him.

Raphael yanked on her hair and snapped her back into dark reality.

"Don't even think of it. There is no escaping, *ma chérie*. Not this time."

Or so you believe.

SÉBASTIEN THRASHED in his sleep as his mind was transported back to that tragic eve twenty-five years ago...

He raced through the Castle Delacroix's corridors with one goal in mind. He had to find the crown prince and princess before it was too late.

I must set things right or at least die trying.

It was what his father would have done anyway.

He battled to shake away the images and sounds from only moments ago. Should he live to see a hundred years, he'd never forget the sight of the king and queen's severed heads on spikes... how the mob had paraded them about the courtyard, the crowd cheering and waving their tricolored freedom flags. Those memories were forever burned into his thoughts, into his very being. An image of Adam and his parents running through the rose garden invaded his mind and further awakened his tenacity.

The castle rocked and swayed as more cannon fire assaulted the walls. The fortress wouldn't hold much longer. Smoke crept through the halls and infected Sébastien's lungs.

Coughing, he held a handkerchief against his mouth and nose to block out those flames. Regardless, they seeped through the material and charred his insides into ash.

A massive crash shook the castle—and the impact nearly knocked Sébastien off his feet. A lightheaded sensation eclipsed his senses as he tracked through the smoky hallway; he clung to the wall, fought to retain his balance, to stay awake.

If I sleep, I shall never wake up again.

Keeping the handkerchief pressed against his nose and mouth, he slid the opposite hand along the wall and staggered toward the bedchambers. A mighty tapestry wavered at his touch; his eyes ran over the salamander and ignited shield, and he caught himself muttering the Delacroix words.

Sébastien's heart violently plummeted as he stopped in front of the nursery. Fire set the hallway aglow, and sweltering heat wafted from the room.

Flames had devoured everything.

Sébastien prayed the prince was still alive, still hiding somewhere within the castle's shadows.

Prince Adam was the last hope.

Minutes later, he found him tied to the king and queen's four-poster bed. The drapes were on fire. Flames drifted toward Adam's unconscious body. They were red-hot and blazing, like the devil's own tongue.

"Adam! *Mon Dieu...*" His arms already bore brutal burns and welts. Smoke charred Sébastien's lungs and eyes. He gazed through his stinging vision in dejected horror, staring down at the king and queen's decapitated bodies. Blood oozed and pooled from the stumps of their necks, covering the parquet flooring.

Was Adam still alive? Was it even possible to survive such a thing?

Sébastien covered his mouth as vomit seethed from his lips and dampened the handkerchief. Whispering words to the prince, he worked as fast as his trembling hands allowed, untying the ropes that bound the boy's wrists. Thick smoke rose into his face and clotted his lungs. Every breath was a battle... The pain was excruciating. Sébastien's heart pounded, fighting to burst its way out of his chest. Blackness fringed his consciousness; he battled the haze and focused his attention on the knotted rope.

Then he pulled Adam's unconscious body from the bedpost, cradling the prince like a newborn babe…

LIKE ALL OTHER nights for the past few weeks, Sébastien found no sleep. No sleep and certainly no rest or peace of mind. He woke from the nightmare, drenched in his sweat and guilt. He tossed and turned for hours on end, punching his feather pillow into submission. Dejectedly he watched as moonlight shimmered through his chamber's sole window and set his carved furniture aglow. Furniture he'd purchased with Adam's generous salary. A fucking feather pillow he'd purchased with Adam's salary.

It was inescapable. Every time he closed his eyes, he saw Adam tied to his parents' bedpost, saw those hungry flames wafting toward his motionless body, saw himself unfastening the binds and shouting words of reassurance over the roaring flames.

What have I done?

Guilt consumed Sébastien, tearing him asunder.

Every morning, he'd race to the newsstands and flip to the engagement announcements. And every morning, not a single mention of Vicomte Dumont and Isabelle Rose met his eyes.

He lied—played me for a fool.

He jolted upright, panting, both hands trembling. Stumbling from the bed, he tossed a wool coat about his shoulders and set off into the darkness.

Over an hour later, Sébastien parked his phaeton and stood in front of Isabelle's humble cottage. The interior was blacker than pitch. *They're probably sleeping, you fool. Or possibly out on a social call.* Yet the uneasy sensation expanded in his chest. The urge to shatter a window and search the home overwhelmed him. He moved closer to the peeling door, drawn to it like a moth to a flame. His breaths were sucked from his lungs as he edged nearer; a wooden plank boarded the front door.

Shadows shifted and moved, manipulated by the flickering street lanterns. He raced through the cold, curving walkways, suddenly needing to be away from here. He ached to return to Adam's castle, to sit with him and Stranger beside the hearth and reminisce on past times. Better times. Just two old friends, more different than day and night, yet linked together by a dark stroke of fate. And a love for aged wine.

A young whore blocked his path. She bowed her face in shame; stick-straight hair draped over her body and hid her features like some secretive curtain. The ill-fitted bodice drooped from dangerously slim, birdlike shoulders in harsh and irregular folds, flaunting her deprivation rather than sensuality. Sébastien felt the compelling desire to sweep away those locks, to peer into eyes that were undoubtedly filled with sorrow, and reassure her that everything would be fine. Instead, he hustled past the creature without a second glance.

A tiny, trembling hand grasped his coat. Her fingers curled into the material in a desperate pull. When she finally spoke, the tremor in her voice overpowered all sensuality. "*Bonsoir.* Care to have your bed warmed on this lonely night, monsieur?"

A rigid breath escaped him.

In an attempt to flee, the young whore inhaled a strained breath and instantly pulled away. Sébastien gripped her shoulders and realigned their bodies. His gloved fingertips pushed against the curve of her chin, forcing her face up and back. He felt his eyes sharpen as they bore into her own. "Clarice! What—what are you thinking? What, in God's teeth, have you done to yourself?"

When she refused to speak, he tossed the hood from her head, confirming the inevitable.

The girl shattered into tears. "It was the vicomte, the wretch! The government—they know Papa has died! Raphael Dumont... he had our property confiscated. Elizabeth and I had no choice!" Sébastien didn't need to hear the rest; he already knew how this tragedy had played out. Women couldn't own property. The two sisters had likely exhausted Adam's funds in a matter of days, leaving them destitute and starving.

Just as Sébastien's heart warmed to the creature, she sneered, "I pray Isabelle followed her father into the grave! It's all her fault. Hers and the old man's!"

Sébastien heaved a sigh, fished a hand inside his cloak, and deposited a sum of francs into the chit's bony hand. And without another word or backward glance, he set off.

He'd found all the evidence he needed.

ADAM'S HANDS TREMBLED as he loaded his leather satchel with a small revolver. Another revolver went into his coat pocket, as well as a gem-studded dagger and extra shot. He tried to focus on the task at hand, but knowing Isabelle was in danger nearly broke him. He inhaled deeply. Fought to hold himself together. For her. Without the warmth of her body... the musical cadence of her voice... the simple feel of her fingers sliding against his own... he was so very lost. Lost, filled with pain, and incomplete.

He withdrew the map with shaking fingers and paced toward the study's conservatory window, urging the moonlight to illuminate its yellowed parchment.

He knew the general location of the Dumont Chateau in Chassiers, Demrov—the journey would be long and tedious—and Adam prayed he wouldn't arrive too late. The plan was very simple, his goal simpler yet. Once he stepped foot in Laché, he'd need to ask for directions. That thought sent a trickle of apprehension down his spine.

He hadn't engaged with the world for over two decades. Adam braced his palms on the writing desk and fought to steady his breathing. The mere thought of Raphael Dumont's hands on Isabelle left him trembling and blind with rage. Testing the cocking mechanism on his revolver, Adam muttered a halfhearted prayer and slipped the weapon inside his coat again. He gazed out the window to the shimmering night that lay beyond—and Adam knew, without question, that he'd brave any storm for Isabelle. She was all that mattered now, and he'd give everything to ensure her safety and happiness.

Even his own wretched life.

Adam stared into the wavering hearth, willing his courage to come forth. In that reflective moment, his entire fate seemed to travel full circle.

I must be brave. Just like Papa said I should...

Knocking ruptured the silence. Adam jolted from the blunt sound and jerked upright.

Isabelle?

Not sparing another thought, he sprinted across the drawing room and chased after the persistent knocking. The sound echoed and snaked through the castle's stone walls, swelling the darkness with a frantic banging. The rhythm of the knock sounded desperate—almost like a cry for help. Adam hastened his steps, then wrenched open the hefty wooden door. The thing emitted a splintering groan as he pushed it open and met Sébastien's panicked gaze.

Adam would have strangled him then and there, but the pain in Sébastien's sea-green eyes rendered him momentarily immobile. Remorse. Regret and empathy. He appeared to have aged a good twenty years since Adam last saw him. Regardless, once he gathered his wits, Adam clasped Sébastien's lapels, pulled him inside, and slammed his back against the wall.

"Adam, please. You must hear me out, *mon ami*. Isabelle's life may very well—"

"*Mon ami?* Never call me that again," Adam snarled as he rounded on Sébastien again. He pinned him against the wall with one hand firmly pressed against the man's neck. Sébastien struggled against the pressure of his fingers, coughing, battling for air. "And never speak her name. You are not worthy of her name." Adam felt his voice grow thin and wary. His anger warped into a painful despair and agony as he lifted Sébastien off the ground.

Then he swept back with a curse, dislodging his hand from Sébastien's neck. He thrust his fingers through his hairline and paced back and forth. "Don't deny it—that worthless vicomte has spirited her away because of you. Because of your treachery and betrayal."

Sébastien audibly battled for the right words. Hearing him stammer and stutter, when he was usually so smooth and quick-witted, filled Adam with an unwanted empathy.

"Hear me out. I beg you—"

"I trusted you, Sébastien. I'd turned my back on society, learned to trust no one... yet I had believed in our friendship." Adam's voice turned soft, thoughtful, each syllable weighed down by a sudden heartache he didn't dare comprehend. "You have thought ill of me for a long time now—perhaps you always have. You made it clear last time we talked that you regarded me as a monster."

He locked on to Sébastien's hazy eyes and swept forward, closing the space between them again. "I would have nothing left to believe in if it weren't for Isabelle. And now, she's been taken away because of you. I love her, Sébastien! I love her more than I've ever loved anything. Should any harm befall her, I—"

"I didn't know, Adam! What was I supposed to think—you were so damn secretive... and she appeared trapped, so lost!"

"You were supposed to believe there was still good left in me."

Sébastien's head lolled forward. When he spoke again, his voice sounded broken and weary. "But I do believe that, *mon ami*. That's why I have returned. Raphael deceived me. I was a fool to have fallen for such deception. But I've come to make things right again. Adam, let me lead you to them. Let me help you avenge Isabelle. You two deserve a life together—and I shall do everything in my power, damn it all, to help you achieve it."

Several minutes crawled by. Finally Adam inhaled a steadying breath. He returned to the drawing room and removed a revolver from the satchel. Passing it into Sébastien's hands, he said beneath a long-suffering sigh, "Then you'd best be ready."

Chapter Twenty-Three

APPREHENSION RACED DOWN Isabelle's spine as the footman ushered her into the withdrawing room. Raphael lounged in his customary wingback chair, positioned close to the hearth, and blankly stared into those wavering flames. Isabelle eyed him with revulsion and a pulsating hatred; she had nearly escaped this hellhole nights ago. Raphael had caught her sneaking out through the servants' quarters. The wretch had made it abundantly clear that Adam would pay in blood, should she attempt another escape. Raphael had truly imprisoned her; she would sooner forfeit her own life rather than risk Adam's.

Adam. My Adam Delacroix. Her thoughts crept inward as a sob lodged in her throat; she closed her eyes, sinking into her own private solace.

"Come, come," Raphael muttered, shattering her thoughts. She hesitated for a heartbeat—then swiftly stepped forward. She yearned to get his daily scorn and mockery out of the way.

Raphael turned from the fire, swirled his glass of brandy, then gave her body a once-over. She was wearing a lovely emerald green walking dress—a garment that had belonged to Raphael's late mother. He'd forced the damn thing on her, as a child might dress his doll. Absently Isabelle tracked her hand over the damask lace detail, her stomach curdling. As of late, Raphael always seemed to be deep in his cups and never sober.

"I apologize," he drawled, his stare admiring the dress, "for tearing you from those chores I know you love so much."

He paused, physically gauging her reaction. Isabelle brushed off the dress's hem and forced a painful, sardonic smile to her face; she could only imagine what Raphael would do if he caught sight of soot on the dress. "It's quite all right. I enjoy our nightly conversations even more if that's even possible." The words actually pained her.

He surrendered to a small chuckle—an eerie, husky sound that made her skin tighten and crawl. Then her thoughts reverted to that long-ago night... how his hands had invaded her most intimate parts... how he'd laughed and found pleasure in her distress... in this very room...

Sadistic animal.

Anger pulsated through her. *I'm no longer the weak and naive girl I'd once been. If he thinks he can threaten me again, then he's a damned fool.*

A damned fool with nothing to lose now...

That last thought sent another shiver of fear through her. She watched with mounting apprehension as he adjusted his body and then signaled her forward with his index finger. Every fiber of her being urged her to run, yet she knew well there was nowhere to escape to.

She slipped forward, her heart beating out of her chest. Their eyes locked for several moments of silence. Then he reached out, grabbed the hem of her skirts, and yanked her body to him with a rough gesture. He chuckled as she fell across his lap, stomach-first. Alas, his lower region protruded and jerked against her abdomen.

She cried out and battled to return to her feet with her dignity still intact. He merely chuckled again, steadying her movements with two unyielding hands on her lower and upper back. Indeed, he laid her across his knee, as if she were a naughty schoolgirl in need of reprimanding.

The heat of the fire, which lurked painfully close, flashed over her face and drew sweat from her brow. Raphael's vile fingers snaked up and down her back in a slow perusal... up and down... before settling on the curve of her backside. Her tears mixed with perspiration as she silently wept.

Please don't let him hear me. Let me retain at least that much of my pride...

She stared straight into the flames with an unwavering, unblinking intensity. The insufferable heat burned her eyes, yet she did not look away; the heat in Raphael's voice burned far more as he lowered his head and whispered against her scalp. "Don't fight it any longer, *ma chérie*. It's over now, can't you see that? Don't fight me any longer..."

Isabelle bit her tongue until the metallic flavor of blood filled her mouth. His hand glided down her leg... down, down, down... then moved under her skirts in a painfully slow motion.

She couldn't hold back the words any longer. "I shall die fighting." She cursed the quaver in her voice, praying Raphael was too deaf to her emotions to hear it.

Her gaze abandoned the hearth and planted on the medallion-style rug. Dejectedly she watched as blood from her mouth lightly splattered the fine material.

He responded with amused laughter. "My darling, you always know just what to say. I cannot help but think you secretly yearn for me... and for my touches..." She shivered, filled only with revulsion, as his hand caressed her backside... then dipped lower, underneath, his fingers invading her most intimate place all over again. "That monster," he huskily said, as if whispering a twisted endearment, "did you let him take you? Did he dare touch what belongs to me?"

Isabelle said nothing, though the silence felt painful. The words she burned to shout nearly burst her lungs apart.

"That's quite fine. Say nothing if you wish. I shall find out with one, eh, slip of the finger, shall I say?"

You had already stolen my maidenhead, stupid fool.

Isabelle eyed the fire poker, which lurked enticingly in front of the hearth.

Do I dare? Could I dare?

As his intrusive finger slipped a centimeter away, her heart and mind screamed in unison, *Yes, I dare.* It wasn't poison—

but it'd serve her purpose quite eloquently. Just as she prepared to propel her body forward—to sacrifice herself to preserve what remained of her dignity—an astonished voice floated in the air.

"Raphael! What... what is this?"

Isabelle breathed a sigh of relief as his hand wrenched away; he behaved like a lad who'd been caught invading a jar of sweets. He twisted his fingers in her hair instead and yanked her upright. Her throat pumped like a furnace while he stretched her neck in a painful backward arch.

"Answer me!" Vivian demanded in a panicked voice.

He responded with an amused chuckle, lightening his words. "You mustn't feel envious, my love. You know there's no one for me but you. She... Why, Isabelle is nothing more than a plaything. *Our* plaything, if you so desire."

Isabelle frantically scrambled from Raphael's lap and onto the floor. She stared up at Vivian, who stood quiet and still in the archway. Her eyes took on a new fierceness, and her fair hands clenched into fists on either side of her body. Her penetrating green gaze slipped over Isabelle, taking in the dress.

"What is she wearing?" Silence. "How—how could you, Raphael? She disgraced you—made a fool of your entire family with her flight! How could you do this to *me*?"

Raphael's gaze darkened for a moment, then he looked amused again. "Even more reason for us to amuse ourselves with her," he whispered, speaking of Isabelle as if she were their pet. Or a pitiful lapdog.

Vivian threatened her with an icy look—one that chilled Isabelle to her marrow. She felt imprisoned as she mutely sat on the floor, encased between Raphael and Vivian.

Alas, they were unraveling before her eyes. Isabelle strongly suspected she'd be the one to suffer their agony. Raphael and Vivian were two dams on the verge of bursting open. And Isabelle was fated to drown in those murky, unquiet waters

ADAM AND SÉBASTIEN traveled through the heart of Demrov for two days and nights. Adam urged Spirit forward at a pace that should have broken her, yet she surged on, as if she knew the importance of their hasty journey. A hard rain hammered down the second day, which brought their pace to a frustrating slowdown.

Only when mere kilometers lurked between them and Chateau Dumont did Adam and Sébastien break their fast. They sat in companionable silence, observing as the rain fell in harsh sheets. The silence eventually slipped into strained small talk—then warped into amicable reminiscing about past times. Memories washed over Adam, as palpable and chilling as the thrashing rain. When the conversation turned to the birth of Rosemary, an excruciating ache pressed against his heart. Sébastien mercifully pushed the topic aside and gave his shoulder a comforting pat. He felt himself soften at Sébastien's tenderness; he fought to remember his recent betrayal, yet all he saw when he met Sébastien's gaze was compassion, regret—the eyes of his friend.

"What really happened that night, Adam? When Isabelle and her father came to your door?"

Adam sighed and shook his downcast head. "About what you would have expected from me. I turned them away. Her father was on death's door, quite literally, and I refused them shelter."

"Ah, yes. You always have lacked, er, a gentleman's hospitality. But that's not the way it went."

"No," Adam agreed as a small smile slipped into his voice. "Isabelle stood her ground—for her father. She wouldn't allow me to turn them away. She was prepared to sacrifice everything for him." Adam shook his head again, reached into his coat, and withdrew the revolver. He rotated it between his thumb and forefinger as the words poured out. "She changed me,

Sébastien, every moment she was here—starting with that first. I didn't believe such loyalty, such profound love, still existed in the world before she and her father stumbled upon my door."

Hours later, Chateau Dumont seeped into sight. Adam pulled on Spirit's reins and brought the phaeton to a halt. She pawed at the muddy ground and tossed her great silver mane with defiance.

Spirit, indeed.

Adam wiped the rain from his brow and surveyed the property. Per Sébastien's story, he and Raphael had struck up a sort of friendship during their encounter. Adam considered having Sébastien call upon Raphael to act as a distraction. He turned the scenario in his head, trying to weigh the possible risks and outcomes.

No, he knows Sébastien will be aware about what he's done. It would only put him on alert. We need to strike while he's completely in the dark—defenseless, vulnerable, and unsuspecting...

Besides—the hour was late. *Raphael and his servants may be sleeping if we're lucky.*

A half hour later, Adam pulled the phaeton inside the carriage house and led Spirit to the stable. Afterward, he and Sébastien circled the chateau's towering walls as they hunted for a way inside.

"Damn you, Adam, we have nearly circled the whole wretched thing. I'm not as young as I used to be, I'm afraid. I may very well have to sit the next thousand meters out. I dare say—"

"Quiet," Adam hissed. "And lower yourself to the ground, you fool."

They crouched before a sweeping conservatory window. A flowerbed surrounded them; small buds decorated the leafy branches. A light flashed on inside the stunning parlor, illuminating the mahogany furniture and fine upholstery. A least a dozen animal heads hung from the darkly paneled walls and decorated the room.

"That's him," Sébastien spat as a handsome man in his mid-thirties swept inside the room. He looked vibrant and in the prime of his youth. He was everything Adam was not. His blond locks, swept back to expose the fine architecture of an aristocratic face, glinted in the lantern's illumination. Adam felt a tide of jealousy crash down.

Sébastien must have read his discomfort. He cleared his throat, then gave a wry smile. "Ah, the spell of his golden beauty is not so different than being too deep in your cups. At first, it's positively alluring—and a short time later, once the effects of his personality cut through, you're left feeling nothing but nausea."

Adam held back his smile and felt as the venom drained. Inside the parlor, Raphael Dumont staggered behind a satinwood bar and rustled through the collection of spirits. His hands visibly shook, and when he moved closer, Adam saw his eyes were hazy and bloodshot. Wiping the rain from his stare, Adam murmured, "He's a fucking drunk."

Sébastien surrendered to a devil-may-care shrug. "I can't say I blame him with the comte being his father."

Raphael drank his fill—straight from the bottle. Swaying with each step, he crossed the parlor, bumping into the hulking furniture along the way, and glared up at the salon wall. Portraits covered the chinoiserie wallpaper from floor to ceiling. The hand clutching the bottle shook in midair, and Adam saw his lips move as he whispered something to a framed portrait. Then he scrubbed his fingers over his face and through his hairline, disheveling the slick golden mane.

Vicomte Raphael Dumont was coming undone before their eyes.

"I've seen enough."

Adam shot onto his feet and wheeled around the chateau's curved facade. A half an hour later, he stopped in front of a small window. Inside, the kitchens were visible; shadows obscured the room, transforming the vast table and chairs into crouching monsters. Adam breathed a sigh of relief. Everything was dark and cleared; the servants had already turned it over for the evening.

Adam searched the ground for a rock—and found one in a nearby flowerbed. Rainwater made it slippery to the touch; he adjusted his hold, then cocked his arm back and hurled it straight at the window. The glass shattered with a splintering crack.

Adam used his elbow to knock away the remaining shards. Then he gestured to Sébastien and climbed through the opening.

MINUTES LATER, Adam and Sébastien tracked down the dark corridors. The servants had settled into their quarters for the night, and the hallways were eerily quiet and still.

He felt like he'd dropped through a black mirror—a portal into the past.

Inside his mind, Adam was eleven years old again, slipping through Castle Delacroix in search of his loved ones. His heart beat in his chest like a caged bird, and a blast of thunder rendered him momentarily immobile; only his love for Isabelle and his determination to free her kept him anchored. He clutched the revolver between his clammy fingers and signaled Sébastien to do likewise.

After ten minutes of sneaking through the shadows, Adam heard the muffled sound of sobs and a woman's voice. He sprinted down the long hallway, his revolver drawn and cocked, ready to fire. He fought to deaden the sound of his footfalls as he and Sébastien gained on the panicked voice.

His heart thrashed as he paused outside a door left ajar. For a moment, he was sure he'd see Maman and Papa gagged and standing in front of their four-poster bed. Holding his breath, he peeked inside—and the sight purged the air from his lungs.

A beautiful woman with flaming red hair clasped a dagger. He couldn't see her face—but her curls were slick with sweat.

Her pale hand violently trembled—and Adam noticed that *red* covered the tip of that dagger.

Adam shifted his body to grant himself a better angle. *Isabelle.* The woman had cornered her against the wall. Isabelle was sitting, her legs pulled up against her chest. Frantic sobs shook her body as she clasped her shoulder. A ring of blood stained the material of her servant's garb. Adam felt a wave of red-hot rage bubble inside. It took every gram of his willpower not to burst into the room and strangle the redheaded woman.

"I know her," Sébastien muttered. "Vivian Brazin—Raphael's mistress. She—"

"I don't care who the fuck she is." Adam gestured for him to keep quiet and tightened his grasp on the revolver. In spite of the cold, sweat drenched his palms and made the barrel quite slippery. "Follow my lead. Be my shadow." Venom leaked from every word; so dark and distorted was Adam's voice, he hardly recognized it as his own.

"I have been, *mon ami*, for over twenty-five years."

ISABELLE'S HEART BANGED against her ribs as she stared into Vivian's wild gaze. Tears streamed down the woman's cheeks, and the dagger faltered in her trembling hand. Isabelle felt herself growing fainter... felt herself slipping into blackness. Although the wound was not deep, it summoned a fierce pain in her shoulder and urged her jaw to clench against the discomfort. Cursing her weakness, she recalled the insurmountable pain Adam had suffered as a young boy.

Red curls flurried against Vivian's tearstained cheeks like wisps of fire. She'd gone mad. The evening had started out normal enough; Vivian had requested Isabelle in her chamber while Raphael was out on a social call. Isabelle had spent over an hour brushing out Vivian's hair and suffering her insults. Afterward, she'd stopped by the library, hoping to find an escape.

Then Vivian had appeared.

Isabelle chose her words carefully, for once not succumbing to her wagging tongue and sharp retorts.

Her very life depended on it.

"Vivian... please, listen to me... Raphael loves you—*only you*..." Each word took a monumental effort and heightened the throbbing pain in her shoulder. She gasped for breaths, trying to stay conscious—afraid of what would happen if she descended into that seductive darkness. "I'm nothing to him. Nothing! Just a plaything, a way for him to thwart his father and pass—"

"Do you think I'm daft? So long as you draw breath, he shall never belong to me. Raphael shall always keep you close. You have bewitched him, stolen him away; he sees his wretched mother when he looks at you!" Vivian edged forward, tears streaming down her pale cheeks. She raised the dagger, and her wobbly hand suddenly grew steady and sure. She struck again—Isabelle gave a pained cry and spun out of the arc of the blade.

A cloaked figure flashed into her peripheral vision, quick and smooth as a lightning strike. Vivian's arm was still in midair; a hand had enclosed over her wrist, keeping it securely in place. Isabelle struggled to her feet, gripping the writing desk for support as she watched the scene unfold.

Adam. Her dark angel. Her prince.

He twisted her arm, causing a nauseating snap to resound and her cry to swell the library. The dagger fell from her grasp and landed on the wooden floor with a muffled clink. Behind him stood a second man.

Sébastien. He drew his firearm—aimed directly at Vivian. Adam shoved Vivian to the ground and withdrew his own revolver in a swift, predatory motion.

She turned to Adam; Vivian screamed as her gaze tracked over his deformed face. He truly looked frightening. Rage twisted his features into something terrible. Something built from nightmares and anguish.

Beast-like. Beautiful. Vengeful.

Vivian scurried away on all fours and reached for her fallen dagger. Adam stepped on her hand and knelt to his knees, his blue eyes filled with fire.

"You—you monster! Raphael shall kill you for this! You and your little whore! I shall take great pleasure in watching him put you down, just like the wretched beast you are!"

Calm and composed, Adam slid the dagger out from her wriggling fingers. She flipped onto her back and scurried away like a hermit crab. Adam followed her every movement, slow and frightfully steady. He lifted his leather-clad hand and pointed the dagger at her abdomen. "Poor choice of words." He swept the bloody point up the length of her chest—paused directly over her heart—then continued an upward quest. His enraged stare fixed on her terrified expression; he dug the point into the apex of her shoulder and neck ever so slightly...

Vivian cried out and attempted to crawl backward some more. Sébastien stood behind her, his revolver drawn, sufficiently blocking her path.

"Adam, no! Please!" Lunged out of a strange inward trance, Adam glanced at Isabelle and lowered the dagger. "What good would it do?" Isabelle implored in a panicked voice, groping at her shoulder.

"She hurt you," he snapped, his hands shaking with uncontrollable anger. "She caused you pain—"

"She already knows suffering and pain, Adam!" Isabelle clasped her seething shoulder and edged forward, holding the furniture for support. "Let us leave—quickly! We must hurry! Please... let's go *home*."

Those words snapped Adam from his stupor. He pocketed the dagger and his revolver, then gave Sébastien a nod. "You don't deserve her mercy," he shot at Vivian. "But you shall have it nonetheless."

Adam wrapped his arms around Isabelle, and the pain in her shoulder ebbed away at his touch. Her heart rejoiced at his nearness, at the feel of his body pressed against her own, at the sensation of his breaths on her cheeks. He peered down at her wound, that fury still alive in his penetrating gaze.

"It's not deep," she breathed, holding him closer, relishing the thunderous beat of his heart pressed against her own. She relaxed as his arms wound about her waist. He tentatively swayed on his booted heels, rocking her back and forth within the security of his embrace. Closing both eyes, she nestled against the planes of his chest, never wanting to let him go. "Just quite painful."

Adam's breaths brushed against her temple like a soft summer breeze. He whispered comforting words against her hairline. Then she felt herself floating as he hooked his arms under her knees, carrying her bridal-style. "I shall never let pain come to you again, *ma belle*. Now and always." She stared up at the opposing sides of his face, in awe of his powerful presence. He turned toward Sébastien, leaving only the scarred half in sight. "Come. We must go."

As they crossed the room and headed for the hallway, a piercing scream rang out.

Vivian.

Adam spun toward her, cursed at her to shut her damn mouth. But the damage was done. Raphael Dumont appeared in the archway within moments, a look of genuine concern in his gaze. Isabelle slid to the floor as Adam dropped her and wrestled for his revolver again.

Raphael's eyes, which looked hazy, flickered to Vivian. She was stumbling to her feet and muttering incoherent words. She appeared mad—as if she were mentally unraveling.

"What the fuck did you do to her?" he said, his glazed eyes planted on Vivian's broken wrist. "I shall kill you for this, you worthless freak!" His eyes narrowed on Isabelle, who hid behind Adam's strong back. Indeed, he'd swept in front of her body, forging a barricade between her and Raphael. "This—this *thing*—this is what you choose? This abomination? This—monster?"

"Big words for a boy with no arms to defend himself," Sébastien cut in, his tone a low sneer.

"You?" A look of recognition crossed Raphael's eyes as they roamed over Sébastien's livid features. Releasing a haunting chuckle, he shook his head and circled around Adam with a scrutinizing gaze. "Look at you. You're little more than a pathetic monster. A sniveling coward. Indeed, your dear Sebastian told me your tragic story... how you've holed yourself up in that decrepit castle all these years, licking your wounds." He stopped circling Adam and swayed drunkenly on his feet. "You are no man. Alas, you are barely human. You are a grave disappointment. A failure. An embarrassment—"

Isabelle's own voice sounded colder than ice. "Adam is more of a man than you could ever hope to be."

"Allow us to pass in peace," Adam cut in, his beautiful tone a bone-chilling growl. "You owe her that much. Now move aside, or I shall gladly riddle your pretty body with lead."

"And a poor waste it would be," Sébastien added.

Neither Isabelle nor Adam nor Sébastien heard as Vivian Brazin rustled through a bureau, withdrew a revolver with shaking hands, and loaded the crude weapon. They never anticipated the shot that rang out, the shot that pierced Sébastien near his heart.

"Go, Isabelle—go now!" Adam yelled as he maneuvered around her and locked eyes with his friend. "Wait outside for me!" Isabelle gave a backward glance, her heart heavier than a stone, then flew into the corridor.

PAIN BLASTED THROUGH Sébastien as he clasped his seething chest. A hot slide of blood rushed from the gun wound and dampened his fingers. His teeth chattered against the agony and rattled inside his skull.

Fighting to anchor himself, he collapsed to the floor and watched the scene in mingled horror and awe.

A maniacal fury had seized Adam Delacroix.

He punched Raphael straight in the gut while Vivian tried to intercede.

Bang! She fired a shot that almost grazed Adam's shoulder. Groaning in pain, Sébastien smacked her legs from his spot on the ground, sending her tumbling onto the floor. The revolver fell from her good hand and slid across the smooth parquet wood. Meanwhile, Adam and Raphael broke into a merciless fight. They battled like two animals—like two wild dogs.

Nearby Adam struggled to aim the revolver—a difficult feat in such close quarters. Raphael clumsily knocked the weapon from his hand and punched him straight in the gut. The sounds of skidding boots, deafening blows, and puttering rain impregnated the room.

Sébastien fumbled for his own revolver—but alas, it was too far away. He grabbed Vivian's dress as she attempted to crawl across the floor, her hand straining for the weapon...

Then the she-devil flipped onto her back and kicked him square in the jaw. His head rang with the sound of shattering teeth. The impact caused him to bite down hard and sever his own tongue. Blood filled his jaw, pooling inside his mouth. Cursing, he spat out broken teeth and a chunk of his tongue, slithered forward, and twisted Vivian's ankle. The delicate bones yielded to the turn of his hand... He felt as they snapped and shifted under his gripping fingers, which were tighter than a manacle. Her piercing scream swelled the room, and a flash of lightning stabbed the library. Thunder roared in the distance. All the while, Adam punched Raphael in the stomach and jaw, transforming his handsome features into a bloody pulp...

Sébastien tried to block out the mind-bending pain... tried to fight off the awareness that his own life's blood was pooling under his body. Hands madly shaking, he glanced at a nearby sideboard, where a lantern sat, its candle flickering within the glass prison...

He struggled to stay conscious as he strained his arm, reaching up... The sideboard seemed to lurk kilometers away...

Adam broke away from Raphael—thrust him to the floor. Then he slammed his balled fist straight into those handsome, aristocratic features. Again and again. Raphael returned the favor with jerky, drunken movements, clawing at Adam's deformity, dragging his nails through the marred skin and drawing blood.

Adam gave a wild roar. Grasped hold of Raphael's lapels

and drove his body into the wooden floorboards. He withdrew a dagger from his coat and brought the blade down in a deathly arc. Raphael rolled out of its path and gave a low, taunting laugh. The blade's point sank into the wooden floor at least ten centimeters deep.

Raphael was at it again—pounding Adam's face like a wild animal, knocking the breath from his lungs with his boots. Coughing up blood, Adam wrenched the dagger free. Then he brought it down with a savage vengeance—burying it almost hilt-deep centimeters above Raphael's heart...

The vicomte crashed to the floor. A crimson ring blossomed where the blade impaled him.

"*Non!* Raphael, *mon amour! Non...*" Vivian cried out and scrambled over to him on all fours. She fisted handfuls of his coat while her body trembled with choked sobs and incoherent words.

Drawing the blade from his flesh, Raphael surrendered to another dark chuckle. "Very good. *Bravo*, monsieur—yet... you... shall lose all the same. Once they find me, you will hang. You... you and your little whore. And that alone gives me peace."

Vivian thrust the revolver into Raphael's quivering hands. "Kill him, Raphael," she hissed, her eyes flashing, the tone of her voice eerily calm and steady. "But make him suffer first."

Raphael aimed the weapon with a last surge of energy; Sébastien watched as Adam charged across the library, storming toward his strewn body.

"Are—are you mad? Go—go with your Isabelle!"

Fighting the darkening haze, Sébastien seized the sideboard and hoisted himself up. He gasped for breaths. Grabbed the edge and dragged the lantern forward. Blood dribbled from his chin and splattered onto the polished surface.

"Now, Adam, you damn fool!"

"I won't leave you here," Adam called out from a meter away, the sound of his voice growing fainter.

"You must." Using the edge of the sideboard to prop himself up, he stared at the flickering candle—making his intent unmistakable. "Good-bye, my friend. *Nutrisco et extinguo.*"

Without another word, Adam slammed the library's door shut. Vivian released Raphael's body and crawled across the parquet floor. She threw her body against the closed door with inhuman cries and choked sobs. Loud screeching resonated from the corridor as Adam barricaded the door with some piece of furniture.

The last thing Sébastien perceived was Vivian frantically pounding at the panels until her hands bled and the wood reddened.

Feeling strangely at peace, he knocked the lantern onto the ground. The glass case shattered—and, within minutes, flames devoured the library.

DECADES AGO, fire had condemned him; now, it would be his escape and salvation. Isabelle, damn her, had remained inside the corridor, waiting for him. Approaching footfalls thundered in the distance as they rushed through the chateau's halls. The servants had awoken and were rushing for the burning library with buckets of water.

Swiping at the blood on his face, he swept Isabelle into his arms. He carried her past the parlor and withdrawing room, out into the safety of the night, his legs eating up the distance at a record speed. Behind them, the fire steadily grew and raged, consuming the library.

Adam fought to remain anchored and focused on his task of getting Isabelle to safety. But the image of Sébastien lying on the floor burned into his thoughts and slowed his steps.

Sébastien Villeneuve had rescued him once again.

Adam stopped to glance at the chateau one last time. Clashing emotions warred inside him—gratitude, appreciation for Sébastien's sacrifice and final loyalty, relief, and an aching sorrow for the loss of a dear friend. Adam whispered a heartfelt good-bye, held back his tears, and hurried past the carriage house and toward the stable.

As the crisp air entered his lungs and he hugged Isabelle to his chest, part of him felt like he was leaving the ghosts of his past behind.

Minutes later, the musky scents of hay and wet dirt surrounded Isabelle. Indeed, they were in a stable. Moonlight streamed through the wooden panels, reaching for her like grasping fingers. The comforting sound of Spirit's nicker and pattering rain imbued the walls. Breathless from the pain, she turned her gaze back to Adam—her dark angel. She watched beneath hooded lids as he tore away his coat. Using a dagger, he cut a sleeve off the garment, then fastened it around her shoulder.

Isabelle reached out and cupped either side of his face. "You are bleeding! You—"

"Don't worry about me, *ma belle*. I am fine." He hesitated, then added beneath a whisper, "He's gone. It's just us now."

Raphael Dumont is gone. A weight lifted from her chest as she echoed Adam's words. "Just us..."

Staring into the depths of his sapphire gaze, she groaned as he applied a firm pressure to her shoulder. "Thank God. It's only a superficial wound," he breathed, his mouth nearly touching her own. "I've stopped the bleeding. You shall be fine until I get you to an infirmary."

She clasped his face again; the blood smeared across his cheeks, painting the contrasting sides of his features. She urged him forward, connecting their lips in a soul-searing kiss. Tears of mingled pain and relief swam down her cheeks and seeped past the seam of her mouth. The salty tang flavored their kiss, as well as the metallic trace of blood. "Better than fine," she reverently murmured into his mouth. Adam chased her words with his tongue and drew her closer. "Perfect..."

Moments later, he broke off their kiss and silently shook his head. He echoed the words that stirred in her own heart, speaking from the deepest reaches of his soul. "Thank you for setting me free. I love you, Isabelle. Today, tomorrow, always."

"Always us. I love you, Adam Delacroix—heart, body, and soul. There's nothing I would change about you; you're a beautiful song, a symphony of light and dark, and I love every shade, every note. I love you—*all* of you."

He withdrew the engagement ring from inside his coat; the crystal-clear diamond and encircling rubies sparkled in the moonlight. Isabelle's voice hitched, while Adam's own emotions threatened to overwhelm him. He slid the ring onto her wedding finger, his gaze never parting from her own. Then he lifted her hand in midair, fastened both eyes shut, and pressed a kiss to her knuckles. Isabelle Rose had become his joy, his hope, his everything.

"My Isabelle. My light, my love..."

Always together.

Epilogue

SEVEN YEARS LATER

I SABELLE SILENTLY OBSERVED Adam and little Rosemary from the music room's doorway. Her heart soared at the way her husband's large body dwarfed their daughter. Strong hands engulfed Rosemary's and guided her slender fingers over the pianoforte's ivory keys. A breathtaking melody infused the room and reached into the deepest corners of Isabelle's soul. Her heart lightened at the genuine happiness on Adam's face... how he appeared utterly at peace, his blue eyes glistening with an unmistakable joy. Indeed, with each passing year, he'd transformed before her very eyes—much like a butterfly emerging from a cocoon.

Adam Delacroix's infiltration into society had been a remarkable journey. Shortly after Isabelle and Adam had married, Louis Philippe of France granted parliament power to Demrov; Adam gained a seat on the council, and citizens and politicians alike welcomed the voice of their long-lost prince. With Isabelle's persistent encouragement and urging, he even shared his musical compositions with the world. Their unique brilliance quickly gathered fame, transforming him into a well-adored and eccentric figure in Demrov. Even after seven years, however, he still shied away from prying eyes and preferred the company of his family and home. Isabelle didn't mind in the least; it allowed ample time for them to pursue the things they loved—and to pursue each other.

"That's it, *ma petite*," Adam said in a tender, reassuring tone. He sat just beside Rosemary, who was only six years old, his massive arm protectively wrapped around her shoulder. "I knew you could do it."

Rosemary's sleek, dark curls bounced about her shoulders as she shook her head. Her bright laughter joined with the melody and brought a smile to Adam's mouth. Rosemary gazed at her father free from horror or disgust, regarding him with only love and admiration. Indeed, in her eyes, he was a hero—a knight from the pages of her cherished storybooks.

"*You* are doing it, Papa!"

He removed a hand from the keys, surrendered to an audible sigh, then smoothed down her errant curls. The melody subsided, and a poignant quiet fell upon the music room. Chuckling, he pressed a kiss to her hairline and gave another sigh. "We are doing it. Together."

Always together.

Isabelle's chest constricted at the tenderness in Adam's gaze—the incalculable love and affection. Then their eyes met from across the room. An entire conversation, the renewal of a promise, surged between them.

ADAM CHERISHED NIGHTS like these most. The chateau had grown silent and still, and now a peaceful contentment swelled his spirit. He'd watched Isabelle sleep for close to an hour, still mesmerized by the sight of her seven years later.

He stepped through their bedchamber's French doors and out into the crisp, cool air. He gazed at Lavoncourt's bejeweled skyline, where a calm sea kissed the sky. The earth and horizon joined in perfect union, a marriage so complete it was almost impossible to see where one ended and the other began. He inhaled deeply, welcoming the air of his homeland into his lungs. He listened to the distant crash of the waves, urging it to stroke his imagination with the beauty of a concerto. The melody flowed through his consciousness, igniting memories that had lived for three decades yet never faded with time.

Then he felt a gentle touch upon his shoulder—one that seduced him from his thoughts and back into the present moment. He gazed at Isabelle's expression, fascinated by how the moonlight bathed her features and brightened the sparkle in her velvety eyes. She embraced him, enfolding his body in her slender arms. Adam melted against her and inhaled the intoxicating scents of her hair and skin.

"This is always my favorite moment," he whispered against the shell of her ear. She shivered in his arms, shutting her eyes as a low moan fled her lips. Her reaction set his blood on fire. *Mon Dieu*, he often made her climax with only his voice. "When the world falls asleep, and it's only us. Nothing brings me more happiness or contentment than simply holding you in my arms." He nibbled on her earlobe, then skimmed his lips across the back of her neck. "Speak my name, Isabelle."

"Adam Delacroix," she said, releasing the words on a long sigh.

"Again."

"Adam Delacroix." All the while, he tracked his lips across her neck in a hot, wet slide of desire.

"Again."

"My Adam Delacroix..."

Adam wheeled her slender body around to face him. Instantly he lost himself within her beauty. Dark hair cascaded over her curves, framing them with the elegance of a dark mantle. A natural flush brightened her porcelain cheeks, and her gaze ignited with an unmistakable passion. Her night rail was a delicate cream color, set off with intricate lace and charming detail. Small-flowered swags decorated the flowing neckline. The luxurious train flowed behind her, spilling across the balcony's floor like a queen's regal gown. Emotion pressed hard on his chest, preventing him from speaking.

So he spoke with his touch.

He latched on to her waist, unable to suppress his burning desire, and spun her round full circle. Her body jolted against the banister, wedged between the stone railing and his abdomen. She returned his hunger and knotted both arms around his neck.

Their lips came together, sensually moving in flawless synchronization. It was an age-old song—one they'd both mastered over the past seven years. He murmured low in his throat while her fingertips frantically worked at his coat buttons. Her resounding moan echoed off the stone walls as he undid the ties of her night rail and shoved the fabric aside in an urgent movement.

With labored breaths, he skimmed his lips across her throat and deftly urged the night rail to the floor, revealing her breasts to his mouth. Moonlight danced across the creamy flesh and pink nipples, kindling his inner fire. He skimmed his lips over each one, drawing a soul-deep moan from her throat. Her eyes fell shut again, and she fisted a hand in his hair, gently urging his mouth against her breast.

His tongue sought her nipple, swirled around the bundle of nerves, and then sucked it into his mouth. Her fingers found his arousal and traced his size through the trousers. Chords of pleasure sang through his body. His hand kneaded her opposite breast, caressing and fondling—cupping the delectable weight in his scarred palm.

Thumb and forefinger rolled over her dusty, veiled nipple, urging it into submission. She obeyed with a moan as the sensitive bud tightened under his shifting palm. His lips detached from her nipple and sought the center of her throat. He felt her pulse quicken under the slick pressure of his mouth, hurdling to life as his lips traced her collarbone.

His body grew harder than stone, and every one of his nerve endings caught fire. Isabelle twisted her fingertips in the thick waves of his hair and pulled him from her neck. Their lips worked in unison, as if they were each attempting to consume the other's spirit. She jerked her head back again, placing a few centimeters of space between their bruised lips. Then she stared straight into his eyes and caressed the disfigured half of his face.

Groaning deeply, emotions crashing within, he dipped into her touch, and a ragged breath pierced the air.

She leaned forward as her fingers slid down his coat in urgent perusal.

"Touch me, Isabelle. Put your fingers on me… around me." At the gruff, commanding note in his voice, he felt a trill of anticipation surge through her body.

Reaching into the high waistline, she dove inside his trousers and claimed him. A husky groan erupted from his throat and echoed in the darkness. His head fell forward as she enveloped him with her slender fingers, sliding up and down his turgid length…

"Remove the trousers."

She paused her movements, grasped his trousers, and urged them downward in a fluid motion. Along with his undergarment, they slid down both thighs until his manhood sprang free.

A strangled sound rattled his chest as she worked his silky-smooth erection between both palms. She dampened her lips. Adam peered down to where her hands rested—pale white against his skin. Shallow breaths stirred her curls. His face slumped forward, and he touched his forehead to hers. His hands landed on the banister, encaging either side of her body, anchoring her in place. One hand slipped downward, beneath the material of her pantalettes, and skimmed the wet material. He found the slit, and a strong, hooked finger eased inside her very center. It nudged against her feminine cleft, drawing a moan from her throat.

"Open to me, Isabelle." His voice sounded clipped. Guttural. Almost beast-like. She trembled against him and leaned against the banister for support. "*Mon Dieu*, you are already wet for me… hot and wet and ready, *mon amour*."

"I always am."

Lavoncourt swirled and rotated, blending everything into a surreal blur. The hold on his manhood faltered. Their breaths grew shallow and irregular. Biting back a moan, she arched against his erotic ministrations. He slid the pantalettes down her thighs while her body opened for him, inviting him inside, and two thick fingers sank knuckle-deep.

He felt as she reached that plateau. Then in a solid, consuming motion that screamed *now and always*, he thrust forward and joined their quivering bodies.

Adam glanced at the star-speckled sky, and the world spun on its axis as he swiftly thrust inside her wet walls.

She embraced him with both arms, while the feel of his wife's warm body and the distant melody of crashing waves brought him to completion.

Holding her against him with their bodies still joined, heartbeat to heartbeat, he sighed into her damp curls, "*Amore é gioia, amore é soffrire, amore é tenerezza, amore é bello. Amore sei tu.*"

Love is joy, love is suffering, love is tenderness, love is beautiful. Love is you.

BURSTING WITH A RUSH OF LOVE, Isabelle's heart contracted at the sight of Rosemary buried beneath the silk coverlet. Her sweet, small hands still held a trace of baby-plumpness, and whenever she lowered her blue eyes, dark lashes rested upon the roundness of her cheeks.

The coverlet stirred. Isabelle jumped back with a start. A guilty smile curved Rosemary's mouth as a small puppy wriggled free of the material. Scrambling to break free of the confines, little Stranger squirmed her body while a black, wet nose erratically twitched. The adorable creature was a plump thing, bearing a round tummy and oversized feet.

"Rosie!" Isabelle scolded, even as laughter erupted from her lips.

"I'm sorry, Maman! She jus' looked so lonely and sad."

Shaking her head, Isabelle ran her fingers over Stranger's coarse, dark coat. "Very well, then. But my word—she's not a prisoner, *ma petite*. You must let her breathe."

Yipping and yapping, Stranger waddled over and splashed Isabelle's face with a barrage of kisses. She wrinkled her nose at the assault and gently urged him away. Tiny, daggerlike teeth nipped at her palm. She muttered *no* and secured her jaws shut. As if in retaliation, the puppy grabbed a mouthful of coverlet and vigorously shook it back and forth.

Rosemary gathered the puppy against her chest and kissed the tip of its nose. The kerosene lamp's illumination flickered across her sleepy, serene expression, reflecting the contentment Isabelle felt in her soul. A small smile curled Rosemary's lips, and her sapphire eyes suddenly grew brighter. She shifted against her pillow, sitting up against the lush coverings.

"Maman... tell me the story again. Please, I want to hear!"

Isabelle reached forward and tucked an errant curl behind Rosemary's ear. She pulled the coverlet up to her chin and combated a smile. "Oh, but it's so very late, *ma petite*. Perhaps tomorrow night—"

"Please, Maman? Tell me about you and Papa." Isabelle couldn't suppress her laughter. She couldn't recall how many times she'd recited the story to Rosemary—even so, she never tired of it.

And neither do I.

She began the tale in the same fashion, just as she had almost every night before. Yet Isabelle caught herself falling beneath its spell. She floated into another time and place while her heart grew heavier and her eyes misted over...

"Once upon a time, in a very far-off country, there lived a merchant who had been fortunate in all his undertakings..."

She didn't need to glance over her shoulder. There was no need to sneak a look at the doorway, where she knew Adam Delacroix stood listening, falling under the same spell as she and their little one...

"When his youngest daughter was little, everybody admired her and called her 'the little Beauty' so that, as she grew up, she still went by the name of Beauty, which made her sisters very jealous..."

She smiled as the mattress shifted, manipulated by the pull of Adam's body weight. His deep, velvety voice picked up where Isabelle left off—and when he spoke, she knew the words were meant only for her.

The End.

RACHEL L. DEMETER

Rachel L. Demeter lives in the beautiful hills of Anaheim, California with Teddy, her goofy lowland sheepdog, and her high school sweetheart of fourteen years. She holds a Screenwriting B.A. from Chapman University's School of Film and Media Arts. She enjoys writing dark, emotionally poignant romances that challenge the reader's emotions and explore the redeeming power of love.

Rachel loves connecting and interacting with her readers!

Twitter: @RachelLDemeter
Facebook: facebook.com/RLDemeter
Goodreads: goodreads.com/RachelLDemeter
Official Website: RachelDemeter.net

CPSIA information can be obtained
at www.ICGtesting.com
Printed in the USA
LVHW031113261218
601494LV00001B/32/P

9 781542 972567